June Taylor was a TV promotions writer and producer for many years before turning to writing plays and fiction. She was runner-up in the 2011 *Times*/Chicken House Children's Fiction competition with Young Adult novel *Lovely me, Lovely You*. *Losing Juliet* is her debut novel for Adults. June is active in the Yorkshire writing scene, including serving on the board of Script Yorkshire and taking part in Leeds Big bookend.

🐦 @joonLT
www.junetaylor.co.uk

JUNE TAYLOR

Losing Juliet

KILLER READS

An imprint of HarperCollins*Publishers*
www.harpercollins.co.uk

Killer Reads
An imprint of HarperCollins*Publishers*
1 London Bridge Street
London SE1 9GF

www.harpercollins.co.uk

This paperback edition 2017
1

First published in Great Britain by
HarperCollins*Publishers* 2016

A catalogue record for this book is
available from the British Library

ISBN: 9780008215095

Set in Minion by Palimpsest Book Production Limited,
Falkirk, Stirlingshire

MIX
Paper from
responsible sources
FSC **FSC® C007454**

FSC™ is a non-profit international organisation established to promote
the responsible management of the world's forests. Products carrying the
FSC label are independently certified to assure consumers that they come
from forests that are managed to meet the social, economic and
ecological needs of present and future generations,
and other controlled sources.

Find out more about HarperCollins and the environment at
www.harpercollins.co.uk/green

for Pearl
my big sister

PROLOGUE

The words sounded blurred and far away, as if someone had pushed her head underwater. She ran off into the rain and into the darkness. Her mother shouted her name but didn't come after her. In any case she was too quick. She cast off her shoes, tossing them into the air, wishing they would explode into little pieces. She wanted to break something. Hit something.

The water running down her face was a mixture of rainwater and tears. She wasn't cold but her dress was stuck to her skin, which was visible through the thin fabric. She didn't know where she was heading and somehow found herself by the side of the lake. How different it felt to the last time she was here.

She removed her clothes, all of them, ripping her dress in the process. What did it matter? What did any of this matter?

The rocks tore at her feet. But what couldn't be seen couldn't hurt you. She knew that now. It's what you *could* see. It's what you did know. That's what hurt the most.

The icy chill of the water seemed to take away some of her pain.

'*There is no better freedom,*' she wanted to say, but the words froze as soon as her lips tried to shape them. She swam to keep warm, soon becoming disorientated. Where was the shore and where was the middle of the lake? Impossible to tell with the darkness wrapped around her and the rain coming down again. The middle of the lake was too deep, she remembered. Soon she would be out of her depth and was already getting tired.

Did it matter? Did any of it matter?

Treading water she turned full circle on herself. The shadows and outlines all looked the same. Her knees scraped against rocks. Crawling over them she managed to stand up, the water to her waist, and she began to wade through it, pushing hard against the lake, feeling exhausted and numb with cold.

Gradually her steps became easier. Somehow she had reached the lakeshore and looked around, hugging her shoulders, searching for her dress swallowed up in the gloom. She ran. She must have, because suddenly she found herself at the tiny hut by the side of the tennis court where the racquets and balls were kept. The director's chair was in the doorway, wet beneath her skin when she sank into it. Pressing her hands hard against her ears she slumped over her knees. If only Chrissy's words would stop echoing inside her head.

She was shivering; naked, alone, and curled up like a foetus.

To think that only a few weeks ago she hadn't known any of this. Was it better now that she knew the truth? She had wanted it so desperately.

PART ONE

CHAPTER 1

Manchester: 2007

The phone rang. She picked up.

'Hello,' said a voice. 'I wonder: can you tell me, does someone by the name of Chrissy live there?'

She tried to tune in to the sounds at the other end for clues. Music. Opera, was it? A clanking of cups, possibly in a café?

'Erm, who wants to know?'

'I'm Juliet, an old friend from uni. We were best friends.'

The voice had a late-night feel to it, deep and smoky; the sort you might want to get to know.

'Chrissy's my mother,' she said, seeing no reason to keep that from her.

'Oh that's brilliant! I thought I'd never find her, been trying for ages. Can I speak to her?'

'She's not here at the moment.'

'Okay, well I'll give you my number. If you could tell her I phoned?'

'Okay.'

'And you are?'

'Eloise.'

'Eloise. What a beautiful name. She chose a French name for you, that's interesting.'

'Is it?'

'It's a lovely name. She's never mentioned me to you, Eloise?'

'No.'

'Well, it was a long time ago, must be nearly twenty years in fact. Getting on for that. It would be so lovely to see her. And to meet you, too. How old are you?'

'Seventeen.'

'Well, tell Chrissy to hurry up and get in touch or you'll have left home!'

'I'll try.'

***

'Are you *absolutely* sure she said Juliet?'

'Yes, for the hundredth time, I'm sure,' said Eloise, throwing her hands up in exasperation.

'And she definitely asked for Chrissy? Not – oh, I don't know – Flissy. Or just Chris? I bet she said Chris.'

Eloise gave her papers a shove down the end of the table to make some room, causing a pen to roll off the edge before she could catch it. But Chrissy made no effort to pick it up, so immersed was she in her thoughts. Eloise slid a slice of pizza onto her mother's plate, hoping the conversation could move on from this now.

'There you go, *Pizza à la Freezer* with some extra Cheese Eloise,' she announced. But Chrissy was giving her a pleading look. 'Oh, Mum, I told you. How many times? Definitely Chrissy. I said that you were my mother, and ... What? What's wrong with that?'

Chrissy was sawing at her crust, her fingers turning white at the ends. She caught Eloise's eye and put down her knife, pushed away her plate and sank back against the chair. It sliced through Eloise's optimism; she was already pinning her hopes on this long-lost friend.

6

'She sounded all right to me, Mum. Why have you never mentioned her?'

Her mother tapped her lips whilst she considered her answer. 'It's just a surprise to hear from her after all this time,' she said finally, allowing a sigh to escape through her fingers. 'I never expected to. That's all.' She seemed to linger on that for a while until the phone started to ring, then she jolted into the air with her hand to her chest.

Eloise let it ring a couple more times. She knew her mother wouldn't answer it; she never did.

'Should I get it?'

Chrissy shook her head.

'CLICK: Hi, Eloise, we spoke earlier. And Chrissy, if you're listening to this I just thought I'd try you again, but you're obviously out enjoying yourselves. Well, it is Friday night. I would love to see you after all these years. I hope you think it is okay for me to contact you now. You have my number but I'll keep trying. *Ciao* for now. Oh, it's Juliet, by the way. Juliet Ricci. Well, Juliet Shaw, as I was then. Remember me?'

Juliet's words drifted into every corner of their room, twisting like smoke, fading too quickly.

'What did she mean?' asked Eloise, trying to hang onto them for as long as she could. 'Why wouldn't you think it's okay for her to contact you now?'

Her mother stood still for a moment – she had begun to pace – frowning at the answer machine.

'Did you fall out or something?'

Dropping forwards over her knees, the way she did when she came back from a run, Eloise was about to repeat her question when Chrissy straightened up again. Her breathing seemed normal but her hands had a slight tremble as she scooped her hair back into a ponytail, quickly letting go again.

'No, we never fell out. Hey, shall we go and see a film tonight? I'll skip my yoga class.'

7

'Mum!'

'What?'

'I'm seeing Anya later. I told you that.'

'Did you?' said Chrissy, rubbing her forehead.

'Oh come on, Mum. We're going to plan our Inter-Rail trip, remember? Well you could at least try and be a bit excited for me.'

Eloise watched her mother move across to the window. It wasn't dark yet but she snapped down the blind.

'You're not going Inter-Railing, I've changed my mind. You're too young.'

'What?' Eloise let out a mocking laugh. 'I'm seventeen for god's sake.'

'Besides, I don't know Anya well enough.'

'Of course you do.' Eloise let her body go limp in the chair, one arm dangling by her side. She didn't want a fight. 'You can't treat me like a kid, Mum. You should have done that when I actually was a kid.'

'That's enough, Eloise. And if she calls again, just say you were winding her up; it's the wrong number; there's no Chrissy living here.'

Eloise almost laughed at that too, stopping herself when she realized her mother was being serious. 'I can't do that. Anyway, why?' She glanced at the time on her phone; still nearly an hour before she needed to set off. 'So is this Juliet the reason you dropped out of uni then?'

'Of course not,' Chrissy replied, sounding irritated. 'You know that was my decision.'

'Well how would I know that? You never tell me anything.' Then she panicked, noticing her mother was drifting, and said: 'Okay, so you had some embarrassing girl-on-girl thing that you're too ashamed to talk about. Is that it?'

At least it got a bit of a smile. She racked her brain for more possibilities.

'Well did she try and steal Dad away? Did she know my dad?'

'Yes,' said Chrissy. 'I mean, yes she knew him.'

'But was it over a boy though? Was it? I bet it was.'

Chrissy got up and walked around the back of Eloise's chair, but didn't respond to the question.

'God, it's like living in a tunnel with you sometimes,' said Eloise, trying to prise her mother's hands off her shoulders. She wanted to turn round, but couldn't.

'It never goes away, Eloise. It never can.'

'What doesn't?'

Eloise gave her a moment then snapped herself free from her mother's grasp, rubbing her shoulders where she had been pressing down. 'Right okay, I'll just call this Juliet woman and ask her. I have her number.' Eloise waved her phone defiantly into her mother's face.

For one brief second the world went dark. Chrissy had slapped her on the cheek.

'What the hell was that for?'

'Oh god, I'm so sorry, Eloise. You know I'd never hurt you.'

'You just did!'

'I'm sorry, so sorry. Of course I'll tell you.'

'Well you better had now. My god, Mum!'

Chrissy sat down and took hold of her hand, staring at their interlocking fingers whilst focusing on her breathing. Eloise grabbed some air for herself. Sometimes there just wasn't enough to go round. When Chrissy retreated back into her silence, Eloise kicked out at the chair leg, giving her a jolt.

'Maybe you could start by telling me how you two met, Mum,' she said, opting for a gentler approach. Inside, she was still screaming at her.

Chrissy closed her eyes and frowned, as though the memory hung by a delicate thread.

CHAPTER 2

Bristol: 1988

The first lecture, French Literature in the twentieth century, was not until eleven o'clock. But Chrissy's nerves were not prepared to wait and she set off much earlier than was necessary. New Order's 'Blue Monday' was thumping out from across the corridor as she stepped out of her room. She had no idea who lived there, or anywhere else on her floor for that matter.

The School of Modern Languages was housed in a series of grand old Victorian villas along Woodland Road. At nine thirty, she left her halls, Cliff Lawn Halls of Residence, down the hill, but with so much time to spare she decided to meander first. The sponge covers of her Walkman had been lost, causing the plastic to nip into her ears, but The Smiths was the perfect soundtrack for her mood.

A dense fog lingered in the air, giving the streets of Clifton an eerie feel. The way it clung to her was like a damp cloak, even entering her nostrils as she reflected on why she hadn't yet clicked with anyone when she had been here for almost a fortnight. It wasn't due to a lack of trying on her part. During Freshers' Week she had joined the Film Soc, French Soc, been to Happy Hours with people on stage giving blowjobs to hotdogs, and drinking a yard of ale in their underwear. She had even forced herself to do the three-legged bar crawl and that hadn't yielded anything either. To make matters worse, she had woken up this morning paralyzed by fear, convinced that all the other students on her course would have been to better schools and read far more books. Plus, that she had been given someone else's A-level results by mistake and had no right to be here in the first place.

Dan assured her it was still early days and things would get better once lectures had begun. Speaking to him daily on the payphone downstairs she assured him she wouldn't call so often once she had found a bunch of people to hang out with. Looking around her now as the tiered rows curving round the lecture theatre filled up and the noise level reached an almost deafening crescendo, she was not so sure she ever would. Everyone else was in full-flow conversation; she was the only person sitting on her own.

How many times could she lace up her Docs? Rub at the coffee stain on her stonewashed jeans? Or keep going over the date she had written in the top right-hand corner of her A4 notepad: ruled narrow feint and margin? The coffee stain was still wet and she could see her leg, red and sore, through the rip in her jeans. She had gone into the common room just before the lecture in the hope of meeting a few people off her course, but had to settle for the vending machine's buzzing and clanking for company as it squirted a dirty brown liquid into a polystyrene cup. Then, whilst she was pretending to read the noticeboard someone had bumped into her without realizing she was even there. And no apology for causing her to tip hot coffee down herself either.

It was a relief when the lecturer walked in. The place fell immediately silent as a small, rotund man with a long beard, tweed jacket and yellow cravat, placed his notes on the lectern, sweeping his eyes over each student, already weeding out the Firsts from the Fails.

'What is existentialism?' his voice boomed round the lecture theatre. 'Who wants to have a shot?'

11

There was no other hand up, only hers. Suddenly sixty pairs of eyes were upon her and she flushed, feeling like a swot. A phoney swot at that because no words were coming out. On the verge of putting her hand back down, she suddenly remembered something she had read.

'A view of the world in which man is condemned to a life of freedom and has the full burden of responsibility?'

She felt her cheeks catch fire.

'Meaning?' said the lecturer.

Meaning? That was good enough, surely.

'Erm, well, meaning that he can't hide behind God or science but he makes his own choices about absolutely everything. Even under pressure, in a split second. I think.'

A commotion at the back of the lecture theatre, a latecomer, made everyone turn round. The lecturer was annoyed, it broke his flow, but then his face melted. Suddenly this student was the most important person in the whole room. Chrissy couldn't help noticing this girl's *je ne sais quoi* factor either, but she was furious with her for stealing her moment.

Most people would have settled on the first gap they came to at the end of a row, keen to end their embarrassment, but this girl had people moving bags, A4 files, coats, legs, arms, to let her through. And to Chrissy's horror she was making for the centre of the middle row where there was an empty seat next to hers. Chrissy looked helplessly at the lecturer, feeling herself flush again, as though this was all her fault. The girl flipped down the seat and held out her hand, refusing to sit down until Chrissy had shaken it.

'Juliet,' she whispered, as she settled down at last.

Chrissy tried to ignore her as the lecturer resumed. She didn't want him to think they were friends, especially as she had made an impression on him and she actually felt worthy of being here now. Juliet scribbled something on her notepad and pushed it towards her. When Chrissy paid no attention she received a gentle nudge in the ribs. '*Qui es-tu?*' the note said. Realizing she would get no peace unless she responded she scribbled her name down quickly, still focusing on the lecturer and not prepared to engage any further.

When the session finished, Chrissy zipped up her bag and stood up.

'Does my head in, all this existential stuff,' said Juliet.

'So what are you doing here then?'

Chrissy turned her back, ready to shuffle along the row.

'Long story. I came to sit with you, by the way, because you looked like the least boring person in the room.'

'Am I meant to be flattered?' said Chrissy, half-twisting her head.

'I don't suppose there's any chance I can borrow your lecture notes, is there?'

Chrissy pulled down the notepad that Juliet was clutching to her chest and saw it was full of sketches of what looked like fashion designs. She shook her head, turning away again.

'You want to get a coffee?'

Even if this girl was rather irritating, and certainly not the sort of friend she was looking for, at least she was showing some interest. 'Sorry, I can't,' Chrissy replied. 'But thanks for asking.'

'I don't mean that shit from the vending machine either.'

'I still can't,' said Chrissy, laughing.

Once she was out into the corridor, narrow with a low-hanging roof, it would be easier to lose herself in the crowd, she told herself. But she was wrong.

'I like The Smiths, too,' said Juliet, referring to Chrissy's T-shirt and suddenly by her side again. 'Saw them twice.'

'Three times for me,' said Chrissy. 'Look, I can't hang about. I've got to go and meet my tutor.' She speeded up again, heading for the stairs.

'You know, the reason I was late was because I saw a dog run over and I couldn't decide if the dog had *chosen* to run in front of the car, or if it was just an accident.'

'Really?' said Chrissy, stopping.

'Oh. Actually, no, I was trying to be existential. I slept in; I don't have an alarm clock.'

'Well maybe you should go buy one then.' Chrissy carried on up the stairs, reminding herself to trust first instincts.

'Do you want to come to a party?'

It was just loud enough to pick out above all the other voices. Chrissy reached for the handrail and turned round.

'Fuck's sake!' snapped a girl with pink hair and alarmingly plucked eyebrows. 'Do you have to stop on the stairs?'

'When?' shouted Chrissy, ignoring the complaints.

'Wednesday. Bring a friend, or friends if you've made some. The more the merrier.'

She found herself going to claim the photocopied invite that Juliet was tantalizingly waving at the bottom of the stairs.

'Where is it?'

'Cowper Road.'

She was about to ask where that was when Juliet helpfully added: 'There's a map on the back of the invite.'

'Aren't you in halls?'

'Stoke Bishop. Miles from bloody anywhere. Luckily I know a couple of people in Redland. Do you know it? Just head up St Michael's Hill away from town. It's not far. Where are you?'

'Clifton,' she said, tugging the piece of paper out of Juliet's fingers, giving the map a quick scan. 'I'll find it.' She tucked it into her jeans pocket and then found herself weakening. Handing over her lecture notes, she said: 'And if you lose those I will kill you.'

'You're all right you are, Chrissy Wotsit,' she heard Juliet shout as she galloped up the stairs, not wanting to be late for her tutor. She turned round and gave Juliet the finger.

But for the first time in days, she had a smile on her face.

CHAPTER 3

Manchester: 2007

'So did you go to the party?'

Eloise was desperate to know more but Chrissy had come to an abrupt halt. It was time to go in any case. Her cheek still felt sore as it brushed against her mother's, kissing her goodbye, reminding her of the slap she had received earlier and for no apparent reason. It was more the shock than any physical pain that had bothered her, but it was a sign that she would have to tread carefully.

Something Eloise had been doing for years.

'Wouldn't you like to see her again, Mum?'

Chrissy shook her head, a small movement at first, as if a tiny part of her was still undecided. Then, an emphatic, 'No.'

'Well, tell me some more later, yeah? When I get back.'

'Do you have to go?' said Chrissy.

'What, to meet Anya? Or do you mean Inter-Railing?'

The lack of reply annoyed Eloise, almost as much as her question. She bent down to pick up her bag, feeling her mother's gaze burning into her back. She stood up again, moving towards her until their faces were almost touching.

'Goodbye, Mum,' she said, meeting her glare, confident she would not be the one to back down first. She just had the edge in her shoes. But in the end Eloise did look away first, her mother's face was so full of anguish, and she turned to leave before she felt that she couldn't.

'How're you getting home?' she heard Chrissy shout as she made for the door.

'Dunno.' She was already halfway out.

'Well, can you walk back with Anya?'

'Yeah, whatever.'

The Mancunian Way rumbled on like a Big Dipper ride over the Stockport Road, the grey-white tower of the university protruding above it. Clouds had closed in on the sun, stealing the warmth out of their summer's evening. The estate was quieter now, apart from the murmur of traffic.

The key turned in the lock behind her, startling Eloise; she had been using the door as a backrest. Then the chain slid across. She kicked out at a piece of Lego, shooting it off the walkway, and moved over to grab the railings, fingernails digging into her palms. If her mother thought a harmless bit of Inter-Railing around Europe was a problem, what would she be like with a whole gap year after A-levels? And what about Bournemouth Uni? Eloise had convinced herself, and her mother, that it was by far the best course in Travel and Tourism. It was also the furthest away.

Of course she would go Inter-Railing; there was never any doubt about that. If she couldn't get Chrissy to agree to it, she would still go. It was for four weeks, not forever. Nevertheless, she could still hear her dad's words, as if it was only yesterday when he had uttered them: 'Look after your mother, Eloise. You're all she's got now.'

At the bottom of the stairwell, these thoughts still pinballed around inside her head. As she walked along Grosvenor Street the pair of trainers looped over the telephone wires swung back and forth. She watched them; they had been there for years, condemned to a life of futile hanging in the breeze. This was not a bad area by any means. The centre of Manchester was less than a mile away, and with the university close by they had the whole world on their doorstep. 'So why go anywhere else?' her mother would say. She had even suggested that Eloise could go to Manchester Uni and live at home. 'It'd be so much cheaper,' she insisted, but they both knew that wasn't the real reason.

The pedestrian crossing on Upper Brook Street was beeping insistently at her. When she failed to cross, a sleek black car with tinted windows allowed her to go, and the motorist in the car behind sounded his horn, revving his engine impatiently. Eloise walked over to the other side, oblivious to the real world. Chrissy would never get in touch with Juliet, of that she was sure. Why did she never allow anyone else into her life? No one could even get close. Even when her dad was alive it was probably just the same, she realized. Except, when her dad was alive it didn't matter, because her mother always had him.

Without Eloise, Chrissy had no one.

Turning right onto Oxford Road there was something of a Friday night buzz. The sleek black car with tinted windows was making slow progress, crawling along beside her in the slow-moving traffic. Up ahead, Eloise could see a crowd of smokers gathered outside Maria's Café. The green sign distinguished it from the kebab shop and the music shop on either side. It was a popular spot, especially with students.

Eloise pushed open the glass door. She smiled at a group of regulars, squeezing between the benches, and waved at a couple of Sixth Formers from her college that she recognized. She was glad not to be working tonight.

Maria looked up from the spurting coffee machine and nodded towards the end computer. After a while she came over. 'Someone was in here looking for you earlier.'

'Really?' said Eloise. 'Who?'

'A man. Wearing some sort of uniform, not sure what he was.'

'Could be Anya's dad, he's some kind of security guard. Did he leave a message?' Maria shook her head. 'He was probably looking for Anya then.'

'He asked for you.'

Eloise smiled, hoping she would go away. It was only when she brought up the Inter-Rail website that Maria took the hint.

'Who is Juliet Ricci?' she typed once she had gone.

The computer fired a string of results back at her. She checked to see if anyone was watching before scanning down the list. They all sounded rather dull, except for one. She clicked on the link.

A website of translucent greys and whites began to unfurl. Moody images of long, pale models, dressed in outfits that looked more like works of art than clothing, appeared across the screen.

'Enter the exclusive World of Ricci. Shop the latest collections of this luxury Italian fashion house. Read the latest news about the brand …'

It was ridiculous even to imagine this Juliet Ricci in the same room as her mother, let alone breathing the same air.

'ENTER: Juliet and Luca Ricci, internationally acclaimed designers producing iconic work as seen on red carpets and catwalks throughout the world. Two major collections a year, distinctive designs.'

A selection of menus along the top enticed her further:

'Womenswear, Menswear, Accessories, Evening Wear, Lingerie, Shoes, Fragrance'

The prices were eye-watering.

'CONTACT'

There she was: Juliet Ricci, standing back-to-back with her Italian husband, Luca, a fluffy white cat intertwined through his legs. She had a beehive, dark with red streaks running through it, and something silver, like a big hairslide pinned into it. She wore a blue and silver Japanese-looking tunic, silver platform shoes.

Eloise clicked on a map of the world covered in white arrows: '*There are Ricci stores in all the major capitals and over 120 concessions within the world's most prestigious department stores.*'

She imagined the possibilities. Trips to Italy. New York. Tokyo. Paris. Long weekends in London. A never-ending supply of free designer clothes for her and Chrissy.

The website disappeared off the screen. Eloise needed to force herself back to reality. She pulled her phone from her pocket and brought up Juliet's number, telling herself that, even if it turned out to be the boring Juliet in IT from Cambridge, it really didn't matter. What did matter was that this woman should become her mother's best friend again. Someone else to share the burden.

'*Pronto? Chi parla?*'

That seductively husky voice. Maybe she lived in Italy?

'Hello?' it said again.

Italy would be perfect.

'Juliet Ricci speaking. Who is this?'

Eloise cut the call. What could she possibly say to Juliet when her mother didn't seem to want to know? A text message, she suddenly thought, wishing she had done this in the first place instead of making a fool of herself. It would also give her time to plan. Several attempts later, she settled for:

'*Would love to meet you Juliet.*
Please don't call again.
Email me – Eloise.lundy@tiscali.co.uk XXX'

Her finger hovered over the 'Send' button.

'Sorry I'm late.'

'Christ Almighty, Anya! You frightened the life out of me.'

Eloise stared at the words:

'*MESSAGE SENT*'

***

Eloise assumed her mother was out when she didn't answer her shout through the letterbox; something she was meant to do before unlocking the door – if she remembered to do it. Rooting in her bag for her keys, Eloise stuck her head over the side of the railings, discreetly, just to be sure. At one point she had thought she was being followed, but when the man had turned off before the Salvation Army building she changed her mind. Besides, he seemed more interested in his phone than anywhere she might be going. Nonetheless it had shaken her; she had quickened her pace, taking the stairs two at a time when she reached them, checking behind her all the way.

When the door wouldn't open she banged on it loudly with her fist.

'Mum, why is the bolt on? I can't get in. It's me.'

It clunked across, top and bottom. The place was in darkness, apart from a candle flickering on the coffee table.

'What's going on? Are you okay?'

Chrissy nodded. She seemed calm enough.

'Has there been a power cut or something?'

'No, I'm just meditating,' she replied.

'Oh,' said Eloise, trying to weigh up her mood and eliminate the flashbacks from earlier, walking home.

Chrissy returned to the sofa, sitting down cross-legged. The TV was on but muted, some talk show with a sofa full of vaguely recognizable people on it, and Eloise noticed a plate of toast and Marmite on the coffee table next to a half-drunk glass of wine.

She wondered whether to remove the bottle that was down at her feet but left it where it was.

'So did you make it to your yoga class?' asked Eloise, bouncing down next to her.

Chrissy shuffled along, continuing to stare at the TV. 'No. I went for a run instead.'

'Oh. How many circuits did you do?' Eloise wasn't at all interested, but running was her mother's thing and sometimes a good way to engage. As far as Eloise was concerned, running was a form of torture.

'Actually I ran into town and back.'

'You never,' said Eloise, screwing up her face. 'Centre of Manchester on a Friday night? What's that about?' Her usual circuit was down to the Apollo, weaving back through the Brunswick Estate. She had been doing that for years, never deviated.

'I changed my mind.'

'Why though?'

'Just a feeling,' she said, still not making eye contact.

'Well, what sort of a feeling?'

'I wanted to be in a crowded place, that's all.'

Eloise grabbed the remote and zapped the TV off. 'Can we talk, Mum?'

'Why, what's wrong? What's happened?'

Chrissy lunged for her glass and turned her body round to face Eloise, who was slightly regretting this tactic now. It had crossed her mind to mention that she thought she had been followed, but didn't dare do that now; it would only play into her mother's paranoia. Besides, it was just in her head, so hardly worth a mention.

'No, nothing's happened. I'm fine. I've just been wondering about your friend, Juliet, and what she did after uni. Have you any idea?'

Chrissy polished off her wine and poured herself another. 'Is that what you want to talk about, Eloise? Because if it is I'm not in the mood.'

Eloise wished she had taken the bottle away now.

Chrissy was looking at her awkwardly. 'Listen, I'm sorry for slapping you,' she said. 'I shouldn't have done that. I don't know what came over me.'

'It's okay,' Eloise replied, knowing her mother's guilt was to her advantage. 'So, when will you be in the mood?'

But instead of answering, Chrissy sank another large mouthful. Before leaning back again, she began rearranging the cushions behind her, pulling out the little yellow bear, a present to Eloise from her dad. It had become a game of theirs, putting the bear in unusual places so the other person would find it: in the biscuit tin, swinging from a light fitting, it could even be found hiding in a pocket. A smile spread across Chrissy's face at the discovery, and Eloise felt herself softening towards her again.

Her cheeks were still flushed from her run, hair swept back in a ponytail and tiny beads of sweat glistened in the fine creases around her mouth. Eloise wished she had her mother's lips; they were heart-shaped and she was lovely when she smiled. This thought saddened her all of a sudden, although she didn't quite know why, not until she started speaking. 'Do you remember, Mum, that time when Dad told me you'd gone running? I thought he meant you'd run away, like forever, and were never coming back. I cried for days.'

She put down her glass and pulled Eloise into her side. 'I'd never run away from you. You know that, don't you?'

'Yes, 'course I do,' Eloise replied, leaving it a moment before adding: 'But I don't know why you run away from everyone else. Why won't you see Juliet? She's your best friend.'

'Was.'

'Okay "was", but you said yourself that you never fell out.'

Chrissy stood up. 'I'm going to run a bath,' she said. She left the room clutching her glass, and Eloise tossed a cushion across the floor.

'Damn thing,' said her mother, shaking her head at the trickle coming out of the hot tap.

'Can't you just tell me?' said Eloise, kicking the doorframe.

Chrissy sank down onto the side of the bath, tucking her hands between her thighs. 'Look, do you have to keep on at me, Eloise?'

'Just tell me why you don't want to see her again.'

'Because …'

She let the word drift into the sound of the water. The tap was flowing now, which seemed to soothe her, then she remembered her wine and tipped the final dregs into her mouth. Eloise took the glass out of her hand and put it down by the sink.

'It's complicated,' said Chrissy. Her face was red from the steam and from rubbing it so much. 'Anyway, it's not possible to see her again.'

'Of course it is, Mum. You just get in touch and say—'

'It's *not* possible.'

She made a chopping motion with her hands as if to say 'The End'. It caught the stem of the glass, clattering it into the sink.

'I'll sort it,' said Chrissy, shunting Eloise out of the way.

Eloise backed off, her hands up in submission, and went to get some newspaper. When she returned, Chrissy was holding out the remnants in her T-shirt.

'Oh, you've cut your finger,' Eloise remarked as the glass clinked down onto the paper.

'It's nothing,' she replied, giving her finger a suck before folding the newspaper into a parcel. She held out her injury for Eloise to inspect. 'Think I'll live, don't you?' Putting her hand to Eloise's cheek, she added, 'I know you're curious.'

'Well then tell me!' she snapped, swiping Chrissy's hand away. 'Or maybe I'll just ask Juliet myself.'

'Don't think you can blackmail me,' said Chrissy, narrowing

her eyes. Her lips also had a habit of drawing in when something bothered her, which they were doing now.

'What are you going to do? Slap me again?'

Chrissy looked down at the vinyl flooring, the edges starting to curl where it wasn't stuck down properly. She let out a sigh before she spoke. 'Look, I will tell you about Juliet. But …' She raised her hand to prevent Eloise from butting in. '… but you can only hear it from me. Do you understand that? Never Juliet. Just give me some time to think.'

'You've had twenty years to think, Mum!'

'Not quite,' she said. 'Please, that's all I ask.'

Eloise nodded, though she was unconvinced. Suddenly a vision of herself, twenty years from now, forced itself into her head. Still crouched by this bath beside her mother, never having left home. Never having a life of her own. She had always thought it was because of her father's death that her mother was this way, but perhaps it was something else. Whatever it was, Juliet was the key – and Eloise had no intention of letting the opportunity slip away.

***

A sharp triangle of light cut across Eloise's bed where the curtains had not quite come together. She had slept lightly in any case, waking up in a panic, trying to unlock a door that she could never quite reach.

Pulling back the curtains she opened the window to let in the familiar hum of traffic. It sounded different this morning, as if it were going somewhere meaningful and not just the dreary commute into Manchester.

Eloise shuffled into the kitchen, grinning to herself, checking her phone as she went.

'Don't you have to get yourself to work?' asked Chrissy when she was presented with a mug of tea, and Eloise climbed into bed next to her.

24

'It's Saturday, you know.'

Chrissy reached for her alarm clock, spilling tea on the bed. 'Oh fuck!' she blurted, setting the mug down and then smiling at Eloise, remembering her as a cross little girl with a swear box. 'Sorry, Eloise. I meant *fluck*,' she insisted.

'Well, I'll let you off if you tell me some more. I want to know about that party Juliet invited you to. Did you go?'

Her mother began folding the duvet into neat rolls, focusing on the wall opposite as though she could see images projected onto it.

'I did,' she said finally.

CHAPTER 4

Bristol: 1988

Chrissy didn't need to look at the numbers down Cowper Road to know where the party was. There was already a huddle gathered outside on the front steps and music was blaring into the street. The house was in a row of Victorian terraces, much shabbier than the ones either side of it. She closed the *A-Z* before anyone saw it and dropped it into the inside pocket of her overcoat; she didn't completely trust other people's maps. The heavy reggae beat pumped through her chest as she got nearer. Clutching her cheap bottle of wine, she pushed her way through the smokers in the doorway. The wisps of a joint weaved up her nostrils as drinks were held aloft, and she repeatedly said 'excuse me' and 'sorry'.

She was heading for the kitchen but somehow ended up in the front room where people were dancing. A beige sofa had been turned on its end to make more space and the gas fire had a CONDEMNED sign across it. Her eyes were drawn to a glitter ball, casting coloured spots over the walls and people's faces as it spun round. The smell of beer, sweat and hairspray hung in the air and took some getting used to.

She had almost made it into the kitchen when the music changed to The Smiths and she felt a hand pulling her back in.

'Chrissy, come and dance,' someone shouted. She assumed it was Juliet, although wasn't sure, and almost stumbled.

Whoever it was wore a fascinator-style hat with a net over her face and looked stunning in a fitted tartan jacket, black shorts, high heels and fishnets. 'Really glad you've come,' she said, lifting up the net and taking a drag from a roll-up, releasing a trail of smoke from the side of her mouth.

'Hi. I wasn't sure if it was you,' said Chrissy. She quickly looked around for somewhere to put her wine bottle, embarrassed that she still had it, then danced to 'Panic' with a group of people who all seemed to know Juliet.

'Drink?' said Juliet when it had finished.

She ushered Chrissy into the kitchen, sloshing wine into a glass as she made some introductions. 'Paula, Leo, Ali, Jazz.' Chrissy smiled as they were being pointed out to her. 'Carl, Vernon, Gabby.' They had to be the coolest crowd in Bristol, an indie fusion of every fashion style going – punk, New Romantic, Hippie chic, and anything in between. Despite feeling under-dressed in her jeans, Docs and purple lipstick, Chrissy was soon chatting away about music, gigs, Glastonbury and Dan's band. To think that she had very nearly talked herself out of coming tonight.

Most people at the party, as far as she could tell, were Second Years, perhaps herself and Juliet the only freshers, so when the conversation in the kitchen turned to housemates' banter she moved over to the wall where she could observe Juliet more easily. Juliet was dancing again, but every so often she would get a tap on the shoulder and briefly stop. Seemed like everyone wanted to speak to her.

How did she do it? A mere fresher.

'Chrissy!' Juliet called when she spotted her again. 'Have you met my friend Chrissy, everyone?' She placed a drunken arm around her neck, pulling her in to dance. Chrissy tried not to spill her drink as they swayed to some reggae beat.

'How do you know all these people, Juliet?'

'Oh well let's see ... Ali and Jazz, I know from school. They were the year above me. Hang on a sec.' She turned away to talk to someone momentarily then came back. 'Sorry. Yeah, so I visited them in Bristol a few times last year. It's their party, in case you hadn't worked that out.'

'I had.'

She was just about to ask a further question when Juliet got an arm around her shoulder and a joint pushed into her mouth. Chrissy realized her moment was up.

'Let's have a proper chat later,' she shouted, waving the joint in the air. 'Really glad you showed.'

'Me too,' Chrissy replied, but Juliet had already flitted.

Chrissy ventured upstairs to find the toilet, climbing over drunken bodies. The first door she tried opened on a couple having sex on a pile of coats, so she shut it again quickly. In the next she was invited to do a line, but eventually found the queue for the toilet and, instead, stood in line.

Juliet was nowhere to be seen when she went back downstairs. Chrissy danced for a while, but soon tired of being on her own and looked for somewhere to put herself. One of the Rasta guys tried to pull her back as she moved away. She gave him a friendly smile, accepting the remains of a joint he was offering her, and began to pick her way through the empty Red Stripe cans, squashing peanuts into the slug-trailed carpet and fanning herself with her T-shirt. The glitter ball spots made the whole ceiling go round as she flopped into a beanbag kicked into the corner. She took a sly look at her watch. One thirty, and more people seemed to be arriving. Perhaps it was time to go.

'So how do you know Ju then?'

It was a girl from the kitchen whose name she couldn't remember. She slid down the wall and sat beside her, and Chrissy thought her eyes looked strange, like she had taken something. The girl's question puzzled her at first, until she realized. 'Oh, you mean Juliet. She's on my course. But I don't know her very well.'

Chrissy took the final drag on the spliff, seeing that the girl had one of her own.

'Her stuff's incredible, isn't it?' the girl said, putting hers to her mouth.

'Is it?' Chrissy replied.

'There you are. I've been looking all over for you!'

Juliet was carrying a stack of white toast smeared in Marmite, holding the plate aloft. She offered it to Chrissy just as several hands descended from all directions. 'Hang on, hang on. Play nicely you lot.' Despite not feeling hungry, and not even sure whether she liked Marmite that much, Chrissy helped herself to a piece.

Juliet handed the plate over to the greedy pack and they moved away.

'Watch her, she's trouble that one,' said Jazz, winking at Chrissy.

'Sod off,' Juliet replied, collapsing into the beanbag, sending Chrissy into the air. The taste of Marmite stuck in Chrissy's throat through laughing so much.

'I might have to head off soon actually,' she said as the room started to spin. 'Great party though.'

'You can't go yet!' Juliet shrieked through a mouthful of toast. 'We've got hash cookies for pudding. Or magic mushroom cake if you're feeling particularly trippy.'

'Well, I don't really do that stuff. The odd spliff but—'

She was persuaded to stay nonetheless, and Juliet began asking questions about her love life, music, friends, jobs, usual topics really. Although Chrissy had trotted this stuff out a million times over the past couple of weeks it sounded vaguely interesting when she shared it with Juliet. She seemed particularly keen to hear about Dan, his band and his music. They talked a lot about Dan.

'So what about you?' said Chrissy, realizing the focus had been almost entirely on her.

'Me?' Juliet took off her hat, shaking out her hair. A trail of shiny black waves fell over her shoulders. 'Jeez, it's hot under there.' She had an olive complexion, dark eyes, and with her hair down she was even more striking. 'I'll fill you in sometime, not now.'

Chrissy hadn't shared those things about Dan with anyone else in Bristol, and the disappointment at not getting anything in return must have shown on her face.

'I generally don't tell people my stuff,' said Juliet, lighting another cigarette. She looked quite forlorn all of a sudden. 'Anyway it's very boring, and to be honest no one ever asks.'

Chrissy wafted the smoke away and looked at her watch. 'I really need my bed,' she said, attempting to get out of the beanbag.

Juliet managed to stand up before her and held out her hand.

'Thanks,' said Chrissy.

Suddenly both Juliet's arms were draped round her neck and she made her sway in time to the music. 'You can always crash here,' she said with a wink. 'It's what I normally do.'

'Thought you were in halls.'

'I use my room for work mainly. They let me kip down here for free whenever I want.'

She saw Juliet give a nod to a seventies-style punk standing by the door. He looked high as a kite.

'How come for free?' she asked.

'Guess they feel sorry for me. Look, please stay. Come on, it'll be fun.'

'No, honestly. I'll tag along with that lot heading back to Clifton.'

'What about that coffee then?' said Juliet, kissing her cheek. 'When are we next in?'

'Friday. Do you know Gianni's?' She was pleased when Juliet didn't. 'It's on St Michael's Hill. I recommend the hot chocolate though.'

Juliet followed her to the pile of coats in the corner. 'Sounds like a date,' she said, kissing her other cheek as Chrissy was buttoning her overcoat. 'I'll give you your notes back then too,' she added, pretending to throttle herself, making choking noises. 'So you don't have to kill me.'

Chrissy looked down at her Docs, embarrassed now for saying that, and gave Juliet a grin.

'Ooh. One more thing,' said Juliet, disappearing for a moment. She had found someone to take a photo of the two of them and placed her arm around Chrissy's shoulder. The Polaroid camera clunked and whirred. After a few minutes it spewed out the picture, wet and shiny, as if by magic. Juliet blew on it, wafting it back and forth then handed it to Chrissy. 'One for me, one for you,' she said. So they had to do it all over again.

CHAPTER 5

Manchester: 2007

'Anyway, get yourself ready,' said her mother. 'You'll get the sack if you're late again.'

Eloise checked her inbox first, before taking a shower. Nothing. And again after her shower. Still nothing. And every five minutes after that. So Juliet had abandoned them already. She could hardly blame her for giving up on her mother. Chrissy was probably the worst friend ever.

Then, just as she was about to turn off her computer, there it was.

From: juliet124ricci@yahoo.com
Dearest Eloise,
I'm sorry, I should have realized that my popping up after all this time would give your mum a bit of a shock. I've been trying to find her for so long now. I tried all the usual ways on the internet but she never comes up. I thought she'd disappeared forever. Then one day I had a brainwave, remembered the name of Dan's band and found their website. After several dead ends and great confusion, which I won't bore you with, I eventually

tracked you down. One of their old band members – good friend of Dan? – gave me an address and a number to try. I can't tell you how amazing it was to hear your voice yesterday, Eloise.

I was terribly sad to hear about Dan. Is he by any chance your father? You'll have to forgive me because I know nothing about what happened after Chrissy left university. We were forced to sever all ties. It was a difficult time for both of us. I can't say any more than that really, except she was a true friend. She did something very important for me once and I never got the chance to thank her, not properly. So I hope that with all these years behind us now, she will want to see me again.

I hope to meet you one day very soon, Eloise. In fact, we have a new collection out so I am currently in the UK promoting it. I will let you know when I'll be coming North.

Much love to you both
Juliet Ricci
Xx

PS My assistant Laura has just brought in my schedule for next week. I will be in Yorkshire and Manchester on Monday. Scotland Tuesday. I could fly up tomorrow (Sunday) and come and see you if you think that's at all possible.

Tomorrow?

Tomorrow felt too soon even for Eloise. It would be foolish to rush into anything. But at the same time she didn't want to lose the opportunity to reunite Juliet and her mother.

It was only after reading Juliet's email another three times that she trusted herself to reply:

'Hi Juliet,

Thanks for getting in touch. I'm working on my mum and hope we can meet very soon. Yes, you are right. Dan is my dad and I miss him loads.

Can you make it Monday instead?
Eloise xx

PS Much better if we meet in town. Not here.'

Anywhere but here, she thought. She wandered about their flat, squirming at the mad colour scheme. The furniture in the lounge was looking rather shabby and everywhere needed a fresh lick of paint. The clock in the kitchen no longer worked, the pictures in there were dire: one of spoons dancing, and another of chubby peasants at a country fair. Suddenly these things mattered in a way they hadn't ever before.

She poured herself a glass of orange juice from the fridge. Her throat throbbed from the ice-cold shock.

When another mail landed in her inbox, she pounced:

'*Eloise,*
    Of course. One thing you should know is that, for Chrissy, I'll do anything. I'll get Laura to arrange it.
    See you Monday.
    Juliet x'

She was already running fifteen minutes late, and Maria would not be pleased, but there was one more thing she had to do before she left.

'Do I really deserve this?' said Chrissy, accepting the plate of toast and Marmite.

'Just wanted to spoil you, Mum.'

Chrissy propped herself against the pillow, her head on one side. 'You're turning into such a young woman, Eloise. Smart and beautiful.'

'Yeah, I know.'

'Your dad would be so proud of you.' She turned to his photo by her bedside. 'I wish he was here to see you grow up.'

34

'Me too. Hey, but listen. I can show you a picture of Juliet if you like. She has a website.' Chrissy gave the duvet a sharp tug. 'I don't mean now. I've got to go to work.'

Their discussion was interrupted by a heavy pounding on the door, followed by an insistent ringing of the bell. Surely Juliet would not just appear on their doorstep without warning? Not after all that had been said. Was Chrissy having similar thoughts too? She was as white as her pillow.

'I'm coming,' shouted Eloise, twisting her ankle in her haste to see who it was.

It was the police.

'Who is it?' said Chrissy, coming out in her dressing gown. She froze when she saw the female officer standing there.

Afraid she might faint, the officer quickly stepped inside and helped Chrissy to sit down. Eloise was told to make her mother a hot drink. 'I'm sorry to give you a scare,' she said. 'It was just to alert you about a break-in next door last night, and we wondered if you'd heard anything.'

They told her they hadn't, that they were in most of the evening, apart from when Chrissy went out for a run, which seemed to fit in with the timing of the break-in.

Everyone got done once on the estate; it was known as 'the housewarming'. And the next-door neighbours were fairly new, so it was to be expected really. That said, their own flat had never been broken into, not with Chrissy's stringent security measures, and they had lived in it for more than ten years.

When the police officer had gone, Eloise phoned Maria to say that she would be in work a bit later. Maria was fine once she explained why.

'I'll be okay,' said Chrissy. 'It was just a bit of a shock, that's all. You don't need to stay.'

'Yes I do,' Eloise insisted. Her mother's face had turned a peculiar shade of grey and she was still trembling. 'I'll put the kettle on shall I?'

Chrissy nodded and soon they were both settled in the living room with steaming mugs of tea.

'So,' began Eloise tentatively, 'did Juliet meet you in that place for coffee?'

Chrissy gave a tut, rolling her eyes at her daughter's persistence.

'Did she? Gino's, was it?'

'Gianni's.'

'Or I can show you her website.' Eloise ignored the stab of guilt she was feeling, pushing her mother like this in the state she was in. 'Your choice, Mum.'

CHAPTER 6

Bristol: 1988

Sitting in Gianni's on St Michael's Hill, her fingers coiled round a mug of hot chocolate that she had been sipping for well over an hour, more cold now than hot, Chrissy was wondering whether she should be offended, or worried. There was no way of getting in touch with Juliet; she could be anywhere. She hadn't shown up to the lecture either, on Nineteenth-Century Romanticism. This probably meant Juliet would ask for Chrissy's notes again, and she couldn't quite make up her mind what to do if she did.

She was just about to leave when a purple raincoat came into view. 'Where've you been, Juliet? I've been worried sick about you.'

'Am I that late? Sorry, I had stuff to do.' She kissed Chrissy on both cheeks, holding her cigarette out of the way, then wafting at the smoke slowly creeping back into Chrissy's face.

'Have you got my notes?' Chrissy asked, sternly.

'Blimey, you don't mess about, do you?'

With her cigarette balanced stylishly between her fingers Juliet rummaged in her bag, proudly holding up three sheets of paper. Chrissy snatched them out of her hands.

'Don't be mad at me,' said Juliet, childishly pleading. When she saw it hadn't dented Chrissy's anger, she tried: 'Let me buy you a coffee.'

'I've already had a drink,' said Chrissy, snapping together the metal rings of her binder.

Juliet put her hand to her forehead. 'Stupid. I mean hot chocolate, don't I?' Waiting for a response, she twisted her hair around her fingers. She wore it down today, and the black went well against the purple raincoat. 'Oh, but do you have to go already?' she said when she saw Chrissy was still gathering up her things.

'*Already*? Juliet, I've been here for over an hour.'

She considered asking what had been so important to keep her waiting for so long. At the same time, she didn't want to feel insulted by the response, so she kept silent. Chrissy feared, somewhere in the back of her mind, there may be a part of Juliet's life she didn't want to have anything to do with. Thrusting her hands into her pockets she made for the door.

'I'll walk back to Clifton with you,' said Juliet, quickly linking her arm through hers. 'We can go shopping.'

Chrissy looked down at Juliet's hand, contemplating whether to remove it or not. 'I'm on a budget,' she replied. Only that morning, in fact, when she had drawn a £5 note out of the hole-in-the-wall, she was shocked at how little was left of her grant money once the halls of residence had been paid. And when it was gone, it was gone.

Broke.

Judging by the cut of Juliet's clothes, she was way out of her price range. Either her parents were rich or she made a lot of money by some other means.

'Well, me too,' said Juliet. 'But people throw away some great stuff in Clifton.' She gave her arm a squeeze. 'Come on! Live a little.'

Chrissy found herself smiling. Juliet was hard to resist.

The sunshine was dazzling as they walked back along Tyndalls Park Road, yet despite an almost perfect blue sky there was still a wintry sting in the air. Chrissy pushed her chin down into her scarf and was glad when Juliet huddled into her. Crossing Queens Road into Clifton the wind suddenly whipped bundles of leaves into brown swirls, as if they were under some spell, and Chrissy quickened her pace.

'Oxfam on Princess Victoria Street is pretty good,' said Juliet, trying to keep up.

'What exactly do you buy in second-hand shops, Juliet?'

Juliet stopped for a moment, giving Chrissy a quizzical look, then started walking again. 'You full-grant students assume that if we've been to boarding school then we're loaded. Don't you? But just 'cos your parents have money doesn't mean they give you any.'

'You went to boarding school?'

'Several. Hated them all.'

They had entered the Oxfam shop and Chrissy pulled her scarf up over her nose to try to diffuse the musty smell. Whenever she bought anything second-hand she couldn't wait to get it home, stick it on a hot wash and spray it with perfume. It didn't feel like hers until she'd washed it three or four times.

Juliet was busily sifting through the knitwear rail, the first one they came to, and Chrissy was horrified when she picked out a chunky mohair jumper, removed it from its hanger then stuffed it inside her coat.

'Juliet!' she said in an overly loud whisper, causing the woman at the till to peer over her glasses on the end of a long chain.

'Money ...' said Juliet, strutting about the shop in a pompous manner, impersonating someone with a very large stomach. '... is for education. *Not* for the enjoyment of oneself.'

'What are you doing?' Chrissy couldn't help laughing, despite not wanting to encourage her.

'That,' said Juliet, extracting the jumper, 'is my dad.' She held it up so the woman could see her putting it back on the hanger. 'He's a fat, fucking idiot.'

Chrissy laughed again, more out of relief that Juliet was not shoplifting than anything else. Chrissy put the jumper back on the rail, giving the woman a look of apology. After that she stuck close to Juliet as they went through the rest of the rails. It was an education in itself watching her. Everything she pulled out she would look at from all angles, nip it in at the waist, turn up the sleeves, weighing up all the possibilities.

'This would suit you,' she said, fishing out a green dress. Chrissy pulled a face. 'Trust me, Chrissy. I'm going to get it for you. What size are you? Twelve?'

'Yes, but—'

'It's 50p. Won't break the bank.'

'I don't even like it. Juliet!'

She was already heading for the till.

'You will,' she shouted back.

They carried on walking to the Suspension Bridge. As this stunning feat of Victorian engineering came into view, slung across the Avon Gorge with its iron chains draped effortlessly between the two towers, it began to rain. Lightly at first, soon getting heavier. Rather than run for shelter, Chrissy and Juliet stood on the bridge, spinning round in the downpour, arms outstretched like children, oblivious to the cars honking as they made their way across the bridge.

'I'm soaked,' said Chrissy, stumbling over to the barrier, laughing because her head was still in a spin.

Juliet didn't respond. She was asking a passing tourist to take a photo of the two of them. They posed like models, pouting at the camera, then Chrissy turned to look at the view. Her eyes struggled to take it all in. The River Avon was a muddy brown colour 245 feet below. Trees clung to its steep banks like green, woolly sheep, and a road snaked around one side with toy-sized cars which looked to be stationary, although were probably moving quickly. On the other side of the bridge was Bristol, stretching out towards the Mendip Hills. Up ahead, the white, sandy terraces of Clifton. 'It's incredible, isn't it?' she said.

'I love bridges,' said Juliet, looping her fingers through the diamond-shaped holes of the barrier. Raising her arm had caused her coat sleeve to slip a little, enough to make the tiny scars on her skin visible. She put it down again quickly. 'Golden Gate Bridge, you ever seen that?' Chrissy shook her head. 'What's your favourite one in Paris? Mine's Pont Neuf.'

'I've never been to Paris,' Chrissy replied.

'What? You're studying French and you've never been to Paris?'

She wanted to say that she had been to Brittany on a school trip, but Juliet cut in with: 'We should go.' Which prompted Chrissy to look at her watch.

'No!' said Juliet, laughing. 'I mean we should go to France. You and me, this summer.'

'Oh.' Chrissy was still frantically trying to process the last ten seconds, including the marks on Juliet's arm. 'Okay … I mean yeah, why not?'

There was the whole year to get through first, but Chrissy felt the beginnings of excitement stir in her stomach.

***

Chrissy was happily enjoying everything that Juliet brought in her wake: the parties, the gigs, and all the interesting people she didn't seem to meet anywhere else. The drug taking was a concern, but as long as Chrissy could stay clear of it herself, it was really none of her business.

'It's only the odd happy pill and a bit of weed,' Juliet insisted. 'And some white powder now and again. You should try some, do you good.'

To be fair, it was pretty harmless in the scheme of things, and plenty of other people were doing it. Even Dan, occasionally, when the mood took him.

'How do you afford all of this?' Chrissy had asked Juliet one evening, gesturing at the spliff they were sharing.

Juliet smiled and grabbed her arm.

'Come on, I'll show you if you like. Let's go to my place.'

Chrissy was surprised. In all the weeks of knowing each other she had never gone to Juliet's room; it was always the other way round.

Feeling slightly apprehensive, she followed her.

***

Chrissy thought she had stepped into Aladdin's cave when she walked through the door.

'My god, Ju. So this is what you get up to?'

She had a sewing machine set up on the desk and piles of clothes everywhere: on the bed, the floor, some in bin bags, some laid out, some cut to pieces, some hanging up. Even the curtain rail was loaded. It soon became clear that the bulk of Juliet's time and a significant portion of her funds was spent on buying second-hand clothes and customizing them. She had a real eye for snapping up bargains and a rare talent for adding frills, collars, fishtails, pleats, belts, zips, buttons, chains and buckles.

'You do all this?' said Chrissy, turning full circle to take in the scale of it. 'Where do you sleep? When do you sleep?'

'I must admit, these help,' she said, popping a pill out of a brown envelope.

Chrissy felt something constrict in her chest. Drugs at a party were one thing, but taking them on your own? She brushed her uneasiness aside, however, and moved about the room inspecting all the clothes in their various stages of transformation. She realized that Juliet was waiting for some kind of approval. 'I'm speechless,' Chrissy said. 'Honestly, Ju, I don't know what to say.'

She did, but it wasn't related to the clothes. She said nothing.

***

The clanking of cups and animated banter in Gianni's was proving too much for Chrissy today. Juliet had even set the time herself, stating that she wouldn't dream of being late, but by five past one Chrissy had had enough and decided to head back. They were four weeks into their course and Juliet had shown her face at only a couple of lectures. She had also skipped a tutorial and missed a deadline.

'Ta-dah,' said a voice behind her as Chrissy gathered up her things. When she turned round, Juliet was holding up a green dress that she vaguely recognized.

'Oh my god,' she said, instantly forgetting how annoyed she was.

'Like it?'

'Like it? I love it. Must have taken you ages.'

She had added an exaggerated scooped black collar, put buttons all the way down the front and made it flare out from the waist. Her trademark label was sewn into the neck: 'JustSoJu'.

'Look great with woolly tights and Docs,' said Juliet.

'But, I can't—'

'Yes, you can. Take it. It's for all the help you're giving me.'

'No. Juliet.'

Shaking the dress temptingly, she added: 'I washed it three times. Doesn't smell of charity shops any more.'

She put it to Chrissy's nose, forcing her to sniff it and break into a grin. 'Well, I really do love it. Thanks.' It was only then that she noticed the dark circles under Juliet's eyes, how her face was slightly drawn and her skin lacklustre. 'Are you okay, Ju? I mean is everything—?'

''Course it is,' she snapped. 'Why wouldn't it be?'

'I just thought—'

'Why do you always worry so much?' She rubbed the back of her neck. 'Sorry, didn't mean to bite your head off; I was up late finishing the dress. I wanted to give it to you today.' She linked her arm through Chrissy's. 'Shall we walk back to yours?'

The first thing Chrissy did on entering her room was to check that the radiator was working. She had shoved newspaper into the gaps around the window to try to stop the heat escaping.

Meanwhile Juliet was rooting through her box of records. 'Are all these yours?' she asked.

'What? Oh, no, some are Dan's.'

Juliet put on The Smiths and started dancing to keep warm, whilst Chrissy admired her new dress. 'So, when do I get to meet this amazing Dan then?' she shouted above the music. 'Are you afraid he won't like me or something?'

Chrissy tried not to let the excitement of seeing him again show on her face. 'I think he's coming next weekend. ''Course he'll like you, Ju. Who doesn't?'

Juliet shrugged. She stopped dancing, inspecting the books on the shelf above Chrissy's desk, running her fingers along the spines, starting with Camus and Sartre and ending up at the enormous French–English/English–French dictionary.

'You bought them all, didn't you?' she remarked.

'Well yeah. We were meant to.' Chrissy tossed the dress down onto the bed and spun Juliet round to look at it. 'Why are you even doing this course anyway? That's what you should be doing, Ju. A degree in fashion, not French.'

Juliet slumped onto the bed, her eyes filling with tears. 'My dad doesn't believe in Mickey Mouse degrees,' she said. 'If I change courses he'll stop giving me any money at all and then I'm stuffed. I'd never survive on my own.' She took a tissue out of her pocket, dabbing at the mascara smudges. 'Cowper Road's okay for a crash pad now and then but they'd soon get sick of me if I had to stay there all the time.' Chrissy thought it best to let her offload without interrupting. 'And I can't live at home either because I don't even know where that is. Hong Kong, Singapore, Australia, Europe. Fuck knows. Any old place where my parents happen to be.' She blew her nose. 'I can speak four languages but what good is that if you never get to know anyone? They really should write a *How to Fuck Up Your Kids* manual.'

Chrissy stroked her arm, pleased that Juliet was opening up to her at last. She noticed some freshly made cuts on the milky-white skin above her wrist. 'Oh, Ju. Why do you do this to yourself?'

'Thanks for listening, I appreciate it,' she said, wrenching her arm back. 'I'm really worried about my essay though. The Proust one.'

'What? So when's that due in?'

'Tomorrow.'

Chrissy let out a moan.

'But not until the afternoon.'

'Oh, well—'

'I have started it.'

Chrissy sighed. 'Okay,' she said, holding out her hand. 'Give.'

Juliet's face brightened and she rummaged in her bag for the essay. Six pages of scrappy handwriting. She hadn't even bothered to number them. Then she sprang up. Her eyes lingered on the essay for a moment but she clapped her hands together as if summoning the real Juliet back. 'Right. We're going to have ourselves a blast tonight and I want to see you in that dress.' Slinging her beaten-up leather bag over her shoulder, she made for the door.

'It's way too glam for the Union disco,' Chrissy protested.

'You have to wear it. I really want you to.'

Juliet blew her a kiss and was gone.

***

The air was thick with cigarette haze and there was an almost tropical humidity coming off the dance floor. Wednesday night was indie night. The fabric-draped ceiling and strobe lighting

45

gave the place a nightclub vibe, and by the time they got there the floor was already tacky underfoot, the music ear-throbbing. It had all the makings of a great night. Chrissy felt overdressed, she knew she would, although she was enjoying having a share in the attention for a change. Admirers usually gravitated towards Juliet, understandably, and Chrissy was fine with that as long as she could find someone to chat to, or dance with, in the intervening period. Hanging out with Juliet this wasn't usually a problem; Juliet drew in the cool crowd wherever she went.

They came off the dance floor and made for the bar, standing to one side clutching plastic pints of lager. Juliet scrounged a cigarette from a guy who was hoping to get lucky. 'Huh. Not a chance,' she said after giving him the brush-off. Juliet then alerted Chrissy to a good-looking guy on the other side of the bar who was clearly checking her out for a change. 'Would you ever, do you think? He's definitely doable, that one.'

'Doable? Honestly, Ju! What sort of a term is that? ''Course I wouldn't; I could never do that to Dan.'

Juliet held a gulp of lager in her mouth, contemplating Chrissy before she swallowed it. 'Hmm, you say that.'

'I definitely wouldn't. Not ever.'

Juliet took a long drag of her cigarette. 'I wouldn't tell him, you know,' she said, giving Chrissy a nudge. 'If that's what you're worried about.'

'I'm not!'

'Just saying. Got to keep your options open. You only live once.' After a few more puffs of her cigarette she seemed to turn gloomy. 'Well, anyway, you're lucky to have him. He sounds great.'

Chrissy tapped her glass against hers. 'Don't be like that. And cheers. I'm lucky to have you both.'

Around midnight, Chrissy returned from the toilet to find Juliet getting it on with the guy who didn't stand a chance earlier. Now, clearly he did. 'I'm going to go, Ju,' she said, patting her on the shoulder. 'Come and get your essay after lunch. I'll see what

I can do with it in the morning.' She didn't think Juliet had heard, but suddenly her arms were around her neck.

'Love you,' said Juliet.

'Love you too.' Chrissy noticed her pupils were like saucers. 'Night then, Ju.' She was going to add *and be careful* but didn't fancy being mocked all over again.

CHAPTER 7

Eloise was wiping down tables, a million questions still racing through her mind. The more she learned about Juliet, the more she was fascinated by her. Her mother fascinated her, too. To think she would have been friends with someone as carefree as that. She couldn't wait to meet Juliet, although had to keep reminding herself that, as yet, her mother had no idea what she was up to. She hadn't quite made up her mind whether to tell her or not.

'They're going to get a ticket if they don't move soon,' said Maria, standing by the window. 'Think they're above the law when they have fancy cars like that.'

Eloise went to take a look.

It struck her that she had seen that car before, or certainly one like it. Cars like that stood out: sleek and black, with tinted windows. The door on the driver's side opened, a man got out wearing a dark suit, and for a brief moment Eloise thought he looked directly at her. She pulled back out of view, a flash of irrational fear passing through her. But five minutes later he was gone, and even if it was the same car from last night it really wasn't that remarkable. So what if the man had caught her eye?

The old woman walking past now was looking right at her, as was the child running along behind. The group of students just did it too. This was a café; people looked in all the time.

**

The smell of cigarettes immediately hit her when she got home. As soon as she opened the door, in fact. Chrissy hated smoke, it made her wheezy, and Eloise had never had any desire to take up the habit. The only thing she could think of was that someone had been to see her mother whilst she had been at work. 'Hello?' she called, telling herself she wasn't frightened, even though her voice felt trapped inside her throat and her stomach muscles were so tight she thought they might snap. 'Mum? Are you in?'

She could be out running, or sometimes she liked to do the charity shops on a Saturday.

Checking in each of the rooms she discovered that the window in her bedroom wasn't shut properly. Strange for Chrissy to have missed this: her security checks were always so thorough, and really she ought to have been extra vigilant after last night's break-in next door. However, as the whole place was untouched, and nothing to suggest that anyone had been in, the simple explanation must be that, for once, the window had been left slightly open, the man next door had been puffing on his cigarettes out on the walkway, as he sometimes did, and the smoke had drifted in.

Eloise closed the window and switched on her computer, continuing to look around as she waited for it to boot up. The only thing missing from her room was the yellow bear from her dad, which, she was almost certain, was back on top of her book-shelf when she had left for work. But Chrissy had no doubt hidden it again somewhere. She would ask her about it when she got in.

Meanwhile *The Exclusive World of Ricci* was coming to life on her screen. Eloise gazed longingly at the gorgeous clothes, then clicked again on the picture of Juliet and her Italian husband, the furry white cat entwined in his legs. If she didn't mess this up, kept a level head, Eloise could be a part of this world too.

On impulse, she sent Juliet another text:

'*Can't wait for Monday!*
Eloise xxx
PS What's your cat called? It's very sweet'

She didn't hear the key being turned in the lock. Or the door opening. And when she did she panicked, dropping her phone onto the floor with a thump. Then it was too late to zap the website off the screen.

As soon as she heard the noise, Chrissy came rushing in.

Eloise saw the way her body stiffened. How her hands turned white gripping the back of the chair. The shock of Juliet smiling back at her after all of these years.

'Erm. I wasn't sure which Juliet it was at first, Mum. But after what you've told me I'm pretty sure it's this one. What do you think?'

She felt the chair sigh as Chrissy removed her hands. Her fingers were trembling, moving slowly towards Juliet's face. But she withdrew them again quickly, as though it was too painful even to touch the screen.

Then she gasped and put her hand over her mouth.

'What is it?'

'She married Luca. I don't believe it.' Her voice was far away. She began to laugh but in a peculiar way.

'Who's Luca?'

'Turn it off. Get rid of it.'

'But she was your best friend, Mum.'

'I'm going for a run.'

Fortunately, Chrissy had already left the room when the reply came through:

'Me neither. See you soon, Eloise.
xx

PS Our cat is called Chrissy!'

***

Eloise snapped her book shut. Whilst her mother was out running she hadn't been able to read a single word. Her head was pounding with too many questions. Was it right to be encouraging this? She thought of the impenetrable darkness in her mother's eyes every time Juliet's name was mentioned. If only her mother had other friends, then perhaps Eloise could ask them for advice. But apart from Juliet, there was no one.

'Phew, that was tough going,' she said, leaning on the door-frame, hunched over to get her breath back. She came up sniffing the air. 'Smell of smoke to you in here?'

'Oh. Yeah, it was the bloke next door, smoking outside my window.'

'Charming,' she said, heading for the kitchen.

Water ran off her hands like sparks as she waited for the tap to run cold, then she filled up a glass and drank thirstily. 'Wow,' she said, banging it down on the unit, swiping the drips from her chin. 'Needed that.' She turned the tap on again, this time dousing her cheeks with cold water, burying her face in the towel.

'Who's Luca, Mum?'

Chrissy screwed up the towel and dropped it onto the unit.

'Come on, Mum, you practically had a fit when you saw him. Why won't you tell me?'

'I've been telling you haven't I?' Chrissy said, reaching for another glass to fill it up with wine. 'About Juliet, how we met? Just not … I can't … There are some things you're better off not knowing, okay?'

'I can take it, Mum. I'm tough, remember. Like you.'

She felt her mother's hand on her cheek.

'You're young, Eloise.'

Eloise flicked it away again. 'I'm not a child. And anyway, you had me when you were nineteen. You probably wish you hadn't. And Dad.' Her words tailed off at the end.

'Don't you ever say that,' said Chrissy, pointing her finger in her face. 'Ever. When you know it's not true.'

Eloise backed off. She didn't know what to expect from her mother since Juliet had appeared on the scene. Receiving one slap was more than enough.

'The last thing I want is for you to get hurt,' said Chrissy, her voice softening again. 'Please, let's not fall out.'

'You didn't care about that when you were drinking yourself to death after Dad died, did you? So why do you care so much about me now, eh?'

The neighbour's dog started barking. Eloise could feel tears pricking her eyes like pins. She blinked them away. Chrissy walked across to the window and peered through the slats of the blinds.

Then she spun round.

'Okay,' she said. 'Okay. Show me the website again.'

'What? Are you serious?'

Another text came through on her phone but Eloise ignored it. This was more important.

***

In a matter of seconds Juliet was back in the room with them.

'Can you zoom in? I need to see that thing in her hair.' Chrissy's face was almost touching the screen. 'My god,' she said in a whisper.

'What? What is it? Is it that silver slide thing in her hair?'

'It's not a slide, it's a brooch.'

52

'Let's see.' Eloise peered at it. 'It's got something on it but I can't really see.'

'It's a cat. I sent her it for her twentieth birthday.'

She was about to tell her that Juliet's white cat was also called Chrissy, but stopped herself in time. Nearly twenty years had gone by and Juliet was still wearing the brooch. Not only that, she had named her cat Chrissy. It would only freak her out more if she knew.

Eloise took a breath. 'So, what if Juliet wants to see you again?' Chrissy shook her head. 'But it's obvious that's why she's trying to get in touch with you, Mum.'

'I don't want to see her.'

'Well, what about the brooch, and the cat? I mean the cat brooch that she still—'

'Will you stop going on about that bloody thing?' Chrissy put her hands to her temples. 'You're driving me insane.'

'Why though, Mum?'

'Because I bloody stole it, if you must know! Okay? Happy now?'

'Oh.'

Eloise was stunned, her brain overloaded. 'So … so Juliet doesn't know that?'

'Of course she doesn't know.'

And then it seemed almost comical. What was a stolen brooch between friends? Hardly the crime of the century, even if the brooch was ugly as sin. Eloise smiled to herself. Things had suddenly got a whole lot easier as far as she was concerned.

'I'm going to have a bath,' said Chrissy, pressing her hands into the small of her back. 'Before I seize up.'

'I'll run it for you.'

Eloise almost knocked the wineglass out of her hand in her eagerness to please. She darted into the bathroom where the hot tap began its slow, pitiful trickle, and she placed a stack of travel magazines on the side to try and tempt her mother.

She appeared a little while later, wrapped in a towel.

'Lovely smell,' she said. 'What will I do without you, eh? All your special baths and breakfasts in bed. You're so good to me, Eloise.'

Eloise felt her cheeks ignite on hearing those words. 'Well, I try,' she said, moving out of her way.

'And that's the best any of us can do.' Chrissy skimmed the water, shaking the drips off her fingers. 'Perfect, thanks.' Then she picked up the magazines and handed them to Eloise. 'They'll just go crinkly in here.'

Eloise forced a smile. 'Okay. Well, enjoy,' she said, closing the door.

Her mother would be in the bath for the next hour at least. Eloise looked down at her phone.

'*On my way. Hope that's okay*
J
xxxx'

She stared at the words. They didn't make any sense.
She was about to send a reply when the doorbell went.
Please. Don't let it be.
'Juliet?'

***

She was exactly as she was on her website. But what was she doing here? On their walkway, outside their flat, the Mancunian Way rumbling on behind her? Juliet Ricci, big shades, big hair with red streaks. Vivid red linen dress with long slits up the sides. Massive bottle of champagne in her hand.

On completely the wrong day.

Juliet put a cigarette to her lips, cheeks sucked in drawing heavily on it, nodding her head as she contemplated Eloise. Eloise noticed the silver cat brooch pinned to her dress. The late evening sunlight gave it a sparkle. It certainly didn't look cheap. Juliet dropped the cigarette onto the walkway, crushing it with her shoe. Then she flung her arms open wide. Eloise resisted, terrified this might lead to some loud 'it's so lovely to meet you' greetings. She managed, somehow, to communicate: *PLEASE DON'T DO THAT*.

'You must be the beautiful Eloise,' Juliet whispered. Her voice was even deeper and more sensual in real life. She kissed Eloise on both cheeks. Her skin was soft.

'*Bella ragazza*. You look so like your mother when I knew her.' She took a step back to inspect her further, chewing one arm of her sunglasses. 'Does she know?'

'I – I don't understand. Why are you here now, Juliet?'

'You didn't get my messages?'

She came closer, smoothing down Eloise's hair where she had been nervously scrunching it. Juliet's nails were red and immaculate, she smelt of roses, jasmine, musk.

Eloise could feel herself shaking. 'I got one text. But—'

Juliet placed her hand on her shoulder. 'I was in London and decided to fly up this evening. I messaged you to say that I didn't think it was a good idea to meet for the first time anywhere public. Much better here.' She gave her shoulder a squeeze. 'We really don't know how she's going to react, do we?' Taking another step back, she asked: 'Is she in?'

'She's – she's in the bath.'

'What do you think, should I wait?'

'Well—'

'Okay,' said Juliet, putting her shades back on. 'Don't worry, Eloise. I'll see you Monday evening as planned. But I'll come here. Okay?' Juliet kissed her on both cheeks again. 'You are even more beautiful than your mother was.' She put her finger on her lips, then pressed it gently to Eloise's nose. 'Best not tell her that. *Ciao*.'

She smiled, waving her fingers like they were playing the piano mid-air.

'Bye.' Eloise felt her racing heartbeat slow as Juliet's heels click-clacked away from her.

Holding the bottle of champagne out to the side, she stopped, spun round, and was heading back again.

No! Go! Before Mum sees you.

'I nearly forgot,' she said, handing over the bottle.

This time she disappeared, the sound of her heels fading into the rumble of traffic.

Eloise had no time to reflect because her mother was shouting from the bathroom: 'Who was that, Eloise?'

'No one. Just someone got the wrong flat again. Delivering pizza.'

'You should've kept it, I'm starving.'

She put down the bottle, ridiculously heavy, and picked up the crushed tab end off the floor, breathing in Juliet's perfume. There was lipstick on the tip. She ran her finger over it, making a red streak on the back of her hand.

'You smoking?' said Chrissy.

Her mother was standing right behind her, pulling the belt through the loop of her bathrobe.

'Erm … Yeah.'

She managed to shut the door quickly on the bottle of champagne, still out on the walkway.

'I knew I could smell it. You're a fool, Eloise.'

'I hardly ever,' she replied, darting into the kitchen to dispose of the evidence.

Chrissy went to sit down. She was about to turn on the TV but Eloise stopped her.

There was still so much more Chrissy needed to tell her. And time was running out.

CHAPTER 8

Bristol: 1988/89

Dan arrived in a howling gale the first weekend in November. She waited for him at Temple Meads, pacing up and down in an effort to keep warm, but also to calm her nerves. So much had changed. She had changed. She couldn't say how exactly, she just knew that she had. But as soon as Dan stepped off the train she was certain that her feelings were the same, and when he began to recount stories about the band, people she had left behind in Manchester, it was like being back there again. Yet at the same time, she could still feel good about being in Bristol.

They spent hours hiding away in her room, trying not to fall out of her single bed, clearly designed to keep visitors away. After such a long separation it still felt right with Dan. And not just the sex. Everything. She was still nervous about him meeting Juliet. Having told him so much about their friendship, Chrissy was desperate for him to like her, and vice versa.

They had arranged to go for a curry at Nazmin's on Union Street, a cheap, no frills sort of a place with Formica tables and a lack of cutlery. Juliet arrived before them.

'Don't look so astonished, Chrissy. She'll have told you I'm

57

always late,' she said, greeting Dan with her customary kiss on both cheeks. She was nearly as tall as him in her high wedge boots, and had gone for a contemporary take on a Sixties' look: tartan miniskirt with a New Romantic frilly shirt. Her hair was in a beehive. 'And it's just so not true,' she added with a wry smile as she sat down opposite them both.

Chrissy screwed up her napkin and threw it at her. She was wearing the green dress that Juliet had customized for her. It seemed only right to wear it tonight, and it led to a discussion about Juliet's business enterprise. They moved on to Dan's band after that, and Chrissy watched the two of them, enjoying the flow of their conversation without really hearing the words, content that both strands of her life were coming together.

By the end of the night Juliet seemed more drunk than she ought to have been, which led Chrissy to believe that maybe she had taken something. Dan noticed it too, especially when she put her head on his shoulder, saying: 'Wish I had a guy like you. I wouldn't let a girl like me dribble on him all night though.' Sitting up again, she added: 'Hey. We could share him, Chrissy. Best friends share everything. It's the law.'

'Think it's time to get you home, Ju,' said Chrissy. She mouthed the word *sorry* to Dan. But he seemed unfazed, amused more than anything, and Chrissy was relieved.

'Oh, all right then,' Juliet said in her sulky voice. 'No! Wait.'

She almost fell off her chair reaching down for her bag, and pulled out her Polaroid camera.

Dan laughed when he saw it. 'What're you lugging that around for?'

'I'm that kind of girl.' She winked at him again, making a clicking sound with her mouth, then dived back down into her bag. 'Ooh! And I found this on the bus.' She produced a small yellow bear, slightly forlorn-looking and rather dirty. 'It's for you,' she said, presenting it to Dan.

Chrissy was instructed to take the photo. Dan put his arm

around Juliet's waist, clutching the bear in his other hand whilst Juliet held a kiss to his cheek. Then they waited for it to develop, amused by Dan's startled expression as it began to emerge. Juliet slipped the photo into her pocket as they bundled her out of the restaurant before she embarrassed herself any further.

***

Dan didn't take much persuading to stay on another night, but it meant a painfully early start on Monday morning. Clouds of mist gathered on the platform, like steam from a bygone era, as they waited for his train at Temple Meads. It was still only seven thirty; they had been up most of the night.

Chrissy rested her head on his shoulder and yawned. 'So what do you really think of her?'

'Who?' Dan replied, but she knew he was teasing.

'She can be a bit full on, can't she? When she gets off her face, I mean. It's like she has to get as far away from herself as she can sometimes.'

'Don't we all?'

'Suppose.'

But Chrissy's big fear was that one day she might go too far. She was about to share this with Dan when he said: 'As long as she doesn't lead you astray then I like her.'

The tannoy crackled into life. His train was approaching.

Chrissy sprang up. 'Oh god, I really can't bear this again.'

'I'll see you in a few weeks,' said Dan. He held her hand reassuringly, stepping forwards as the train pulled in.

'Wait! … Dan! … Chrissy, tell him to hang on.'

Someone was tearing down the platform.

'I did you these,' said Juliet, gasping for breath by the time she reached them. She managed to unfurl from her bag a white T-shirt with the word 'MashUp' on the front in blue letters. Underneath were dancing stickmen with crazy hands and hair.

'Wow, Juliet! That is so cool.' Dan lifted her off her feet and spun her round.

'There's one for all of you,' she said, exhilarated. He set her down again. 'Oh, and erm, I'm sorry about the other night. I hope I wasn't out of order. Think I took something weird.'

'The guys are going to be well chuffed with these,' said Dan, looking wide-eyed at Chrissy, who gave him a shrug to say that she had no idea about them.

'I'd love to see you play sometime,' said Juliet.

Dan picked up his bag, draping his arm round Chrissy in the same movement. 'You can be on the guest list whenever you like, Juliet.'

Juliet was still waving long after his train had disappeared. Chrissy was already halfway up the platform.

'You really should hang on to him, you know,' said Juliet, catching up with her. 'Definitely a keeper that one.'

***

Juliet's creations were beginning to cause such a stir she couldn't keep up with demand, and soon everyone had heard of JustSoJu.

Sometimes they went shopping together, Chrissy occasionally managing to pick things out which Juliet deemed suitable, and she would often sit on her stall in the Student's Union, for which Juliet would pay her very generously in clothes. Juliet was starting to build up quite a reputation for herself. But increased demand meant less time for her coursework and the more pressure she put herself under, the more substances she seemed to be taking. Her drug habit was spiralling out of control. Chrissy tried many times to start 'the conversation'. She had been meaning to have it for some time. But it was out of her sphere of experience and she always ended up saying nothing.

'You're asking me to write this essay for you from scratch?' said Chrissy, sitting on the floor with a can of cider in Juliet's room. There was nowhere else to sit except for a tiny patch of carpet. 'You haven't even read the book, Ju.'

'Well, I haven't had time.' She rubbed her nose. She looked terrible. It was hard to distinguish the highs from the lows these days. She had lost weight, the dark circles under her eyes were even more pronounced, and most of that Juliet sparkle had faded. 'I'll give you this,' she said, throwing the purple raincoat at her. Chrissy caught it before it hit her in the face. She knew it was special. A one-off. It had a silk lining, pleated fishtail, and was Juliet's favourite too.

She refused the coat; it seemed too much like a bribe. But she weakened on the essay front. 'This is the very last time, Ju. I don't want to get chucked out as well.'

***

When she handed the essay over to Juliet a week later she placed a booklet on top of it.

'What's this? Fashion and Textiles. Bristol Poly.'

'You've got to do it. Does your dad even need to know? I mean, at graduation he'll have a heart attack, but if you come through with a First … And what about this? Look.' She pointed to where it explained about a post-qualification bursary to help set up your own business.

'Thanks,' said Juliet. She tore out the page and ripped it into tiny pieces, scattering them above her head. 'Now get off my case, Miss Goody Fucking Two Shoes.'

Chrissy snatched up the purple raincoat and left. She still felt that payment was unnecessary. Until now.

***

It was three in the morning when the pounding came to her door.

61

'Chrissy, are you in there?' said a voice. 'It's your mate. Juliet.'

She sprung out of bed, pulling a jumper over her head. She didn't know the guy who had come to get her, although vaguely recognized him as one of Juliet's 'sleeping partners', as she liked to call them.

She hadn't seen Juliet in over a week.

'What's happened? Is she hurt?'

'She's on the Suspension Bridge.'

'What?'

They ran through drizzle. The pavements, wet and shiny under the streetlamps, were littered with Chinese takeaways. The wind had got up too. On her way out, Chrissy had grabbed the purple raincoat from the back of her chair, which she was glad of now, pushing her arms through the sleeves as she ran. Her pumps were soon squelching from the dampness, and she realized just how unfit she was. There was no time to stop and catch her breath.

By the time they reached the bridge her chest was heaving. She could see a female silhouette balancing precariously on the railings. Chrissy recognized the style of dancing immediately. Juliet was holding onto one of the steel cables, weaving her free hand through the air.

'Juliet!'

A police officer held her back.

'This is the friend I was telling you about,' said the guy.

'I'm her best friend. I'm Chrissy. Let me go to her, she'll listen to me.'

It was a female officer who escorted her through. A large crowd had gathered, late-night party people mostly, but a few local residents in their dressing gowns also looking on anxiously. The traffic had backed up on either side of the bridge, blocked by police barriers. An ambulance and fire engine were standing by.

Juliet was in her underwear. She was holding her face up to the rain as the wind raced through her hair, playing a game of its own – trying to sweep her off. It reminded Chrissy of the time they had been on the bridge together that day, catching raindrops on their tongues. It seemed like a long time ago now.

Juliet took her hand off the cable. The crowd let out a gasp as she teetered precariously, wondering which way she would fall. She was barefoot, and the railings looked slippery in the wet. Her arms made frantic circles in the air, until, somehow, they managed to grab hold again. Juliet let out a whoop as she steadied herself.

'Hey Ju,' Chrissy shouted, trying not to sound alarmed. 'What're you doing up there?'

'Chrissy! Come up onto our bridge.'

'It's the middle of the night, Ju. Let's go back to mine, have a mug of hot chocolate.'

'"I would go out tonight, but I haven't got a stitch to wear" ...' Juliet began to sing.

Chrissy caught a whiff of something that suggested she might be smoking a joint up there.

'Have you any idea what she might have taken?' the officer asked.

'No,' said Chrissy. 'None at all.' She didn't want Juliet getting arrested the moment she came down. The truth was, she could have taken a whole cocktail of stuff.

'Has she ever done this before?'

'Not to my knowledge,' Chrissy replied. As far as she knew she hadn't, but this had been her fear all along. 'Ju, come on down! You must be freezing up there in your knickers. What're you like?'

'Freezing my tits off! It's great.' Suddenly her tone changed. 'It's all so fucking great.'

'Ju, you're scaring me now. Just turn around – carefully – and we'll catch you. I promise.'

Juliet looked down into the Gorge, almost losing her grip. 'Wahoo!' she shrieked.

'Ju!'

Without warning, she had jumped.

Her landing was softened by Chrissy on one side and the police officer on the other. Fortunately, her limbs were loose, due to her inebriated state. Someone threw a foil blanket over her, which she immediately shrugged off again. 'Are we keepers, Chrissy?' she asked, smothering her in kisses as she was leading her away from the applauding spectators. The paramedics steered them towards the ambulance.

'Sure we are, Ju.' She slipped the purple raincoat over Juliet's shoulders. 'Come on, let me help you.'

'We're going to France, you and me. Gonna be a blast.'

'Yeah, we'll see,' said Chrissy.

Juliet stopped in her tracks and flung the coat back at her. 'Fuck you then, Chrissy Wotsit.' She burst into tears. 'I thought you were my friend.'

'I am, Ju. Ju!' But Juliet was pushing her away as the paramedics tried to get her into the ambulance.

'She'll be fine,' one of the paramedics told Chrissy. 'Best not cause her any further distress.'

'Juliet!'

The rain flickered like ticker tape in the headlights of passing cars. Chrissy watched the guy who had come to her door earlier climb up into the ambulance with Juliet, and she just wished there was more she could do to help her friend.

***

It was nearing the end of the third term and most students had finished their exams. There was a sense of relief in the air, and thick woolly jumpers had been replaced with T-shirts, shorts and white summer legs. A heavy-duty lawnmower could be heard in the distance. Chrissy had opened her window as far as it would go to let in some air. With it came wafts of barbecued sausages and cheap burgers, drifting in on random bursts of laughter. She gazed out at the huddles of First and Second Years spread out across the grass, and sighed.

A tentative knock on her door broke her from her trance.

'Juliet,' said Chrissy, narrowing her eyes. Her initial elation was soon tainted by the hurt she still felt.

'Can I come in?' asked Juliet, as tentatively as she had knocked. ''Course.'

Juliet was in a pair of chequered hot pants and red halter-neck top, her hair piled high in a beehive. She sat down on the edge of the bed with a nervy smile which seemed to convey both remorse and shame. The dark circles under her eyes were faded; she had put some of the weight back on, and her face had lost that sad, hollowed-out look. She looked fabulous in fact.

'Dan came to see me,' she said.

'Yeah, I told him to,' Chrissy replied, tersely. 'We were worried about you.'

Juliet paused for a moment. 'So how were your exams? Thought it best to stay away, let you get on with your revision and stuff.' Chrissy nodded. 'Still on for that First, are we?'

'We'll see,' she replied with a modest grin.

Juliet glanced out of the window and then down at a piece of paper on her lap. 'I wanted to say I'm sorry, Chrissy. Yeah, I know. And also … to show you this.'

It was a letter of acceptance onto the Fashion and Textiles course at Bristol Poly.

'Oh my god, Ju. Well done!' she said, rushing towards her.

'My dad doesn't know. Obviously.'

'It's the best news, Ju. Dead proud of you.'

'I've found us a house for next year too. So … well … if you're interested that is. It's in Redland, with three other housemates.'

'You have been busy.'

'And before you ask – because you're bound to – it's booze and fags from now on. Nothing else. Never again.'

'That's good too.'

'Yeah … Well, anyway, I thought you might want to celebrate.' She fished out a cheap bottle of plonk from her duffel bag. Chrissy rinsed out two mugs, the least chipped ones, and they sat on the bed trying to think of a toast.

'How about "to the big road trip"?' Juliet suggested, like she had only just thought of it.

Chrissy's heart lifted, ignoring the warning voice in her head. She had zero plans for the summer and Dan was away teaching guitar at summer school, followed by a music festival with the band.

'I'd love that,' Chrissy replied, chinking mugs. She took one mouthful and began to sputter. 'Oh god! It's absolute *merde*.'

Juliet and Chrissy broke into fits of laughter, a mixture of excitement and relief from both sides.

'Slight problem though,' said Chrissy. 'How do we pay for it?' Her grant money had long run out, the overdraft was gone and she had reached the credit limit on her card. 'Suppose I could ask my parents to stump up for a coach ticket maybe …'

Juliet held up two tickets, waving them in front of her face. 'Proceeds from JustSoJu. Instead of frittering it away on … well, that's all history now.' Chrissy's mouth fell open. 'I knew you'd say yes, Chrissy. Two open returns, London to Paris. Bit slow by coach, but hey, we have the whole summer. And once we get down to the coast we'll get jobs dead easy. It'll be a blast.'

Chrissy didn't doubt that. Life was always a blast with Juliet. 'But we get to Paris and then what?'

Juliet stuck her thumb out, as if that should have been obvious.

'Hitch-hike? Is it safe?'

''Course it's safe. Trust me: I've done it all over the world and never had a problem yet. Even on my own.'

'Not on your own. God.'

'Well, only once, and I knew the guy. Friend of my parents; an absolute gent. Pity really, as I quite fancied him. I'll get you back to Dan in one piece, don't you worry.'

Juliet put up a convincing case: two young girls with rucksacks on their backs, cardboard sign, friendly smiles. They could take a tent, too, and be free, roaming spirits. Not many male motorists would leave Juliet standing by the side of the road with her thumb out, that was for sure.

'I think we should avoid the Côte d'Azur and aim more for the south-west,' said Chrissy, suddenly embarrassed by her eagerness. 'Okay, so I already looked at my map. Why are you laughing? It'll be cheaper on that side of the coast.'

'You kind of just take the lifts you can get,' Juliet responded with her usual breeze. 'You'll soon get the hang of it,' she added, patting Chrissy's leg. Then she held up her mug. '*Cul sec* and *vive les vacances.*'

Chrissy held onto her nose as she downed it in one, recoiling from the aftershock.

'Can't wait,' she said, coughing and spluttering.

CHAPTER 9

Manchester: 2007

'Sounds great,' said Eloise. 'So was it easy to get lifts? Is that what you did?'

'Don't even think about it.'

'I'm not!'

'Well, lots of people did it then. That didn't take away the risks, but it wasn't considered totally mad.'

'Did you just take off then, without any more planning than that?' Eloise was reflecting on her own trip with Anya.

'There was no internet then, you know.' Chrissy laughed at herself. 'Can you believe it? How reckless.'

For a fleeting moment Eloise thought she saw the teenage girl her mother had once been. But she noticed how quickly her expression changed. 'So why don't people hitch any more, do you reckon?' she asked her.

'Oh, I don't know. Maybe there was more trust then. Or more fear now, what with all the media and—'

'The internet,' Eloise chipped in, sarcastically. Her mother hated it; she didn't know why. Then another thought occurred to her. 'That yellow bear … ' Eloise stopped for a moment. 'That's not the one Dad gave to me, is it? I thought it was a present – for me, I mean. But, so, Juliet gave it to him?'

'Well, I guess he wanted you to look after it. He was fond of it.'

Eloise still couldn't help feeling disappointed. 'Where is it, by the way?'

'Oh,' said Chrissy, trying to think. 'Haven't seen it in a while. You've hidden it and forgotten where, haven't you? Don't worry, it'll turn up. I'm off to bed.'

'No! I want to hear about your trip.'

''Night, Eloise.'

***

Eloise's first thought on Sunday morning was to check the fridge. In her haste to hide the enormous bottle of champagne from Chrissy, she feared she may not have disguised it well enough.

'Morning,' said Chrissy, suddenly appearing.

The fridge juddered as Eloise slammed the door shut.

'You look a bit tired, Eloise. Do you feel okay?'

She forced a smile. It had been a restless night, worrying that her mother would be angry with her, instead of grateful, when she finally came face-to-face with her best friend again.

Her fists clenched when she saw Chrissy opening the fridge.

The champagne bottle was still wrapped in the carrier bag, wedged behind the leftovers from Maria. Eloise watched anxiously as Chrissy removed the carton of milk and took it to the table. A small part of her wished that her mother had discovered it, and then she could tell her the truth; the rest of her was glad because that might just ruin things completely.

With so many knots in her stomach, Eloise merely pushed her cereal round the bowl. 'I have a theory about Juliet,' she said. 'Do you want to hear it?'

'Depends what it is,' said Chrissy, licking butter off her fingers.

69

'Well, it's about that brooch.' She winced as she said the word 'brooch', sensing this was a bit of a trigger.

Chrissy put down her toast and folded her arms, resting them on the edge of the table. 'Okay. Fine. Let's hear it.'

'Well, I think Juliet's been trying to communicate with you. I mean, for ages.'

'What, via the brooch?' Chrissy scoffed. 'Like some telepathic thought transfer through the cat?'

'Sort of.'

Eloise knew her theory was a good one. Most people used the internet these days; it was almost impossible to function without it. Unless, of course, you were Chrissy: 'It's too nosey, too public, too Big Brother-like,' she would say. 'You give it bits of information and soon the whole world knows your business and where you are.'

'I just think, Mum, that she hopes you might try and Google her sometime.'

'Like you did to her you mean?'

'Well, yeah, it's what people do. And when you find her website, there she is: wearing the silver cat brooch in her hair that you didn't even think she liked.'

'So?'

'So, almost twenty years have gone by and she still has this thing in her hair. Don't you get it? She wants you to see it. It's a message just for you.'

'Saying what?'

'Saying: she cares about you; she misses you; still thinks about you – all of those things. Saying, get in touch.'

Chrissy took another bite of her toast, but Eloise could see that she had sent her to some distant place.

'Don't you think it's a bit mean not calling her back?'

'"Mean"?' Chrissy sprang up and started clearing the table before either of them had finished. 'It's not easy for me all this dredging up of the past, Eloise. You seem to think—'

A text had pinged through on her phone. It was too risky to

ignore after what had happened the last time, but Chrissy was staring at her, almost challenging her. Eloise stuck it out, and when she heard her washing up, she seized the moment to take a look:

'*Open the door.*'

It wasn't Juliet's number. Or anyone else in her Contacts.

Could it be dangerous? Should she tell her mother?

Sliding the chain across, she released it as silently as possible. Using both hands, she attempted to get a firm grip on the handle, and with her body butted up against the door, opened it a little way, preparing to shut it again quickly if necessary.

The walkway was deserted. Only the neighbour's dog, tied up. It was trying to sniff the huge bouquet of flowers left in front of their doorway. Eloise was surprised that it hadn't barked. She leapt over the flowers and peered over the side of the railings.

A man was just stepping into a car.

Cars like that stood out.

So her instincts had been right all along. That man really had looked directly at her yesterday when Maria had commented on the car. And quite possibly had followed her home the other night; she hadn't imagined that either. Was he linked to Juliet? Or someone else who knew her mother? But Chrissy didn't socialize with anyone except for her.

Leaving flowers was hardly threatening. Despite this, Eloise still couldn't shake the unsettled feeling. She scooped them up, closing the door with her foot. Their flat immediately burst into colour. An exotic scent drifted into every corner of the room. The cellophane made a crinkling noise, causing Chrissy to come out of the kitchen to see what was happening. She looked puzzled when she saw the flowers, her body rigid.

'Someone loves you, big style,' said Eloise, putting them down on the table when she refused to take them.

Chrissy stared at the words printed on the card:

She began to examine each flower individually. 'Must have cost a fortune,' she said.

'Have you any idea who they're from though, Mum? They were just left outside the door.'

Eloise could see she was struggling to work it all out.

'But how could they find us?' she said, after what seemed a long time.

'Who? Mum, who?'

She was sinking into her memories again like they were quick-sand.

'Well, maybe someone from Dad's band told them where we live,' said Eloise, hoping that might lead to something. 'I'm just guessing, obviously. But why don't they know you're called Chrissy Lundy? Juliet knows you married my dad.' Then she realized that Juliet hadn't actually known they had got married, not until Eloise confirmed it for her. 'Well, I'm assuming she did. She was your best friend.'

'I'll see to these,' said Chrissy, handling the flowers roughly. 'Let go, Eloise.'

***

She found them in the wheelie bin outside, tossed upside down. By the time she got back upstairs, Chrissy was in her full kit and running shoes.

'I'm sorry, Eloise' she said, twisting side to side. 'I shouldn't have got angry.'

Eloise held them out to her like a limp corpse. They were still in their cellophane, ruined. 'These haven't done anything wrong, Mum.'

Chrissy stared at them, narrowing her eyes. Gradually her face softened. 'No. No, you're right. And nor have you. I suppose they'll brighten the place up a bit, won't they? Do your best, eh? And I'll see you in a little while.'

Eloise rummaged in the kitchen drawer for some scissors. She would make sure these flowers would be the first thing her mother saw when she came back from her run, and then she would have to tell her who they were from.

***

'Juliet sent these. Didn't she?'

Chrissy wiped the sweat off her face with her sleeve. 'I don't know,' she said, heading into the kitchen.

'Who else could it be?'

Eloise stayed close.

'I've no idea.'

'Yes, you have. Don't lie to me.' She felt her cheeks redden at the accusation, squirming under the pile of lies that had spilled out of her own mouth lately.

Chrissy began to pour herself a large glass of wine.

'Isn't it a bit early for that, Mum? Look, maybe Juliet wants to make it up to you.'

'For what?' said Chrissy, eyeing her with suspicion.

'Well, maybe for saving her from doing anything stupid on that bridge. And she wouldn't have changed courses if it wasn't for you. And look where she is now.' Eloise gave her a moment before pushing it further. 'Unless, Mum, there's something you're not telling me. You know who sent the flowers, I know you do. Was there someone else besides my dad? You can tell me ... Mum.'

There was no response.

'Would Juliet know then – if I asked her?'

'Don't you dare, Eloise.'

'You can't stop me.'

'No,' said Chrissy, glowering at her. 'But I'm asking you – again – not to do that. And I will know if you have.'

'How? How could you know?'

'Oh, believe me, Eloise, I will know.'

She stole the glass out of her mother's hand. 'Right. You can have this back if you tell me some more. Tell me about France.'

CHAPTER 10

France: summer, 1989

'Told you it'd be easy,' Juliet shouted as they jogged towards the truck in the blinding sun, rucksacks bouncing on their backs.

They had trudged out to the recommended spot near Porte d'Orléans station at the end of Ligne 4 on the Paris Métro. Eleven fifteen, and they already had their first lift out of Paris.

Chrissy had been feeling stiff from the long coach journey, queasy from the rough Channel crossing and weary from lack of sleep in a couchette that refused to recline. The cheaper overnight ferry meant arriving in Calais around four in the morning with stinging eyes and grinding stomachs, yet all of this fell away the moment she stepped off the boat.

'Ça sent bon,' she said, taking her first breath of France.

'Must be something wrong with your nose,' said Juliet. 'We're still in the port and ça *pue*!'

'Don't spoil it, Ju. I just want to savour the moment.'

On the five-hour coach journey into Paris, Juliet only wanted to sleep but Chrissy made constant observations about driving on the wrong side of the road and how much she wanted a Citroën 2CV. Once they hit Paris she talked dreamily of strolling by the Seine or meandering through the labyrinth of streets in the Latin Quarter; she wanted to browse the flea markets and eat Proustian madeleines in a *salon de thé*, drink wine with the ghosts of her literary heroes in Café de Flore or Les Deux Magots.

Sadly, on this occasion, Paris was well beyond their budget and as soon as they got off the coach they were straight onto the Métro. For Chrissy, though, even the smells and sounds of the Paris Métro were a delight. 'How many times have you been to Paris, Ju?' she asked as a distant rumble came down the tunnel.

'Four or five,' said Juliet, yawning. 'Plus, I went to a summer school here once. Can't remember where.' They stood back as the train pulled in. 'Kind of wish I was seeing it through your eyes.' She glanced at Chrissy as they stepped onto the carriage.

They didn't even attempt to get a seat, clinging to the handrail facing one another with their rucksacks still glued to their backs. Chrissy could feel her dress sticking to her skin and she noticed fellow passengers were frowning, no doubt jealous of their great adventure. The doors beeped shut. She grinned at Juliet, screwing her eyes to suppress her excitement as the train jerked on its way.

In spite of all that Paris had to offer, Chrissy was keen to move on. '*Tant de choses à faire et si peu de temps,*' she said as they had emerged at ground level at Porte d'Orléans. But her romantic notions soon vanished when they were confronted by booming traffic, tall buildings, wide boulevards and a frenetic intersection of roads. 'What now, Ju?'

'Not sure, I haven't hitched from here before.'

'Well, I thought you had.'

'I never said that,' Juliet protested, removing her rucksack. '*On parle bien le français, hein*? You stay here with the bags. Someone's bound to know where the *Périphérique* is.'

Chrissy watched her go, massaging her shoulders as she walked; envious that Juliet could still look that good even in their dishevelled state. As she waited, she looked around, taking in the street names: Boulevard Jourdan, Avenue du Général Leclerc, Boulevards des Maréchaux. They didn't mean much and she hated not knowing where she was.

'Right,' said Juliet, returning with a paper bag, a smiling orange *croissant* on the front. 'We need to be opposite those traffic lights.'

'Which traffic lights? There's hundreds of traffic lights.'

She waved a map in front of Chrissy's face. 'Knew that would make you happy,' she said.

Chrissy stuck her tongue out and snatched it from her. They ate their *croissants* as they went, but a sense of unease began to set in when cars honked their horns and well-dressed Parisian women on their way to work shook their heads in disapproval. *Was this a crazy thing to be doing?* Chrissy asked herself. Putting themselves at the mercy of complete strangers, with their false smiles and Juliet's cardboard sign that said '*La côte SVP!*'

'Why can't it be somewhere more specific, instead of just saying "the coast please"?' Chrissy had queried. 'Like Lyon? Or Autoroute du Soleil?'

'Trust me, will you? I've done this a zillion times.'

Juliet stuffed the screwed-up paper bag into Chrissy's hand.

'Well, not from here you haven't.'

She tapped Chrissy over the head with the cardboard sign, saying: 'Told you, you always worry too much. Finish your *croissant*. You're so tetchy when you're hungry.'

They were not the only ones hoping for a lift. Chrissy counted four young men spaced at intervals by the side of the road with their thumbs out, and one middle-aged woman with a ferocious-looking dog.

'I bet you we get a lift before any of them,' said Juliet.

Twenty minutes later a lorry pulled in. Juliet could have choreographed it herself. The driver shook his head at the four young men bounding towards him, pointing to the two of them instead. The woman's dog began to bark, upset at the unfairness of it all, but she held it back, resigned to the fact that the lift wasn't hers either.

He was a Spanish trucker, obsessed with The Beatles, and had to finish off his rendition of 'Let It Be' before he spoke, unfazed by all the horns blasting in protest of his stopping.

'*Buenos días*. I'm going as far as Dijon,' he said in a mix of French and Spanish. 'Ça va?'

'Yes,' said Juliet. She turned to Chrissy for approval.

'Don't we need to go more like Orléans, Ju?' She was about to get her Michelin road atlas out, but was getting 'that look' from Juliet.

'It's not a taxi service, Chrissy. And it's still south. The main thing is, do we get a good vibe?'

Chrissy peered inside his cab. A photograph, presumably of his wife and daughters, was attached to the mirror. 'Well, I guess so. Do you? You're the expert.'

Juliet tossed her bag in and climbed up.

Chrissy had never ridden in a full-sized truck before. It was even better than her dad's van, giving her a real sense of the open road. She noticed Juliet grinning at her, mocking her innocence, so she gave her leg a sharp pinch.

'Ouch. What's that for?'

'Looking smug.'

It was a while before they cleared the sprawl of Paris, and Chrissy was still desperate to get out the road atlas to see where they were heading, but couldn't because her bag was trapped behind the seat. Juliet would only give her grief in any case. She began to feel more at ease when it became clear that the only thing the trucker wanted in exchange for the ride was a translation of Beatles' songs. He fished out a bundle of shabby, handwritten lyrics and Juliet set to work. Chrissy must have fallen asleep because, the next thing she knew, a whole four hours had gone by and they seemed to be pulling onto the hard shoulder.

'This is where I drop you,' she heard him say. 'The turn off for Dijon is in seven, ten *kilomètres*. You should stay on this road.'

Chrissy looked out of the window. This really didn't seem like the ideal spot to try and pick up another lift.

'Here?' said Juliet, also surprised.

But they thanked him for getting them this far and he pushed their bags out onto the tarmac, wishing them luck as they jumped down. The traffic thundered past, kicking up swirls of dust.

'Don't let *les flics* see you,' he shouted as he swung his door shut.

'What did he mean?' yelled Chrissy, rolling her rucksack out of the way of the motorway blast, pinning her hair down with her hand. She got out her Michelin road atlas and felt slightly better, climbing up onto the metal crash barrier where it felt that bit safer.

'What are you doing?' Juliet screamed. 'Get your thumb out; it's the only way out of here, Chrissy. You should dump that. We don't need it.'

Chrissy ignored her. She remembered seeing signs for Lyon. At a quick glance she noted it was almost due south of Dijon so this was taking them in the right direction. Slapping the atlas shut again she put it back inside her rucksack and began slowly edging her way towards the wall of traffic. She took hold of her corner of their cardboard sign, trying her best to smile even though she feared for her life. 'You never said it was breaking the law, Ju.'

'Just look gorgeous and we'll be on our way again. Laws are for breaking in any case.'

It seemed like hours before any lift came, but when Chrissy looked at her watch it had only taken twenty minutes for a bright green Renault to come crawling along the inside lane, a line of juggernauts hot on its tail. The one immediately behind flashed its lights at the late indication to pull in, and Juliet nudged Chrissy out of the way just in case.

It was a French family from a town north of Paris. The mother was driving and the father was in the back, a baby on his knee. 'Which part of the coast are you trying to get to exactly?' said the mother, referring to their sign. She spoke French, shouting over the roar of the traffic.

'Montpellier,' Juliet yelled back. 'Marseille. That sort of area.'

The woman raised her eyebrows. 'Well, we are actually going to the Alps but we have to go via Lyon. Ça vous va?'

Chrissy nodded to Juliet. She wasted no time in clambering into the front seat with her rucksack, leaving Chrissy to get into the back with Papa and the baby.

'*Bonjour, Monsieur*,' she said, trying to smile as she wedged her bag between her legs. She held a finger out to the baby, surprised when he grabbed it and then wouldn't let go. The car smelt of regurgitated milk. She wound the window down, hoping that wasn't too impolite.

'It's very dangerous what you are doing,' said the mother.

The same could be said about her for stopping, thought Chrissy, but she just smiled and let Juliet do the talking.

'So are you on holiday? Or maybe you have jobs for the summer?'

'Yes,' said Juliet. 'Well, we hope to find work.'

The baby began to emit piercing little shrieks which bounced off the car's interior and drilled down into Chrissy's eardrums. Papa gave her a pleading look and she was suddenly landed with it, along with a bottle of milk.

'Oh!' she said, trying to look pleased. She waved the bottle in front of its mouth, forcing the rubber teat between its tiny lips. Then, something rather ghastly began to waft up from its nappy. She hung onto her breath for as long as she could, holding her nose to the open window and just praying that she wouldn't be given that job as well.

Juliet turned round and smiled. 'Aw look, so cute. Quite the *petite maman*, aren't you, Chrissy?'

Chrissy mouthed the words 'piss off'.

It was a slow journey, and they made several stops, but despite the inconvenience of the baby and its dreadful odours, Chrissy drifted into a contented doze whilst Juliet chatted with the mother in the front. Two free rides across God knows how many miles. Maybe hitch-hiking wasn't so bad after all.

Five and a half hours later they arrived in Lyon. By now it was dark; it would be impossible for them to get to the coast tonight. They were dropped off at Camping Soleil in Dardilly on the outskirts of Lyon: not far from the Autoroute du Soleil, so they were told.

The woman handed Chrissy a piece of paper with a telephone number scribbled on it. 'Call me if you want au pair work,' she said.

Chrissy ripped up the number as soon as they were gone, much to Juliet's amusement.

It had been a long day and their lack of sleep the previous night was catching up with them, and even though it was dark there was no let-up in the heat. Chrissy let out a loud moan when Juliet helped with her bag, lifting it onto her back. Adjusting the straps made little difference to the soreness in her shoulders. They set off down the dusty track to the campsite.

'Do you know how to put this tent up?' said Chrissy.

'No, do you?'

'I thought you did.'

'I thought you did.'

They linked arms, giggling their way into Reception, the smell of barbecues suddenly making them feel ravenous, reminding their poor stomachs that they hadn't eaten anything since breakfast.

Chrissy woke in the middle of the night with a stiff neck, scratchy mouth and pounding head. 'You awake, Ju?' she whispered, giving herself a scare when the sagginess of the tent touched her face. Juliet had managed to befriend some hippy types who had put the tent up for them, and afterwards they binged on bread and *saucisson*, getting drunk on ridiculously cheap table wine which they had dragged back from the campsite shop in a large plastic container. 'Ju,' she said, louder this time, reaching out to feel for her in the dark.

Juliet was gone.

The campsite was full. She stumbled repeatedly over guy ropes and protruding tent pegs; the cheap batteries in her torch were already fading. She went first to the toilet block, calling Juliet's name every few seconds. Then she tried walking between the tents, up and down, still calling out, startled by every noise or silhouette that moved. She was getting horribly lost too. And soon she would have to alert someone that her friend was missing.

Then she spotted it, the hippy tent: a wigwam-shaped structure they had been in earlier. Cursing as she stumbled towards it, she could hear Juliet's distinctive laughter coming from inside. She hovered for a while, listening to their voices, eventually satisfied that she could return to her own tent and get some sleep. It took at least half an hour to find it again.

***

'I was worried sick about you,' said Chrissy the next morning as they stood at the side of the heat-hazed road, thumbs out, wearing their fake smiles and munching on bits of leftover baguette, clutching a corner of their cardboard sign.

'So I got an offer to have some fun. What's the big deal?'

'You didn't tell me you were going.'

'Well, you were fast asleep. Look, if you weren't with your precious Dan you'd be doing that too. You can't expect me to live like a nun, Chrissy.'

Juliet tossed two paracetamols down her throat and swigged from a bottle of mineral water that had been perspiring in the morning sun.

'And why did you give a T-shirt to all four of them?' Chrissy asked.

'Because they put the tent up for us, *and* took it down again this morning. That's got to be worth something. Come on.'

'I thought the idea was to sell them, Ju. Did they give you anything besides?'

Juliet raised her eyebrows, as if that should have been obvious, then she pulled a cigarette from behind both her ears.

'Is that it? Two bloody fags.'

Juliet extracted something from her shorts pocket: a polythene bag full of weed. 'That'll keep us going,' she said. 'Oh come on Chrissy, you like it too. I got it for us both. And they're my T-shirts, you know. Lighten up; we'll get jobs in no time when we get there.'

'We'll bloody starve at this rate. And get where exactly?'

A horn honked loudly, speeding past them with an assortment of body parts hanging out of windows. Then whistles, shrieks and more horn blasts as the car seemed to be slowing.

'What the hell is that?' said Chrissy.

'Dunno, but it looks promising.' Juliet was already running towards it. A Fiat, the size of a bubble, had come to a screeching halt just up the road. 'Some Italian lads on their way to Spain,' she shouted back. 'Quick.'

'Spain?'

Chrissy had to slow to a walk: a painful stitch jabbed into her side. She didn't know which was worse: that, or the sizzling heat. Not forgetting the ludicrous weight on her back.

'Spain, Ju?'

'They're going to a wedding but they can drop us at the coast,' she replied. 'It's a gift! *Faut pas refuser un cadeau.*'

'We'll never fit in there!' said Chrissy, counting five beaming faces, as well as the driver's.

Juliet had already surrendered her bag. Shortly after, her legs disappeared too. Chrissy eased herself in as best she could. With europop blaring from tinny speakers, windows fully down so they could all take turns to breathe, they were on their way again.

Chrissy felt sorry for the poor boy whose lap she was crushing, although he didn't seem to mind. Mostly she chatted to him on the journey in English whilst Juliet entertained the others in her fluent Italian. At some point Chrissy must have fallen asleep, as the next time she looked at her watch she saw that they had been going for three hours.

And Juliet was in full snog with one of her new friends.

***

Chrissy was sure she could smell the sea blowing in through the windows. She stuck her head out as they were passing a vast stretch of water. It didn't look much like the sea.

'It's a lagoon,' said the driver. 'A salt water lake. Have you heard of La Camargue and the wild horses?'

'The white ones?' said Chrissy. 'Are we near there?'

'This side Montpellier, that side La Camargue.'

'Show me on the map,' she said, pulling out her road atlas.

'*Allora.*' His friend took over the steering. 'So, for you, I'm thinking La Grande Motte … Watch out!' They swerved to avoid a car. 'On your map … it's … ah, here it is,' he said, pointing to it. 'If you don't find work in La Grande Motte you won't find it anywhere.'

'Lots of people on holidays,' one of the others said.

The next time they passed a sign for La Grande Motte, Chrissy felt a wave of excitement. She desperately wanted to share it with Juliet but couldn't because she was still attached to her Italian lover's lips. Leaning out of the window the wind caught her hair; the moment spoiled, however, when someone pinched her back-side. The boy whose lap she was sitting on put his hands in the air to protest his innocence. One of the others winked at her.

She tapped Juliet on the shoulder. 'Hey, what do you think about this place, Ju?'

It was a purpose-built resort with giant pyramids rising out of an incredibly flat landscape, creating an almost futuristic skyline. Chrissy couldn't decide whether it was attractive or ugly, not that it mattered. Palm trees lined the side of the road, with holidaymakers strolling casually either side along wide pavements, eating ice creams, carrying bags of shopping or heading to the beach with all their paraphernalia. A blue dolphin structure came into view as they got close to the marina, where brightly coloured flags wafted lazily in the breeze.

'La Grande Motte,' said the driver, bringing them to an unnecessary screeching halt.

'Ju. For god's sake, Ju, put him down, will you?'

She finally came up for air, her hair in chaos and her lips looking like they couldn't take much more. 'What? Oh, this looks okay,' she said, wiping her mouth with the back of her hand. Her neck was still being caressed as she peered out of the window. 'Yeah. Looks great. Drop us in *Centre Ville*.'

'We're already in *Centre Ville*,' said Chrissy.

'Anywhere here then.'

They spilled onto the pavement like their spaceship had just crash-landed. Whilst their bags were being squeezed out onto the kerb the driver honked his horn, then an array of hands began waving out of the windows as they pulled away. Chrissy lost count of the number of times she said '*grazie*', and anyone would think Juliet was sending her sweetheart off to war with all her kisses and cries of '*Ti amo*'.

Chrissy ran her fingers across her cheekbones to wipe away the sweat beneath her sunglasses. She could already feel the sun burning through her skin as she waited for Juliet. The enormous pyramid on Allée de la Grande Pyramide towered above the others. Further down the street she could see the Tourist Information symbol and a sign for the campsite. Meanwhile Juliet was still waving enthusiastically.

'They've gone, Ju,' she said, hoisting her rucksack onto her back. 'You can stop now.'

'I'm in love.'

'In under four hours? A record, even for you.' Chrissy saw that she was clutching a folded piece of paper to her chest. 'You got his number? I don't believe you sometimes.' She laughed. But then a thought struck her. 'Which one was it you were snogging?'

'Luca,' said Juliet, dreamily.

'Didn't they say it's Luca who is getting married?'

'Final fling.' She grinned at Chrissy, enjoying her disapproval. 'Never kissed an English girl before.'

'Oh well, that makes it all right then.'

'I didn't force him. We can't all be saints like you, Chrissy.'

'You're not going to look him up, are you?'

'Well, I might. One day.'

With that, she tucked the piece of paper into her bra and slung her rucksack onto her back. 'Who knows? *On ne sait jamais.*' She gave Chrissy a kiss on the cheek and Chrissy wiped it off again like a sulky child. 'Hey, guess what?' said Juliet, linking arms.

'What?' said Chrissy, pretending to be mad at her.

'We fucking made it!'

Their cheering caught the attention of a group of old men playing *pétanque*. The metal *boules* clattered together in a cloud of dust and the men seemed to think that the cheers were for them, waving as the girls walked past.

'Seems like a friendly enough place,' said Juliet, waving back.

'If you tap off with any one of those, Ju, I'm going to disown you.'

'I think they're more your type. Steady and sensible.'

'Excuse me. Dan's not steady and sensible, he's a musician. Actually, maybe he is. You're just jealous in any case.'

Juliet came to an abrupt stop. She pressed her hand to her heart and, with her eyes closed, said: 'Yes, but now I have my Luca.'

'*Tu es complètement folle,*' said Chrissy, amused by her theatrics all the same.

They continued walking.

'Ah, but you love me because I am mad,' said Juliet in her mock French accent.

Chrissy shielded her eyes from the sun. They had reached the marina, and the sea was glistening, as though someone had scattered tiny diamonds across it. Halyards clanked against the masts, sounding random xylophone notes. Motorboats and handsome yachts bobbed up and down on the silky water, and a neat row of masts protruded into the sky like giant cocktail sticks. Further along the shoreline they could see the beach with swimmers' heads bouncing up and down on the waves.

'This is perfect,' said Chrissy, sighing. She could already taste the salty spray on her lips.

A boy selling ice creams weaved in and out of holidaymakers on the beach, stretched out on sunloungers beneath their straw parasols. But it was a group of fit-looking men playing volleyball that had caught Juliet's eye.

'Let's stay here forever,' she said.

Chrissy elbowed her in the ribs when she realized what she was gazing at. 'You might get through the whole team, Ju, if we stay here long enough.'

'You're just jealous that I can.'

'No, I'm not.'

'Really, you should step outside the box sometime, you know.'

'Piss off, Juliet.'

'Just saying.'

'You're always saying. Saying I should sleep with someone else, be unfaithful to Dan. Why? Why do you always do that? Are you trying to break us up?'

''Course I'm not. But if Dan's box is the only one you ever sample, you might be missing out.'

'On what? It's called a relationship, Juliet. You won't be familiar with that concept because you screw everything that moves.'

'That's a bit harsh,' replied Juliet. 'I only screw the good-looking ones.'

'Seriously, Ju. What if you get yourself up the duff? You take too many risks.'

Juliet shrugged. 'Well maybe you don't take enough.'

CHAPTER 11

France: summer, 1989

Dan would love it here, Chrissy mused.

She was sitting cross-legged in front of their tent eating a *pain au chocolat* in the morning sunshine, contemplating the view of Pic St-Loup in the distance. She had already looked it up: 638 metres, and the thought of climbing it one day with Dan filled her with joy. But right now, she could not be happier. Somehow or other they had stumbled upon a campsite with a 24-hour festival vibe. Dancing, campfires, bongo drums and ghetto blasters going on well into the small hours.

They became known as *Les Anglaises.*

Yan's Bar was the place to find work. Word of mouth spread quickly on the dance floor as to who was hiring, and by the third night they had potentially found their first job. A new restaurant was opening in town on Avenue Plein Soleil, in need of a paint job inside and out. After some clever negotiation and mild flirtation on Juliet's part, they were hired, but Chrissy later discovered this was largely because she had agreed to do the work for next to nothing and committed them to complete in four days.

'Four days? We'll have to work our bloody arses off. I thought you had a head for business.'

'Don't know what gave you that idea.'

She therefore took great pleasure in shouting down Juliet's ear at six thirty on their first morning: 'Last one in the sea is a piece of *merde*!'

'Are you insane?' Juliet protested, tugging the sleeping bag over her head. But when she saw Chrissy pulling on her bikini she joined in the race to get down to the sea.

They had the beach pretty much to themselves at this hour. Wake-up swim, *pain au chocolat,* off to work by seven; it became their routine.

By day three they were exhausted. Juliet trundled wearily up the stepladder with her tray of paint, gripping the paintbrush between her teeth. She yawned, and then began scratching the top of her head with the handle. 'Is it Saturday today?' she asked.

'Think so,' said Chrissy. 'Why?'

'In that case it's a very sad day. Luca's getting married.'

Chrissy rolled her eyes and flicked paint at her.

'Oiy!' shouted Juliet, although they were already covered in paint. 'Do that again and I won't invite you to our wedding.' She stuck her tongue out at Chrissy, who then fired another round of paint. Before long they were both white from head-to-toe.

'I wonder where we'll be in twenty years' time,' said Chrissy, a few hours later during a short lunch break. She was picking paint out of Juliet's hair, who was lying across her lap. 'I just hope we've got better jobs than this.'

'Well, you will for certain. You'll be a high flyer. In London, probably. Married to Dan. Start firing out kids at thirty-three, thirty-four, then back to your career.'

Chrissy considered it for a moment. 'Yeah, I'd settle for that. And you'll be some big shot in the fashion world.'

Juliet shook her head. 'Nah. I'll be happy with just a little shop in a place like this, making clothes that people come in and love. And buy, obviously.'

'Do you think you'll get married, Ju? Do the kids thing? And don't say you'll marry that Luca bloke because it's just so ridiculous.'

'Oh, I don't know. Suppose I'll have kids. Doesn't everyone? Or I could just be part of your extended family.'

Chrissy tugged at Juliet's matted hair, and said: '*Tante* Juliet.'

'Don't! That makes me sound so old.'

'Right, come on,' said Chrissy, throwing Juliet off her lap. 'We need to finish this job before we're twenty, or neither of us will have a future.'

***

Once the paint job came to an end, Chrissy found work in Frankie's Ice Palace along the seafront. More of a kiosk than a palace, it was wedged between a long line of restaurants with beautifully laid tables under large white canopies, serving food they could never afford. Juliet sold the remainder of her T-shirts, scarves and small canvas bags to holidaymakers coming on and off the beach, keeping under the radar of any *gendarmes* on the prowl. In addition, the odd hour of babysitting and English lessons was enough to give them a hand-to-mouth existence.

'Chrissy,' whispered Juliet.

It was 4 a.m. and they had just crawled back into their tent from an all-night beach party. Their legs ached from dancing non-stop on sand for nearly six hours.

'Mm?' Chrissy was almost asleep.

'Don't be angry with me.'

'Why, what have you done now?'

'I bought a little something with today's earnings.'

'Like what? Oh, you'd better not have, Ju. What did you spend it on?'

'Some magic beans at the party.'

She sputtered and giggled like a child. Chrissy pulled the sleeping bag over her head. She was too exhausted for this right now. And it wasn't the first time Juliet had done this either.

***

Their final job was working as *femmes de chambre* in a tourist-class hotel on Avenue du Général Leclerc: making beds, polishing mirrors, hoovering carpets, and holding their noses as they cleaned out toilets. But as the season was slowly drawing to its close there was a growing sense of the town emptying out. In the mornings when they left for work they would see people packing up their tents, then, in the evenings, all that remained were the faint outlines of where they had been. Increasingly, thoughts of home crept into Chrissy's mind. Back to Manchester. Dan. Family. Friends. The second year at university. And for Juliet, a fresh start at Bristol Poly.

'Do we have to go?' said Juliet, making a sad face when Chrissy suggested they should think about heading back.

'Can't stay here forever, Ju. And we'll be into September soon.'

'Kind of wish we could.' Juliet dug her toes into the grey sand as she spoke.

They had no fixed-return coach tickets booked from Paris to aim for but Chrissy had worked out, based on their journey down, that they could be home by the following Saturday teatime, if they were lucky. The long hitch-hike back up to Paris filled her with dread, yet she knew Juliet viewed it differently; it was still part of their big adventure and she was in no hurry to get home, especially as her dad still didn't know about her changing courses.

Finally, Juliet agreed it was time to leave.

Chrissy called Dan to tell him the good news.

'Okay, well, ring me when you get to London,' he shouted, racing to beat the dreaded pips. 'Let me know what time your coach gets into Manchester and I'll be there. God, I can't wait to see you again.'

'I've no coins left, Dan!'

'Leave a message if I'm not in. See you Saturday.'

'I will. I love—'

The line went dead.

It was to be a morning departure, to make the most of any long-distance traffic heading for Paris. However, by the time they had shaken off their hangovers, got packed up and said their goodbyes, it was already late afternoon. Four thirty, according to Chrissy's watch, when they finally headed out of town with their thumbs in the air, the reverse of their cardboard sign saying *'Paris SVP!'*

The sun showed no signs of it being the end of the summer, and their rucksacks seemed heavier than ever. To make matters worse, Chrissy was furious with Juliet for blowing their last bit of money on partying the night before.

'Well, you helped me spend it. Some of it,' said Juliet, looking guilty. 'Great night though.'

'I didn't know it was our travel money you were dipping into.'

'Who cares? It's just money, Chrissy.'

'So how the hell are we supposed to eat now?'

Juliet shrugged. 'Something'll turn up, always does.'

'Oh. Like starvation and dehydration, you mean? Well, thanks a lot, Ju.' She was trying to smile at a man in his car but he shot past them shaking his finger. 'And how do we pay for another night's camping?'

'We'll do a runner.'

'I'm not a thief.'

Chrissy's side of their cardboard sign had drooped and Juliet pushed it up again. 'Maybe it's time you did something mad and crazy, Chrissy Plumber.'

An hour later, Juliet apologized. They still didn't have a lift. Where was the family with the stinking baby? The friendly Spanish truck driver? The fun-loving Italian guys?

Why wasn't anyone stopping?

Another hour slipped by. They had gone less than two miles up the road and that was by flip-flop. By now it was six thirty and they were beginning to feel hungry. The only thing they had eaten all day was a handful of stale baguette when they eventually crawled out of their sleeping bags.

'We still friends?' said Juliet, sheepishly kicking at sand drifted into the kerb. She twisted a strand of hair round her finger. 'It's just, you haven't said anything for a whole two hours now.'

'Do you even have to ask that?' Chrissy snapped. But she laughed once she realized how angry that sounded.

Standing by the side of the road in an affectionate make-up hug, they heard a loud horn blast from a truck that was thundering past. All the skidding and screeching seemed to suggest it was actually trying to stop. With whoops and shrieks they grabbed their bags and ran as fast as their flip-flops would allow.

The trucker was eagerly climbing down to greet them. '*Bonjour, Mesdemoiselles,*' he said. He didn't sound French.

'*Bonjour,*' said Juliet, her chest panting from the exertion. '*Vous allez vers Paris?*'

'*Mais oui.*'

He was already taking her bag off her shoulders and tossing it into his cab, wedging it behind the seat. He did the same with Chrissy's. They climbed up and, barely inside, the door was pushed against them; the lock button immediately clicked and disappeared. Turning to one another they realized it was too late. His sweaty gut was already behind the wheel.

'Wiktor,' he said, giving Juliet a salivary grin.

They presumed that was his name.

'Erm. Sister Rosa,' Juliet replied, shuffling into Chrissy, trying to make her shorts stretch further down her legs. 'And this is Sister Theresa.' She held onto Chrissy's hand. Any earlier bad feeling between them was now evaporating into the cab, which reeked of smoke and sweat.

When he saw they were holding hands he winked at them and started up the engine.

'Where do you think he's from?' said Chrissy, squeezing the words out of the side of her mouth just in case he spoke any English.

'No idea. Weird accent.'

As they pulled away, he took a swig from a bottle of what smelt like whisky. He offered them some, an invitation to join his party. Even if it had been a glass of the coolest iced water, the only fantasy in their heads right now, they would still have said no.

'It'll be fine,' said Chrissy, speaking quickly. 'We'll get him to stop at the next services. We grab our bags and we leg it.'

CHAPTER 12

Manchester: 2007

'Bloody hell, Mum. What happened? Did he hurt you?'

'He was a moron, that's all. I'm still here, aren't I?' She pushed Eloise's hair out of her face, leaving her hand to rest on her cheek. 'There's no hurry for you to know any of this stuff, Eloise.'

Of course there was. Juliet would be here soon and Eloise still hadn't got to the bottom of what had happened between them.

They took a tram out to Heaton Park. It was a good day for views, far-reaching over central Manchester and beyond. Wisps of cloud stretched lazily across the sky, and Eloise thought back to the times they used to do this as a family. If only her dad was still here, then she wouldn't be in this mess.

Chrissy walked at her usual brisk pace and every so often Eloise had to break into a jog to keep up. They were heading for the lake. 'Don't come where you're not wanted,' shouted Chrissy, waving her foot at a dog that seemed keen to join them. 'We don't want any uninvited guests, thank you.'

Eloise swallowed, observing her closely as she lay down on the grass. She was gazing up at the sky, one arm across her forehead shielding her eyes from the sun, and when the wind caught her hair Eloise could almost imagine her being nineteen again.

She tossed a stone into the water. 'How could you be so naive, Mum, with that lorry driver? Is he the reason you and Juliet don't speak any more?'

'No. I told you, he was just a moron.' She sat up, hugging her knees into her chest. 'Things were very different then; the world wasn't like it is now.' She let out a sigh before carrying on. 'There was no Bank of Mum and Dad to bail us out. No mobile phones, no internet, no social media or 24-hour news. I suppose it gave us a sort of blind trust in people.'

Eloise threw another stone into the water, watching the circles ripple out. Suddenly her mobile pinged, causing them both to jump. She hoped she wasn't catching her mother's fear-of-the-phone syndrome.

'Will come round for 7.
J xxx'

'Who's that?' said Chrissy, trying to look.
'No one. Just Anya.'

***

Chrissy taught at the School of English near Piccadilly on a Monday, and was usually exhausted when she got in. '*Salut!*' she shouted, tossing her keys onto the table, kicking off her shoes.

Eloise didn't want her to get too comfortable. She had to look her best this evening, and her mother would want that too if she knew who was coming. Maybe she had taken the easy way out by not telling her about Juliet. It certainly didn't feel easy.

Chrissy assured her that she hadn't forgotten they were going out. Suddenly she noticed how neat the place was. 'Oh, I get it now,' she said, pointing her finger. 'I know what you're up to.'

Eloise felt herself go weak. 'Really?'

'It's a boy. That's what all this is about.'

'No!' She was grateful on this occasion for the confusion. Her mother was weird about boys at the best of times and Eloise would never dream of bringing one home, even if it was serious. 'Anya said she might pop round later,' she splurged. 'Well, after we get back. But she probably won't; you know what she's like. I thought the place could do with a bit of a tidy, that's all.'

***

'So. What do we do now?' said Chrissy, rubbing her thighs in that slightly fidgety way when she was all dressed up.

'Just waiting for the taxi. You look great, Mum.'

She did look good in her own relaxed style. Eloise had also opted for jeans, like her mother. Plus, vest top, black with white zigzag splashes across the front. Juliet could probably spot a past season a mile off, but it didn't matter. That wasn't what tonight was about.

'Taxi?' said Chrissy. 'What's wrong with the bus?'

'I got a pay rise.'

'I don't want you to blow all your hard-earned cash on me, Eloise. I appreciate you wanting to treat me but—'

As she was speaking, another text message sounded on her phone. It was Eloise who shot into the air.

'*On my way*
J xxx'

'Are you sure you've not got a boy coming round?'

Eloise tried to swallow the guilt wedged in her throat. There was no time to dwell on it, however, because the doorbell went through her like an electric shock.

'I'll just see if that's the taxi,' she said, relieved to see that her mother was in no hurry to get up. She was unusually calm in fact.

'Take two,' Juliet whispered. Eloise pulled the door to, so that Chrissy wouldn't see. 'Are we all set?'

Juliet looked like she had just stepped out of *Vogue* magazine. A black leather bag was slung over her shoulder. Soft. Italian-looking. Expensive. On the other shoulder she had a shiny white carrier bag with long black handles and the letter 'R' on the side.

Juliet removed her shades and slipped them into her bag.

'Is it the taxi, Eloise?'

She could feel her mother pulling on the door. She wasn't ready, not at all. But couldn't hold onto it.

Chrissy stood with her arms folded, her eyes firmly fixed on Juliet. 'Go,' she said, in a tone of voice Eloise didn't recognize. 'Leave us alone, Juliet. I don't know why you're here.'

Then she turned to Eloise, silently accusing her.

'Chrissy, I know this is a real shock for you,' Juliet pleaded. 'But—'

'I don't want to know. Just go.'

'I want her to stay, Mum.'

'I'd be quiet if I were you, Eloise. This isn't about you.'

Eloise hesitated. 'I think it sort of is now.'

Chrissy thought for a moment, slowly stepping to one side. Her arms were folded solidly and her face remained stern.

It unnerved Eloise to see Juliet looking to her for clues. Surely it was for Juliet to take the lead now; she had played her part.

Perhaps Juliet picked up on that because she moved forwards, stepping cautiously into their poky little flat. A scent of jasmine and musk trailed behind her. Chrissy didn't take her eyes off her for a second, but Eloise hung back thinking maybe she should leave them to it. Her mother dragged her in and closed the door.

Juliet flinched at the sound of the chain. Like a knife being sharpened, Eloise thought, immediately trying to stop herself from thinking that. 'Erm, sit down,' she said, wanting to reassure their guest.

'She's not stopping.'

Juliet looked to Eloise once again, but all she got in return was a helpless shrug.

'Look … Chrissy—'

'What?'

'I'm sorry for showing up again like this. I really thought it'd be okay. Don't be hard on Elle. I persuaded her to get involved.'

'She doesn't like being called Elle,' said Chrissy, trampling over her words.

'Yeah, I don't,' Eloise confirmed, almost apologetically. 'It rhymes with smell.'

'Oh god, so it does,' said Juliet, mouthing the word *sorry*. 'Look, all I want to do, Chrissy, is say thank you for what you did for me.'

'You've said it. Now you can go.' She nodded towards the door.

'Please don't be like that. All this time I've wondered how you are—'

'You can see I'm fine.'

'… what you're doing, who you're with. I've missed you.' She beamed at Eloise. 'And you have a very beautiful daughter.' Juliet began to rummage in her bag. 'I wrote you a letter, Chrissy.' She fished out an envelope that was grubby and creased. Then she fished out another one, more pristine.

Eloise offered to take her bags; she seemed to be struggling.

'There's something for you both in that one,' said Juliet, referring to the shiny white carrier with the letter 'R' on the side.

'Thanks, Juliet.' Eloise glanced nervously at her mother and took a step back.

She noticed Juliet's hand was lightly trembling as she held one of the letters out to Chrissy. It was met with a look of disdain, and Juliet cleared her throat, preparing to speak.

'I wrote this just after you left me in Bristol,' she began. 'Of

99

course, I never sent it because I knew you wouldn't want me to.' She paused for a reaction, but didn't get one. 'I was scared too you know, Chrissy.'

Eloise observed her mother, who was taking in every last detail of Juliet. Like a blind person suddenly able to see her friend for the very first time. She lingered over the cat brooch, then said: 'It was me they wanted. You know it was.'

'No!' said Juliet, stepping in closer, immediately retreating again. 'That's just not true. We were both in it together, Chrissy. And still are. I'm here now, aren't I?' She held out the newer-looking envelope. 'This one I wrote last night. Everything I ever wanted to say to you is in these letters. Read them, Chrissy, and tomorrow night I'll send a car round, we'll go somewhere special. I've arranged to stay on in Manchester, so let's just enjoy ourselves. Please, Chrissy, for old times' sake. We don't even have to talk about any of that stuff. Give me one more night, and then if you really don't want to have any more to do with me I'll stay out of your life forever. I promise.'

'You promised last time, Juliet.'

'But it's getting on for twenty years. I wanted to see you. Is that a crime?'

'Of course it's a crime!' Chrissy yelled. 'Just go. Leave us alone. And you can take *these* with you.' She seized the vase of sorry-looking flowers and thrust it towards Juliet. Juliet was so startled she backed away and the vase smashed, scattering fragments of blue glass in all directions.

Water seeped into the carpet. Eloise quickly put down the bags and got onto her hands and knees. She removed a battered white lily from Juliet's shoe, not daring to look at her, gathering all the stems into as neat a pile as possible. When she eventually stood up again, Juliet had gone. And Chrissy was standing with her hands over her face.

'You okay, Mum?'

She slid down the wall, her head falling between her knees, hands over the top as if to protect herself.

Eloise crouched down beside her. 'I'm sorry,' she said.
'It's not your fault, Eloise. None of this is your fault.'
'I just thought … she was your best friend.'
Chrissy reached for her hand. 'She was.'
'So what happened?'

CHAPTER 13

France: summer, 1989

Juliet was almost sitting on her lap. Every so often his hand would wander across to her thigh, golden-brown from two months of sunshine, and she would politely return it to the steering wheel. Chrissy wondered how long Juliet would be able to keep her cool. She could usually handle her men. What concerned Chrissy even more, though, was they appeared not to be going in the direction of the autoroute. But she kept that to herself.

He made some attempt at conversation, blowing smoke into their faces. He asked, in French, what they had been doing and where were they from. Juliet's insistence that they were nuns only made him more excitable, particularly given their attire, and it was not long before he was asking whether their suntans were all over, or were there any white bits. He laughed at his own crude remarks, eyebrows bouncing up and down on his sweaty forehead. His teeth, the few he had left, were nicotine-stained from all the chain-smoking; the stench from his mouth enough to make anyone retch.

'*Combien pour une baise? Je vous donne cinq mille francs,*' he said, flicking his cigarette out of the window. '*Hein?*'

They knew the word *baiser* meant either to kiss or to fuck, and they understood perfectly which one he meant. It was a lot of money, enough to get them home quickly – the equivalent of around five hundred pounds. How often had they sat and played the *What if?* game in Bristol: *What if you were offered a million quid?* The outcome was always: *Depends on how badly you need the money at the time.* Well, wasn't this the time? Didn't they desperately need the money? But when reality was staring them in the face with piss breath, bad teeth and rancid yellow tongue, they both knew there was no way they could do it even for five billion pounds. Besides, he didn't look like he had more than five francs to his name, let alone five thousand.

Chrissy smiled politely. '*Non merci.*'

'If we don't get out of here soon I'm going to have to crash this fucking lorry myself,' Juliet declared, speaking quickly in a Scottish accent. They were pretty sure he didn't speak any English, but better safe than sorry. 'And where are we? We seem to be on pissy little roads.'

'Keep calm,' said Chrissy, pretending Juliet had told her something wildly funny. 'Look like you're enjoying yourself.'

'Enjoying myself?'

'It's okay, I have a plan,' she tried to say reassuringly. 'We just need to wait until we get to civilization.'

'Well, hurry up, Chrissy, because I swear I am this close to grabbing that steering wheel and swinging us off the road.'

'Please don't do that, Ju.'

'Where the hell is he taking us? We should be on the motorway by now.'

'I don't know. He's probably trying to avoid paying tolls.'

Chrissy didn't believe that for a minute. It was at least an hour since she had seen a sign for the motorway or for Paris. They seemed to be going in the direction of Toulouse for some reason when they ought to have been heading back up the Autoroute du Soleil towards Lyon. They could be anywhere now.

She didn't recognize any of these smaller places on the signs: Fumel, Cazals, Salviac, *Le Back of Beyond*. It would help if she could get her road atlas out of her bag, but it was firmly wedged behind their seat.

'Okay, here goes,' said Chrissy, beaming. 'I want you to smile and look as flirty and dirty as you can at him.'

'What?'

'Just do it, Ju. Smile.'

'Think I'm going to puke.'

'That's great, just keep it up. No matter what I say … *Excusez-moi, Monsieur.*'

'*Oui? Qu'est-ce qu'il y a?*'

Chrissy continued in French, smiling and flirting: 'We're actually really hungry. Maybe we can stop and get something to eat at the next services, or maybe if we pass a bar that's open …? We'll make it worth your while. Won't we, Sister Rosa? We'd like to accept your kind offer.'

Juliet looked like she really was going to throw up. Chrissy gave her a sharp dig in the ribs.

'Sure. Sure we will.'

'Flirt, Ju. Flirt. Talk dirty. In English, then you can let rip. Do it.'

'Okay … me and Mother Theresa will suck and fuck the shitty arse off you if that's what you want, you slobbering, slimy dickhead piece of shit.'

'Lick your lips,' said Chrissy.

'Oh please.'

'Look sleazy and like you mean it.'

Juliet managed to make some suggestive motions with her tongue. He laughed like a drooling idiot. Meanwhile Chrissy kept an eye out for a place to stop. The sky was darkening, making it difficult to read signs or see any trace of civilization that might be out there. Everything was firmly shuttered up. He pointed to an Aire de Repos, but Chrissy shook her head. It had to be somewhere with real signs of life if they were to have any chance of escape.

He began to get desperate, keen to pull in to secluded lay-bys or go down any old rough track. Juliet had gone worryingly quiet and Chrissy had to keep reminding her to flirt. How much longer could they hold him off like this? Did she need a Plan B?

What was Plan A?

'*Non, non, non,*' Chrissy insisted when he began to veer off again. '*C'est nous qui décidons.*'

Almost another hour slipped by and darkness engulfed everything, including their hope of ever getting out of this.

A light, shining up ahead, provided them with a faint trace of optimism.

'*Là! Arrêtez là!*' said Chrissy, thinking it could even be a small service station as they got nearer to it.

The place was disappointingly empty. A few lights on here and there, three large juggernauts parked up in some sort of desolate car park. Beyond that, nothing.

A car was just pulling away from the pump. They hadn't spotted it until now as the driver had no headlamps on. For a brief moment their faith was restored – vanishing quickly again when they drove into an area completely unlit, away from the main forecourt.

As the truck jerked to a standstill he grinned at them greedily. There was sweat nesting in his brows. A few moments later he was round their side, grubby paws at the ready.

Chrissy tried to free her rucksack from behind the seat.

'*Non, non, non,*' he said. 'No bag.'

'But we need them,' she said in French.

'No bag.'

'He can't be serious,' Juliet yelled.

'It's okay, Ju, we'll get them after.'

'But I put everything in there. Passport, tickets, everything.'

'I know. Me too. It's okay, I have a plan.'

She didn't. But they were stuck with him until they could retrieve their bags. They jumped down, powerlessly watching as he double-checked the doors were securely locked. Chrissy's eyes struggled to adjust to another layer of darkness. It was unnerving to hear the trees blowing back and forth, unable to see them. The cool air made her arms feel tender. She ran her hands up and down to keep the chill off.

Juliet nudged her.

He was loosening his flies, laughing at the horror on their faces as he got into position to pee on his front tyres.

'Wait!' said Chrissy. 'We need to go, too. But to the WC. *Toilette.*'

He nodded, zipping up. They followed him towards the main building. There was one toilet, which they could smell long before they got to it.

'What are we going to do?' said Juliet, her voice thin and shaky.

He had gone in first, safe in the knowledge that they couldn't get far without him. Before Chrissy could think of an answer, the toilet door opened again.

It gave him a thrill when they both went in there together.

'Look, Ju, you've got to keep your head,' she said, pulling the bolt firmly across. 'I'll get us out of this, I promise. Just go along with anything I say and do.'

'Well, what are you going to say and do for god's sake? He has our sodding bags.'

The stench of raw sewage hit them. They covered their faces, trying not to inhale as they each took a turn squatting over the hole in the ground. But if that hole had been any bigger they would have used it as their escape route, because crawling through a sewer was preferable to what was on offer outside.

Juliet stuck her face over the tiny sink. She splashed a dribble of cold water onto her cheeks whilst Chrissy stroked her back, trying to calm her.

'We're going to steal his keys, Ju. You're going to go down for the blow-job whilst I go through his pockets.'

'No way! Why can't I go through his pockets?'

'Because you're his favourite.'

Juliet wiped her hand across her mouth.

'Look, you don't have to do it for real. You just take your time, work him into a frenzy. When I have his keys I'll shout "Run", then we leg it to the truck. If there's time I'll kick him in the bollocks.'

'Right, okay,' said Juliet, puffing out her cheeks like a boxer before stepping into the ring. 'That's actually brilliant. I love you.'

She clung to Chrissy.

'You ready, Ju?'

She nodded.

'Let's go get the fucker then.'

He was nowhere to be seen. It unsettled them. Either he was hiding, about to pounce, or had driven off with their bags, passports, tickets, dirty washing, the lot. Probably the dirty washing he would be most interested in.

He emerged from a door with a battered *Tabac* sign above it, a packet of Gauloises stuffed into his shirt pocket. A foul odour wafted up as he put his arms around them, pulling them into his sides and slobbering down their cheeks. His breath smelt like he had just licked out the hole in the ground and then smoked a hundred fags. They were heading back to his truck, but Chrissy was trying to work out the best place to steer him. If he shoved them out of sight, there would be no telling what he might do to them. She had to ensure they would have enough time to retrieve their bags, and then, somehow, run for safety. He didn't look in good shape, one thing in their favour; he'd been coughing and spluttering throughout their journey. His hairy belly hung over his jeans like dough.

Definitely get that kick in the bollocks, she thought.

Maybe, just maybe, they could pull this off.

'*Par ici*,' she said, indicating to some trees. It was a risk, rather secluded, but Chrissy reckoned they could still be seen if someone was to pull up onto the forecourt, which might just save them.

'How quickly can you run fifty metres?' she asked Juliet, this time in an Australian accent.

'Believe me,' Juliet replied with an Aussie twang, 'I can break the world record if it means we get shut of this greasy arsehole.'

Juliet was getting into her part now. Whenever he went for a grope she would tell him not to rush, to take his time; he ought to get his full five thousand francs' worth. She pouted and teased, patted his groin, blowing saucy, suggestive kisses. Meanwhile Chrissy ran her hands over his chest, checking his shirt pockets for keys, keeping an eye on the trees to make sure they were heading in the right direction.

'Stop,' she said, hoping they had gone far enough.

It wasn't perfect. But it would do. It would have to. She grabbed him, slamming his back hard against a tree. He let out a growl of approval, which set him off coughing and gave them a chance to go through the plan again.

One last time.

'When I shout "Run", you just run like your shorts are on fire, Ju. Okay? And don't look back; I'll be right behind. Okay?'

Juliet took off her flip-flops and closed her eyes.

The coughing stopped.

It was time.

Chrissy watched Juliet zigzag down his fat body. It seemed like none of this was for real; she could be watching it on TV.

But it was real.

And now it was her turn.

Chrissy slipped her fingers into the back pocket of his jeans. He moaned at her touch, which made her stomach heave. Nothing. Sliding her hand to the other pocket, squeezing his saggy backside for good measure, she managed to hook her index finger around what felt like a key fob. No sooner had she got it when she lost it again; his jeans had plummeted to his ankles.

They hadn't discussed this. Juliet had unfastened them

completely. Despite slowing him up once they started making a run for it, Chrissy would first have to grovel down at his feet.

'Haven't you got them yet?' cried Juliet, desperation in her voice. He had hold of her head, pressing it into his yellow-stained Y-fronts. 'I'm not sure how much more of this I can stand. The fucking stench. Camembert!'

He slammed her head into his groin as if to say: *Stop talking and get on with it.*

Juliet screamed.

'Okay run!' Chrissy yelled.

As Juliet tried to escape he grabbed her by the hair and she let out another scream. Chrissy reacted quickly, biting his hand so hard he was forced to let go, but when they both set off again, Chrissy felt herself being pulled back and it was her turn to scream.

Juliet stalled. She didn't have the keys. 'Here,' Chrissy shouted, tossing them at her feet. 'Just go, Ju. Get the truck open, get our bags.' Juliet came up again, slowly, holding the keys, unsure what to do.

'I'll handle it, Ju. Just leg it. Fuck's sake. Go!'

He fired a tirade of abuse as she finally took off, and Chrissy seized upon the distraction, managing to swing herself around. As she did so her hair twisted in his hand, pulling her scalp so tight it made her eyes water, but she was able to raise her knee to his groin, enough to make him crumple to the ground.

'Please let Juliet have our bags, please let Juliet have our bags,' she chanted as she ran, flip-flops in hand, her bare feet shredding on the concrete. In the background she could hear him launching a barrage of things he was going to do to them. It seemed a long way back to the truck, much further than she thought. A hundred metres, not fifty.

She found Juliet pounding hysterically on the door, kicking at the tyres. 'What are you doing?' said Chrissy, trying to get her breath back. 'Where are the bags?'

'They don't fit.'

'What do you mean "they don't fit"?'

'I can't open the doors,' Juliet wailed. 'I've tried both.'

Precious time had been lost and they could hear his curses approaching. Aware that no one would be able to see them in this dark, lonely corner, Chrissy wondered if they should just abandon their bags and run. Before she even had time to suggest this, however, she was shunted out of the way, the keys ripped from her hand.

Instinctively, she stood in front of Juliet to protect her, but when he spat in Chrissy's face Juliet shot out from behind, landing a kick on his shin with one of those slender, bronzed legs he had been admiring. He grabbed Juliet's arm, ramming her into the side of his truck with a violent slap to put a stop to her yelling, holding her by the throat.

'You fucking arsehole!' Chrissy screamed. Out of the corner of her eye she spotted someone getting into a car. It was a long way off. She shouted and waved, knowing it was useless. The car disappeared and she broke down in tears. Then she realized it was doing a U-turn. She waved her arms again in despair.

A smartly dressed businessman got out and was coming towards them.

Chrissy stood back to let him through.

'Let her go,' he said in French.

Juliet was still pinned against the truck.

The lorry driver shot him a look of contempt, slyly sizing him up. The man was tall and looked like he worked out at the gym.

'*I said*, let her go.'

Chrissy ran to Juliet, who was rubbing her neck where his fingers had been pressing hard into her skin. He had given her a shaking before releasing her, and her cheek was inflamed where she had been struck.

'Now drive.'

'No! Wait,' Chrissy shouted. 'He has our bags. He won't let us have them.'

Hauling himself up into his cab, the trucker tossed down one bag then the other. He swore at them, calling them filthy English prostitutes then slammed the door. The engine coughed sluggishly into life, jerking the truck forwards. Huge, hefty tyres were thundering towards them.

The man was quick to react, pushing their bags out of the way, steering them to safety.

They stood and watched the truck turn bulkily into the road, until it disappeared into the gloom.

'Oh god, thank you so, so much,' said Chrissy in French. 'What a *cochon*! What a disgusting pig of a man.'

'*Pas de problè*me. Are you okay?'

'Well, thanks to you,' said Juliet. 'If you hadn't showed up—' She looked away, tearful.

He explained that he had been on the road all day, just pulled in to buy petrol and a coffee. 'I could see that something was wrong,' he said. 'But really I did nothing.'

Chrissy wanted to throw her arms round him. He was about the same age as her father, handsome in that French way, and seemed embarrassed that they were thanking him so much.

'*Vous avez faim*?' he asked, continuing in French. 'Because, if you are hungry I will buy you something to eat.'

Chrissy felt her stomach grind at the mention of food. 'Thanks,' she said. 'But we just need to get to a campsite now.'

'Where are you heading?'

'Paris,' said Juliet.

'I'm hoping to get to Paris tonight, if that's of interest. My wife is expecting me. It's my son's birthday and I'm terribly late.' He started walking back to his car.

'He seems decent enough,' said Juliet, watching him go. 'It'll be late when we get to Paris but we can always kip down in the coach station, get the first bus out tomorrow morning.'

'We don't even know where we are,' replied Chrissy, dragging her rucksack over. 'Let me get the map out.'

'Are you mental? We can't let him drive off. How many more nutjobs are out there? And what if that one comes back?'

Maybe she had a point.

'Okay,' said Chrissy, fastening her rucksack back up again.

He loaded their bags into the boot of his car, a brand new white Citroën, flashy and expensive-looking. Five minutes later he appeared with a *gruyère* baguette and a large bottle of Evian. Juliet almost took his fingers off when he offered it to them, and they tore into the bread like feral cats. Chrissy tipped the bottle of water vertically over her mouth and, with a gratifying sigh, wiped the droplets off her chin. Juliet grabbed the bottle and did the same.

'*Pas faim, hein?*' he said, shaking his head. 'You English are just too polite.'

Chrissy was mortified that he had witnessed their feeding frenzy.

The headlights cut through the darkness as they pulled away, tyres crunching on loose stones. She kept imagining the terrible phone call that her parents would have received from the French police. Also Dan. Poor Dan.

'It's a five or six-hour drive to Paris, I think,' he said. 'I will try to get us there much faster.'

Juliet put her head on Chrissy's shoulder and it wasn't long before she started to doze. Chrissy, on the other hand, remained alert. Every time she saw a truck, her heart began to race. It bothered her that they were heading in the same direction.

CHAPTER 14

Manchester: 2007

'I'm going to bed,' said Chrissy, sliding herself back up the wall.
She was still clutching Juliet's letters.

'Christ, Mum. Thank god you got away from him.'

Chrissy pulled Eloise to her feet. 'Now do you see why I'm so
worried about you?'

She wanted to say that she would never be that stupid or naive,
not like her mother and Juliet had been.

'You think you're invincible at that age,' Chrissy added. 'When
really, you're not. Goodnight, Eloise.' She disappeared into the
bathroom and closed the door.

Eloise heard a thump.

'Mum. You okay?'

'I thought I'd made myself very clear about Juliet, that's all.'

The soap dish clattered into the sink, and when she heard her
cleaning her teeth Eloise could picture the blood swirling round
the plughole from such vigorous brushing, audible even through
the door. She took a deep breath before she dared say anything.
'Well, maybe you should let me read her letters. So I know what's
going on between you two.'

Chrissy burst out of the bathroom, pushing past Eloise. 'You never let go, do you? You just never let go.'

The bedroom door closed, putting an end to their argument.

Eloise contemplated the mess. Petals and bits of green foliage still strewn across the carpet, possibly shards of glass that she had missed, too. The wet patch had almost doubled in size. And Juliet could well be on the next plane back to Italy by now. Who could blame her?

'Sorry about tonight, Juliet.
Thanks for the prezzies.
Eloise xxx'

A message came straight back, saying:

'To be expected.
See you tomorrow.
J xxx'

Eloise hugged the carrier bag into her chest, then peered inside it. There were two boxes, each wrapped in purple tissue paper and tied with a gold bow. *'For my most beautiful Eloise'* it said on one of the glossy labels.

Eloise fell asleep with the gift next to her bed, the scent of Juliet drifting into her dreams.

With or without her mother, she would still be going out with Juliet tomorrow night.

***

Chrissy had to be there when she read the letters; that was the deal. But she was still in the bath, taking so long to get ready, and besides, what harm would it do?

The envelopes lay next to her on the bed. Eloise could just see the words:

'Your best friend forever, Juliet xxx'

The one that resembled an old teabag needed some gentle coaxing out of the envelope. She took great care not to rip any of its six pages as she opened them out. To think that Juliet had written them nearly twenty years ago.

'My Dearest Chrissy, 24ᵗʰ October, 1989 …'

But that was as far as she got before they were snatched from her hands.

'*Never* go behind my back again, Eloise.'

'But you said I could read them before we went out and there's hardly any time left.' Their eyes locked together. 'Juliet said we don't even have to talk about any of that stuff, Mum. Didn't you hear her? … What? What's wrong?'

Chrissy was looking at her aghast.

'My god, look at you. You look stunning, Eloise. Let me see.'

She forced a smile, giving her the full twirl, spinning on one heel and holding out the ends of the dress. Her hair was pinned up in a messy backcombed style for a grungy-chic look.

'Is that from—?'

'Juliet.'

'It fits you perfectly.'

It was a short, floral print summer dress in red and black. Beautifully made: *100% pure silk crêpe de chine*. Juliet had put a note inside the box:

'Eloise, I am basing your shape on what I remember your mother's to be. If it's not suitable you must choose something out of any of the collections. Love Juliet xx'

'Why don't you wear yours?' Eloise asked, her eyes drawn to the piles of clothes scattered across the floor. She picked out the

115

purple box and offered it to her mother. When she refused it yet again, Eloise pulled on the gold ribbon, parted the purple tissue paper and unfurled a Fifties-style black dress. 'Wow! That is just lush.' It had lace detail in a V-shape around the neckline. Sleeveless, pinched in at the waist with a full flowing skirt and just a hint of net underskirt below the hem. Simple, but elegantly beautiful.

Her mother didn't react.

'Let me quickly dry your hair,' said Eloise. 'Get the full effect.'

After that she helped her slide the dress over her head, being careful with the waves she had just created. Eloise admired the way the dress drew in around her curves when she zipped it up at the back.

'Blimey, it's tight,' Chrissy gasped.

It was a perfect fit for her slim, athletic figure. She had a slight tan due to all the running that she did, and the dress complemented her golden skin tone.

'Look, you have a waist, Mum. And boobs. You look gorgeous.'

Chrissy allowed herself only the briefest moment in the mirror before she was tugging at the zip again. 'I can't come out tonight,' she said.

'Why? Wear something else then.'

'It's not the dress.' She was getting more and more impatient with the zip.

Eloise rushed over before she damaged it.

'I won't tell Juliet about the brooch, if that's what you're worried about. That you stole it.'

Chrissy stepped over the dress, catching it with her toe and flicking it off. 'It's not about the brooch either.'

Eloise picked up the dress, folding it neatly with the respect it deserved. But she could feel her anger building. 'You just can't let anyone else get close, can you?' she snapped, stepping into her mother's face. 'Stuck in the same old house in the same old city, forever and ever. Doesn't matter what I want. You don't bloody care!'

By now Chrissy was in her dressing gown. She looked at Eloise, shell-shocked, then yanked on the belt pulling it into a tight knot. 'Actually, Eloise, this may surprise you, but you're all I care about.'

'Yeah, right.'

As she tried to leave the room, her mother blocked her way.

'I'm sorry it's not how you'd like it to be. And I'm sorry if you feel trapped,' she said stiffly. 'But, like it or not, Juliet is not the answer. I can't just welcome her back into my life. There's a lot to consider. One day you'll understand that.'

'How?' Eloise yelled, barging her way through.

'Where are you going?' Chrissy shouted after her.

'Round to Anya's.'

She had already asked Anya to cover for her, if questions were asked. Because that's what friends did for each other.

As Eloise raced blindly down the stairs she realized she felt secretly pleased that her mother wasn't coming out this evening. It meant she could have Juliet all to herself.

***

'She really isn't coming?' said Juliet as Eloise piled into the car. She had to be quick in case Chrissy was out on the walkway.

The driver shut the door. She hadn't even realized he was standing there; in so much of a hurry to get in.

'She says it's because she wants *you* to tell me the rest of the story, Juliet.'

Eloise felt herself flush.

Juliet smiled. 'So she hasn't let you read my letters?'

'Not yet, but she's started to tell me stuff. I know she saved you from the lorry driver.'

'The lorry driver?'

'Yeah, the one who was really horrible to you.'

Juliet tapped on the glass; they moved off slowly.

'It fits you well,' she said, turning to admire the dress.

'Oh, it's perfect. Thank you so much. Mum loves hers too. You should see her in it, she looks like a film star. I hardly recognized her.'

She saw that Juliet had toned it down tonight, wearing a simple navy blue dress with a white short-sleeved cardigan. She obviously wanted Chrissy to be the one to shine this evening. The cardigan was secured at the top with the silver cat brooch. There were tiny cuts in the metal, creating stripes along its back. Didn't she ever take it off? Surely she hadn't been wearing it every day for the past twenty years.

As they drove round the grassy island in front of their block, Eloise felt the need to say: 'This is just a temporary place, by the way. We're sort of between houses.'

Juliet smiled and linked arms. 'Well, let's have ourselves a good time, you and me, Eloise. It's a chance to get to know each other a bit.'

Already Juliet had begun to unravel the knots in Eloise's stomach.

It was only as she began to relax that she registered the car.

Black. One-way glass.

She tried to get a look at the driver's face. His profile alone told her enough. Something was not right about this.

'Where are we going?' she asked.

'You'll see,' was all Juliet would say.

CHAPTER 15

Manchester: 2007

Eloise felt slightly more at ease when they continued up Oxford Road, heading into town.

'This is where I work,' she said as they passed Maria's Café. She wanted to bring some normality to the situation. The bars and fast food places on Oxford Road were busy with students. A small crowd was gathered in front of the Cornerhouse; on the other side, the queue was growing for the Palace Theatre. Their car moved slowly through the traffic as people were being dropped off and taxis tried to push their way in.

'Yes,' said Juliet. 'But you go to Sixth Form College.'

'How did you know that? I – I never told you that.'

'Forgive me, Eloise. You see, I had to make some enquiries. Anton followed you on a couple of occasions. I hope you don't mind.'

She must have looked shocked because Juliet touched her hand and said: 'Oh gosh, I'm so sorry. I really didn't mean to scare you. If I'd got the wrong Chrissy it would have been terrible. Can you imagine?' She let out a laugh. 'Anton's a much better chauffeur than he is a spy.'

Eloise wondered how many times she had been followed and not even known about it. And when had it started?

'It's okay. I – I get it,' she replied, trying to convince herself that it was. The knots in her stomach were beginning to re-form.

'Your mother, on the other hand, proved much more elusive.'

'Yeah, I bet. She runs everywhere, doesn't she?'

A tram was just pulling into St Peter's Square and as their tyres rattled over the tracks, the Midland Hotel on their left, Eloise thought this could be their destination. It seemed the sort of place Juliet might stay. Instead, they turned down Mount Street towards Albert Square. The Town Hall shone magnificently in the evening sunlight. At least Manchester was not letting her down.

'I'm so sorry to hear about your dad,' said Juliet when the traffic began to slow again. 'So young, as well. It must be hard for you, Eloise. And your mum.'

'Did you know him well?'

'Yes.' Juliet beamed at her. 'I bet he was a great dad. Oh, but I'm not upsetting you by talking about him, am I?'

'No, it's okay. I do miss him.'

'I'm glad Chrissy got her happy ending,' she said, pulling Eloise into her side. 'I truly am.'

Eloise wasn't sure what she meant by that exactly; she had never considered herself a happy ending before. The remark made them both pensive for a while, although the traffic was a distraction crawling around the Square.

Finally, she spotted the sweeping curve of the Lowry Hotel. As they pulled into the car park the impressive Trinity Footbridge was just visible and Eloise found herself wishing, rather guiltily, that her mother could be here to experience this too. She was so distracted she hadn't realized that Anton was waiting for her to get out of the car. He gave her a steely stare, and she was relieved when Juliet took her arm.

They were escorted up to the terrace bar, where chairs were pulled out for them and a pianist played a Frank Sinatra song which Eloise vaguely recognized. Juliet ordered two glasses of champagne.

'Ssh. You look old enough,' she whispered. 'And we won't tell your mum.'

'She won't mind as long as I don't go home arseholed.'

Eloise squirmed, wanting the evening to begin again.

'Well, here's to us,' said Juliet. 'And to your wonderful mother, who is very, very dear to me.'

Eloise thought she could see tears in her eyes and felt the need to look away out of politeness. Sipping her drink, she focused on the bridge instead. From here it was like a giant harp suspended across the River Irwell, reflecting wavy reds and purples on the water.

Then she became aware of Juliet rooting around in her bag.

'Ah!' she said when she had located her cigarettes and lighter. But as she was putting her bag back down by her feet, some of the contents spilled out onto the floor.

Eloise jumped up to help.

Confusion flooded her brain when she saw it.

'My god, Juliet. How come you have that?'

She picked up the little yellow bear that had gone missing from their flat a few days earlier.

'I can explain,' said Juliet, scooping the rest of her things into her bag. She took the bear from Eloise and held it up. 'Do you know where this came from?'

'My dad gave it to me,' she replied, feeling the disappointment all over again that it wasn't a special present just for her, as she had always thought. 'But why have you got it?'

Juliet winced. 'Anton again, I'm afraid. He was a little too keen to prove that he'd found the right Chrissy.'

'So he came into our flat and took it?' Eloise was trying to work out when that might have been, thinking back to the incident when her window was open and their flat smelt of cigarette smoke.

'I can only apologize, Eloise. You see, I'd shown him photos of what your mum used to look like. In among them was one taken of me and your dad with this little fellow, in Bristol. Anton was only meant to find out where you lived and report back to me. When he returned with the bear … well … I'm so terribly sorry.'

'You found it on the bus. My mum told me.'

'That's right,' said Juliet, handing it back to Eloise.

'You might as well keep it now,' she said sulkily. 'I've got other things to remember him by.'

'Are you sure? Well that's very kind of you. I shall treasure it.'

Eloise wasn't sure, but it was too late now; she couldn't ask for it back. She would have to say she had lost it, or the neighbour's dog had got it, if her mother should ask.

Juliet went out onto the terrace for a smoke before their meal arrived. Eloise could see her talking on the phone. Probably a business call. Or maybe Luca. Other people were staring at her as well; she was that sort of person.

The dinner was confusing; French, and a never-ending array of courses. Eloise was flattered when a waitress thought she was Juliet's daughter, and she could tell Juliet was pleased too. Then she found herself wondering what it would be like to have Juliet as her mother, and may even have wished that she was.

'Don't you have any children?' she blurted. Not only was it an inappropriate question, it felt like she had betrayed her own mother by asking it.

'No,' Juliet replied, tearing her bread roll. 'Luca already has a family. Besides, he lives in Italy and I prefer London.'

'Oh, I see,' said Eloise. She didn't at all, and searched for a much safer question. 'What are you doing in Manchester?'

'Seeing you.' Juliet took a sip of water. 'And promoting the new collection. I'd also like to open a couple of boutiques in the North of England. We have small concessions in Manchester – Harvey Nichols and Selfridges – but we only have one Ricci store in the whole of the UK.'

'London. I looked at your website.'

Juliet was clearly impressed. She put down her glass, planting it thoughtfully. 'You know, you really should come and stay. You and Chrissy. I have a flat on the river … the River Thames?'

'Yes, I realized that,' Eloise replied, laughing. 'I'm just in shock. My god, I'd love to.'

Juliet gave the waiter a signal to say that they had finished, and held off a moment until their plates were cleared before continuing. 'There's plenty of room. Just me rattling around in the place most of the time. And if you ever want work experience, please say. Whenever you want, just come.'

'Your life sounds amazing,' said Eloise, registering just how small hers seemed in comparison.

Juliet answered with a shrug, briefly turning her attention to the other diners in the restaurant. It had got busier, couples mostly, and one or two businessmen dining alone. She returned to Eloise and asked: 'When do you finish school? Have you any plans for the summer?'

Eloise rolled her eyes. 'None that ever get off the ground.'

So Juliet got it all then … the Inter-Rail trip, still nothing more than a wish list of cool places to go; the gap year that she worried about taking because she didn't like leaving Chrissy on her own; the dilemma of Bournemouth Uni …

'Nothing nearer to home than Bournemouth?' Juliet queried.

'Yes but—'

She gave her a look of sympathy. 'I hear what you're saying, Eloise.'

'It's been a bit difficult, you know, since my dad died,' Eloise said tearfully. Juliet handed her a packet of tissues with the Ricci logo on them. Eloise smiled gratefully.

'I'm here now, Eloise.'

She felt so relieved to have shared all of this at last with someone. Even if she was practically a stranger.

'Thanks, Juliet.'

'I only wish I'd come sooner. But I can fix all of that.' She waved both her hands, as though wiping the slate clean. 'Come to London, stay in my flat. Come to Italy, stay in Rome. You have the whole summer. We can talk about your gap year later.'

Juliet seemed to be waiting for an immediate answer.

'Erm. Well, my mum doesn't know about any gap year yet. Might be good not to—'

'I won't breathe a word,' she said, putting her finger to her lips. 'So what does your mum do?'

'She teaches French. And English as a foreign language.'

'In a high school?'

'She works freelance. Like a tutor. I mean not like a tutor – she is a tutor. Language schools, private lessons mostly. She's quite choosy, but always seems to be busy.'

'Strange, I never found her website. Does she have some exotic French name she goes by?'

Eloise sat on her hands. 'She doesn't do the internet. Don't ask me why.'

Juliet nodded, as if she understood, then asked for the bill.

**

The mood in the car was more subdued on the way home. They seemed to take a different route and a drunken rowdiness had spilled out into the streets. Juliet began brushing non-existent marks off her dress then reached into her bag for a packet of cigarettes. She offered one to Eloise, who declined, and then proceeded to light up two cigarettes, giving one to Anton through a flap in the screen.

'Sorry. Disgusting habit,' she said, opening the windows. 'You don't mind, do you?'

Eloise shook her head. Then she noticed a tear rolling down Juliet's cheek. There was something about Juliet which she couldn't quite put her finger on. Eloise fished out the Ricci tissues from her pocket. 'I didn't use all of them,' she said, trying to lighten things a little.

Juliet took one and dabbed her eyes. 'You keep them,' she said. 'They're just to promote the new collection.'

Eloise was used to her mother crying on her. Not so much now – after her dad died mostly – but she never expected she would have to console Juliet. Strong, successful, fun-loving Juliet. She had no idea what to say. Luckily Juliet seemed caught up in her own thoughts so she probably didn't need to say anything.

After a while, she took a pill out of a silver tin, tipped her head back and swallowed it. 'It's screwed up her life,' she said, tracing round the edges of the cat brooch. 'You must hate me, Eloise.'

Hate?

Why should she hate her?

***

It was a relief to be out of the car. For all its luxury it was starting to feel prison-like and stuffy. And Anton gave her the creeps. It was a clear summer's evening, the air still warm. Even so, Eloise felt a chill up her spine and goose bumps down her arms.

'I probably shouldn't come up,' said Juliet.

It seemed more of a question. And then it struck Eloise that she hadn't informed Juliet that she had come out without her mother's consent.

'Why don't I call her?' she asked.

'Oh god, no! Don't do that. My mum hates phones.'

She considered it a moment. 'Sod it. Let's give it a try, Eloise.' She grabbed Eloise by the hand and set off at a marching pace. 'Life's too short.'

The click-clack of their heels was almost in sync as they went up the metal stairway, heading towards the door.

'Look, Juliet, my mum doesn't kn—'

Too late. She heard the key turn in the lock, the rattle of the chain being released, and knew she had made a big mistake.

Thankfully, Chrissy had got dressed. She looked good in her jeans and long-sleeved top and hadn't destroyed her hair and make-up. But she also looked furious.

'I'm just returning your lovely daughter,' said Juliet. 'Thank you for allowing me to borrow her this evening. It was very special.'

'Juliet … my mum didn't know.'

'Oh.'

Chrissy's demeanour never altered as she held the door open. Juliet edged tentatively across the threshold, checking that Eloise was following.

Chrissy slid the chain back across and left them to stew in the silence.

'Right,' said Eloise, sensing that an apology would only ignite her anger. 'We should have the champagne.' She darted into the kitchen without waiting for a response and returned with the bottle from Juliet, clutching it with both hands. Her mother was clearly puzzled that it seemed to have come from their fridge. Eloise got in there first before she could comment. 'God, this weighs a ton. Better not drink it all tonight, eh?'

She handed it to Juliet, who passed it to Chrissy, and whilst the two of them passed it back and forth between them as if it were a bomb, Eloise rummaged in the box of vinyl, blowing off the layer of dust. She wasn't used to playing records and the arm of the needle was broken so she had to bring it down manually into the groove. It landed with a thump, followed by a series of crackles. Before long The Smiths were playing loudly through her dad's old speakers.

The champagne cork exploded out of the bottle. Chrissy was making no effort to help Juliet, and Eloise gave her a disapproving look as she brushed past her into the kitchen. 'These are all we've got, I'm afraid, Juliet,' she said, producing three wineglasses. She knew the lack of flutes was the least of her worries.

The tiny bubbles rose to the top in playful anticipation, but no one seemed to want to propose a toast. Eloise didn't think it was her place. Eventually Juliet stepped forwards and raised her glass. 'To friendship and the future.' She made it sound more like a question.

'To friendship and the future,' said Eloise, chinking her glass against Juliet's. 'And Cheese Eloise, Mum.' Juliet looked bemused. 'Oh, it's just a daft thing me and my dad used to say.' She felt foolish for saying it now, especially given her mother's lack of response.

'Well, cheers,' said Juliet, holding her glass up to Chrissy before taking a sip.

Chrissy sank hers in one go.

'Blimey. You were thirsty, Mum. Top up?'

'No,' she said, sitting down.

They took it as their cue to do the same.

Morrissey's voice came through the crackly speakers, filling the awkward void. It was 'Girlfriend in a Coma'. Eloise cringed at the lyrics, something about there being times when he could have murdered her. But Juliet tapped her glass in time to the music with her perfectly manicured fingernails, probably immune to the words, having heard them so many times.

Eloise tried to imitate the way she was sitting, perched on the edge of the chair with her legs tucked to one side.

'I often put The Smiths on even now,' said Juliet. 'Takes me back. Happy days.'

'Some were,' said Chrissy. She seemed to be concentrating on the brooch, but then her eyes latched onto Juliet's.

Juliet made out she needed to cough so she could look away.

'My mum's told me all about the parties you used to go to,' said Eloise, knowing what it was like to be gripped by one of her mother's pale-blue stares. 'They sounded brilliant.' She felt like a piece of cling film stretched between them, being pulled tighter and tighter.

Juliet gave her a grateful smile. But Eloise wasn't sure for how much longer she could keep this up. She topped up their champagne and could hear herself babbling. 'Don't worry, Mum, I only had the smallest glass at the restaurant. Which was amazing, by the way; we should go there sometime. You get more cutlery for your starter than we have in our cutlery drawer. The waitress thought I was Juliet's daughter—'

If only she had some cling film to put over her own mouth. The silence came down between them again like a shutter.

The song changed to 'Sheila Take a Bow', hissing and crackling in the background.

'It's a shame they broke up, The Smiths, isn't it?' said Juliet.

'They'd already split up by the time we met,' Chrissy replied tersely.

'Really? I don't remember.'

Even though Juliet was still tapping her fingernails in time to the music, Eloise could tell it was a forced gesture, and a few moments later she was preparing to leave. Eloise was distraught. If she left now she may never come back.

'I remember when you fell off the table dancing to this,' said Chrissy.

Juliet was clearly taken aback, but settled herself again. 'Do you?' She beamed at Chrissy like a child desperate for praise.

'We had to wrap your ankle in frozen peas and I had to push you home in a shopping trolley.'

There was a pause before anyone laughed. Eloise wasn't sure which one of them laughed first, though it didn't matter. Actually, perhaps Chrissy didn't laugh, not really.

But almost.

'I had those ridiculous wedge boots on, didn't I?' said Juliet. She dabbed at her smudged mascara, still laughing. Or crying. Eloise couldn't tell. 'You won't believe it, Chrissy, but that bloody ankle still plays up. And when it does, I always think of … you.' She tailed off at the end.

It brought the silence back again.

'Tell me about your course,' said Chrissy. Her tone was harsh but at least she was engaging a bit more. 'I'm assuming it must have gone reasonably well for you to end up being Queen of the Ricci Empire.'

Juliet held up her hands. 'I've so much to thank your mum for, Eloise. I don't know how much she's told you, but—'

'She knows enough,' said Chrissy. 'At least for now.'

'Until I read your letters, Juliet.'

Juliet nodded, taking a moment before she said anything else. 'Well, I got that business bursary at the end of my degree. I was dying to tell you – obviously I couldn't. So I decided to get out there and make a name for myself in the hope that one day you'd see how much you'd done for me. I set up the Juliet label, which did okay. And then, as you say, the Ricci Empire.' She laughed quietly to herself. 'But it wasn't through ambition at all. None of it. Just the love of a good friend.'

Chrissy dropped her head, pressing her fingers into her temples. 'Mum, are you okay?'

'I'm fine,' she said, glancing up again.

Eloise sensed it was time for her to leave. They would speak more freely without her, no matter how much she wanted to stay. She made some pretence of checking the time and stood up. 'I know you two have loads to catch up on, and some of us have Double Geography in the morning. Thanks for a lovely evening, Juliet.'

Juliet waved, the same wave as before, her fingers playing an imaginary piano.

'Goodnight, Mum.' As she leant in to kiss her she was about to say something about reading the letters, and then didn't bother.

But later, when she went hunting for them, she wished that she had.

Because there they were, in the bin. Nothing more than black-ened remnants.

'*And. Motel. The. His. Friend forever. Shower. Glass. Juliet xxx*'

All the words Juliet had so carefully written, and all the answers Eloise desperately needed, were lost forever. Juliet should know about this. She could hear the music still playing next door.

'Where is she? Where's Juliet?'

Chrissy was crouching over the record player. 'She's gone,' she replied calmly.

'What do you mean "gone"? Gone where?'

The needle dragged across the record, making a deep scratchy sound. It seemed like an accident, not that it mattered.

'Why? What did you say to her?'

Chrissy blew on the stylus, her breath travelled through the speakers.

'I can't believe you, Mum. Why would you do that?'

'Because I had to.' The record player clicked when she turned it off. 'For both our sakes.' Then she disappeared into her room and closed the door. 'And you had no business to see her behind my back, Eloise,' she heard her shout.

Eloise burst into her mother's room, a fireball of frustration.

'And you had no right to burn those letters! Tell me why you did it.'

Chrissy was sitting on her bed, head in her hands. She looked up, her eyes falling on random objects so as to avoid Eloise.

'I had to do it, Eloise. It was evidence.'

CHAPTER 16

France: summer, 1989

'*Je suis fatigué*,' he declared, rubbing the back of his neck. 'I am tired.'

They thought he meant to pull in for a comfort break, stretch his legs, that kind of thing. They had been driving for nearly three hours. So it unnerved them when he went on to say that maybe Paris was overambitious in view of the distance they still had to go. Could he propose setting off early again in the morning when he would be refreshed and safe behind the wheel?

'I have a motel where I usually stop. It's just off at the next junction.'

Chrissy saw her own turmoil reflected in Juliet as they looked to each other for guidance. All they could see outside was the blur of headlights and a never-ending black sky. Suddenly the rules had changed. They had no idea where they were and they had no money. How could they get a room? It threw up a whole host of other issues, besides who would pay for it.

After a brief and hushed discussion, in a coded Welsh accent, they came to their decision. 'If you could drop us at the nearest campsite that would be great,' said Chrissy. They could do a runner first thing in the morning, as Juliet had rather flippantly suggested earlier.

He tutted. '*Non, non*. It's okay, I will get my usual room. It has two beds, and they know me here. You just let me check in and then I give you the signal.'

It sounded like he was suggesting they would have to sneak their way in. They, too, felt tired, but getting to Paris tonight, however late, was their agreed objective. This new plan seemed rather complicated.

'Obviously it doesn't look good for you to come through Reception with me. They will think the worst. French people make terrible assumptions.'

They smiled politely. It hadn't occurred to them they would look like a pair of prostitutes. Of course they would have to sneak in; it was obvious now that he had said it.

'No really, the campsite will be easier,' said Chrissy. 'We'll get another lift in the morning. We can't put you through all that.'

He tutted again. '*Non*, I insist. I cannot abandon you at this hour. What if the campsite is not open? I'd never forgive myself. Trust me, it will be very simple. The room is on the ground floor. So … I check in; I go to the room; I open the window and when you see the light go on and off again you run across the car park with your bags. Then, you climb in through the window and nobody will ever know you are there. We all get some rest. And *allez, hop* … in the morning we are on our way to Paris. Arrive by ten. Ça vous va? Okay?'

Although it still sounded rather complicated, it had been a long and turbulent day and the thought of erecting a tent in the dark was not an enticing prospect, especially as they *still* didn't know how to put it up properly. How could they not, after all this time? Chrissy thought angrily to herself.

The motel was largely in darkness, apart from a dim light over the entranceway through which they watched him disappear.

'At least we get to sleep in a proper bed tonight,' said Juliet through an exaggerated yawn. 'So where the fuck are we?'

It was a rectangular shoebox sort of a place, flat-roofed and soulless, and seemed pretty downmarket. But maybe that was what businessmen did who were clocking up the road miles and just needed to get their head down until morning. There were three other cars parked up for the night, all with a similar newness and flashiness.

'I'm going to get my road atlas out of the boot,' said Chrissy.

'Do you really think that's going to help?'

Chrissy stuck her head through the window. 'Yes, Ju!'

The night was much warmer than she imagined it to be, but goose bumps still rippled over her bare arms and legs. She lifted both bags out of the boot, handed them to Juliet and sprung back into the car. 'You know, I'd be more than happy kipping in here for the night. Wish we'd said that now.'

'God no! Give me a bed and a shower. Think I've got fleas,' said Juliet, scratching herself. 'Must have caught them off you.'

Chrissy was trying to find the correct page in the atlas, in no mood for banter. She spread it across her lap. 'I know we've passed Poitiers because I saw signs for the turn-off. I think we're some-where here.' She ran her finger up and down the A10 between Poitiers and Tours. Looking out of the window there was little else to go on. The car park's perimeter was lined with mature-looking trees, which, although would give good shade during the day, only hemmed in the darkness at night. The reason they knew the trees existed in the first place was because they were lit up by the headlights when they had pulled in, but now were bulging, menacing outlines and gave the place a remoteness and sense of seclusion. Chrissy just hoped she was right in her theory that they were not too far from Tours.

'No one around,' said Juliet.

'What if we just stay here when he gives us the signal? He'll assume we're sleeping in the car,' Chrissy suggested.

'You heard what he said: he'd be worried about us. And he's right to be. What if that nutjob truck driver suddenly pulls in?'

'Seems unlikely.' Chrissy felt her scalp tightening at the thought of him.

Juliet was the first to spot the light flashing on and off. '*Allez, allez, allez.*'

'Hey shush, Ju. If we're seen, we're done for.'

The light had gone off, but they knew which window to aim for and could see him as they got closer to it. The window was open for them. He leant down for their bags, hoisting them up one at a time like some dubious cargo that had to be disposed of quickly. Then he pointed to a small gap in the brickwork for Juliet to use as a footrest. Chrissy stood beneath her, ready to give her backside a helpful shove.

Juliet giggled.

'Ssh, *les filles*,' he said in a loud whisper.

Even as she was guiding Juliet's foot to where he had indicated, the thought still crossed her mind that they should spend the night in the car. But once Juliet's legs disappeared through the window, she knew it was too late to change their minds, and grew anxious when Juliet failed to show herself again. Moments later, Chrissy herself was being pulled over the ledge, hitting the floor with a thump. Juliet was standing over her, offering to help her up.

The room was as described: two beds, one of which was single, presumably theirs. They would insist on that; it seemed only fair. The decor was not too offensive, pale lemon colour scheme. Juliet bounced onto their single bed and let out a grateful moan as she lay down on it. 'Ça c'est le grand luxe.'

Meanwhile Chrissy was dragging their rucksacks over, wiping sweat from her face. 'Is it okay to use the bathroom, *Monsieur*?' she asked in French.

Loosening his tie, he seemed once again amused by her English politeness. 'But of course. Make yourselves at home.'

'You need to go as well, Ju,' she said, grabbing her foot.

'What? No, I don't. I'm fine.' Juliet looked at her blankly. It was a command not a question. 'Actually I'm peeing my pants,' she added.

There was no lock on the bathroom door, Chrissy pointed out. 'And we'll sleep in our clothes tonight, Ju. Okay?'

'Whatever you say. I wish you'd just relax.'

'How can we after that shitty truck driver incident?'

'That was hours ago. And we escaped that shitty truck driver *because* of this guy. Are you having a pee or what?'

He was phoning through to the bar when they went back into the bedroom. Ten minutes later there was a knock on the door, which startled all three of them. They had to make sure they were out of sight before he answered.

Juliet silently clapped her hands as he waved the bottle in front of their faces. He disappeared into the bathroom, emerging a few minutes later with two full glasses of velvety Shiraz; one, a wine-glass, the other a plastic toothbrush holder, which he gave to Chrissy.

'*Santé*,' he said, raising the bottle.

'Oh here, have mine,' said Chrissy, seeing he was without a glass. She didn't feel much like drinking in any case.

'*Non, non.* It's for you. I will leave you to freshen up. Take a shower if you want. I'm going to the bar to get something to eat. Would you like me to bring you something back? It's basic *cuisine* – *hamburger-frites*, something like that, but it's okay.'

They declined, reminding him that he had already bought them something earlier. They didn't want to take advantage.

'*Fa-ti-guée*!' declared Juliet, collapsing onto the double bed and somehow managing to turn on the TV as she fell backwards. Her black hair had come loose and was spread across the duvet. She stretched out in a star shape, her long, tanned legs hanging over the end. 'Jeez, I'd forgotten what a proper mattress feels like.' She curled up into the duvet. 'Wow, clean sheets. Bliss.' Then she sat up, reached across for her wine that was on the chest of drawers next to the bed. She shook her empty glass at Chrissy in the hope of a refill.

'Blimey. Go easy, Ju. We still need to stay sober. And for god's sake, that's not our bed. Get a grip, will you?'

Juliet giggled. 'That's good stuff. Gone straight to my head. I'm so knackered. Aren't you knackered, Chrissy?'

'Yes, but I'm having a shower whilst the going's good. No more wine for you, Ju, and get off his bloody bed. Don't you dare fall asleep.'

Chrissy removed her clothes, grimy and dusty from a long day on the road. In her head she was already under that cool jet of water.

***

Juliet told Chrissy she must have slept for a while. At least, it felt like sleep but she had a splitting headache. She may have had some more wine, but couldn't quite remember. At some point she possibly switched beds again. The TV was on, she remembered that clearly enough. When she tried to sit up, her head felt like it was filled with concrete, and then everything started to spin: the people on the TV, the carpet, the window, the lamps. Everything. The whole lemon-coloured room.

She probably staggered back to the double bed to see if that helped. *It's not our bed,* she kept telling herself. *Chrissy will get mad.* Same pale lemon sheets, same cheap soap powder smell. *It's for somebody else, though, not for us.* She couldn't quite remember who that somebody else was.

If she closed her eyes everything was calm again.

She wasn't sure how long it was after that.

There were voices, but possibly from the TV. A tremendous weight came down on her chest, which felt like it was about to cave in, and her head was still pounding. Opening her eyes only gave her room-spin again. In fact, the only thing that wasn't spinning was the brown stain above her head on the ceiling. It helped if she fixed on that.

She wanted the heaviness to stop, and for her clothes not to be pulled and torn. But she could do little about it.

She tried to fight and scratch and scream but no sound would come out, no matter how hard she tried to cry out for help. She could barely move her limbs were so heavy. And he was heavy. It wasn't a dream; she knew it wasn't. She kept telling him to stop. She tried to put her hand over his mouth to prevent him from kissing her. Why was this handsome, older guy – the man who had rescued them from the shitty lorry driver – the man who had a wife and son and lived in Paris – why was he doing this?

It made no sense.

She focused on the brown stain on the ceiling above her head as he got rougher and angrier …

Waiting.

And hoping …

… for Chrissy to come to her rescue.

***

Chrissy realized she had been in the shower for too long. She never heard him come in; he must have slithered in like a snake. As soon as she realized, she had a terrible feeling.

What if?

Grabbing a towel, she wrapped it around herself, securing it with wet, trembling fingers, asking herself: why had she not thought of it sooner. *Why?*

She found him on top of Juliet, pinning her down, tearing at her clothes. He was naked, apart from a towel round his waist. Chrissy launched herself at him, pulling on his shoulders trying to budge him, repulsed by the feel of his bare skin.

He turned and glowered at her, pushing her away with such force that she fell over.

She tried again but hit the floor with a smack that time and realized it was useless. Her nails gripped the carpet as she scanned the room. Pick up the phone? They weren't meant to be here in the first place. Shout for help? Same problem. In those brief moments her eyes jumped from one desperate thing to another. The wine bottle on the chest of drawers was almost empty. The TV was still on, as if everything was normal. And, strangely, he had taken the time to fold his clothes into a neat pile on the pillow.

That seemed like the ultimate insult.

Chrissy hurled herself at his clothes, tossing them onto the floor. The belt in his trousers came loose in her hand. She shook it free.

Suddenly she was standing behind him, jerking the belt taut in her fingers.

Breathe Chrissy, breathe. Snap it round his neck then pull back hard.

One quick movement.

That's all it would take.

She moved in closer, caught her shin on the bed frame but was immune to the pain.

As far as she could tell he was still trying to remove Juliet's clothes. She had to act now before it was too late.

Breathe Chrissy. Breathe.

One, two, three.

She gave the belt another tug.

Next time, she told herself. But in that final second she froze every time.

Something, an instinct, made him turn round.

He seemed to find it amusing when he saw what she was trying to do, towering over her as he stood up. Chrissy backed off. The contours of his upper body were defined and solid. Feeling trapped as he came towards her, and angry because he was still laughing at her, she whipped the belt back behind her head, lashing it forwards so fast she heard it whistle by her ear.

The buckle caught him in the eye. He reeled backwards.

An old woman on the TV was laughing as he put his hands over his eye, blood seeping through his fingers. He staggered, still coming at her though, and there was nowhere left to go. Her legs bashed against the bed frame, causing her to stumble.

She hit the floor hard.

The broken stem of the wineglass was standing proud on the carpet. She hadn't noticed it until now and had almost landed on it.

He seemed to be struggling to see, which gave her a few seconds to think. The blood had entered the front chamber of his eye. It looked horrific.

She seized the broken glass and stood up, holding the lethal spike out in front of her as she edged towards him.

This time, no hesitation.

The blood trickled down his stomach like a thickening raindrop on a windowpane. It wasn't a deep slash, but enough to make him fall backwards. As he went down, his head burst open on the corner of the chest of drawers, and he landed on the bed with one arm across Juliet.

'Mm. No,' Juliet muttered. She had barely moved until now.

Chrissy removed his arm from her neck, trying to ignore the bloody halo that was forming around his head, soaking into the sheet. Apart from the shallow rise and fall of his chest he was motionless, and she was able to concentrate on Juliet.

Her clothes were ripped. He hadn't quite succeeded in removing her shorts.

Chrissy stroked her face. 'Ju-Ju. It's me. Chrissy.'

Her head thrashed side to side, panicking that it was starting over again.

'You're okay now, Ju. You're okay.'

She managed to pull her up into a sitting position. A limp rag doll in her arms, Juliet began to weep down her shoulder with Chrissy rocking her back and forth.

The wine bottle on the chest of drawers suddenly caught Chrissy's eye.

And then she knew.

The bastard must have put something in their drink.

***

She couldn't bear it. Hearing it once was terrible enough, but Juliet wanted to keep going over and over what she thought had just happened to her, each time adding in another painful detail. The heaviness, the roughness, the spinning, the pushing, the shoving, the tearing, and the brown stain above her head on the ceiling. And just when Chrissy thought she might be returning to normal she would say something like: 'Look, Chrissy. Someone's shat on our ceiling.' Then she would laugh, making it plain to see that she was still under the influence of whatever he had put into that wine.

Juliet was incapable of holding her head up for more than a few seconds.

'Come on, Ju. Please. I think we need to get out of here.'

'Whoops,' said Juliet as her chin flopped down onto her chest again, causing further amusement. During all of this, Juliet didn't seem aware of her assailant lying next to her.

Finally, she spotted him.

'*Monsieur*,' she said, prodding his arm. '*Monsieur*.' When she didn't get a response she looked at Chrissy. 'I'm very cross with him, you know.'

'I know,' said Chrissy. 'Me too.'

Juliet nudged him again.

'Wake up. Wake him up. I want a word. Tell him I want a word. A cross word.' She giggled. 'A crossword.'

Chrissy put her finger to Juliet's lips.

'Oops, sorry,' whispered Juliet. 'Sssh, *les filles*. Don't make a sound. Okay, okay let's play. Come on, *Monsieur*. Six across: the clue is *cross words*, four and three.'

140

Nothing.

'Hellooo,' Juliet sang in his ear. She gave him another nudge. Still nothing.

'You don't know the answer? Okay, I'll tell you. Four and three. *Fuck. You.*'

She managed to stifle her giggles as she lay back down, curling up close to him, almost spooning him. Chrissy was repulsed, about to move her, when Juliet began tapping him on the shoulder. She gave his leg a firm kick, and asked: 'Is he dead, Chrissy?'

'I don't think so.'

From somewhere deep inside, he let out a long, drawn-out moan.

Juliet sat up quickly. 'Oh god, he said something then, Chrissy. What did he say?'

'Nothing,' she replied.

But actually, she thought he had said: 'No, fuck you.'

CHAPTER 17

Manchester: 2007

Eloise could see the fear and anger still burning in Chrissy's eyes. A sense of regret squeezed her heart for having pushed her mother this far. No wonder she had been so reluctant.

For the first time, she wanted her to stop talking.

But what had possessed them to get into that car and end up in a motel?

Admittedly, in those circumstances – lost and alone at night in a foreign country, with no money, no credit card, without mobile phones or any internet to rely on, and a sex-crazed trucker still at large – she would probably have done the same. Eloise could understand their desperation. After all, this man had saved them. A respectable businessman. Husband. Father.

She remembered her mother's phrase, 'blind trust'.

'But you got away from him, Mum. You and Juliet: you lived to tell the tale.'

In that moment she knew she could fix this. Now that it was out in the open, Chrissy could finally put this ordeal behind her.

Eloise just had to say the right things.

'What he tried to do to Juliet was the crime, Mum. Don't you see that? Not what you did to him. You shouldn't be punishing yourself all these years on. He will have gone to hospital, got his eye stitched up and his stomach, and then gone back to his wife with his tail between his legs.'

'I expect so,' she said, quietly.

'And all these years have gone by, no one's come after you. If he'd gone to the police they'd have caught you by now – with CCTV, DNA and all that stuff.'

Chrissy was still in a trance. 'The world wasn't like that then. I told you: we didn't even have digital cameras.'

'Exactly. So then why are you worried? You're not scared, are you; that he might try and find you? Is that it?'

'What? Oh no, he'd never be able to.'

'Well, then.'

Eloise understood how hard it must be to let go of this terrible memory. She also understood that by removing Juliet from her life it would give her a better chance of doing that. But, clearly, it hadn't worked. Nearly twenty years on, it really was time to forget. And time to welcome her old friend back into her life again.

'So why did you burn the letters before I'd seen them? It would've been much easier if you'd just let me read them first. And Juliet wanted me to.'

She drifted for so long that Eloise feared she had lost her. Still in a trance, eventually she spoke. 'I keep telling you, Eloise, you need to hear this from me.'

'But we can still see her again though, right?'

Chrissy shook her head.

'What, like never?'

'No.'

'But why?'

***

143

Manchester was shrouded in a light drizzle and there was more of a chill to the air than the past few days. Eloise had left college early. At this rate she would never get the grades for uni, be it near to home or as far away as possible, but if she allowed Juliet to slip from their lives forever that would surely be worse. Without Juliet, nothing would change. And no matter where she was or what she did, Eloise could never escape the guilt of leaving Chrissy on her own. She adored her mother, but she would always be trapped.

Chrissy was due to finish at the Language Institute any time soon. She had tried to call her, going through to voicemail, so now she was scurrying through the Arndale, dodging kids in school uniforms, mothers with pushchairs, hoping to catch her on her way home. Eloise tried calling her again. If Chrissy saw it was Eloise, then she would answer. Anyone else, she would just ignore it.

'Eloise. Are you okay, what's wrong? You left a message. I haven't listened to it yet. I was teaching; I'm so sorry. What's wrong?'

'I'm fine, Mum. I'm fine. I just wondered if you fancied meeting me at Maria's? There's something I need to tell you.'

**

Maria's was bustling, but luckily the table in the far corner was unoccupied. It was a little on the cramped side, and wedged in by the computer shelf, but it would give them a degree of privacy.

Maria brought their drinks over.

'What an asset your daughter is to this place,' she said, as if Eloise wasn't there. 'I'll be sorry to lose her when she goes. No doubt you will be too.' Then Maria flatly refused to take any money for the drinks.

'I'm not sure why she's so friendly,' Chrissy whispered when she had gone.

'Because she likes you?'

'She hardly knows me.' Chrissy began stirring her coffee. 'She's very good to you though, sending you home with leftovers, giving you a pay rise. I suppose she does do a good trade in here,' she added, looking around.

Eloise had forgotten about the invention of the pay rise and squirmed at the reminder. It was difficult to keep up with all the lying she had been doing recently. But from now on, things would be different.

'I've thought about what you said, Mum.'

Chrissy put down her mug and leaned in, keeping her voice low. 'I've said a lot recently, Eloise.'

'Yes, I know that. But shouldn't we just focus on the future now?'

She seemed to relax and sat back in her chair.

'Weren't you pleased to see Juliet just a tiny bit?'

Chrissy looked around before she answered. 'I told you, we never fell out. But we can't discuss this in here.'

'Well, it's just that Juliet said we could go and stay at her place in London. And in Rome. Wouldn't that be great?'

Chrissy's eyes narrowed. 'What did you say to her last night exactly?' She jabbed her finger into the table. 'You made us sound like a charity case, didn't you?'

'No!'

'Offering us free holidays. You played the sympathy card, Eloise, and don't you deny it.'

'I didn't. She just asked about college and uni, that's all.' Eloise felt flattened by the sudden lashing, and it seemed unfair. 'I didn't play the sympathy card, Mum. You do that all by yourself.'

She hadn't meant it to come out like that. The more she tried to repair the damage the worse it became. People were looking over. Chrissy snatched her jacket off the back of her chair, took out four pound coins and slammed them onto the table. 'Tell her we don't need her charity either.'

'Mum!'

Eloise sensed it was best to let her go. She watched her step out onto the street and pull up the hood of her jacket. The drizzle didn't seem to be clearing, people scurried about like ghosts, and Chrissy soon blurred into them. Eloise thought she saw Juliet's face in the misty outlines, but it was only because she wanted her to be there. In the same way that she wanted her dad to be there and he never was.

She sat for a while, playing with her phone, texting Anya in the hope that she might be able to meet her at the café, but Anya replied to say that she couldn't. Now, even Anya was angry with her. Since Juliet had come on the scene, Eloise had more or less abandoned planning their trip. Countless missed calls and several irate text messages later, she had confessed she might be going to Italy instead of Inter-Railing. She knew it was ridiculous; why was she pinning all her hopes on Juliet, a woman she barely knew? But if Eloise could convince her mother to go, perhaps she could finally break out of the protective shell that Chrissy had built around them both for so long.

And if Chrissy refused to go, well, maybe she'd just go alone.

Scooping up the coins that Chrissy had left on the table, Eloise went to drop them in the 'Tip Jar' over by the till. Maria waved but she couldn't bring herself to wave back. She stepped out into the drizzle and became a ghost herself.

***

Chrissy had no idea about London. She hadn't told her yet that she was going.

College was over, the holidays had begun, Anya wasn't really speaking to her, and all that was on offer were some extra shifts at the café. Even if Chrissy still flatly refused to come, Eloise felt she had nothing to lose by just going on her own.

Juliet was ecstatic when she told her. 'That's fantastic!' she squealed almost as insanely as Eloise on the other end of the phone. 'Just tell Laura and she'll arrange everything for you. And I'll see you on Sunday then. Right, I must fly. Literally. My plane's ready for boarding. I actually get to see Luca on this one.'

'Luca?'

'Yes, exactly. Who's Luca? He's my husband.'

'Oh, right, yes.'

'*Ciao, bella.* See you soon'

'*Ciao*, Juliet. And thanks. Really, really, really thanks.'

Eloise assumed that was the end of the call.

'Eloise.'

'Yes?'

'Don't keep thanking me.'

'Sorry.'

'You do know now what your mother did for me, don't you?'

She didn't tell her about the burnt letters, but Eloise knew that if it had not been for Chrissy, Juliet would almost certainly have been raped.

'Yes.'

'So you see there's absolutely no need to thank me.'

'No, okay.'

Eloise was still in bed, flicking through the pages of a travel magazine, wondering when and how to break the news to her mother. She hadn't even packed yet, in case it aroused suspicion. The car was coming at two to take her to the station. She had tried to persuade Juliet that she could get herself there, not wishing to be alone in the car with Anton. He made her skin crawl, and the fact he had been in their flat, rooting through her things, bothered her immensely. But Juliet wouldn't hear of it.

Eloise pulled the suitcase out from under her bed. It had been on top of Chrissy's wardrobe for years gathering a thick layer of dust. The last time they had used it was for Bruges after her dad died.

Seven years' worth of dust.

Predictably, her mother was furious when she told her. But Eloise tried to style it out.

'Juliet thinks the world of you, Mum, and she's not even going to be there till Sunday in any case. We can hang out. You and me. In London.' She flung open the suitcase and Chrissy looked on, too stunned and angry to respond. 'So I'm going to take this for you, okay?' Eloise blustered on. 'Because we're bound to be going somewhere posh, knowing Juliet. What's that place where all the celebs go? The Ivy. I bet we go there.' She carefully placed her mother's dress, still in its purple tissue paper, on top of the things she had already packed.

Chrissy picked up the nearest thing she could find, Eloise's washbag, and fired it into the case. It landed like a bomb on top of the dress, exposing the black lacy neckline.

'Bloody hell, Mum! I wish you'd just get a life.'

Chrissy turned her back. She was clearly upset.

'Oh god, I'm sorry, Mum. I just want you to come, that's all.'

Eloise wanted to hug her but she couldn't bring herself to. Her mother's voice sounded broken when she did eventually speak.

'The only reason I'm still here, Eloise, is because of you. You and your dad were, are, my whole life.'

'So start living it then. Where are you going? Mum! The car's coming for us at two,' she shouted after her.

Five minutes later Eloise heard the door slam, and when she looked out she saw her mother going off for a run.

CHAPTER 18

London: 2007

Eloise did a final check of each room to make sure that she hadn't forgotten anything. There was still no sign of Chrissy.

'I know what I'm doing,' she said, picking up her dad's photo, putting it straight back down again. She remembered very clearly the day he had given them that picture. It was one of those memories forever glued onto her heart. He had known for a while that he was ill – months, two to three at most, remaining – and this was his way of breaking the news. 'I don't want you choosing a really shit photo of me when I'm gone,' he had said. Typical of her dad to make a joke out of something as morbid as this. 'The frame's a bit crap, mind,' he added. 'Probably fall apart in a few years. Maybe buy a new one when you're a bit older.' She remembered the way he had looked at her, too, as if he was trying to tell her something.

Swinging her bag over her shoulder she sent the frame crashing to the floor. The glass shattered. She picked it up, careful not to let any fall out. It was just at the moment when a car horn sounded outside. Her suitcase was holding the door open so she could keep an eye out for Anton. She didn't want him coming up here when she was in the flat on her own.

There was no time to do much with the frame now, apart from getting rid of the broken glass. Tipping it out onto the table the photograph came loose from the cardboard mount and she spotted a note tucked in between, folded in half. She could smell her dad's aftershave, cinamonny, peppery. Her hands trembled as she removed the piece of paper, running her fingers over the letters of her name. She felt a familiar pain in her chest, a reminder of how raw her grief had once been. But seeing the words '*My darling Cheese Eloise*' made her laugh out loud.

A tap on her shoulder gave her a start, disrupting the memory, and she quickly pushed the note into her jeans pocket. Praying it would be Chrissy when she turned around, she screamed when it wasn't.

'Anton! God, you gave me a heart attack.'

She watched the fingers of his leather gloves wrap round the handles of her suitcase, and made sure he was first out of the door so she could keep him within her sights.

***

Beyond the sprawl of Manchester, the view began to open up into green countryside. Pylons planted in fields were like giant wire scarecrows. The power lines that linked them bounced up and down in one continuous motion, broken only by roads or a row of houses.

The note was resting on her lap; she hadn't read it yet, having felt much too uncomfortable during the car journey to do so. It may have been her imagination but she was sure Anton was looking at her; his eyes darting away every time she glanced up. Maybe Eloise could ask Juliet if she could send another driver in future. Then she cringed. *Another driver? Who do I think I am?*

Now that she was safely on the train, she was finally able to dismiss Anton from her thoughts, and she began to read the note. Seeing her dad's handwriting instantly made her cry.

150

*'Take care of your mother, Eloise. See that she's never
alone. And no matter what you hear, always try
and forgive her. Don't be afraid to ask questions.
But remember, we both love you.
Always at your side,
Dad X'*

She stared at the words.

He must have known what had happened.

Suddenly Eloise's stomach lurched with guilt. She really had
no idea how her mother felt; how that dreadful summer had
affected her. And now she had abandoned her for the one person
who brought back all those painful memories.

She had to get off this train.

'I might have known she'd have put us in First Class. I've been
up and down, up and down, looking for you.'

'Mum!'

Eloise quickly folded the note back up and stuffed it into her
pocket, blinking away her tears, hoping they wouldn't be noticed.
She stood up to help Chrissy put her bag onto the luggage rack.

'Did Anton come to get you?'

'Who's Anton? I've no idea what the driver's name was. I called
a taxi.'

'I'm so glad you've come,' said Eloise, squeezing her arm as
they sat down together.

'Well, let's get one thing clear,' Chrissy replied in a stern voice.
'I came for you. Not because I want to see Juliet.'

'I'm still glad.'

Eloise watched her mother's eyes as they tried to keep up with
the blurring landscape. It made her consider all the things she
now knew about her.

*'Take care of your mother, Eloise … And no matter what you
hear, always try and forgive her.'*

Of course she could forgive her. What she had found out changed nothing.

'I think what you did for Juliet was very brave, Mum,' she suddenly felt the need to say.

Chrissy continued to stare out of the window. She just wished that her mother could forget what had happened, not live this life of torment and fear when, clearly, that man had it coming to him. Even if he was blinded in one eye as a result of what Chrissy did to him, as far as Eloise was concerned he had got off lightly. Was her mother *really* afraid that he might one day come for her? Had she lied about that? If so, maybe Juliet could help convince her they were safe. And maybe Eloise also needed to hear that, for her own peace of mind.

***

Juliet's London flat turned out to be a penthouse on the South Bank, directly opposite the dome of St Paul's. Chrissy had barely slipped off her shoes when Eloise began pulling her across the floor of the open-plan living area and out onto the terrace. She had already seen pictures but wanted the real thing to be a complete surprise for her mother.

The river traffic slid along at a leisurely pace. Faint cries from hungry gulls could be heard in the distance, criss-crossing over boats and bridges, swooping low every now and then. Standing on the curved balcony looking out across the city, the view stretched from Canary Wharf down to Westminster. To think that Juliet woke up to this skyline every morning, eating her *croissants* and jam, flicking through the fashion pages of her glossy magazine, Eloise did wonder whether the decadence of it all would simply annoy her mother.

'She always did go over the top with everything,' Chrissy remarked, shaking her head in every direction. Even at the sky, as if Juliet owned that as well.

'I dunno,' said Eloise, taking a ridiculous number of photos, 'I reckon I could get used to this.'

'Well, don't,' said Chrissy, playfully shaking her. 'And don't you dare point that thing at me.'

'As if, Mum. Come on, let me show you the rest.'

Juliet had left an itinerary out for them in Chrissy's room. Eloise skimmed over it before offering it to her, but Chrissy was distracted by a picture hanging on the wall above the bed. A colour photograph, enlarged, in a Shabby-chic frame. The only picture on display in the whole apartment, come to think of it.

'Oh wow!' said Eloise, going over. She soon realized why Chrissy was so mesmerized by it. 'Is that you and Juliet?'

Eloise had only ever seen her mother in a single photograph and that was on her wedding day. Here she was, a smiling happy teenager on the beach, one arm casually slung around her best friend's neck, with a bottle of beer in each hand. They were wearing bikinis and probably dancing. A fire flickered behind them, bathing their youthful bodies in an orangey-red glow.

'So ... is that in France then? Is that the beach you were telling me about?'

Chrissy attempted to unhook the picture off the wall, gently at first, but when it wouldn't release she tugged so hard that the hook came out with it, leaving a gaping hole where it had been. It was because she was so eager to show it to her, Eloise thought; hence she was shocked when the picture was slammed face down in a drawer and shut away, as though it had no right to be on display in the first place.

Then Chrissy left the room without a word.

A few moments later she wheeled in the suitcase, making deep grooves in the carpet, and Eloise rushed at her with the itinerary, relieved that they were not heading straight back up to Manchester.

'Would you like to see what Juliet has planned for us, Mum?'

Chrissy hoisted the suitcase onto the bed. 'We can just do our own thing, Eloise.'

They took a late afternoon stroll along the river. Having dispensed with the itinerary they were free to wander as they pleased, and seeing Juliet on Sunday was now their only deadline. Eloise didn't mind one way or the other; she was glad to be away from home – something they rarely got to do together.

Chrissy seemed much more at ease down in the hustle and bustle of the South Bank, instead of watching it from above. They weaved through a constant flow of people out strolling by the river, enjoying the sunshine. They would stop every now and then to watch a street performer. A break-dancer was spinning on his head to the sound of a beat machine. Further along, a girl was attempting to rollerblade through the crowd, causing chaos.

That was when she spotted Anton.

He couldn't possibly have driven down here faster than the train. Could he? Maybe he was even on the train?

Eloise pulled on Chrissy's arm, dragging her into Gabriel's Wharf.

She relaxed again when she saw him walk straight past. But why was he still following them, and was Juliet aware of it?

After browsing the shops, and then a drink in one of the quieter courtyard cafés, Eloise felt a safe amount of time had elapsed and they continued on. They found a spot on a wall overlooking the river. The waves from a City Cruiser slapped into those from another boat, making the water look choppy. On the far side, a vessel was dragging containers along on a large platform: a reminder that the Thames did far more than just ferry tourists up and down it. A police boat suddenly whizzed by. Chrissy kept a close eye until it disappeared towards Greenwich.

Eloise hitched herself up onto the wall, sitting with her back to the river, still keeping a lookout for Anton. But they seemed to have lost him. Chrissy jumped up next to her, playfully grabbing her shoulder, saying, 'Whooh, don't fall in, Eloise!'

Eloise only wished she could be like this more often. She watched her mother bounce her feet off the wall observing the people going by, as casual and free as the teenage girl in the photo. Without a care.

'I wouldn't fancy your chances running through that lot, would you, Mum?' said Eloise, giving her a nudge.

It became obvious that she wasn't without a care, even in that brief moment, because she said: 'I always used to look for your dad's face in a crowd.'

'Yeah, me too,' Eloise replied, realizing how much she still missed him.

'Once, I was so convinced it was him I followed a complete stranger all the way to Stockport. Can you believe it?' She laughed at the memory, pulling Eloise into her. 'Grief's a strange thing. But we get through it, don't we?' Eloise nodded. 'And we were very lucky to have him in our lives,' she added, patting her leg.

It made her think of her dad's note.

'Did Dad know about any of that stuff, Mum?'

'What stuff?'

'What happened in France?'

'Does it matter? He's not here now.'

'It matters to me,' she said, kicking her heels back against the wall.

Chrissy detected her frustration. 'The answer is, yes. He did know, Eloise.'

'Everything?'

'Yes. And I know it matters to you. Of course it matters.'

For a brief second, Eloise wondered whether she should show the note to her mother, but thought better of it. Even a coded reference to what she had done would most likely send her into a panic. And the note into the river. She gave her mother a side-ways look and changed the subject. 'Juliet's jealous of you, you know. No, seriously, she is.'

'What?' Chrissy laughed. 'How did you figure that one out?'

'Because you got your happy ending and she didn't. She told me.'

'When?'

'When we went out together. The night you didn't come.'

'Hm. That one. Well what did she mean by "happy ending"?'

Eloise shrugged. 'I guess because Luca's her fourth husband, and they don't seem to spend much time together. Plus, she hasn't got any kids.'

Chrissy pulled her knees up to her chest, hugging them into herself.

'I mean, she knows Dad died and everything. And those things that happened in France, she knows they still bother you. I mean, like, a lot.'

'So what else did she say?'

'Not much really. Just that you have a lovely daughter.'

'And?'

'How talented and gorgeous she is.'

Chrissy pretended to tip her over the edge.

'Mum!'

'Don't worry, I won't let you drown,' she said, pulling her back up.

Chrissy slid off the wall and offered Eloise a hand. She jumped down, getting her hair ruffled when she landed, and she gave her mother a reluctant smile, squinting into the sun.

As they were heading back, Eloise began to feel the nerves kicking in at the thought of seeing Juliet again on Sunday. The last time was in Manchester when Chrissy had told her to leave and never come back. That seemed like an age ago now, yet only two weeks had gone by.

'How are you feeling about seeing Juliet again, Mum?'

It was a mistake to ask. It changed her mood and she quickened her pace, saying: 'I told you, I'm here because of you, Eloise. Not Juliet.'

CHAPTER 19

London: 2007

The photo weighed heavily on her mind. Still lying face down in that drawer, and Juliet was bound to notice it missing, not least because of the damage it had done to her bedroom wall. Eloise had considered hanging it up again but wasn't sure if it would only make things worse between them, and she desperately wanted to steer them away from yet another disaster.

There was another hour to go before Juliet was due back. Chrissy seemed surprisingly relaxed, sitting out on the terrace with a book, and Eloise badly needed to occupy herself, unable to concentrate, pacing about the apartment.

Juliet's office was a room she had been in before, even sat at her desk, spun round in the chair in front of the white Mac next to the white telephone. Everything in there was white. The only splash of colour came from the fashion magazines and glossy art books in the bookcase, which was also white.

Without realizing she was even doing it, Eloise began to pull open the drawers in the desk. There was nothing of interest in any of them, although the top one was locked. Telling herself she shouldn't really be snooping anyway she stood up to leave, running her fingers along the array of fashion mags on her way out. Then she noticed a key poking out of one of them.

She tried it in the drawer, smiling to herself when it unlocked.

Not quite what she had expected to find: the Polaroid that her mother had told her about, of Juliet with her dad holding the yellow bear, was resting on top of an old-fashioned photo album.

Eloise gave the office door a quick shove with her foot. She didn't want Chrissy to suddenly appear. Then she began flicking through the pages.

It was all there: the picture of them on Clifton Suspension Bridge, the party in Cowper Road, one of her mum in the purple raincoat, another of her dancing in the green dress, several more of the two of them together in Bristol. Two best friends. Her mother, happy, in another life. There were no others of France, she noticed.

She was just about to lock the drawer again when she saw something else tucked towards the back. It was a purple notebook. She pulled it out and began to leaf through its graph-paper pages. There were columns of numbers, things recorded in blocks. It seemed boring at first, maybe a book of accounts, and then she looked more closely at one of the entries.

'*Daughter: 8.40 left flat. Daughter: 9.10 arrived Maria's Café, Oxford Rd.*'

Then another:

'*Daughter: Eloise. Manchester Sixth Form College.*'

And so it went on. It mentioned her mother too: the times she had left the flat, but no record of where she went.

A shiver ran down her spine. How long had Juliet been watching them?

'Hello?' called a familiar voice.

Juliet was back early.

Eloise put the notebook and album back in the drawer, remembering to put the loose photo on top. Her fingers fumbled trying to lock it again. She also had to remember to replace the key between the pages of the magazine where she had found it.

'Hi! Sorry, didn't hear you come in. I've just been looking at all your fashion books,' she tried to say nonchalantly when she ran into Juliet in the hallway.

To her relief, Juliet threw her arms wide and gave Eloise the biggest hug.

She noticed her mother hovering. When she caught her eye she immediately let go of Juliet, launching into an account of what they had been up to and what a fabulous time they were having in London.

It seemed to work.

'Eloise! At least let Juliet get her bags in,' said Chrissy.

Helping to carry her things through, Eloise tried to give Juliet a coded message that she needed to speak to her urgently. She wanted to warn her about the photograph missing from the wall. But Chrissy was hot on their trail, following them into the bedroom. When she realized that Juliet had given up her own room for her, Chrissy seemed embarrassed.

Juliet held up her hands, saying: 'As long as you're having the best time—' coming to an abrupt stop.

She had spotted it.

'... that's all that matters to me.'

'You need to destroy that photograph, Juliet. You should have done it years ago.'

Chrissy stormed out, and Juliet sank down onto the bed.

'How is she?' she said, quietly.

'She's been okay actually.' Eloise pointed to the drawer. 'On the whole.'

Juliet nodded.

They found Chrissy staring out of the window, chewing

on her fingernails. She turned round when she heard them come in.

'So,' said Juliet, rubbing her hands together, 'are we all set for a spin on The 'Eye? We're booked on for five thirty. If that's okay with you guys? I've just a few calls to make, emails to send, boring stuff, and then I'm done.'

'Fine,' said Chrissy. 'Would you like me to make a cup of tea, Ju?' She paused, as if she had startled herself. 'Juliet,' she said, disappearing quickly.

Juliet pulled Eloise out onto the balcony. 'So what about Italy? Are we on?'

It hadn't even occurred to her since they had been in London, and even if it had she probably wouldn't have mentioned it.

Chrissy reappeared. Did Juliet still take one sugar in her tea? Weak, without milk? Unless she preferred Earl Grey. If so, she would leave the teabag in for five minutes.

It was Juliet's turn to look perturbed. 'Yes,' she replied, her voice shaky. 'One sugar, no milk. Oh god, sorry. Really sorry.' She fished out a tissue from her jacket and dabbed at her eyes, being careful not to smudge her make-up.

Eloise hadn't noticed until now but that was where the cat brooch was pinned today, on her pocket.

Juliet blew her nose. 'You remembered, Chrissy. After all this time. Sorry, I'm being stupid.'

Chrissy lingered, weighing up her response. 'No, it's not stupid. Some things you can't forget.'

***

The capsule doors swished together, sealing them in. Juliet had organized a private flight on the London Eye, so they had it all to themselves. Chrissy immediately began fanning herself with the souvenir brochure. 'How long does it take?' she asked.

'About thirty minutes,' Juliet replied. 'Are you okay?'

Chrissy nodded. 'Sitting down I'll be fine. I didn't realize it would be quite so hot.'

The view changed by small degrees, although it hardly felt like they were rotating at all. Juliet pointed out Wimbledon, Hampton Court, Battersea Power Station, other places on the outskirts. 'That's Windsor Castle over there. You can just about see it. And we live …' Her finger traced a rough outline on the glass as she tried to locate it. They were almost at the top now. '… Well, there's the wall you were sitting on this afternoon. So if we just—'

'Hang on a minute,' said Chrissy. 'How do you know that?'

'What?'

'That we were sitting on a wall.'

'Anton saw us, Mum. He's Juliet's driver. I didn't think he'd seen us, but obviously he had.' She threw Juliet a look, but Juliet merely smiled and carried on.

'Okay. So, round about there … where my finger is … see it? … that's where we live.' Turning to Chrissy, she added: 'You know, I always think of Bristol when I see the Millennium Footbridge. Maybe that's why I chose it.'

'So you could dance on it in your knickers?' Eloise sniggered. She got a frown from her mother, and Juliet seemed embarrassed. Then she remembered the seriousness of the incident and regretted her comment.

'You really have told her everything,' said Juliet.

'Just about.' Chrissy gave Juliet a sarcastic smile.

'Well, anyway, they had to close the bloody thing soon after it opened because it swayed too much and people were terrified.'

'I'm not surprised,' said Chrissy. She was concentrating on her breathing, still fanning herself.

'I never knew you had a thing with heights,' said Juliet. 'You used to be fine in Bristol.'

'I think it's the confined space,' Eloise explained.

'I'm fine,' said Chrissy. 'It's warm in here, that's all.'

'Hope you'll be all right in Rome,' said Juliet.

Her remark was left suspended mid-air. But as their capsule was nearing the end of its rotation, Eloise couldn't hold back any longer.

'We can go to Rome, Mum. Can't we?'

'Does this thing go any faster?' Chrissy replied. 'I swear it's getting hotter.' The early evening sunshine was flooding in, a spotlight bearing down on them. 'And no. We are not going to Italy, Eloise.'

'Oh, but Mum—'

'I *said*, no.'

'Why "no"?' She watched her mother wiping sweat from her forehead. 'Is it because you think you might get caught? Is that the reason?'

Juliet remained silent, even though Eloise was looking to her for backup.

'We went to Bruges, Mum, and that was okay. I know it was only a long weekend, but even so.'

Not a word. Not from either of them.

'And why would they even be looking for you? You didn't do anything wrong. It's not like anyone died.'

Juliet sat down next to Chrissy. 'She doesn't know?'

'Of course I know,' said Eloise. 'She whacked him in the face with his belt and made a gash down his stomach. He deserved it.'

And then it struck Eloise: the way they were both staring at her.

'Oh god, he didn't … Did he?'

They were moments away from the capsule doors opening.

'I killed him, Eloise.'

'It was an accident,' said Juliet.

Suddenly the heat was getting to Eloise, too. She felt trapped inside this strange glass bubble. 'But you can't have, Mum. That's ridiculous.'

She sat on the other side of her mother, who was nodding her head in small movements.

'Well, are you sure? Maybe he wasn't dead.'

'He was,' she said in a whisper.

The doors opened; they had to get off.

Juliet helped Chrissy onto the platform; she was beginning to hyperventilate. Eloise stood apart, trying to make sense of what she had just heard. She couldn't bear to be near them and felt sick.

Running – fast – made her feel even more sick, so she slowed to a walking pace. A sign for the Underground gave her something to aim for. Green Park, Bond Street, St John's Wood, Swiss Cottage; she hadn't even heard of some of these places, but she didn't care. She needed to get away, be among strangers.

Then she felt someone grab her arm.

'Where are you going?'

Anton's steely glare emerged above the crush of people. The tube doors were about to close. She leapt from the train and ran across to the opposite platform where another train's doors snapped shut behind her. He couldn't possibly have been that quick.

The carriage was half-empty and Eloise returned to a state of calm.

For hours she rode aimlessly up and down the Tube network, until she was eventually apprehended by the Transport Police for jumping the barrier and not having a ticket.

It was Juliet who came to her rescue.

'I'll pay the fine,' she said, elbowing her way through into the tiny office waving her credit card around. 'How much is it? This poor girl has been through a lot, you know. Her father died and her mother's very ill.'

In the end Juliet only had to pay for a travel card.

Afterwards they went into some luminous pink-fronted café near the tube station, where Eloise burst into tears.

'It's okay, Eloise. You have a good cry.'

Juliet put a chocolate milkshake down in front of her, which

Eloise hadn't ordered but she didn't complain. Then she sat beside her, pulling the chair in closer.

'Why is Anton still following me?' asked Eloise. 'I don't like it.'

Juliet stroked her hair. 'Oh, well I just asked him to keep an eye on you both in London. It's such a big city, I assumed you wouldn't know it very well. If at all. I'll tell him to back off, shall I?'

Eloise nodded and Juliet held her shoulders, which made her feel safe again.

'Where's Mum?' she asked, sweeping the tears off her face.

'Oh, she's fine, don't worry. She's back at my place.'

Eloise slurped the chocolate milkshake up through the straw, feeling a childish glow from Juliet's kindness wrapped round her like a comfort blanket.

'I'm sorry, Juliet.'

'*You* don't have to be sorry. I thought she'd told you everything. She told you about me prancing about on the Suspension Bridge in my underwear, but not that she – well anyway.'

'She's not actually ill though, is she?'

'No, no. I only said that so they'd let you off. She is traumatized though. It never really goes away.'

'I can't believe she killed him,' Eloise whispered.

Juliet stared into her espresso. 'For me. She did it for me.' She sighed. 'You must really hate me for that, Eloise.'

'I don't hate you. What happened, it wasn't your fault. But, oh god …' She felt the tears returning. 'Please don't give up on her, Juliet. She needs a friend. Someone who knows what happened.'

'Of course not,' she replied, giving her hand a reassuring squeeze. 'I'm not going anywhere. And besides,' she added, drumming her fingernails against her cup, 'I have an idea.'

'What?'

'Just persuade her to come to Italy.'

***

164

It wasn't until they were back in Manchester that Chrissy would say any more. Eloise couldn't even remember the train journey home. It seemed they had entered a tunnel and never come out again. Not a word was said. But the moment they stepped through the door she fired questions at her mother: 'You should have told me. Why didn't you? Why keep that bit from me?'

Chrissy threw down her bags and walked to the other side of the room, crushing her head with her hands. 'How do you tell your own daughter such a thing, Eloise? I killed someone.'

Eloise took her arm and made her sit down. She realized this wasn't about her any more.

'So when did you know, Mum?'

She didn't want to hear it, any more than Chrissy wanted to share it, but they had reached the point of no return.

CHAPTER 20

France: summer, 1989

'Go get cleaned up, Ju. Go take a shower.'

Chrissy even thought she was beginning to pull round, being more like Juliet again, but as her eyes drifted back to her attacker laid out on the bed, blood slowly creeping across the pale lemon sheets, Juliet began to shake. So Chrissy could only assume that she had gone into shock.

'It's okay, I'll sort this,' she said. 'Give me your clothes.'

'What? What clothes?'

'The ones you have on. We need to take everything with us, Ju. Can't leave a trace.'

'No, we can't leave a trace,' she said, dreamily.

Chrissy helped her. Her clothes were ripped, her shorts already half off.

'What are we going to do, Chrissy? What's to do?'

She noticed there were deep scratch marks down Juliet's stomach and legs. On her arms the bruises were already showing where he had pinned her to the bed. It sickened her to see Juliet's perfect skin disfigured in this way, his brutal imprint etched into it. It was bad enough seeing the scars she had inflicted on herself, although those were fading now. Juliet hadn't noticed any of this for herself yet, or she appeared not to have. At least, over time, *his* marks would heal and disappear. Maybe Juliet was drugged sufficiently so that the mental scars would heal completely too.

'Shower first, Ju. You'll feel better then.'

Juliet nodded, did as she was told and went into the bathroom.

Chrissy became aware of someone in the mirror watching her: a young girl she barely recognized. She couldn't bear to look, but couldn't escape her. The mirror was smeary. Whoever cleaned it had done a terrible job; she would never have left it in that state. How could it only be a few days since they were cleaning hotel rooms in La Grande Motte?

It seemed a lifetime ago.

And there was no escaping *him* either. He was there when she looked in the mirror, and he was there when she turned back to the bed. There was still a trace of a smirk on his face.

His pulse had been present when she had checked it before. Faint, but still a pulse. It wasn't there now. She was certain of that. Hard to believe the amount of blood that had oozed out of him. Harder still to think that she had done this. The muscles in her legs locked as she removed her towel, standing over his body. She threw it over his face so she no longer had to look at it.

That face.

The sound of running water began to soothe her mind. It was Juliet taking a shower; she was not alone.

There was work to be done.

First she hunted in the wardrobe for a motel laundry bag, stuffing Juliet's clothes into it as well as her own. The towels. She must remember the towels. Everything. Leave no trace; even the towel under his foot. It made her retch when she raised his leg to pull it out. She needed to wipe down surfaces too: door handles, drawers, TV remote, window frame, mirror. Everything. As soon as Juliet was done in the bathroom she would clean in there as well.

Next she checked under the bed for any stray piece of jewellery that might give them away: an earring yanked off in the struggle. She needed to get dressed, pulling out some warm clothes from her rucksack. Long cotton trousers, long-sleeved T-shirt. Her grey sweatshirt was in dire need of a wash, the sort her mother would give it when she got home.

Home.

It was a long way off yet.

She winced as she put on her trainers, her feet still sore from running barefoot across the car park to escape the trucker.

The trucker.

Might they even have been better off sticking with him? At least they knew what they were dealing with from the moment they stepped into his cab.

'That feels better,' said Juliet, making Chrissy's heart leap. She was wrapped in a white towel, clutching it to her neck.

'Well, that's good,' Chrissy replied, chirpily. 'You get yourself dressed and I'll do some tidying up in the bathroom. You okay, Ju?'

Juliet's face twisted as she pointed to the body. 'Don't leave me,' she wailed.

'Hey. Don't worry; we won't hear another peep from him.' She rubbed Juliet's bare shoulders, trying to transfer some of the strength she had found in herself into her friend. She was used to Juliet being the one in charge.

'Is he …?'

'As a dodo.'

Juliet whimpered.

'Ju, you have to be strong. He would have raped you.'

'I know. I know,' she whispered, the terrifying reality finally hitting home.

'He deserves all he's got. And no one knows we're here, remember. Don't lose your head now, Ju. We can get out of this. We can be home this time tomorrow.'

'Home,' said Juliet, drifting.

'Yes. Home. You get dressed. Pretend he's not even here.'

Juliet laughed crazily.

Even now, Chrissy realized, Juliet must still be under the influence of whatever drug he had slipped into her. She had to put her hand over her mouth. 'We have to be quiet, Ju' she whispered.

'As a mouse,' Juliet giggled, pushing her hand away and noticing there was blood on Chrissy's finger. 'Oh, you poor kitten.'

'What?'

'You cut yourself.'

'It's nothing.'

It must have been from the glass. She ran it under the cold tap, mesmerized by the red swirls dancing round the plughole. When the water ran clear she plunged her face into it, numbing her cheeks, hoping, when she resurfaced, this would all be some weird dream. She stayed down too long and had to silence her coughing with the towel pressed to her mouth.

Come on, Chrissy. Stay strong.

After a few deep breaths she seemed to get her focus back and set to work properly in the bathroom, wiping down surfaces, gathering up the things they had used. Some of it could be flushed down the toilet. The rest had to go with them. Quite what they would do with it on the outside, she wasn't sure; she just knew it was better than leaving it behind to incriminate them.

Incriminate her.

She tipped the last trickle of wine down the sink, rinsing away the drops. It had crossed her mind to leave the bottle behind as some kind of evidence – get rid of their fingerprints, smudge on some fresh ones of his. But that would mean having to touch him again. And who was to say it wasn't the other way around? That they had slipped something into *his* wine and drugged *him*? She tried to dismiss that thought as she rinsed out the plastic tumbler, wrapping it in the towel along with the broken glass. She had found another piece under the bed.

The radio alarm on the bedside table said 2 a.m.

'Okay, Ju. Either we stay here and get a couple of hours' sleep—'

'What? With *that*? You can, I'm not.'

'If we go now we have to sleep outdoors. I mean, we can do that but we'd have to stay out of sight. No tent. It's pretty cold.'

'What the hell are you doing?' asked Juliet, seeing her rifling through his jacket, which he had put over the back of the chair.

'Taking some money.'

'What for?'

'Because we're getting the train into Paris so we can get the first coach back to the UK. We're out of here, Ju. No more lifts.'

'But it's stealing,' she said, and Chrissy let out a sputter. Juliet laughed. 'I guess, after what we've just done, stealing a few hundred francs from a dead man's wallet doesn't really matter, does it?'

'After what *I've* just done you mean, Ju.'

There was a clear outline now where the blood from his stomach had seeped into the sheets. The towel over his face had turned red, sinking in like a shroud.

'Maybe we should call the police,' said Juliet.

Chrissy was quick to explain the reasons why they couldn't. She had been through each and every scenario. Two young English girls in a businessman's motel room: what were they doing there if it wasn't for sex? No one was going to believe them. He hadn't forced them to come here and there was no evidence they had been attacked, apart from a few scratches and bruises on Juliet, which, in the scheme of things, didn't amount to a whole lot. It would not look good, no matter how they tried to explain it. Telling the truth on this occasion would only lead to more trouble. If they wanted to see their families again, go back to university with their lives intact, then calling the police was definitely not the right way to go about it.

'It's a mess,' said Juliet. 'And it's my fault.'

'No, Ju. It's not your fault. He's to blame, not you. Anyway, I'm the one who did it.'

170

Juliet shook her head. She darted to the window and began to climb through it. Chrissy grabbed her firmly by the wrist. A cold blast of night air hit Juliet in the face and she came back in.

'How long do you think we've got before anyone will notice something's up?' she asked. Her voice was on edge. But Chrissy seemed to have all the answers, even the impossible ones.

'If we put the 'Do Not Disturb' sign on the door then I guess till morning.'

'What if someone comes in? I mean by mistake. They'll all have master keys. Like we did. What then?'

Juliet was shivering. Chrissy held onto her shoulders, told her it was going to be okay. She promised she would get them out of this. 'Look, if we sleep for two or three hours,' she said, 'we can leave about five, five thirty.'

Juliet flopped onto the bed: the single bed that had looked so inviting when they first arrived. *Their* bed. Chrissy had said so. Many times. She watched Chrissy hook the 'Do Not Disturb' sign over the door handle, impressed that she remembered to cover her fingers with her sweatshirt. They couldn't afford any slip-ups, after all.

Chrissy sat on the chair over by the desk. No way was she going to risk going to sleep; envious, though, when Juliet went out like a baby. For the first hour her mind wandered. The numbers on the radio alarm glowed a luminous red, and each minute that passed felt like a hammer blow to the head, triggering flashes of the day's events. If only Dan was here. She had never wanted him so badly. Watching the gentle rise and fall of Juliet's body made her want to sleep. Her eyelids felt heavy. She mustn't let go. As a distraction she tried to think of the two of them back in Bristol, what it would be like. How it was before.

Before.

Wondering what it would be like after. There would be an after. She would make sure of that. But how quickly had they gone from being two happy-go-lucky students on a working summer holiday to fugitives on the run.

Did she really just kill someone?

The phone by the side of the bed suddenly sprang into life and Chrissy jolted into the air. Juliet woke up, disorientated, a look of panic spreading across her face. Chrissy put her finger to her lips but Juliet still leapt off the bed, flinging her rucksack onto her back – was making for the window. Despite the cool air blowing in, Chrissy had left it open for a quick getaway.

Juliet glanced back in horror when she realized Chrissy was picking up the phone.

It trembled as she held it to her ear. She had to use both hands, her sweatshirt making the handset slippery.

Holding her nerve, she didn't say a word.

After a few seconds, a voice said: '*Ah pardon, je m'excuse. C'est une autre chambre qu'il me faut.*'

The line went dead. Chrissy hung up and allowed herself to breathe again. A simple mistake. The girl on Reception had dialled their room by accident.

She had taken a risk, and had absolutely no idea what she would have done if the caller had required an answer. But this was surely a good thing now. It gave them more time. The motel had living proof that the occupant was in the room, just trying to sleep. Alive. Breathing. And in the morning, when the house-keeping team showed up, the 'Do Not Disturb' sign would be respected until check out. Which, Chrissy had already found out, was midday. By that time, they could be well on their way to Calais. And from there, a ferry across the Channel to the UK.

It was time to go.

Chrissy made one last attempt to wipe down surfaces and objects, checking under the beds. They left in the same fashion as they had entered: in darkness and in secrecy, without a soul knowing they were ever there at all.

The cold air soon found its way through their thin, summer

clothes and Chrissy felt her teeth clattering together. Once they got going they would be moving quickly, she told herself, and lugging around these rucksacks would soon warm them up.

His car was easy to pick out in the car park, even in the night mist, and Juliet whimpered when she saw it.

'Shush, Ju,' said Chrissy in a stern whisper. Her stomach lurched as they walked past it. There really was no time. As far as she could remember they had removed everything from inside. The key was in his jacket pocket in any case. But she still ran back to the car to make a half-hearted attempt to wipe down the windows and doors. It *had* to be enough. It just had to.

They were on their way at last.

Home.

But which way was home?

Chrissy hoped her instincts were right. She had studied the road atlas again and again. In a cruel twist of fate, it was of little use in their hour of need as they would have to stay clear of the roads. If they were seen by a motorist, even in the dimmest of headlights, they could easily be identified as two figures carrying rucksacks in the vicinity of the motel.

'Which way do we go?' asked Juliet.

'How the fuck should I know?'

Juliet's lip quivered.

'I'm sorry, Ju. I think it's this way.' She steered them towards the trees.

Darkness was their friend – at least for now – and they had to gain some ground whilst they still could. Soon the glowing fingers of dawn would begin to point them out.

CHAPTER 21

France: summer, 1989

They had been walking for two hours, stumbling in the pitch-black over tree roots and stones. Complaining that she couldn't see, Juliet turned on her torch but Chrissy snatched it from her with a ferocity that alarmed both of them. Since then, Chrissy had been making a huge effort to keep her cool and remain calm for both their sakes. She knew that if she lost Juliet, metaphorically or otherwise, they would be finished.

It was a struggle. Chrissy's senses were so on edge they exaggerated the nightmare that was playing repeatedly in her head. Trees were giant monsters. Small animals rooting through the undergrowth were about to attack. The sounds of an owl hooting, a branch snapping, bore into her skull. And every touch, no matter how light – the brush of a spider's web, the leaves on a tree as she felt her way – was like a knife across her skin. She could even smell and taste her own fear.

Every so often they would stop to rest; their rucksacks weighed down by all the extra things Chrissy had stuffed into them. Wine bottle, glass, towels, rubbish.

Evidence.

And already the first signs of morning were poking through the trees. They would soon lose their cover. Streets were coming into view up ahead, and although the houses were still shuttered, the odd car was shooting past. Juliet hadn't yet noticed they had been walking in a circle for the last few kilometres. She was getting weary, probably still suffering from the side effects of the drug.

'If we got rid of these it'd help,' said Juliet, throwing down her rucksack.

'And how do we do that? Magic them into thin air?'

'Don't be cross, Chrissy.'

'Don't be cross? I've just killed someone and you tell me not to be cross. If we don't get out of this I'm going to prison for the rest of my life, Ju. Don't you understand that?'

'You're cross with *me* though. I can tell.'

Juliet wiped her forehead with her sleeve, took off her sweatshirt and tied it round her waist. The scratches and bruises from the assault were clearly visible now on her arms, although she didn't seem to notice.

'We need to get going,' said Chrissy.

Then it struck her that Juliet had perhaps hit on something. 'Wait. You're right, Ju.'

'Am I?'

Chrissy pulled out a small bag from her rucksack. Really all they needed were passports, coach tickets, the money she had stolen, and a change of clothes just in case. Chrissy tossed a book in at the last minute, only because it might make her look a bit less suspicious.

'What the hell do we do with these?' said Juliet, giving her rucksack a kick after following Chrissy's lead.

'Oh something'll turn up, I expect. Always does, Ju. Remember?' Chrissy narrowed her eyes, but Juliet didn't pick up on the sarcasm.

They set off again, creeping like shadows, making sure they couldn't be seen from the road if a car should happen to pass.

Something told Chrissy she had better get used to this. At some point these streets were going to burst into life, and then what? They needed some more good fortune and it had to come soon.

Juliet was heading towards a bus shelter, and Chrissy followed her. It was the advertisement on the side, a picture of a *château*, which seemed to be drawing her in. Juliet pressed her hands against it and read, longingly, '*City of Tours, gateway to the Loire*'.

'What's that?' said Chrissy, wrenching Juliet back into the trees.

'What's what?'

'That beeping and chugging noise.'

From their temporary hideout they could see a large refuse lorry turning into what looked like a housing estate.

It had to be worth a try. There was nothing else.

Chrissy thought she could hear Juliet's heart pounding over the sound of her own; holding onto her until it was safe to go. She was just about to give the signal when three cars sped past, puncturing the dewy stillness of yet another glorious morning. They waited until it was clear, scurrying down the grassy incline to the road and houses on the other side.

Dodging in and out of driveways reminded Chrissy of playing hide-and-seek as a child, giggling and squealing. In the grown-up version they hardly dared breathe; moving only when she said it was safe. Quite how they were going to get to the refuse lorry and toss their bags into it without being seen was another matter. In their favour, though, it was still early and hardly anyone was about.

'How long do we wait?' whispered Juliet. 'Let's just go for it.'

'No!'

Her next suggestion was to go back and dump their bags in the woods, but it would only be a matter of time if they did that. At least this way, despite the enormous risk, the evidence would be totally destroyed.

'Hey, they're off somewhere,' whispered Chrissy, observing the men walking away from the refuse truck.

'Looks like they're going on a fag break,' said Juliet. 'Lucky bastards.'

'Right, this is it, Ju.' Chrissy was attempting to summon up more of that extraordinary strength she had discovered in herself the previous night. 'We only get one crack at this. If we don't manage it, we just leave the bags and run. Okay?'

Juliet nodded.

They made for the truck, intimidated by its bulk once they were standing beneath it. When Chrissy saw how impossible this was she almost made them abort, then saw the determination in Juliet's eyes. On a silent count of three they launched the first bag into the air. It went high, one full rotation, handles and straps flying. Then it dropped, sinking into the gaping mouth they couldn't even see. There was no time to celebrate or to recover because it had to be done all over again.

Juliet grabbed Chrissy's arm, shaking her excitedly when the second bag landed safely. As they turned the corner, walking casually away from it they could hear the lorry on the move again, whirring and beeping, grinding their rucksacks to a pulp.

It was another hour before they found a bridge over the river. Signs for 'Centre Ville' and 'Gare SNCF' meant small shoots of life were beginning to appear on the streets of Tours. The pavements were being washed down, and shutters on some of the bars and *boulangeries* were being removed. It seemed like a lovely place to spend some time, Chrissy thought, despite the screaming inside her head and the gnawing feeling in her gut. She wondered how much longer she could hold it together. Juliet needed constant encouragement and it was draining all her energy having to fill her with false hope that everything was going to be okay.

Because how could it be?

The station was already bustling, a steady stream of commuters trickling in. They tried to blend in as best they could. It saddened Chrissy to think that this country, which she had always adored and dreamt of living in one day, now felt foreign and hostile. Her only desire was to leave it behind as quickly as possible and never return.

The ticket vendor on the other side of the screen was brusque and agitated. For once the lack of eye contact was reassuring, but everyone else was staring at them: the people in the queue, and especially the *gendarme* loitering nearby. Chrissy let out a girlish giggle when they were forced to walk past him, which baffled Juliet to begin with. Then: 'Ooh, you're good at this game,' she said, once she realized why she had done it.

Their train wasn't for another hour. It seemed sensible not to kick about on the concourse looking nervous and guilty. Chrissy found them a busy café, a place where they wouldn't stand out, and they sat down to a spread of fresh orange juice, *croissants* with slices of ham and cheese, and two large *cafés au lait*. Juliet took pleasure in the fact that it wasn't every day they got to spend a dead man's money, and she had a good appetite, too. Chrissy, on the other hand, who had stayed up all night and not eaten for nearly eighteen hours, had to force it down. She was constantly checking her watch. Time seemed to be expanding like elastic, ready to snap back in their faces. She thought about calling Dan but, as yet, had no good reason to speak to him and didn't want to make him think anything was wrong. They were not even clear of Tours yet. A long way to go.

Ditching their bags was definitely the right thing to do, Chrissy thought, when the train glided in. It was almost full, commuters into Paris mostly, some day trippers but certainly no backpackers. The crush and press of bodies was strangely comforting as they fought to get to their reserved seats. The denser the crowd the more inconspicuous they would be. Chrissy had hoped for seats on their own, limiting their interaction with anyone who could identify them later, but the elderly French couple sitting opposite were keen to engage in conversation and she soon realized they were not prepared for this.

She was furious with herself at such a glaring oversight, having had many hours to come up with a strategy. Luckily she managed to launch into a story before Juliet could open her mouth. They were exchange students: she was an American over from New York, and Juliet her exchange partner. Juliet was often being mistaken for a French girl, with her air of insouciance, so it was plausible that she lived with her parents in Paris. Which was where they were making for now, Chrissy permitted Juliet to explain. To avoid having to elaborate they closed their eyes and pretended to sleep, but were both so exhausted that they had to be woken up as they pulled into Paris Gare d'Austerlitz two and a half hours later.

The old man gently touched her arm to try and stir her, and Chrissy let out a scream. Juliet's laughter – however inappropriate in light of what they had just been through – was the best reaction possible. But, in any case, everyone else was gathering up their belongings in the race to get off and no one seemed to react.

After a brief farewell to the elderly couple, they sped off into the crowds and Juliet pushed her arm through Chrissy's. 'You were awesome,' she said in an American accent.

They spilled out into the busy concourse, where armed men in uniforms appeared to be everywhere. Chrissy felt Juliet's grip tighten as she, too, sensed the danger. Any moment now they would be stopped. Sweat was pooling on Chrissy's forehead. The clothes she had put on for warmth through the night were clinging to her now, and she thought she might faint. Juliet spotted the sign for 'Taxis' and began pulling in that direction.

Chrissy felt it revive her.

Disappointment showed on Juliet's face when Chrissy steered them towards the Métro instead, telling her they needed to immerse themselves in the crowds. On the escalator, going down into the tunnel, she noticed Juliet staring at posters for Chanel and Dior as they filed past on the wall. She wondered what was going through her head. How much of the incident could she remember?

Poor Juliet.

The coach station in Paris was even more insane than Gare d'Austerlitz. On any other day they would have found this intolerable. Today, it was perfect. Pushing through hordes of people with bags, pushchairs, suitcases, dogs, children playing games being scolded by their mothers, they made for the screens up ahead with Arrivals and Departures information. Over the sea of heads, they could just make out that the next coach to London Victoria was in two hours.

The waiting room stank of perspiration and babies. Strangely, on this occasion, these things were comforting. A TV was mounted high up on the wall in one corner and an advert was running for some life-changing yoghurt drink, a stunning French woman maintaining this was the secret of her beauty. The morning news reported on a water shortage in Provence, a strike in a factory somewhere in Grenoble.

And then:

'A man was found dead in his hotel room this morning near Tours. It's thought he may have hired the services of a prostitute and the murder was motivated by money. The man's family has been informed. He leaves behind his wife and three-year-old son.'

They got up and walked away as if they had just been listening to the day's weather forecast. Chrissy could hear the thud of her own heartbeat echoing inside her head.

CHAPTER 22

Manchester: 2007

Eloise always knew there was something different about her mother, even when her dad was alive. The hushed conversations as a child; finding her in tears curled up in a quiet corner; the desperate hugs when Eloise didn't want them; the way she jumped at the slightest thing. Not to mention the transience of her friends, keeping them at arm's length until they dropped off the radar altogether. If Eloise had known the reason behind these things, she would never have pushed her mother. She thought back to the words Chrissy had said only a fortnight ago: 'It never goes away.'

From now on it would always be there for Eloise as well. For the rest of *her* life. They were all in it together now. It still didn't make any sense: a story about someone else, someone else's mother. With such an ending, how could it possibly be her own? What do you do with that sort of information? She had acted in the heat of the moment trying to protect her best friend. Would Eloise have done the same if Anya was in that situation? Probably, yes.

Chrissy had not meant to kill him.

When they said their goodbyes at Euston, Juliet had whispered in her ear not to forget about Italy, reaffirming that she still had plans to help her mother. Eloise couldn't even consider that yet. What if she ever did get caught? Could she be put on trial even though it was back in 1989? Would she be found guilty? After all, there was nothing to back up their story. It was perfectly clear to Eloise now why she had severed all ties. Not only was Juliet a terrible reminder of her crime, but the enforced estrangement would also make them much more difficult to trace if the police or Interpol ever came looking. She understood her fear of the internet too. Her mother was right; these days everyone lived around the virtual corner, whether in Timbuktu or Tunbridge Wells. Chrissy didn't want to leave any trace of herself in the digital world because it would make her too easy to find.

***

The first thing Eloise did was to gather up any alcohol they still had in the flat, hide it under her bed. If her mother took refuge in a bottle again she might lose her in the darkness forever. And Eloise would be left on her own once more to deal with it.

She had tried everything.

'Just imagine, Mum, if you'd done nothing, if you hadn't acted like you did, where would that leave Juliet? He might even have killed her. Or you could both be dead. And then I wouldn't be here either, would I?' But it only made Chrissy sob inconsolably. 'Please, Mum. I still love you, and you're still my mum. Why can't you understand that if *I'm* fine with it, and Juliet is too—'

'Juliet didn't kill him.'

'*And* you said my dad was fine with it … It's time you let this go, Mum. Please.'

Of course she wasn't fine with it. Not with any of it. How could she be? Her own mother had left a son without a dad and a wife without a husband. But she would make herself, because this was the only way to move forward.

How long was this going to go on? It already felt like forever.

Eloise went into her room, pressing her face into the pillow so she could scream into it. She had to stop her mother falling apart again.

There was one thing she still hadn't tried. She hadn't thought of it until now. Tortuous, if her mother agreed to it, but Eloise was prepared to do anything.

'How about we go for a run, Mum? I mean both of us, like, together.'

If only she had come up with that sooner. Ten minutes later, Chrissy appeared in her running kit.

***

She followed her mother up Oxford Road then down onto the towpath. Eloise always got a sense of Old Manchester along the canal: the mooring rings for the coal barges, and all the huge brick warehouses and mills, now apartment blocks and bars.

It was impossible to keep up with her, and she was making no allowances for the fact that her daughter hated running and was not in the least bit fit. Eloise's chest was tight and a cold pain in her throat made it difficult to speak.

'Mum,' Eloise shouted, hoping she might slow down a little. 'Mum ... I've been thinking.'

'What about?' Chrissy turned her head slightly but still cracked on at a sprinter's pace.

'Well ... Bournemouth Uni ... is—' Eloise gulped some air into her lungs, 'is a long way from here ... so how about I do what you suggested ... and apply to ... Manchester Uni ... and live at home with you?'

Rather than pausing to consider this information, Chrissy speeded up.

'Mum!'

As Eloise emerged onto Canal Street she felt her legs buckle coming up the ramp. The sight of people sitting out at the street bars did give her a short burst of energy, but she could see that Chrissy had already crossed Sackville Street, heading for Minshull Street Bridge.

'Mum!' she called just before she lost her again.

Then, spotting her rejoining the towpath: 'Mu-um!'

A bike swooshed up from behind, coming at speed down the slope. Eloise heard it, unsure which way to go. Losing her balance, she screamed and toppled into the water. The canal closed in over her head. It smelt of sludge and diesel fumes. A raft of twigs and litter floated in front of her face. She was treading water, desperately trying to find a way to get back up onto the towpath without having to breathe or swallow.

Then she felt herself slowing, her body getting cold, shutting down.

The next thing she knew her mother had hold of one arm, the cyclist the other, and she was being pulled out of the canal.

***

Chrissy came into her room and woke her with a hot mug of tea. She put it down on the bedside table. 'How are you feeling?' she asked, stroking her hair.

'Yeah, better thanks.' Her stomach felt tender and her body still ached, but no real harm done.

'You need to get right for Italy,' said Chrissy.

'Oh. Look, Mum, it's okay. We don't have to go.'

'Yes, we do. You are the most important thing to me in the whole world, Eloise. I can never let you forget that.'

'Manchester's fine. Honestly, Mum.'

'No, it's not. You can't stay here forever. We're going to Italy.'

She should have been ecstatic, but memories of London were still circling in her mind. She feared, even if they did go, it might not all be pizza and ice cream. How could a single trip to Italy put her mother back together again? Juliet was fooling herself; she didn't understand. How could she?

Still, it was as good a place as any to try.

PART TWO

CHAPTER 23

Rome: 2007

'I wish you wouldn't wear that thing all the time,' Chrissy said irritably as they waited in the Executive Lounge. 'Don't you ever take it off?' She was referring to the cat brooch. Juliet had it pinned into her beehive today, the way she wore it on her website.

Chrissy had been fractious ever since they set off for the airport. Juliet had offered her some pills to take before their flight, but she flatly refused. Her behaviour had even prompted a security person to approach at one point.

'Oh, she's a terrible flyer,' Juliet intervened, taking her by the arm. 'Always the same. She'll be fine once we're on the plane.'

'I *was* fine,' said Chrissy, keeping her voice low. 'I was perfectly fine until you showed up again.'

'Mum, you said you wouldn't do this.'

'It's just nerves, Eloise.'

'How do you know that, Juliet? What can you possibly know about my bloody nerves?'

'And you weren't perfectly fine at all, Mum.'

'Please,' said Juliet, 'don't hate me, Chrissy.'

'I don't hate you!' she hissed, in a low whisper.

Juliet waved her arm at someone. 'I think we need a sherry. Calm your nerves.'

'Sweet, medium or dry, Madam?' the lounge attendant asked.

'Sweet what?' said Chrissy, looking directly at Juliet. 'Sorrow? Charity?'

'Get her a double cream sherry, please,' said Juliet. 'I'll have a *fino*. Eloise?' Eloise shook her head. The attendant nodded and went away. 'Look, if you don't want to do this just yet, we can go back. I'll call Anton and—'

'She does want to. Don't you, Mum? We haven't had a proper holiday in years.'

Chrissy managed a smile for Eloise.

'You'll be fine, Mum. I promise.'

Their drinks appeared on a tray and set down on white paper mats. 'Enjoy,' said the attendant.

'Hardly,' muttered Chrissy.

Eloise ran her fingers along the top of her dad's note. She always carried it with her now, safely tucked into the top of her purse. An announcement sounded over the tannoy. A further hour and a half's delay sent Chrissy back to the perfume counter. They could see her contemplating the array of bottles on the shelves. She took one down and sprayed it in front of her face, stepping into the mist.

'I'm really worried about her,' said Eloise. 'She's acting weird.'

'It'll be okay,' Juliet reassured her. 'Sometimes things have to get worse before they can get better.'

'They can't get any worse, Juliet!'

The attendant came to clear their table. Shortly after, Chrissy returned. She smelt like she had sprayed the entire perfume counter over herself.

***

London dissolved beneath them until there was nothing left but sky. Eloise kept checking on Chrissy. Her eyes were closed and she seemed relaxed. Juliet gave her the thumbs up across the aisle. But when the pilot cut in with: 'The "Fasten Seatbelts" sign will remain on due to some light turbulence', Chrissy was suddenly roused.

'That's all we need,' she said. 'More turbulence.' She became agitated again, turning to Juliet, saying: 'And I'd feel a whole lot better if you removed that thing for a start. Every time I look at you I see—'

'What?'

'That stupid brooch.'

'I like it,' said Juliet, putting it to her lips. 'I kiss it every day for good luck and it keeps me safe. I even have the card you sent me. For my twentieth birthday. Remember?'

'Why should I remember?'

Chrissy was aware that Eloise was secretly grinning at her; she didn't react, however. But really, what did stealing the brooch matter in comparison to what else she had done? Chrissy pulled a magazine from her bag, reclining back into her seat, and Eloise rested her head on her shoulder, grateful for the peace. Moments later they heard Juliet ordering champagne. Chrissy gave Eloise a nudge, rolling her eyes, happy to share a private snigger this time.

Eloise could remember starting a text to Anya, missing her all of a sudden, but was told to turn off her phone. She must have fallen asleep after that because when she next looked out of the window they were high above the clouds, the sun streaming through. She was just about to tell Chrissy it was like being in heaven when she heard: 'If you didn't want me to wear it, why did you send it to me for my birthday?'

Their bickering could be heard even over the engine noise.

'I just thought you'd keep it somewhere,' said Chrissy.

Eloise couldn't believe this was still going on. 'Look, does it matter?' she said, leaning forwards, putting herself between them. 'It's only a brooch.'

'It's all I had left of you, Chrissy.' Juliet was almost tearful. 'Why is that so terrible?'

'Oh, because she bloody stole it, that's why!'

Chrissy looked furious with her. Juliet, wide-eyed.

Once Juliet had recovered from the shock she began to laugh, and Eloise joined in.

Chrissy unbuckled her seatbelt and made for the toilet, leaving them to their amusement.

***

Eloise was relieved to see that it wasn't Anton who met them at Fiumicino airport. Juliet had assured her he would not be coming on this trip, but he did have a tendency to appear from nowhere. She knew straight away this man was Luca. He had a loose-fitting white shirt over black linen trousers. His hair was slightly longer in real life than it was on the website, to his shoulders, dark, with a few grey flecks, and he had a sort of rock star presence: handsome but with a lived-in face. He gave Juliet a kiss on both cheeks, which struck Eloise as rather formal: more business partner than husband.

'Luca, this is Chrissy,' she said, smiling at them both. 'You've met, of course, many, many years ago in a tiny little Fiat. She's my best friend from university. And her beautiful daughter, Eloise.'

He shook their hands. '*Benvenute a Roma*. Welcome to Rome,' he said, guiding them towards a newish-looking car with a dented rear-end. Nearly every car they passed seemed to have some battle scar, in fact. Eloise rummaged for her shades and tied her hair up so it wouldn't stick to her neck.

'Rome burns,' said Luca, opening the door for her. 'Forty-two degrees.'

He started up the engine, letting it run a few moments,

examining them in his rearview mirror. But if he or Chrissy remembered each other, neither of them was letting on.

They didn't get very far before car horns rose to a crescendo and arms were gesticulating out of windows at Vespas weaving in and out of impossible gaps in the queue of traffic. Luca slapped the steering wheel, uttering some profanity in Italian. Juliet turned to them, shaking her head as if to apologize for him.

'As you can see, all roads lead to Rome,' he said, blasting his horn and shouting at a young man not wearing a helmet.

'You will get used to Luca's ranting,' said Juliet.

'They are insane,' he said. 'You know, you are fifty times more likely to die on the roads in Rome than you are in London. And these guys, they die like flies.'

'How have you been, my darling? Did you miss me?' Juliet lit up a cigarette as she spoke, putting the windows down.

'No, but the cat has,' Luca replied, wafting the smoke away.

'You have been feeding her, haven't you?'

'Just pizza and beer.'

They were moving again, slowly, and gradually the traffic began to flow. 'Of course, this journey is much quicker by helicopter,' said Luca. 'I'm afraid it's at the garage.'

'Really? You have a helicopter?' said Eloise.

'No, but it would still be quicker to go and buy one.'

Juliet slapped him on the thigh. She turned to them once more and put her finger to her temple. 'Crazy Italian. As I say, you'll get used to him.'

They could only see his eyes in the mirror, framed by thick eyebrows which made them appear cartoonish. His gaze was still fixed on Chrissy whenever possible, and Eloise could detect it was starting to bother her. She tried to distract her mother by pointing to the river.

'*Fiume Tevere*,' said Luca. 'The Tiber.'

Eloise recognized its green tinge from images she had seen on the internet, but wasn't sure if this was a good or a bad thing to mention. 'I've read that some of the bridges are really lovely,' she said instead.

Luca nodded. 'You will see.'

When they hit more stationary traffic he twisted round to Chrissy. 'I've heard many things about you.'

Chrissy wiped the sweat from her lip, glancing at Eloise. 'What things?'

'Don't worry, I left out the really terrible bits,' said Juliet, reaching for her hand, which Chrissy ignored.

'Ah yes, only very good things,' said Luca. 'So good, in fact, I thought I was coming to meet Santa Chrissy today.'

'Huh, I'm no saint,' she said, sounding relieved.

They made good progress after that and everyone fell quiet, including Luca. Soon, however, they got to the Grande Raccordo Anulare where a lane-swapping frenzy began. Luca made circles in the air with his finger. 'Great Ring Road,' he said, unfazed by the near collisions happening all around them as cars swerved in all directions.

'Not for the faint-hearted,' said Juliet. 'As you can see.'

'My wife never drives in Rome.'

'Your wife wants to live, that's why,' she said, extinguishing her cigarette in the ashtray, blowing smoke into his face.

Eloise spotted a sign, making some attempt to read it out loud: 'Roma Centro, Aurelia, and Città del Vaticano.'

Chrissy gave her a pat on the leg. 'Not bad.'

Luca grinned at her through the mirror. 'We live very near to everything,' he said. 'Ten minutes, you are at the top of Spanish Steps. The same for Via Veneto, Piazza Barberini, Fontana di Trevi. Piazza Navona. You know these places?'

'I've heard of them,' Eloise replied.

'You might also have heard of our neighbour, Mister Pope? He has a very nice house, an entire city, in fact.'

Eloise was slowly warming to Luca. She sensed that maybe Chrissy was too; she even smiled at his last remark. The sudden drumming of tyres pounding over cobblestones, however, served as a reminder not to drop their guard. They had turned into a maze of one-way streets, jostling for space along with Vespas and pedestrians; vehicles parked haphazardly on either side. A *panificio* with its display of mouth-watering breads and pastries caught Eloise's eye. A few of the bars had locals standing outside, chatting and smoking. She tried to take in every last detail: the graffiti on doorways of ancient buildings, and all of the street names – Via Francesco Crispi, Via degli Artisti – finding it impossible to keep up.

'So …' said Luca, switching off the engine when they eventually pulled up outside an old Roman Palazzo. It had a light grey façade and elegantly symmetrical windows. 'We are just around the corner from Via Veneto and Villa Borghese. Remember these places and you won't get lost. And we are on the sixth floor. Many, many steps.' He pointed to the top of the building and laughed to himself as he got out of the car.

They followed him into a marble-lined lobby where two white lions stood either side of a sweeping staircase and several big palm plants were dotted about in huge Roman pots. Luca helped with their luggage, but apologized for having to go back to the office. Eloise was relieved to see that there was a lift, just to the right of the staircase, which Luca summoned for them before he left.

'Hope this is okay,' said Juliet, wedging her foot against the door for Chrissy to get in. It was the tiniest of spaces, made worse by the fact that their suitcases had to be rammed in as well.

When the lift door slid across they were pressed in even tighter.

'So, do you remember Luca?' Juliet asked.

It was like an oven inside, and it was obvious that Chrissy was finding it hard going. 'Vaguely,' she replied, letting her head flop back against the back wall. 'But we only met him for two minutes. Look, are you sure he doesn't know any of that stuff in France, Juliet?'

195

'Of course not,' she replied, her voice too loud for such a confined space. 'Not a thing. Swear on my life. Swear on your daughter's life even.'

'Yours will do, thank you,' Chrissy snarled. 'Leave my daughter out of this.'

Eloise gave her mother a nudge and the lift jerked to a standstill.

The apartment was smaller than the London one, giving it a homelier feel. Juliet rushed to pull open the sliding door which led out onto a balcony, where they stood beneath a large blue awning to admire the view over tiled rooftops and the maze of narrow streets below. It was surprisingly peaceful up here. A white, fluffy cat casually appeared from behind one of the large terracotta pots, brushing against their legs then stretching its way indoors to greet Juliet affectionately.

'How cute,' said Chrissy. 'What's he called?'

'She,' Juliet corrected her.

'How old is she?' said Eloise, shooting Juliet a concerned look, suddenly remembering the cat's name was Chrissy. She wasn't sure how the real Chrissy would react to that. Not well, most likely.

'Oh,' said Juliet, calmly acknowledging. 'Well, let me see. She's quite an old lady now, aren't you? Yes, you are. I brought her over from England so I've had her for sixteen years.' Juliet shook a box of cat treats and it followed her into the kitchen.

A commotion down at street level drew Eloise and Chrissy back to the balcony. A car was trying to reverse park into an impossible space and a chorus of Italian voices rang out in a real-life opera.

'Right, I'll show you to your room if you like,' said Juliet, reappearing behind them. 'It's quite *bijou*, but there are two beds.'

She took them up to the next level via some internal stairs. Their room was a good size by their standards. A flimsy white curtain billowed across the tiled floor, revealing French doors that were slightly open and pale blue shutters either side. Eloise was just about to claim the bed nearest the window when Juliet hurried them on again.

They hadn't even noticed the spiral staircase in the corner. They followed the tip-tapping of her feet up wrought iron steps, emerging out onto a roof terrace. Eloise had never seen anything quite so sublime in her life: a panoramic view of Rome with all its domes, spires and rooftop gardens was on display just for them it seemed. In the foreground they could see St Peter's Basilica, the Pantheon, and the church at the top of the Spanish Steps. Juliet gestured further out to the Gianicolo Hill and Villa Borghese. Eloise couldn't wait to be out among it all.

***

The Spanish Steps were teeming with tourists posing for photos. Juliet said they should start by wandering the streets nearby. It was seven o'clock in the evening and everyone was out strolling. They stopped to admire the steps which linked Piazza di Spagna with the upper Piazza Trinità dei Monti. Eloise took picture after picture, being careful not to capture her mother in any. She had always refused to be in any photos, and now Eloise knew why.

They walked along the lively Via della Croce, lined with restaurants and bars. Many of the shops were still open but Juliet assured them they would have plenty of time for shopping. She led them into a tangle of alleyways, large white canopies marking out rows of pink and red tablecloths where waiters stood in readiness by their Cucina Romana chalkboards boasting pizza, pasta, veal and seafood, trying to tempt them in. But they peeled off down a narrow side street to leave the tourist trail behind, taking a seat at an outdoor *trattoria,* not a chalkboard in sight and whose clientele seemed more local.

The heat was still clinging to them.

'Luca was right when he said Rome burns,' Chrissy remarked, fanning herself with the menu.

Juliet poured out some water from a carafe already on the table. 'You see why I prefer to be in London?'

'Is that just for the summer?' asked Eloise.

'Maybe.' Juliet looked away, sipping her water.

The sudden dip in tempo made Eloise wish she was back out in the livelier streets again. But then Chrissy felt comfortable enough to break the silence as the banter on the next table became more animated. She leaned in to Juliet, and said: 'I'm intrigued about Luca.'

'Oh?' Juliet put down her glass, as if preparing for more questions. 'Why's that?'

'Well we hitch a lift with him and his – I don't know how many of his mates were in that car – six, seven? Judging by the number of hands, I'd say about sixty … then, a few days later, he gets married to his childhood sweetheart, and then the next thing I know he's married to you.'

'You're missing out a whole decade there at least,' Juliet replied, laughing. 'And anyway, he was far too young to get married the first time.'

'My mum was only nineteen when she married my dad,' said Eloise.

Juliet reached over and placed her hands on both of theirs. 'Wish I'd been there for that. And in your parents' case it was the perfect match. In Luca's, I'm afraid, fairly disastrous from the start. Why do you think he was getting it on with me on the way to his own wedding?'

'Because you wouldn't leave him alone,' said Chrissy, pulling her hand away.

Eloise wished she would go easy on Juliet.

Juliet smiled, as if to say it didn't matter. 'Your mother's still angry with me for kissing people I shouldn't,' she said.

'You mean Luca,' said Eloise.

Chrissy was looking pointedly at Juliet, who seemed embarrassed, and as the waiter hurried by with a tray of drinks she

198

clicked her fingers and said: '*Fabio, vorremmo ordinare.*' A few moments later he returned, greeting Juliet with a kiss on both cheeks, and they began chatting in Italian. The hand gestures suggested they were discussing food for their table, and this was followed by some introductions from Juliet.

'Chrissy,' said the waiter, shaking her hand. 'Delighted to meet you. Welcome to Italy.'

'And this is her daughter, Eloise.'

He kissed Eloise's hand, holding it to his mouth for what seemed like a long time. She blushed, in the end pulling it away as she could feel the heat coming off her mother.

'*Bellissima ragazza*,' he said with a flourishing bow.

When he had gone, Eloise tried to disguise the fact that he had written his phone number on her wrist. Chrissy was incensed when she saw it.

'He's just trying it on,' said Juliet. 'It's the Italian way.'

'That's no excuse,' said Chrissy, rattling the ice cubes around her glass. 'If you say "it's the Italian way", it will always be "the Italian way".'

'I don't think he meant anything by it.'

'It's not as though I'm going to phone him, Mum.' Eloise dipped her napkin into her water and rubbed the number off her skin. 'Gone. Completely. Look.'

'I can't believe that you, of all people, Juliet, could ever say he didn't mean anything by it.'

Chrissy glowered at her, and Juliet searched for a diversion.

'More water?' Eloise offered, shaking the empty carafe at her. She took it and handed it to a different waiter, whilst Eloise gave her mother a pleading look.

'So when did you get back in touch with Luca?' she asked, taking her daughter's request on board. 'How soon was it after we got back from France?'

'Oh, it was years after. I got through three husbands first.' Juliet wafted the air, as if batting them all away.

'So what happened to them? Divorced, beheaded, died?'

'Mum!'

Chrissy broke into a grin.

'Something like that,' said Juliet. 'Divorced mainly. That seems to be my forte in life. You know, that's what I've really missed about your mum, Eloise. Her razor-sharp tongue. So quick she could kill a man with one lash.'

Juliet froze.

'Shit. I wish I hadn't said that.'

For the first time, Eloise could see a film of sweat forming on Juliet's top lip. She watched her dab it with her napkin.

'I'm so sorry, Chrissy. I didn't think.'

Chrissy took a sip of water. 'Makes a change.' Her glass made a thud as it hit the tablecloth.

Juliet fanned herself with the napkin. She tapped Eloise's foot under the table, but it was Chrissy who threw her the lifeline.

'You were telling us about Luca,' she said.

'Yes. Yes, I was. Well …' She cleared her throat. 'I ran into him at a fashion show in Milan. Amazingly, we recognized one another. He was married to his second wife at the time. Getting divorced. They had two children.'

'And that coincided with you wanting a change of husband, did it?'

Juliet twisted her fork round her fingers, but when she saw Chrissy grinning at her again she shook her head. 'You know me so well, Chrissy.' She put the fork back on the table. 'He wasn't the love of my life but—'

'Then why did you marry him?'

'Oh. Well, I suppose it was our love of fashion, first and foremost. And then—' She paused. 'I think I can say this. The sex was great too.'

Chrissy frowned.

'Oh, she's old enough to know the ways of the world. Aren't you?' said Juliet.

Eloise didn't answer, avoiding eye contact with either of them.

Suddenly Juliet's expression became serious. 'There's another reason though. I mean, besides all that. Do you really want to know?'

'Yes, of course I want to know,' said Chrissy, screwing her eyes at Juliet.

'This might sound a bit odd.' She was twisting her fork again. 'It's just that … well, he reminded me a little bit of you. You met him briefly and—'

'Oh, come on!' said Chrissy. When she saw people looking over she lowered her voice. 'You cannot be serious that's why you married him.'

'I think it did play a part, yes. You left such a massive hole in my life, Chrissy.'

Juliet slid her hand across the table, but Chrissy moved hers out of the way. 'We should get the bill,' she said, reaching down for her bag.

By which time Juliet had handed over her card and paid, much to Chrissy's annoyance.

CHAPTER 24

Rome: 2007

'We can just saunter back if you like,' said Juliet. 'It's been a pretty tiring day for—'

'No!' Eloise protested.

The night-time spell had been cast over Rome and it was just as irresistible. The streets were bathed in a magical glow of yellows, purples and blues. There was an energy and excitement pulsating through them.

'Aren't we near the Trevi?' Eloise asked.

'Yes, actually. And a good time to go in the evening when it's a little quieter.'

Juliet looked to Chrissy for approval.

'Sure. Why not?'

She took them via the Spanish Steps again to experience the Fontana della Barcaccia by night. The sinking boat was flooded in yellow, sad but beautiful, and around the Steps the cameras flashed like exploding stars. People turned to silhouettes as they walked in front of illuminated shop windows, and the obelisk in Piazza Mignanelli was also lit up. They turned left up Via del Nazareno and across Via del Tritone to Via Della Stamperia.

The sound of rushing water could be heard long before they reached the Trevi, and jubilant voices were swept along on its spray. Nothing could prepare Eloise for what was to come, however. Ancient streetlamps created shadows over the pale marble sculptures, bringing them to life. The night sky was reflected in the thick pool of water as the white cascades continued their downward shimmer. Eloise pointed her camera in every direction, pausing for Juliet to explain that at the centre of the fountain was Neptune – or was it Ocean – she could never remember which – standing in his shell-shaped chariot pulled by two sea horses, Tritons on either side. 'One horse is wild. Do you see that? So the Triton on the left is struggling to control it. But the other horse is calm. It's a metaphor for the sea's changing moods.'

Chrissy was rubbing her shoulders as she listened, though it wasn't cold. 'It's like they're frozen in time,' she said.

Her words made all the other sounds fade away, except for the tumbling water.

***

'You must be exhausted,' said Juliet. 'At least I'm used to this heat. Make yourselves at home. I'll put some coffee on.'

Chrissy turned her face to the ceiling fan, busily whirring away above them. The cat jumped onto her lap and she began stroking it, surprised when it curled up, purring loudly. 'Well you certainly know how to make yourself at home … whatever your name is. Do you even have a name? Hm?'

Juliet loaded some cups noisily onto a tray, deliberately avoiding eye contact with Eloise. There was something determined in her expression that worried Eloise.

The cat yawned, extending its paw.

'She's called Chrissy,' Juliet announced.

The cat purred louder, as if to verify. Chrissy was still waiting for the sensible answer. When it didn't come she let out a nervous laugh. 'Okay, you're kidding me, right? Eloise?'

Eloise gave her a neutral shrug.

It was a moment or two before they realized Juliet was crying.

'You probably thought it was easy for me, Chrissy. Well I can assure you it wasn't.' She brushed away the tears and picked up the tray. 'It was like you'd died.'

'Poor Juliet,' said Chrissy, heading towards her with the cat in her arms.

Juliet put the tray down in readiness.

'Here,' said Chrissy, thrusting the white bundle into her chest. She carried on walking and left the room.

The cat let out a meow, objecting to the rough handling, and then to Juliet's wet face being pressed into its fur. When Juliet saw Eloise coming towards her she looked hopeful all over again. But it was only to give her arm a quick squeeze before she went in search of her mother.

***

Chrissy was already in bed when Eloise stormed into the room.

'You didn't even say goodnight, Mum.'

'So. It's been quite a day,' she replied.

The French doors were wide open but it didn't bring the temperature down any. Even the breeze blowing in on the curtain brought with it a flame of heat.

'Look, I know this is a big deal for you, coming to Italy and everything—'

'I said I'd do it for you, didn't I?'

'Well, that's just it,' said Eloise, refusing to be appeased that easily. 'Why are you being so hard on Juliet? It wasn't her fault what happened.' She flopped down onto her bed, stretching out. 'Is there more to this than you're telling me, Mum? Is there?'

The bed creaked as Chrissy turned over. 'How do people survive in these temperatures?'

The curtain rippled in again and Eloise caught it with her hand. 'I just want us to have a nice time here.' She sighed as she let it go again, watching it retreat like a diminishing wave. 'That's all I want.'

'Me too, Eloise. I will try.'

'And I feel sorry for her. Just seems so unfair what happened to you both. I can't stop thinking about it.'

There was a pause before her mother responded, and when she did she sounded tearful. 'I'm so sorry, Eloise. It really breaks my heart.'

'Well, I'm glad that bastard is dead because it means he can't do it to anyone else. I think it will get easier, Mum, from now on.'

'Sure it will,' she replied, faintly.

'Juliet must have missed you a lot, mustn't she, to name the cat after you?' Eloise laughed at the strangeness of it. 'I suppose, though, when you think about it she could still have been a student at the time. So maybe it's not that weird she named it after you, so soon after you'd gone and everything.'

'I guess not.'

Chrissy was clearly not in the mood for talking and Eloise felt herself eventually drifting off. She was almost asleep when she became aware of a light tapping sound somewhere in the room.

'Juliet?' she called out, sliding off the bed. She opened the door a little way, realizing that was where it was coming from.

It was Luca.

'Ah! *Mi scusi.* My wife thought you were still up.'

'Oh. Well, I am, sort of. Erm, you can come in.'

He stepped into the room and didn't seem perturbed to find Chrissy already in bed. She sat up, pulling the sheet into her chin.

'So,' he said, rubbing his hands. 'Juliet tells me you like to run, *no?*'

205

'Oh. Well, I—'

'Yes, she does. And she's brilliant. Really fast.'

'Ah! In that case, tomorrow morning, if you would like to join me—'

'No. But thank you.'

'You should go, Mum. It's your thing.'

'What time?' she asked, being polite.

'Six thirty. So it's not too hot.'

'Well, I'll see. Thank you, Luca.'

He gave her a nod on his way out.

Chrissy shouted to him: 'But please don't wait for me,' and he nodded again, closing the door.

'Why don't you go, Mum?'

'What if he really does know something?' she whispered.

'Juliet says he doesn't. Just trust her. Do you really not see how much she wants to be your friend again? She couldn't make it any clearer. You're still her best friend after all these years.'

***

At first she thought it was an intruder in their room. She froze, not daring to open her eyes. Then she realized it was her mother tiptoeing about.

'What are you doing? What time is it?'

'Six fifteen.'

'It's the middle of the night.'

'I'm going for a run with Luca. At your suggestion.'

'I was wrong, it's insane.' Eloise pulled the thin sheet over her face then threw it off again because even that was too hot.

'Healthy body, healthy mind,' Chrissy said, kissing her on the cheek.

'Well, it's not working,' said Eloise, but only when she was gone.

Juliet was out on the balcony when Eloise eventually surfaced an hour or so later. She was holding a thick white envelope, tapping it against her hand. Eloise was about to go and join her, but hung back when she suddenly tilted her head back to slip down a couple of pills with a drink of water.

She turned round, startled. 'Oh. Morning, Eloise. Did you sleep well?'

'I did until Mum woke me up saying she was going to run a marathon with Luca before breakfast.'

'You didn't fancy it then? We can go for a swim later if you like. Some neighbours have a pool we can use.'

'That'd be great.'

Juliet got her a glass of freshly pressed orange juice, ice cold from the fridge.

'Heavenly,' she said, taking a large mouthful.

'Cheese Eloise,' said Juliet, laughing, as she chinked her glass. 'I still haven't the foggiest what that means, by the way.'

'Oh, it's just something my dad said to me once. What he actually said was "Cheers Eloise", but I was really young and stupid, and I said to him: "Daddy, why did you just call me Cheese Eloise?" The name sort of stuck after that. I don't mind.'

Juliet smiled fondly and indicated that they should go back onto the balcony. She followed with *croissants* and pastries and then poured out some coffee.

'I don't really smoke,' she said, lighting a cigarette. 'Just for emergencies.'

Eloise assumed that must mean anything to do with her mother then. 'She's not always like this,' she said, biting into a pastry. 'What I mean is, my mum can be really lovely. She *is* really lovely.'

Juliet sipped her coffee. 'I know that. We need to take things slowly, that's all.'

Eloise noticed the envelope on the table. It had been opened. 'Listen, if you have to work, Juliet, I don't mind. I can always—'

'What? Oh that. No.' She picked it up and pretended to toss it down onto the street below. 'It's not important,' she said, skimming it across the table instead.

Eloise stared out at the rooftops. 'They've been gone ages, haven't they? Must be roasting out there.'

'Luca normally stops for breakfast on the way home. I suspect they'll be here soon. We'll put your mum back together again, Eloise. You mustn't worry.'

Juliet's hand was hot against her head as she stroked her hair, and Eloise was pleased when the cat began swishing round her legs because she could bend down to pick it up.

'I'm not sure I can call your cat Chrissy, Juliet. Might be a bit weird for my mum.'

Juliet put her finger to her lips when they heard the door open in the hallway. '*Ciao*,' she shouted.

Chrissy was the first to show. Her face was flushed, her hair scraped back with sweat but she had an exhilarated glow about her.

Luca staggered in behind. 'This one doesn't run,' he said, panting heavily. 'She sprints.'

'What a way to see Rome,' said Chrissy. 'They were just setting up the vegetable market in Campo de'Fiori, and all the little places slowly coming to life everywhere. Wonderful. Thank you, Luca.'

'Sit down,' said Juliet. She brought out a large jug of water from the fridge, ice cubes clunking against the sides.

'Hello, little Chrissy,' said Luca to the cat. 'You must feel very honoured to have a human named after you.' Luca raised one eyebrow at Chrissy, as if to say that wasn't his idea.

'Go have a shower, you stink,' said Juliet, followed by something else in Italian. She had the envelope in her hand and was tapping him with it rather aggressively as she pushed him out. Luca was having to shield himself. Then she turned round, forcing herself to smile. 'You're welcome to take a shower, too, Chrissy. Whenever you want.'

'Actually I'd prefer a cold bath, if you don't mind. I saw that you have one.'

'All yours,' said Juliet. She then excused herself to go and find Luca.

It wasn't long before Eloise could hear raised voices. Passionate chitchat, or they were having a row?

***

Despite the heat, Eloise had already decided she wanted to live in Rome as well as London.

'I think my brain is cooking today,' she said, flopping into a chair in Piazza Navona on one of their many excursions. It was a beautiful square, lined with restaurants and elegant palaces with pastel façades. Artists had set up their easels around the Fountain of the Four Rivers. A perfect spot for lunch.

Juliet had set aside the whole day for shopping. At the request of Chrissy, they had spent the morning at Porta Portese flea market on the other side of the Tiber. Despite this being 'for old times' sake', picking out the bargains like in their student days, they nearly came to blows when Chrissy found a pair of earrings which Juliet then surreptitiously bought for her. And Chrissy had been sulky ever since.

'Order whatever you like,' said Juliet when the waiter came over with menus.

'I'll get these,' said Chrissy. 'You're paying for everything. It's too much.'

'Luca says that Rome is like a big Italian feast. And you should feast. You are my guests.'

'In that case, can I have the biggest *gelato* in the whole of Italy?' said Eloise.

Chrissy closed the menu. She ordered a glass of tap water. It was far too hot to try to persuade her otherwise, and even when their ice creams arrived she still would not be tempted.

'Mm,' said Eloise, slowly retracting the spoon from her mouth. 'You really should try some, Mum.'

'I'm okay, thank you.'

'The *frutti di bosco* in this are divine,' said Juliet, pushing her bowl towards Chrissy.

'No. Really.' Chrissy pushed it back again with a tight smile. It became something of a game, teasing Chrissy with dripping spoonfuls of delicious ice cream.

Until she snapped.

'I said no, didn't I? At least one of you ought to know what that word means.'

She banged her fists on the table. They exchanged sheepish glances.

'Chrissy, I'm so sorry,' said Juliet.

'Me too,' said Eloise.

'I wasn't really thinking.'

'As we know, Juliet, never one of your strong points. Unless it was about yourself.'

Juliet put down her spoon, her hands fell limply onto the table. 'Do you really mean that, Chrissy? Is that what you think of me?'

'She doesn't,' said Eloise.

'*Scusi, signore.*' Chrissy waved her arm at the waiter. 'The bill, please.' He gave her a nod and went away again. Chrissy sighed, blowing air down the front of her shirt. 'This heat is something else, isn't it?'

They sat in silence after that, Juliet on the verge of tears. When the bill arrived, Chrissy was allowed to settle it without any fuss. Moments later, Juliet slapped the table. 'Right,' she said, trying to sound cheery again. 'So, are we ready to hit the shops big time?'

Chrissy stood up, pushing her chair back. 'I'm afraid that's me done for the day. What about you, Eloise?'

She looked pleadingly at her mother. She had been promised boutiques and Italian high street this afternoon.

'Right then,' said Chrissy, trying to disguise her hurt. 'I'll see you back at the apartment.' She screwed her eyes at Juliet. 'Don't spend too much. Please.'

Juliet nodded. 'I'm sorry again, Chrissy.'

'I know you are.'

They watched her cross the Square, soon swallowed up by the flow of people.

When she was out of sight, Juliet sprang up. 'Shall we?' she said, offering her arm to Eloise.

Making their way to Via del Corso, Eloise fell into step, and for a moment imagined this woman so full of *joie de vivre* was her mother. She grinned at anyone who gave them a look, but as soon as she realized what she was doing she felt ashamed, freeing herself to walk alongside Juliet, leaving a gap in between.

'Why do you think she's so off with you? She says she blames *him* for what happened, not you.'

'Mm,' Juliet replied, pondering on it. She seemed about to say something and then stopped. But seeing Eloise's expression, imploring her to answer, she tried again. 'Well, I suppose it could be because I was a bit flirty with your dad once. But—' She put her hand up so she could finish. 'But only to test his loyalty, that was all. Chrissy was my best friend and they'd been going out since they were in highchairs. I didn't know your dad that well at the time and didn't want her to get hurt or – or waste her best years. They were living in different cities; I wanted to know that Dan was solid.'

'Oh,' Eloise responded, suddenly thrown off balance. 'So … was he?'

'Of course he was. He loved your mum to bits and nothing was ever going to come between them.'

Eloise was still musing on this as Juliet grabbed her hand and swung it back and forth. 'Let's give that credit card some stick, shall we?'

She was prepared to buy whatever she touched, but Eloise drew the line in the more exclusive designer stores on Via dei Condotti. 'We shouldn't go too mad, Juliet.'

'Why not? She can't stop me spoiling you. You're officially my adopted daughter now.'

***

They could barely get through the door with so many bags and boxes. Remarkably, Chrissy made no further comment. But that night, when they were alone together, Eloise took it upon herself to say something. 'It's just her way of saying thank you, Mum. She's obviously loaded.'

'And if she wasn't loaded?'

'She'd still be great,' she said, giving her a kiss. 'Just like you.' Eloise hesitated before her next question. 'Mum. Be honest. Were you ever worried about Juliet and Dad?'

'What do you mean?'

'You know what I mean.'

Chrissy sighed. She had been brushing her hair and stopped. 'Juliet has a very strange approach to relationships. But her parents are to blame for that.' She gave Eloise a reassuring smile. 'Your dad thought the world of her. They were good friends, nothing more.'

Eloise bounced onto her bed, stretching out, hands behind her head. 'Do you think you would have tried to find Juliet if she hadn't got in touch with you? I mean, like one day.'

Chrissy threw her hairbrush onto the pillow. 'I doubt it.'

'But imagine you'd found out that she'd died.' She had gone into the bathroom so Eloise then had to shout. 'You'd feel awful, wouldn't you, Mum? You hear of people doing that, leaving it too late.'

'Hard to say.'

'Oh come on, Mum, you'd be devastated. Your best friend.'

Chrissy reappeared and climbed into bed. 'I'd much rather never know,' she said, switching off her light.

***

The only tourist box left to tick was the Vatican City.

'I'm not sure I feel like it today,' said Chrissy. 'The queues are awful, and in this heat.'

'We won't have to queue for long,' said Juliet.

'How come?'

'I've got us Fast Track tickets.'

'Don't tell me the Ricci label gets us into the Vatican as well?' said Chrissy. 'Oh, I can just see the Pope in his little Ricci cape. *Comes in red or white, Your Holiness. And look, we have matching papal slippers.*'

It ought to have been funny, but there was an edge to her tone.

'Don't forget the papal underpants,' Eloise added in desperation.

'Anyone can get Fast Track tickets, Chrissy. You just pay a bit more, that's all.'

Chrissy held her face up to the ceiling fan, giving Eloise a sideways look. Eloise was making it perfectly clear that she was not impressed.

'Right, I'll go get ready then,' said Chrissy.

***

The Basilica was relatively peaceful at that time. Early morning sunbeams welcomed them with open arms; an irresistible pull drew them towards their transparent glow. The gold leaf mosaics above their heads glittered as if in fanfare to the vast beauty of the place, and Eloise felt herself shrinking as her eyes tried to gather it all in.

Juliet suggested climbing the Cupola first. 'It's narrow though, Chrissy. You might want to wait for us. You could look around here instead.'

'Why would I want to do that?'

'Oh. Well, like I said it's a bit of a tight squeeze, lots of steps, people in front and behind you all the way. It's high when you reach the top.'

'I'm fine with heights.'

'There's a lift you can get,' Juliet persisted. 'But still over three hundred steps after that.'

'I'll go buy the tickets,' said Chrissy. 'And I'm taking the stairs.'

She insisted on going first, and with no one immediately in front of them, she soon disappeared from view. Once they entered the spiral tunnel there was no turning back. At times even Eloise felt claustrophobic.

They emerged at the first ring, where Chrissy was already admiring the mosaics on the inside of the Dome.

'When did you get so fit?' asked Juliet, gasping. 'Running upstairs like that. Phooph!'

'Mum spends her life running. Don't you, Mum?'

Chrissy shot her a glance then moved off again, rejoining them at the entrance to the next set of stairs. 'More?' she said.

If this was difficult for her then she certainly wasn't showing it. But as they neared the end of the tunnel it began to twist narrower and darker and Eloise detected a sense of panic brewing. Chrissy was clinging to the rope with both hands, her breathing on the edge. She was determined to keep going, however. At last they emerged into daylight, where she made a desperate grab for the railings.

'I'm okay,' she said, holding up her hands, 'before you ask. I just need a minute.'

Juliet held down her hair so it wouldn't blow into her face, rubbing her back gently. After a few minutes Chrissy managed a smile; the colour returned to her cheeks.

'Wow,' she said, when she could finally concentrate on the view.

The colours of Rome stretched out before them: reds, browns, oranges and bold flashes of pink. The sun glinted on a small patch of river they could just make out, lined with bushy clumps of green. Directly below, tiny black dots scuttled across the Piazza.

'Worth every step, eh?' said Juliet, opening her hands out to

St Peter's Square and the Vatican obelisk. She pointed to the Vatican Museums, where they would go next, and then wandered off to have a cigarette despite telling them it wasn't permitted.

Eloise began taking photos.

'Don't you dare point that thing at me,' said Chrissy.

'Mum, I am aware after all these years,' Eloise replied.

***

'Is there really no photography allowed inside the Sistine Chapel?' said Eloise, scowling at the sign as they shuffled along in the queue. 'Not a single, measly photo. How mean is that?'

'I've seen people take them in there before,' Juliet whispered. 'As long as you don't get caught. Here though, let me. I'll be able to talk my way out of it.'

Eloise handed her the camera; it was almost their turn to go in.

'Shush, no talking,' said Chrissy as they entered the Chapel. 'Probably not allowed to breathe either,' she whispered.

Eloise felt herself being pushed slightly ahead of them. And, as a result, she missed Juliet pointing the camera at Chrissy, pretending to take her picture. She didn't hear the click of the shutter either. But she couldn't escape the fallout afterwards.

'What the hell are you doing?' said Chrissy.

Someone shushed them.

'I'm sorry,' Juliet whispered. 'It was a mistake.'

'Delete it. Now.'

'Well, I will, I will. Just give me a second; it's not my camera.'

'What's up?' said Eloise, coming over quickly. 'Everyone's looking at you.' She tried to divert Chrissy by pointing to the Michelangelo frescoes on the ceiling. 'That's the really famous one where they're touching fingers. *The Creation of Adam.* See it?'

'Eloise,' said Juliet behind her in a hushed voice. She was pulling on her arm, which forced her to let go of Chrissy.

215

'What?'

'Can you delete this? I didn't mean to take it.'

Eloise winced when she saw the picture. Somebody 'shushed' them again. The Vatican staff were getting twitchy.

'Has it gone yet? Bloody better have,' said Chrissy.

'Nearly,' said Juliet. 'Look, Chrissy, I really think you need to let this go …'

'Deleted!' Eloise announced. 'Gone forever.'

She hoped that was the end of it, but Chrissy moved in so close to Juliet their faces were almost touching. 'Let go of what exactly? What do you think it is that I have to let go of, Juliet?'

'Sssh.'

'I think we should get out of here,' said Eloise.

'This fear and guilt you still feel,' whispered Juliet. 'After so long.'

'How do you know how I feel? How can you possibly know?'

Chrissy marched off towards the Exit and Eloise ran after her.

'Mum. Are you okay? She didn't mean to do it.' Eloise was struggling to keep up. 'Maybe Juliet's right though. Mum!'

By now they had emerged into Piazza San Pietro. The vast open space and bright sunlight came as a shock to both of them. And there was the heat to get used to again. Chrissy came to an abrupt standstill, and Eloise almost walked into her.

'What do you know either?' her mother said snappily, sweeping the sweat off her brow. Then her expression changed. 'You already know too much, Eloise. That's the problem.'

'There you are!'

Juliet positioned herself on the other side of Chrissy.

'Mum, please. We only want to help. Don't shut us out any more.'

***

216

Juliet was up to something.

Eloise chased her up the spiral steps and out onto the roof terrace, where Chrissy was fanning herself with a wide-brimmed hat that she had bought from a street vendor the day before. She seemed oblivious to the sky turning a delicate pink all around her.

'Listen up,' said Juliet, clapping her hands.

It startled Chrissy. She sat up, raised her sunglasses, giving Juliet a frown.

'Tomorrow I have *una sorpresa* for us.'

'We ought to be booking a flight home actually. No more surprises.'

'So tomorrow,' said Juliet, disregarding what Chrissy had just said, 'we get out of Rome and we go into the Tuscan hills. It's so beautiful, you will love it there, both of you. We catch the train to Chiusi in the morning at eleven.'

Juliet looked encouragingly at Eloise, as if to say: W*ork on your mother,* before heading back down the staircase.

Eloise stood helpless. She knew only one thing: 'I'm not ready to go home yet, Mum. I want to stay, and I think you should, too.'

'There's a flight tomorrow evening,' said Chrissy. 'I checked.'

'No.'

'Yes.'

Eloise moved in, pointing her finger in her mother's face. 'Why don't you go then? I want to be with Juliet.' She was surprised at how angry that came out. It must be the heat.

***

Juliet was in the kitchen. She made out as if she wasn't aware of Eloise standing there, opened the fridge door, humming to herself. Three tall glasses were lined up on the unit. She tipped ice cubes into each one; they clattered against the sides as though in shock at being disturbed.

'Maybe we should stay in Rome, Juliet. She's got used to it here. She can go running with Luca and—'

Juliet was shaking her head. She filled the glasses with water then drank from one of them. 'We need a change of scene,' she said. 'It's very important. Trust me, Eloise, I know what's best. Now go and convince your mother.' She handed her the other two glasses. 'You can come back to Rome anytime you like. With or without her, you'll always be welcome.'

CHAPTER 25

Tuscany: 2007

A woman called Marianna picked them up at Chiusi-Chianciano Terme railway station. She was waiting for them on the platform clutching a pair of folded sunglasses, looking elegant in a pale blue linen dress.

'*Buongiorno.* How was your trip?' She took Chrissy's bag. 'Not too hot on the train, I hope. It's a wonderful journey but can get so crowded.'

'If I can rough it for an hour and a half, anyone can,' said Juliet. 'And it's well worth it.'

'Very beautiful,' Chrissy added.

'We're just over here.' Marianna pointed to a dusty Opel 4x4. They loaded their luggage into the boot then got in. '*Non è molto lontano da qui,*' she said, turning to Eloise. '*Parli Italiano?*'

'If that means, "do I speak Italian?", then no.'

Marianna laughed. 'No problem,' she said in perfect English. 'We don't have far to go. In this heat I expect you'll be glad.'

She chatted to Juliet in Italian for most of the journey, whilst Eloise and Chrissy tried to survive in the back. Even with the air-con it was like a pizza oven, at least to begin with. But once they were past Chiusi Scalo and out into open countryside they didn't notice the heat any more. Huge skies and patchwork fields of green and gold stretched out on either side. Dirt roads lined with cypress trees zigzagged up the hillsides, leading to farmhouses perched right on the hill tops.

'Where are we?' Chrissy asked.

'*Mi dispiace*,' said Marianna. 'You really must forgive me. This is the Val d'Orcia. Beautiful, isn't it?'

'Stunning,' said Chrissy.

'I just love it when the wheat is ripening; it's like a golden desert. Also you see the hills of the Crete Senesi. The soil is clay so it makes a sort of blue-grey colour. In this area they grow a lot of olives. And *Vino rosso*, of course. The wine from Montepulciano and Montalcino is very good. Oh, and you must try the *pecorino* cheese *di Pienza*. It's made from sheep's milk.'

Eloise was so enthralled she hadn't realized that half an hour had gone by, not until they were being bounced about like Lotto balls in the back and she glanced at her phone. They had turned down a winding track, passing through two large iron gates, after which the track became even rougher. At first she thought it was the stone farmhouse they were making for, but as they came to the end of the track, a whole estate came into view. She spotted a swimming pool, tennis court and a number of horses in one of the fields.

'Oh my god!'

'*Bellissimo*, no?' said Marianna, pulling on the handbrake.

'Just a bit.'

Marianna asked Chrissy to pass her jacket from the parcel shelf. They noticed it had a Ricci label in it. Juliet gave Eloise a wink as they got out.

'Follow me,' said Marianna.

There was a serenity about her, and she didn't appear to be at all bothered by the heat. Chrissy's face was red and shiny, Eloise assumed her own must be too, and even Juliet was fanning herself. They walked away from the main buildings passing what looked like the stable block, then alongside the tennis court. Eventually they arrived at a large stone building. Marianna pushed open the door, holding it open for them.

The inside temperature was gloriously cool: oak chestnut beams and terracotta floors. A stone terrace, accessible through sliding glass doors, ran one length of the living/dining area, giving them an uninterrupted view of olive groves, cypress trees and the surprisingly green valley and surrounding hills beyond.

They each had their own bedroom: queen-sized beds with crisp white sheets and fluffy white towels.

'Let me show you the pool,' said Marianna.

They followed her outside underneath a large pergola covered in vine and down some steps. The water rippled like blue silk. It was a decent size, too, Eloise thought. She longed to dive into it; cool off from this searing heat.

At the end of their tour Marianna informed them there was wine and beer in the fridge, plus a few provisions. They must say if they needed anything else, and if they wanted to hire a car she could arrange that too. In addition, there were bicycles and Vespas available for guests, so they only had to ask if they were interested in using them.

'Welcome, and make yourselves at home. There are some people around who can help you. Anyone who doesn't look like a guest, you can ask them. Do you like horses?'

She was directing the question at Eloise.

'Oh. Erm yes.'

'Do you ride?'

'I've never tried actually.'

'Well, maybe this is the time. We do some nice treks in the hills. Come over and see the horses later if you want.'

Eloise nodded.

'Very unusual brooch,' Marianna remarked as she was leaving.

Juliet exchanged glances with Eloise; they couldn't help but grin.

'Thank you,' Juliet replied. 'It was a gift. From a friend.'

'This friend?' said Marianna, looking to Chrissy.

'An old friend,' said Juliet.

When Marianna was out of earshot the pair of them cracked up laughing.

'A cat burglar friend,' Eloise joked.

Chrissy was stony-faced.

Juliet tried to redeem herself. She cupped her hands over her mouth and shouted: 'Last one in the pool is a piece of *merde!*'

Nobody moved. Juliet seemed to be waiting for Chrissy.

'Well, I'm up for it,' said Eloise, diving into her suitcase, and Juliet took this as her cue to do the same. 'Come on, Mum,' she hollered, waving her striped bikini in the air.

Juliet had more luggage than the two of theirs combined. It looked like she would need hours, not seconds, to locate her swimwear. She fished out a sarong, gold flip-flops, suntan cream, floppy sunhat, shades, book, beach towel.

'Look, Mum! You can still catch up,' said Eloise, nodding at Juliet's great pile of stuff. She flew past the pair of them and ran towards the steps leading down to the pool.

'Wait for me,' said a voice behind her. It was Juliet, but she didn't wait. Instead she dive-bombed into the water creating a satisfying explosion. Wiping the drips from her eyes she saw Juliet preparing to dive in and applauded as she hit the water.

When Chrissy finally appeared she put down her book, laid her towel over the back of a chair, removed her flip-flops and entered the pool via the steps.

'Well, I think you're both the piece of *merde,*' said Eloise. 'You've both got far too much baggage.'

Chrissy kicked off the side to swim underwater. Eloise stayed alongside her, but neither of them was a match for Juliet's front crawl; she was soon lapping them.

Juliet got out of the pool, announcing she was going to unpack. Eloise watched her go then turned her attention to her mother, who was already drying herself over by the sunloungers. She stopped for a moment to take in the view, shielding her eyes from the glaring sun. The sweeping valley and rolling hills of Montepulciano were quite a change from Rome. Eloise went to sit by her, although it wasn't long before Chrissy said she could only bear it for another ten minutes.

'If you're staying out here be careful not to burn, Eloise,' were her parting words.

It felt good to be alone. She could fully soak up the peace and quiet of the place. Reaching lazily for her phone, she sent a text to Anya.

'*Wish you were here. xxx*'

Even though Anya had forgiven her, eventually, Eloise had come to realize that there were things she could never share with her best friend; with anyone, in fact. And when things flared up between Juliet and Chrissy she had no one to talk to about it.

Perhaps they would get on better now they were out of Rome. That was probably why Juliet had brought them here.

Eloise got back into the pool, floating aimlessly in the stillness. The sky was a deep blue; the water lapping at her ears the only sound. Gradually, though, a sense of unease began to creep in: the feeling of being watched. Splashing noisily, treading water, she searched all around. There didn't seem to be anyone about. Then a ginger cat strolled lethargically out of the shrubbery, giving her a look that said *so what?*

She flipped herself underwater and swam an entire length, her lungs ready to burst when she reached for the tiles at the other end. Her eyes were stinging then, so she rubbed them with her fists. That was when she heard a voice shout: '*Ciao.*'

At least, she thought she had.

Realizing she was without a towel, as soon as she stepped out of the pool she felt exposed in her bikini, leaving a watery trail behind her.

'*Ciao*,' said the voice again.

Eloise froze.

It seemed to come from the bushes.

Black hair, messy, lots of it falling over his face. That was what she noticed first about him. Then big brown eyes, long eyelashes. He was tall, much taller than she was, seemed friendly enough although he didn't smile. Older, but she couldn't tell by how much. He was pruning the branches of some prickly looking shrub.

'You didn't do the whole thing underwater,' he said in an accent she couldn't quite place.

'Yes, I did,' she replied, wishing her response had been cleverer than that.

'We will have a race; see who wins.'

'What? I don't even know who you are.'

'*Mi chiamo* Nic. Or Nico.'

He offered her his hand. It was tanned, like the rest of him, smooth and strong-looking. She stared at it for a moment, concluding it would be rude not to shake it and that he must work here.

'Eloise. *Mi chi*—?'

'*Mi chiamo*—'

'*Mi chiamo* Eloise.'

It was a firm handshake. Electric. Made her feel even more exposed, and she placed one arm across her chest in an attempt to cover herself. When he started to remove his T-shirt she panicked, wondering what to do, but then a sense of relief as he ran towards the pool. Without thinking, she took a flying dive at the water and they touched the tiles almost together at the other end.

He climbed out, lowering his hand down to her. 'Not bad,' he said, hoisting her up.

'Er, I won that, I think you'll find.' She was far more out of breath than he was, made worse by the fact that she was trying to disguise it.

'*Penso di no*. I think not.'

'*Penso di* yes. And you cheated.'

'*Non è possibile*.'

He put his T-shirt back on, the drips from his hair making wet marks over his shoulders. '*A presto*,' he said, walking away.

'What does that mean?'

'I look after the horses,' he shouted, without turning back.

Eloise smiled to herself watching him go. Maybe she didn't wish Anya was here after all.

***

Juliet rustled up a salade niçoise in the evening. 'When in Rome,' she joked.

'Juliet, what does "*a presto*" mean in Italian?'

'It means "see you later" or "see you soon".'

Eloise flushed, and missed most of what Juliet said next, something about the outdoor pizza oven and Luca. They ate supper out on the terrace to the sound of cicadas in the background. It was easy to get accustomed to this slower pace of life after the frenzy of Rome, and there was no obligation to discuss the following day's itinerary.

A grunting noise began to perplex them.

'What the hell is that?' said Eloise.

'Could be wild boar,' Juliet suggested.

'Sounds like you in the tent, Ju: "*Attention tout le monde! Juliet est en train de lâcher les gaz*".'

'What's that mean?'

'Juliet used to make the air a little fragrant sometimes, shall we say?'

'Mum!'

Juliet seemed way too sophisticated for that, but it was pleasing to see the two of them laughing together, and Juliet's only protest was to flick water at Chrissy who then flicked some back. When they calmed down again, Juliet said, 'Jeez, our diet was appalling that summer. I think I went home with scurvy. What about you?'

Chrissy pushed away her plate and folded her arms on the table. 'I think scurvy was the least of my worries, don't you?' They were staring at each other, rewinding through time together, nineteen again, wondering where all the years had gone in between.

'It was an accident, Mum.'

Another loud grunting came from the field.

'Juliet, really!' said Eloise, which prompted Juliet to throw a wine cork at her. Eloise took it upon herself to refill their glasses, saying: 'Hey, tell us some more about your life, Juliet. It sounds so amazing.'

She seemed to need Chrissy's approval first.

'Go ahead,' said Chrissy. 'I'd really like to hear.'

'What is it you want to know exactly?'

'What's it like being friends with all those famous people?' asked Eloise.

Juliet had gulped her wine too quickly and started to cough. 'Hardly friends. And they're just the same as you and I really. Although …' – she had to clear her throat again – 'admittedly, some of them can be quite tricky, particularly when it comes to their clothes.' Half-covering her mouth she whispered: 'You wouldn't want some of them as your friends, believe me.'

'Like who?'

'Oh, I'm afraid I can't say, Eloise, or I'd have to kill you. I mean … not literally, obviously. Sorry. Sorry, Chrissy.' She had got herself in a fluster, but recovered from it soon enough. 'Confidentiality is a big part of my job. I'm good at keeping my mouth shut.' Her eyes landed on Chrissy as she said it.

'You get to travel the world,' said Eloise. 'That must be fantastic.'

Juliet sat back, pensively stroking the stem of her glass. 'My

226

whole life I've never had anywhere to call home.' Then she pulled a cigarette out of her bag, flicking up her lighter. It took a few attempts. 'Isn't this boring?' she asked.

'How can you say that?' said Eloise, but she realized it could have been for Chrissy's benefit.

'All I ever wanted was a small clothes shop to sell my stuff in. I never meant for it to get so big.' Juliet sounded defensive all of a sudden. She took a sip of wine, delayed swallowing it whilst she focused on Chrissy, and then said: 'Anyway, I think you're the one who's lucky.'

'Me? Why the hell am I lucky? How do you get to that?'

'Because you have Eloise.'

Chrissy flushed, giving Eloise's hand a squeeze. Eloise wasn't offended. If anything, she was pleased that Juliet herself had said these words because Chrissy might actually start to believe them. They each drifted into their own private thoughts after that, and Eloise began to wonder if their worlds had grown too far apart for them to be as close as they used to be. Perhaps the most she dared hope for was that Chrissy might have someone else in her life who knew about her past, someone to replace her dad. This could only be Juliet. As far she knew there *was* no one else. Eloise just needed to ensure that Juliet was here to stay. As a friend, a good friend, even if it wasn't a best friend. And then she would be free to do all the things she wanted to do, without worrying about her mother any more. The conversation turned to their university days, and for a brief moment the two women seemed like two regular friends catching up. Eloise thought she would leave them to it.

'I'm going for a walk.'

'Well, don't go far,' said Chrissy. 'It's getting late.'

The oncoming darkness was beginning to draw the heat out of the day. Eloise understood now why there were torches in all the bedside drawers. The only light to assist her was coming from one of the other villas up ahead. She saw a couple sitting out on

227

their terrace drinking wine and smiled at them as she passed.

This place was even bigger than she imagined. She carried on towards the field where Marianna said the horses liked to graze. There weren't any at this hour so she headed for the stables, where she supposed they would be for the night. The smell of horses led her to believe she was going in the right direction. As she neared the main house, suddenly a light flickered on and she saw someone come out. Retreating slightly, she heard a voice coming from behind her, causing her to stumble backwards.

'Ah!'

It was Nico.

'The girl from the swimming pool. *Buonasera*.' He shone a torch into her face, dazzling her. '*Scusa*,' he said, pointing it downwards.

'I was just taking a walk and—'

'Sure, *va bene*. We allow that. French Fry is sick.'

'Sorry?' She thought she had misheard, or maybe he had got his words wrong.

'French Fry. He's a horse. He was sick today.'

'Oh.'

'I think he's okay now. We will get the vet to him tomorrow. Are you – how do you say – relaxed?'

He spoke quickly, and Eloise was still getting used to his accent. His English was good, all the same, if a little quirky. 'Oh yes. It's so amazing here. The view's awesome.' She curled her tongue back inside her mouth. Referring to the view when they couldn't see a thing was ridiculous.

'*Ma certo*.'

He didn't translate, and they stood in silence after that. The longer it went on the harder it became to think of anything else to talk about, and he seemed to be leaving it to her. He was leaning against the wall, one arm outstretched above his shoulder. And he was very close.

Was he challenging her?

She reckoned he was a couple of years older; maybe she felt intimidated by that. In the end all she could think of was, 'Well, *buonasera.*' But as she turned to go he caught her by the arm. It seemed strange to see his hand on her skin; white, where his fingers were pressing into it.

'You want me to walk with you?' He removed it then. 'Many people get lost *la prima notte.* The first night.'

'Yes, I can see why. Think I'll be okay.'

'*Ecco.*' He handed her his torch. 'I don't need it.'

'Oh, er, *grazie.*' She took it and smiled, but when he didn't smile back she found it unsettling.

She lingered a few more tortured seconds then sped back to their villa the same way she had come. The couple who had been sitting out on the terrace had gone inside, an unfinished wine bottle and two glasses still on the table, as if they had left in a hurry. The light was on in their bedroom; two silhouettes were removing their clothes. At that point Eloise realized she had come along their private pathway and each villa had its own access off the main path. A mistake she would not be making again.

Their place was in darkness. Chrissy and Juliet had gone to bed. She shone the torch into Chrissy's room to see if she was still awake.

'That you, darling?'

Always a sign that she had drunk too much. If ever she said *darling,* she meant Dan.

'It's me,' she whispered.

'Where've you been? Is it late?'

'It's only midnight, Mum.'

But it was clearly not the time to ask about her evening. She kissed her mother goodnight, and Chrissy held onto her for as long as she could without falling out of bed. Eloise had almost reached the door when she heard her say, sleepily: 'Last one in the pool in the morning is a piece of *merde.*'

'Too right!' said Eloise. 'And it won't be me. Do you like it here, Mum?'

229

'Yeah, it's *fantastico*,' she replied through a yawn.

Eloise laughed and closed the door, getting a fright when Juliet stuck her head out of her room.

'Just wanted to make sure you're okay,' she said, waving the yellow bear at her.

'Don't let my mum see that, Juliet!'

'Don't worry, I won't,' she whispered back.

'Well, night Juliet. We both love it here, by the way.'

Eloise got into bed and placed Nico's torch under her pillow. Only because she might need it during the night, she told herself.

***

She panicked when she woke up the next morning and failed to see Chrissy anywhere. Then she remembered they were in Tuscany and shuffled next door to see if she was stirring yet. Chrissy lifted up the duvet without opening her eyes.

Eloise slid in beside her, sitting up. Tugging her hair gently, she asked: 'Did you have a nice night with Juliet then?'

Chrissy moaned, pushing herself up the bed.

'Yes. No. I don't know.' But she saw the determination in her daughter's eyes and knew what she was in for. 'Look, there's only so much you can reminisce about old times before the reality of what happened hits you in the face.'

Eloise nodded. She couldn't imagine what her mother was going through. 'So what happened next – when you got back to England?' Eloise felt bad forcing Chrissy down memory lane again, but she couldn't stop herself.

Chrissy was silent for a moment. Then, rolling the duvet into tight little folds, she slipped back in time.

CHAPTER 26

London: summer, 1989

The announcement came. She knew it wouldn't be long now.

Would all passengers please return to their vehicles. Foot passengers, please wait.

'We made it,' said Juliet, shaking her. 'Chrissy. Chrissy, look. It's the white cliffs again. Look! You okay? You still look a bit green.' She lowered her voice. 'Come on, Chrissy. Don't bomb out on me now. We're almost there. We're so close.'

Juliet was right; she had to pull herself together. Otherwise what had it all been for? She may as well have turned herself in to the French police.

Breathe Chrissy. Breathe.

Clinging to Juliet, waiting to disembark, she could feel herself sinking. She took a step back to lean against the wall. Why was everyone looking at her? Could they tell she was a killer? Did it show on her face?

'Nearly home. Just hold that thought.'

Juliet's voice was too loud and too confident.

'We've still got to clear Passport Control yet. I'm so scared, Ju,' she whispered.

'It's going to be okay.'

How could it be okay? Juliet had no idea what she was feeling inside. No idea at all.

Chrissy had expected to feel better once they stepped off the boat onto British soil. It was this thought that had been keeping her going. But she didn't. If anything, she felt worse. They had made it back from France without getting caught. Now she had her whole life to get through.

***

'You're still in shock,' said Juliet, once they were on their way again. 'I reckon a few stiff drinks with Dan tonight will sort you out.'

Chrissy was silent for most of the journey. When they reached the outskirts of London, Juliet pointed gleefully to a sign for Victoria Coach Station. Holding up her crossed fingers, she said: 'If we get through this, Chrissy, we can do *anything*.' Sliding back down the seat again, she whispered: 'Are you going to tell him? Dan, I mean.'

'I've got to.'

Chrissy stared at her own reflection in the window. The whole journey seemed to have passed in a blur. She couldn't even remember turning in to the coach station, so it came as a surprise when they swung in to Stand C and the driver announced their arrival.

Juliet took her hand so they could step down together. They were the last to get off. Chrissy felt her knees buckle as her feet touched the ground.

'We made it, Chrissy. We've done it.'

Everyone else clamoured to retrieve their bags, find loved ones. They simply stood still, observing the world carrying on around them.

'We should go find out what time your bus is back to Manchester,' said Juliet. 'There's a kiosk thingy there.'

'Ten past three,' the man said. 'Gets in, eight twenty.'

'I can wait with you,' said Juliet. 'We could go get a—'

'No.' Juliet's face dropped. 'You need to go, Juliet.'

'But—'

'I'll see you in Bristol.' Chrissy felt her strength returning. If they hung around for too long someone could identify them later. 'It's only two weeks till the start of term, Ju.' She wiped a tear from Juliet's cheek. 'And don't contact me over the summer, will you? No phone calls, letters. Nothing. It's too risky.'

Juliet shook her head. She was like a lost child. 'I won't,' she said, attempting to hug her.

Chrissy stepped backwards. 'Please go, Ju,' she said. 'I can't bear it, I'm sorry.' And then: 'Wait! Just one thing – would you do me a favour? Phone Dan when you get home and tell him my coach gets in at eight twenty. I'll probably break down if I do it.'

'Yeah, 'course,' she said, glad to be of some use.

Chrissy managed to hold back the tears until she had seen Juliet turn to wave for the last time. When a complete stranger asked if she was okay she realized she had to get a grip.

Making her way through to Domestic Departures she noticed a policeman positioned by the Exit, managing the flow of people.

Do it, Chrissy. Do the right thing. The more time goes by the less believable your version of the truth will be.

'You need to arrest me,' she said, holding her hands out ready for the cuffs. 'I've killed someone.'

He waved her on. In her confused state she could only assume that she hadn't said anything, and turned her face away from him as she passed.

The queue at the booking office was slow. She found herself shaking, shifting from one foot to the other in order to camouflage it.

Don't lose it, Chrissy. Breathe.

Handing over the money for her ticket she caught a whiff of

233

her own body odour. It made her think of home and how much she longed for a shower.

A shower.

The whole scene came flooding back. Juliet on the bed. The bottle of wine. The phone call in the middle of the night. The man with a towel round his waist on top of her best friend. The smug look on his face. His mangled eye. Blood creeping across the sheets.

'*No, fuck you.*'

***

The coffee bar was heaving but she managed to sit down with her polystyrene cup of disappointing English coffee. Still in her pocket was a strip of paracetamol, which Juliet had given her at some point on their journey. Two white pills popped out onto the table and all she could do was stare at them. It was laughable really. How could they possibly make this go away?

The coffee was steaming but she couldn't wait for it to cool. Flinging the pills to the back of her throat, the hot liquid was scalding as it went down. She was still reeling from the pain when a young couple came and sat opposite her without even asking if it was okay. They were roughly the same age as her and Dan, wrapped around each other, in a world all their own. Their kisses stung Chrissy, and seeing their hands secretly disappear under clothes made her recoil.

Brown stain on the ceiling. Red spatters on the wall. Scratches on Juliet, down her stomach and legs. Blood-soaked towel over his head like a shroud. Halo of blood across pale lemon sheets.

And that face.

'*No, fuck you.*'

She decided to go and locate her departure stand, even though she still had a long time to wait. Feeling herself being jostled as she stood up, she saw it was the young couple from her table who were also on the move. The girl mouthed the word *sorry* then turned back to her boyfriend. They carried on walking, lips pressed together, causing everyone else to move out of their way.

Stand 21.

Golders Green, Stockport, Manchester.

She spotted a 'Toilet' sign just behind it.

Completely out of coins, she had to duck under the barrier.

The attendant was waiting for her when she came out. 'You don't pay,' she said, holding out her hand insistently. 'You need pay now.'

'Look, I don't have any English money. I really don't; I was just desperate.'

'You don't pay; I call security guard.'

'No! No, don't do that. Please don't do that. Here. That's fifty francs. That's like five pounds. Get it changed at the currency place and keep some for yourself.'

The woman eyeballed her but took the note and waved her through. It was all the money gone now. She pushed against the turnstile, hearing it grind round like a torture rack.

'*No. Fuck you.*'

She would fight this all the way. Whatever it took.

Arsehole.

Dan was going to help her. Dan would understand.

***

Chrissy searched for him in the sea of faces. It was late when she arrived, and the temperature in Manchester was much cooler than she had been used to in France. She observed her fellow passengers with envy, receiving hugs and kisses from their loved ones.

Perhaps he was stuck in traffic.

She paced up and down, shivering, on the verge of dissolving into tears.

Nearly an hour went by, sitting in the waiting area. Numb.

Like being in a thick fog where sounds were muffled and people were blurry. Realizing she was drawing attention to herself, she tried to think what to do. *I'm in a bus station,* she told herself. *There must be a payphone here somewhere.* Trudging around she finally found one that worked, surprised to hear her own voice asking the operator for a reverse-charges call.

'Why the hell didn't you phone me when you arrived in London?' was the first thing Dan asked. 'I've been really worried about you.'

It was good to hear him again. Even better, to know that he still cared.

'Well, didn't Juliet call you? I asked her to. She was supposed to.'

'No.'

'Look, please Dan, I'm really tired. Don't … just don't, okay?'

'I'm on my way,' she heard him say.

He took one look at her and said: 'God, what's happened? You look awful. Bad journey?'

CHAPTER 27

Tuscany: 2007

'So, wait, Dad wasn't there?' asked Eloise.

Chrissy opened her mouth to continue but was interrupted by a loud '*Buongiorno!*' from just outside their window.

'Who's that?' whispered Chrissy, immediately on the alert.

'Sounded like Marianna.'

'*Croissants.* Fresh bread. Come and get it!'

That was Juliet.

'We should get up,' said Chrissy.

'Wait. Why wasn't he there? Did Juliet … did she tell him what happened?'

Chrissy gave a strangled laugh.

'No, god no. Though that was what I thought, of course. I thought he didn't love me any more. But no, Juliet didn't even call him in the end. I was in such a state when I saw he wasn't there.'

'Juliet didn't call him? What … why?'

'I don't know why. Because she's Juliet?'

'But if Dad wasn't there for you—'

'It's fine,' Chrissy whispered. 'Don't worry.'

Eloise trudged into the living area. The terracotta tiles under her bare feet gave some relief from the already intense heat.

'*Buongiorno*,' she said to Marianna, pointedly ignoring Juliet.

'Morning, Eloise,' said Juliet, clearly perturbed by the snub. 'Pretty *scorchio* again.'

A few moments later Chrissy appeared, fanning herself with a magazine.

'Ah, but a storm is coming,' said Marianna. 'Maybe two, three days away. Everyone is praying for it as we badly need the rain.' She could probably tell from their faces they didn't believe her. The sky looked like it could never be anything other than pure, uninterrupted blue. She changed the subject by asking: 'So, do you have any plans for the day?'

Juliet and Chrissy both said they were happy to chill by the pool. Eloise nearly asked if Nico would be around, stopping herself just in time. Her mother would freak if she thought she already had her 'boy radar' on. Chrissy's phrase, not hers.

'*Va bene*. Well, if you want to use the bicycles or Vespas, just find one of us to help you. And let me know if you want to horse ride,' she said to Eloise on her way out. 'Oh, and if you want to play tennis there are racquets and balls in the small hut just at the side of the tennis court.'

'Isn't she just great?' said Juliet when she was gone. 'I mean look at this place, it's incredible.'

'Have you met her before?' asked Chrissy.

'No, I found it on the internet.'

Chrissy puffed out her cheeks and stood up. Eloise stepped in, sensing her mother's tension. 'Without the internet, Mum, we wouldn't even be here.'

'Exactly. And Juliet would never have found me. I'm going for a swim.'

'Chrissy!'

'If you can find me, Juliet, anyone can. Doesn't that bother you? Because it should.'

'I knew where to look, that's all. But it took me long enough.'

'Doesn't matter,' said Chrissy.

She slung her towel over her shoulder, thumping her bare feet onto the tiles as she walked away.

'Well, who else would know to look up Dan's band?' Juliet shouted after her.

Eloise shot her a look of contempt. Juliet raised an eyebrow.

'What's wrong? What did I do?'

'She doesn't like the internet. You know that. And … how could you forget to call my dad?'

'What?'

'My dad. Dan. Mum asked you to let him know when to pick her up when you got back from France, but you didn't. After everything that happened, you couldn't do that one small thing for her?'

Juliet laughed strangely. 'It wasn't just your mother who was suffering, Eloise. What happened in France happened to me too. So, yes, it slipped my mind. I just forgot. Anyway, it was a long time ago.'

'That's pretty crap though. Wouldn't you say?' For the first time, Eloise was starting to see Juliet through her mother's eyes.

She turned on her heel and followed Chrissy to the pool.

***

Juliet was itching to say something. They were having lunch, the heat blur making waves across the hillside. Eloise spotted a lizard scurrying across the terrace as though it would get its feet burnt if it didn't move fast enough, and all that remained of the ice cubes in her glass was a thin film floating on the top.

'I did some research on *you-know-what* whilst I was on my mission to find you,' said Juliet, tapping the side of her nose, unable to keep it to herself any longer.

239

'I've no idea what you're talking about,' said Chrissy, mimicking her nose-tapping.

'You've nothing to fear.'

'Fear? Why, what sort of research?'

'You know,' said Juliet, pretending to type with her fingers. 'Online.'

'There was no internet then,' said Eloise.

'No, but I found an article from a couple of years ago.'

'A couple of years ago?' Chrissy slammed both hands on the table. Eloise had to shush her. But she felt the same fear. What the hell were they doing crossing borders if the police were still looking for the killer? Why hadn't Juliet mentioned this before?

They had to get Chrissy inside, somewhere cooler. Eloise sat her down, straddling a chair; it sometimes helped if she rested her elbows on the backrest.

'Turn the ceiling fan on,' Eloise instructed.

Juliet kept saying how sorry she was, that she had only meant to reassure her. She had some positive information, apparently.

'Save it for a minute,' said Eloise.

'No, now,' said Chrissy, gasping.

'Mum, it can wait.'

'No, it bloody can't. Say it now!'

'Mum, please.'

She was getting worse. In a way it was a scene Juliet needed to witness. Eloise was beginning to wonder if she viewed this whole 'let's rescue Chrissy thing' thing as some sort of game. She said she wanted to repay her dues but did she really know how?

As Chrissy began to show signs of recovery, Eloise gave Juliet the signal to carry on. She had to prompt her when she didn't take her cue. 'So did they reopen the case, Juliet?'

'Oh god, did they?' said Chrissy.

'*Juliet!*'

Eloise wanted to shake her.

'What? … Yes. Yes, they did. But then closed it again. Are you okay, Chrissy?'

It was unnerving to see Juliet this way. Like seeing a tear in one of her expensive fabrics, a broken heel on her designer shoe. Where was Juliet Ricci?

'So what happened?' said Eloise. 'Please, Juliet.'

She must have seen the desperation in her eyes, imploring her to stop unravelling.

'Well, we know that they always suspected he'd had a prostitute in the motel room …'

Chrissy nodded, and Juliet became animated again.

'And you stealing the money from his wallet was definitely a good move, as it turned out, because it gave some credence to this theory. I mean, I know you only did it so we could get the hell out of there and back to England as quickly as possible, but it suggested a motive. I found all this out in the newspaper article: it gave a summary of the crime.'

'But why was the case reopened?' asked Chrissy, wiping the sweat from her forehead.

'Okay. Apparently they interviewed a number of prostitutes in the area just after you – well after the incident – and they all had alibis. The bloke's wife confirmed he had a few regulars, so they were found – nothing on them either. She also confirmed he had a mistress. The bastard had even bought an apartment for her in Paris, can you believe it? Anyway, she was cleared. So was his wife, by the way, poor woman. Two years ago, it comes to light that he had another mistress and – wait for this – an illegitimate child. The mistress contacts his wife, well, widow, to say that she was entitled to some of his money. She'd lost her job or something like that.'

'The widow?' asked Chrissy.

'No, no, the mistress. So the police investigated, but again there was no evidence to suggest it was her either. The article said that all lines of investigation had been explored and unless any new evidence was found the case was closed. Something like that. But the motel is now a block of HLM in any case.'

'What's "HLM"?' Eloise asked.

'It stands for *Habitation à Loyer Modéré*.'

'Council housing,' said Chrissy.

'So, basically the tone of it was that he was a complete and utter shit and deserved all he got. You know what the French are like, complete hypocrites.'

'What do you mean?' said Eloise.

'They like their bit on the side,' said Juliet. 'A kept mistress isn't unusual.'

'I'm not sure it's still like that, is it?' said Chrissy. 'Oh, maybe it is. What do I know? So no one went down for it? Thank god.'

Eloise hadn't even considered that outcome. Would her mother have turned herself in if she had discovered the wrong person had gone to prison? Knowing her, she probably would.

'I used to buy French newspapers all the time,' Chrissy said quietly, as if reading Eloise's mind. 'I'd scour the pages looking for updates and progress on the case. Listen to French radio obsessively for news, any indication that they were coming for me, so I could be ready. It drove Dan nuts; I was in such a state. So then I stopped. Just like that, buried my head in the sand. And for that I feel really quite ashamed.'

'You shouldn't,' said Juliet.

Chrissy laughed, but in a mocking sort of a way. 'No, you're right. Why should I care if yet another life got completely ruined? A complete stranger's, totally innocent.'

'But no one did get put away for it, that's what I'm saying.'

'Supposing they had, though, Mum? What would you have done?'

Her eyes were glossy when she turned to Eloise. 'I really don't know. It would have depended on so many things.'

'Well, there you have it,' said Juliet, bringing her hands together.

'You're safe. They'd have found you by now, Chrissy.'

'It's just me now is it? No more "we're in this together" and "I'm in this as much as you are"?'

Chrissy stood up and pushed over the chair she had been straddling. It clattered to the floor.

'Wait, no. That's not what I meant. But isn't this good news?'

'Juliet. I killed a man – a person; another human being. You have no fucking idea what that does to someone. What it's done to me. So you were right the first time: it's just me. No us.'

Chrissy grabbed her towel, heading outside again.

'Where are you going?' Juliet said desperately.

'To think, Juliet. Some of us do that.'

Eloise stole a look at Juliet's face. She couldn't read her expression but there was a kind of static coming off her. Shock or anger, Eloise couldn't tell.

***

There was no let-up in the sun, and nobody spoke. They did lazy lengths in the pool. After half an hour they came together on the steps, stretching out where the water was shallow in an attempt to stay cool.

'They would probably have found you first in any case,' said Chrissy.

'You reckon?' said Juliet, surprised by her remark. 'Why is that?'

'Just a feeling.' Chrissy got out and dripped her way across to the steel-framed hammock under the trees, a few of Juliet's magazines scattered beneath it.

Juliet got up too. She stood with her hands on her hips, facing Chrissy, and Eloise worried over what she might say.

'So, then. Does anyone fancy a trip into the village? Or we could get a couple of the scooters, go and explore?'

It was a *no* from Chrissy.

'Eloise?'

Eloise still felt bruised from the earlier incidents. Also, her mother might see it as taking sides. It had nothing to do with the fact she had spotted Nico out in the field with the horses. 'Think I'll just chill,' she said. 'Might take a walk in a bit.'

She watched Juliet wind her sarong around herself, intrigued at how she managed to turn it into a dress, like it had never been a sarong at all.

'Sure?' said Juliet.

Eloise nodded. She needed to return Nico's torch, after all.

Juliet mouthed the word *sorry* and blew her a kiss goodbye.

'I think she means well, Mum,' said Eloise.

'Yes, I suppose.'

'And it's good about what she said, don't you think? About … stuff?'

'Maybe.'

Chrissy flicked the pages of her magazine, not wanting to engage. On this occasion, that suited Eloise.

'Right, I'm off for a walk then. See you in a bit,' she said.

***

She set off without the torch and had to dash back to get it. By the time she got to the field Nico wasn't there any more. Then she spotted him leading a horse out of the stable block. By his careful handling, she assumed it was French Fry.

He looked up. Now she was committed.

The last thing she wanted was a repeat of the awkwardness from last night. He had seemed to enjoy it in some perverse way, making her feel like a tongue-tied schoolgirl. Maybe that was all she was in his eyes.

'*Grazie mille*,' she said, blushing when she handed over the torch.

Still holding onto the reins, he slid it into his pocket. French Fry threw his nose into the air. '*Sta' calmo*,' he said, stroking him.

244

'How is he?'

'A little better. The vet said maybe he has been bitten by some bug – do you say? Insect or something, but he is okay.'

Eloise put her hand on its nose. She had never actually touched a horse before and was amazed at how solid it felt.

'Do you ride?' asked Nico.

'I've never tried.'

'Do you want to?'

'Yeah,' she said. 'But he's not well.'

'I don't mean French Fry. For you, maybe—' He broke off to look at the other six horses dotted about the field pulling up clumps of dried-out grass with their enormous teeth. 'Well, you are quite tall but very light, and you have never ridden before. So therefore I think Cioccolato.'

'He sounds nice.' She laughed. 'Means chocolate, right?'

'You want to try?'

'What, now? I'm not really – I'm wearing flip-flops.'

'Okay. Maybe some other time.'

It opened up another deep silence. But it was Nico who filled it, much to her relief.

'Have you found the lake yet?' he asked. 'Most people miss it. It is so beautiful, very peaceful. You can walk there or take a bicycle. Also swim. It's very – how do you say … *solitario*?'

'I don't know. Solitary? Or maybe, like, private?'

'*Esatto*. If ever you need to escape.'

'Now?' She felt the blood rush to her cheeks again. 'Point me in the right direction I mean.'

'*Andiamo*. I just need to—' The words eluded him. She watched him lead French Fry away to the far end of the field then jog back. 'Oh, but still, your shoes,' he said, staring at her flip-flops.

'I'll be okay to walk in them.'

He set off at a brisk pace. She was cursing her choice of foot-wear, picking her way across the field trying to keep up. After a while he saw that she was struggling and waited for her. But this became the pattern. Until, suddenly, he pulled down on her hands, forcing her to sit. They had reached a grassy, secluded area with plenty of shade.

'Where's the lake?' she asked.

'We are not there yet.'

'Oh.'

She sat cross-legged, fanning herself, racking her brain for something to say. 'How do you manage to work in this heat, Nico?'

He gave her a sideways glance, pulling up a long strand of grass and chewing the end of it.

She tried again. 'So erm, do you always work here?'

He began to study her, which put her even more on edge. 'No. I also manage a bar in Florence with a friend,' he said, in his own time.

'Really? A bar in Florence.' That set her off wondering if the friend was just a friend, or something more.

'He does most of the work; we own it together.'

'Oh wow. So is he your …?'

Nico gave a short laugh. 'I like girls, if that is what you are asking.'

Eloise turned bright red and quickly tried to steer the conversation onto safer ground.

'And erm … Marianna, is she your mother?'

'Sì.'

'She's nice.'

Nico continued to stare at her, chewing on the blade of grass. Eloise couldn't quite put her finger on it. There was a sullenness about him. Maybe it was the language thing. 'Your English is very good,' she said lamely.

He shrugged, then stood up abruptly, offering his hand. She brushed down the back of her shorts as he pulled her to her feet. 'We should go back,' he said. 'Your shoes are very—'

'No! They're fine. Honestly.' It was the heat that bothered her more in any case, and that didn't matter either.

They set off again. Nico was soon ahead.

'Ouch!' she yelled, suddenly feeling her ankle twist.

He was quick to react, running back and guiding her over to a rock. 'Here, sit down, Eloise.'

She winced when he took hold of her leg. 'I went over on a stone.'

'I think you twist it. Does that hurt?'

'Yes. A little bit. Ooch.'

'Would you like me to – wait a minute, in English – carry you? We should go back, I think.'

'No, it's okay. I mean, I think we should go back but I'll manage.'

He scooped her up. 'Are you sure?'

'Whooh,' she yelped, putting her arms around his neck.

He seemed in a terrible hurry, and never once looked at her, so in the end she found it a humiliating experience, and as soon as they got within sight of their villa she asked to be set down. If her mother saw them like this, Eloise would face interrogation.

'*Qui?* Here?' he asked, sounding irritated.

Eloise nodded, trying not to show her disappointment. 'I can walk the rest.'

'You need to put on some ice,' he replied, pointing to her foot.

'I'll do that. Thanks.'

'The lake is only a little bit – erm, not far. I am sure you will find it.'

'Thanks anyway.'

The moment she pressed down on her ankle she felt a sharp pain but was so desperate for a quick exit, she didn't let on.

'I'll take you there tomorrow if you like, Eloise. By scooter. You know, Vespa? Here, take this.'

He handed her a card. She read the words 'Dream Tuscany'.

'You message me tomorrow. In the morning,' he shouted, running off in the direction of the horses.

***

Juliet was still out exploring when she got back, and Chrissy was taking a siesta indoors. She took an ice pack out of the freezer, wrapping a tea towel around it.

'Are you awake, Mum? Can I come in?' she said, gently tapping on her door.

'Of course.'

Chrissy spotted the ice pack right away.

'What's that for?'

'My ankle. It's fine, don't worry. Just a mild sprain.' Eloise stretched out on the bed like a starfish, losing herself in her daydream. 'I went over in my flip-flops. It's really nothing.'

She still insisted on taking a look, but seemed satisfied it wasn't anything serious and placed the ice pack carefully under her ankle. Chrissy plopped back down beside her and, after a few seconds silence, came out with: 'Telling your father was the hardest thing I ever had to do.'

'Pardon?' said Eloise.

Chrissy's eyes were glassy and she was staring off into the distance. Eloise's throat was dry and her ankle throbbed; for once she wasn't in the mood. But her mother carried on talking, and Eloise owed it to her to listen.

CHAPTER 28

Manchester & Bristol: summer, 1989

'So come on then, how was France?'

Chrissy shrugged, choked by the anguish of what she knew she had to tell him.

'That good, eh?' said Dan, making her sit down. They were alone now, everyone else was out.

This was the time.

Chrissy burst into tears; she couldn't help it.

'Hey, what's up? Did something happen?'

She nodded, faintly. Contemplating where on earth to begin. Dan had to know what he was taking on; he deserved that at least. A pattern of behaviour soon set in. She would sob, hyperventilate, spend hours just staring at the floor then fall asleep. Her parents thought she had some kind of bug. A foreign bug. She looked well enough; the suntan gave her a healthy glow. She had lost weight, but with some good home cooking inside her she would soon put it back on. They didn't press her about the trip either. Chrissy said it had gone well, they found jobs, made friends, her French improved. Her parents didn't need to know that their daughter had come home a killer.

She was learning to live the lie.

'You think I should go to the police, don't you?'

By the end of the second day, Dan knew everything.

'I don't know, Chrissy. I just don't know.'

Her fingernails were so badly chewed they were starting to bleed. 'I think that too. Sometimes. So maybe I should. Look, Dan, if you decide to bail out on me I totally understand. I'm not sure I could …'

'Listen,' he said, holding her firmly by the shoulders. 'We don't have to rush this. If you turn yourself in today or in six months it's not going to make much difference. You said yourself there's no evidence in your favour. You'd just be confessing to murder basically. It'd be up to a jury to believe you. Or not.' He tailed off at the end.

'What the fuck is happening to us, Dan?' She sobbed into his chest. But the only face she could see was *his* and she pulled away again.

'*No. Fuck you.*'

Arsehole.

***

The start of term was drawing near. Since she had been back she hadn't picked up a single book or felt the slightest interest in what she would be studying in her second year. Even Sartre and Camus could not inspire her. In fact, all that existential stuff only made things worse. Why had she killed him? What was her motivation? Did she do it out of hate for him or love of Juliet? If only she could become *en-soi*, like a bird or a tree or a pen and be totally without consciousness, then things would be simpler.

Dan was being supportive, as best he could, but it had come close to tearing them apart. At least now, with some gentle coaxing, she was allowing him to get close. He taught her to trust him again with her body, lying naked together for hours. Their love-making had changed, sometimes slower and more intense, but often there was a reckless sense of urgency, as though it could well be their last time.

Juliet was in her thoughts. She missed her but was terrified of seeing her again. Their friendship could never be like it was; Chrissy had worked that out when they were still in the motel room. And Bristol would never be the same either. Her degree was trivial and pointless, a million miles from the person she was now.

Maybe she would feel differently when she went back.

She didn't.

'At least go to one lecture, Chrissy,' Juliet tried to coax her. She laughed at the irony. 'This doesn't feel right, me telling you.'

Chrissy would only shake her head, or say: 'I can't.'

'But it's been nearly four weeks. They'll kick you off the course. Maybe you could get some time off sick, if you actually go and see someone, tell someone. I don't mean tell … well, you know what I mean. Tell them you're ill. There must be some special dispensation. There was that lad in the first year who went off the rails and he came back.'

'And committed suicide,' Chrissy reminded her.

'Hm, bad example.'

'I'm not going to do that.'

''Course you're bloody not. Look, this will pass, Chrissy, I know it will. I feel exactly the same. The whole nightmare keeps playing out every time I shut my eyes. But I won't let it beat me. I won't let *him* beat me. And nor should you. Don't let him.'

'It's not the same though. It's really not the same.'

'Yes, it is.'

'No. No, Ju. I killed him, not you.'

She wished they had never stepped into his car. She wished they had never gone to France. She wished she had gone to a different university, never set foot in Bristol. But, most of all, and no matter how much she tried to push it out of her head, she wished she had never clapped eyes on Juliet.

251

The temptation was to drink herself into a twenty-four-hour oblivion. That was impossible because she had to stay alert at all times. Juliet, on the other hand, was not so disciplined, and Chrissy worried about her drunkenness and what she might say. As time went on she realized this was not really an issue. It became apparent that Juliet's way of dealing with their ordeal was to put it out of her mind altogether, as though it never happened. Something which made Chrissy feel both relieved and envious about in equal measure.

On those rare occasions when Chrissy did leave the house she knew she had to remain vigilant. Who was that man? Why was he following her? Was he still following her? And why did people want to know what she had done over the summer? Why did they keep asking if there was something wrong?

Trust no one. Keep your mouth shut. Distance yourself from everyone, except Dan and Juliet.

'You're punishing yourself too much,' said Juliet. 'We're going to have a party. I'm going to invite Dan, maybe get his band to play. What do you think?'

'I think no.'

Dan did come down that weekend, but without the band. He took Chrissy out for a curry instead, to get her out of the house.

'Chrissy, come and dance,' Juliet called when they got back. The party was in full flow, some of the old crowd were there, and a new lot from Juliet's fashion course. Juliet had put The Smiths on specially.

'I'm going up, Dan. You can stay if you want to.' She was already halfway upstairs.

Dan came up later. Chrissy was almost asleep. He started nuzzling her, hungry for sex, and she felt that she couldn't deny him. Afterwards, though, he noticed she was crying. 'Hey, what's up? What did I do? Tell me.'

'No, it's not you, Dan. I can't live with this for the rest of my life. I've made up my mind to go to the police.'

He was nodding, trying to take in what she was saying. 'They could put you away for a long time, you do realize that?'

'It's okay, I don't expect you to wait for me.'

'I'll support you, whatever you decide.'

She smiled at him, knowing that would be the end.

***

Chrissy squinted up at the sky. She couldn't have chosen a nicer day. Bright sunshine, blue sky, thin clouds breaking across it. Dan was meeting her at eleven. They would drink a coffee together and then he would go with her to the police station. At least that was the plan.

But that couldn't happen now.

Coffee slopped over the sides as Dan set the mugs down on the table, scraping his chair nearer to sit opposite her.

'I keep thinking I'm going to wake up from this nightmare,' he said. 'And I don't.'

Chrissy sat on her hands to stop them from shaking. She had tremors in both legs too. Dan may not want her to go to the police, but he agreed it was the right thing to do. What would he say now she had changed her mind?

'I don't think I can do it, Dan. Despite what I said.'

He was looking at her in turmoil. She knew this was destroying him

'Okay,' he replied, rubbing his face. He was trying to sound patient. 'Well, maybe you just need more time. We can wait a few more days.'

'No. I can't ever do it. Not ever. I'm pregnant.'

He looked at her in bewilderment, waiting to be told it wasn't true. When that didn't come, he put his head in his hands grabbing at thick clumps of hair. 'Fuck me,' he said, banging the table repeatedly with his fist. 'Fuck me!'

'Well, yeah,' she said, trying to calm him. 'I guess we've been

253

a bit careless.' She wanted to say *since France* but couldn't bring herself to. It was too painful to reflect on how much her life had changed. 'I want to go through with it, Dan. I *need* to. I'm not going to the police and I'm going to come home, back to Manchester. Maybe not just yet. I haven't told Mum and Dad. But honestly, I don't want you to feel like you have to do this. You have your music and all the stuff you want to do.'

He sat up straight, still contemplating her.

'Please. Say something,' she said.

Dan blew air out of his cheeks. 'Are you sure?'

'I had it confirmed at the doctor's. It's for real, Dan. This is happening to us.'

He stood up, placed his hands on the wall, leaning his body into it. Someone needed to get past with a tray so he sat down again.

'Look, I'll understand, whatever you decide. But no one knows, okay? Not even Juliet. I need to start again and she can't ever find me.'

Dan placed his hands over hers, like he had suddenly found a solution. 'No one's forcing you to do this either, Chrissy. You *can* change your mind.'

'No. No. That's not an option.' He pulled his hands away again, sat back in his chair. 'You don't have to decide now. But that's my final decision, Dan. I mean, just so you know.'

She held onto his gaze. She knew what was coming next.

'I'm sorry,' he said. 'I'm really sorry, Chrissy.'

***

The next day she thought Dan had already left Bristol and gone back to Manchester. His things had been removed from her room, razor, toothbrush, a few spare clothes. They had all gone. But then, in the afternoon, she heard Juliet talking to someone down-

254

stairs, followed by footsteps on the floorboards leading to her room.

'Can I come in?'

He looked terrible.

'Did you forget something?' she asked when he didn't say anything.

He shook his head, running his fingers through his hair, staring at her in that intense way.

'Well, do you want to—'

'I can't do this, Chrissy.'

'No. No, you said. I understand.' Her voice was tight with hurt.

'No, I mean – I can't lose you, I can't. I'm scared shitless but … I love you. Fuck's sake.'

He held her to his chest, but where there should have been happiness or relief, Chrissy just felt something break inside her. The tears streamed down her face as she contemplated their future. Where would they get the money; where would they live?

And when she closed her eyes, she still saw the face of the man she had killed.

CHAPTER 29

Tuscany: 2007

'So I was the reason you chucked it all in then,' said Eloise, her voice flat. She was running through all the implications in her mind. 'You always said it wasn't, but it was. I screwed up your life. *And* my dad's.'

She flung the ice pack onto the floor. Chrissy held onto her arm as she tried to escape.

'No, Eloise. Wait, no, please don't run off. I'm sorry, that's not what I meant – I was going to quit uni anyway. I was going to hand myself in, for Christ's sake. Instead, I had you, and you became the most important thing in my world. That, and being with your dad. You saved me.'

'But you always said I came along after you went back home. It's not true though, is it?'

'Well, you did. I admit it was a little sooner than we might have planned it. But you and Dan were all I wanted and nothing else mattered to me. I couldn't just go on with life as it had been. You were very special, Eloise. Always. To me and your dad. You *are* very special.'

'But you just said Dad wasn't sure.'

Chrissy looked uncomfortable. Eloise was struck by the notion that, for a minute, Chrissy had forgotten to whom she was telling her story. The floodgates were well and truly open.

'I'm sorry, sweetheart. It was a big decision for both of us. He was sure once he got his head round it. We were just so young.'

Eloise stiffened in her mother's arms, resisting her embrace. A loud knocking suddenly returned them to the present. They had lost all sense of where they were.

'Only *moi*. Anybody home?'

It was Juliet.

Eloise managed to free herself, pulling away sharply.

'I've found us a lovely restaurant for tonight,' Juliet shouted. They could hear her heels clicking on the tiles. 'Booked a table for eight o'clock.'

'You okay with all that?' Chrissy gently brushed the hair out of her eyes, and Eloise gave a shrug. But actually her mother was right. She had to be okay with it because this was the truth she had asked for. There was just so much of the stuff.

'Am I talking to myself again?' Juliet said in a sing-song voice. 'Has anyone seen my cigarettes?'

'Come on, we'd better go or she'll think we've left the country,' said Chrissy. 'She'll be going demented without her fags.'

Eloise managed a smile.

***

Sleep was an ordeal that night. First, her ankle was throbbing. Then when she did drift off, Eloise was plagued by nightmares; her mother, heavily pregnant, being led away in handcuffs; the businessman creeping in, climbing on top of Eloise, leering at her as he had surely done to Juliet. Chrissy clutching a shard of glass, her hands covered in blood, come to save her. When morning finally arrived, Eloise woke up in a cold sweat, bedclothes in a heap on the floor.

'We're taking a car to Siena today,' said Juliet at breakfast, watching Eloise hobble to the table. 'Do you fancy that?'

'You look tired,' Chrissy remarked, sounding apologetic.

'Well, my ankle isn't really up to it. But you two go. I'll be fine just chilling here.'

'No!' said Chrissy. 'I'll stay and keep you company. You go, Juliet.'

'Not on my own. How about Siena tomorrow then? Or the next day?'

Chrissy seemed to bristle. 'We've not spent much time together, you and I. Have we, Eloise? Let me look after you.'

'Told you I'll be fine. I'm going back to bed.'

Eloise limped away again, to her room, praying that her plans would not be scuppered. Shortly after, Chrissy came to see her and sat down on the bed.

'Are you sure you'll be okay? We won't be back till this evening.'

'Hey, who put my cigarettes in the bin?' they heard Juliet shout. Chrissy rolled her eyes.

'That wasn't you, was it?' said Eloise.

'Filthy habit anyway.'

'Mum! Oh look, I'll be fine, I can take care of myself. You go. It'll be good for you and Juliet to spend the day together.' Chrissy pulled a face. 'At least give it a go. Please, Mum. For me.'

'I'm worried about you.'

'My foot's okay.'

'I meant with all the other stuff I've dumped on you, Eloise.'

'It's fine. I just need some space.'

Chrissy nodded. 'Ring me, and I'll head straight back.'

***

The murmur of a scooter engine gave her a brief moment of doubt. What was she doing, going off to the lake with a boy she didn't know? Hadn't she learned anything from Chrissy's story?

After a final check in the mirror, shorts and T-shirt over her bikini, she headed out.

Nico revved the engine in a sort of mock-macho way, giving her a nod to take a seat behind him. His stomach felt firm, sliding her arms around his waist, and she caught a faint trace of horses through his musky scent. The dust kicked up in a swirl as they set off. They passed Marianna, who waved at them from the path. At least someone had seen them going off together.

But what if Marianna told her mother? Too late now.

It seemed no distance at all to the lake. As the track became rockier, Eloise was able to hold onto him tighter, breathing him in without his knowing. Now they were at a standstill she was suddenly struck by the seclusion of this place he had brought her to.

'It is very nice here, no?' he said, pulling out the kickstand with his foot. 'Beautiful and calm.'

She nodded, taking in the view. A line of trees around the lake's circumference made it seem bigger than it probably was. The blue-sky gaps in between the branches created the illusion it extended out further, to the hills beyond. Nico said it was deep towards the middle. There was no movement except for the tiny waves lapping at their feet. He pulled his T-shirt over his head then hurled himself into the water.

'Is it cold?' she shouted.

'Come and see. *Andiamo!*' He bounced down into a dive and disappeared.

Eloise stripped down to her bikini, tentative at first, but when Nico re-emerged and shook his hair into a shimmering water-wheel, she hurried herself along.

'Come, Eloise! Come and swim.'

It was rocky underfoot and her ankle was still tender. Flip-flops would actually have been useful today, had she thought to bring them.

'*Allora*,' said Nico, pushing her head under. She felt him grab her legs, kicking out to swim away from him. He was faster, and came to a stop right in front of her, which forced her to tread water.

The sun danced on the ripples their fingers made.

They swam together for a while but he seemed to want to go much further out into the lake. She watched him fade into the distance before going to lie in the sun. Her towel was spread on the ground as she had left it. She removed her bikini top and lay down, closing her eyes, enjoying the frisson of water drying on her skin.

'I love this lake,' said Nico, suddenly standing over her, rubbing his arms on the towel.

'God, you scared me!'

Eloise grabbed her T-shirt to cover herself, flipping swiftly onto her front. She could feel the drips from his body onto hers.

'Were you sleeping?' he said, tossing the towel aside, putting himself down next to her.

'No.'

She moved up to make some room. He edged nearer, until they were almost touching. How could she stop this? Did she need to? She was desperate to put her T-shirt back on but didn't dare move. In a moment of panic, she asked: 'Do you have a girlfriend, Nico?'

It was as if someone else had said it. She was unable to look him in the eye after that.

He tutted. 'I like to stay free, *come il vento*. Like the wind,' he replied, threading his fingers through hers. 'What about you, Eloise? Do you have a boyfriend?'

'Me? Oh. Not really. Erm, no one serious.'

'I am lucky, then, that you are here all alone.'

She let out a nervous laugh. 'Not quite,' she reminded him.

Her response left a dent in the conversation. She didn't want him to think she was scared. 'Still, it's good to escape from those two,' she added. 'Driving me nuts.' He looked confused. 'Erm, *folle?* I've no idea in Italian. They make me crazy.'

'Ah!' he said. 'So one of them is your mother? Mothers, they are always driving us crazy.'

If only he knew.

'My mother, yes. And Juliet. She's ... a really old friend.'

This was how it would be from now on. She had to be careful, make sure she didn't let slip, reveal too much. Not even to someone she wanted to get close to. She was trapped, burdened with her mother's secret locked away inside her. She felt tears gather in her eyes.

'Eloise, what is it?'

'I'm sorry. I didn't mean ... It's just, I miss my dad sometimes. This is the first proper holiday I've been on since he died, and I sort of wish he was here instead of Juliet.'

This hadn't even occurred to her until now, when it suited as an excuse. That made her feel even worse. Nico wiped away her tears with his towel. Then he sat up, tossing a stone into the water.

She took the opportunity to put her bikini top back on, fumbling with the clasp. Believing he was trying to help, she turned to make it easier for him. Instead, he removed it again, saying: 'You're more beautiful like that, Eloise.'

She smiled, shyly. 'Aren't you supposed to be working?'

'I hardly tell anyone about the lake,' Nico whispered. 'It's very special.'

Stroking her cheek, he moved his body in close again. Eloise thought he was going to kiss her, but his finger traced along her neck then down between her breasts. She drew breath sharply and closed her eyes. When she couldn't stand it any longer she pressed her mouth against his, feeling her body being lowered onto the towel.

Eloise wasn't sure who broke away first but it felt like they needed to. Nico sat up, staring out at the lake. Eloise curled onto her side, relieved to take a moment over what just happened.

'Sometimes I come here at night to swim,' he said. 'You know, totally … erm, naked. Is that the word? Have you ever done that, Eloise?'

'Yes. I mean, no.' She slipped her T-shirt back on and sat up. He didn't look at her. 'What I mean is, naked is the correct word, but I've never done that.'

'You should try it sometime. There is no better freedom.'

'We call it skinny-dipping in English.'

'Skinny?'

'Dipping. I guess it's like dipping your skin in the water.'

'Hm. Well, you really should try it,' he said, throwing another stone in. 'So, do we ride horses tomorrow?'

'Erm, yeah. I guess.'

'Does that mean *sì* or *no*?'

'It means *sì*.'

He pointed to her ankle.

'It's fine,' she said.

He took hold of it, ran his hand up and down her calf, squeezing it gently. 'It hurts?'

'Not really. I put some ice on it, like you said.'

Nico stood up. 'Another swim?'

'Thanks. I'll just watch.'

'Very good. That way you can improve.'

Eloise reached out to grab his leg, but he was already on the move. She loved the way he attacked the water and swam into the middle of the lake like he owned it. Sinking into her daydream, she lost track of how long he'd been gone, and got a shock when the heat from the sun disappeared and he was standing over her again.

'I must go now,' he said as he dried himself. 'But I can come back for you later. If you want me to.'

'It's okay,' she replied, shielding her eyes so she could see him properly. He had stepped to one side and the sun was glaring into her face. 'I'll walk back when I'm ready.'

Eloise watched him get onto his Vespa. She hung on to the noise of the engine for as long as she could.

As the silence deepened, she removed her T-shirt and lay down on her towel. It wasn't long before the remoteness of the place made her feel uneasy again.

***

The rest of the afternoon she lazed by the pool. It felt safer here than being at the lake by herself, and she was able to swim without getting out of her depth. As she dozed in the sun, she noticed that her body was sensitive to every touch. Even the sweep of the breeze across her skin.

'She sleeps,' a voice whispered in her ear.

Eloise felt a cold sensation on her back, the smell of sun cream, and strong hands massaging it into her skin. A hand slid underneath her bikini and out again.

'Nico,' she whispered.

He lowered himself onto her, his body pressing down, pushing her breasts into the towel. She could feel him between her buttocks.

'Stop,' she whispered, but she didn't want him to.

He raised himself up so she could turn over onto her back. She smiled, gazing up at him. She wanted to stay like this forever. Suddenly her arms were pushed out wide, she felt his tongue zigzagging down her body. When he reached her stomach, her muscles tensed, creating a gap for his tongue to slide under the waistband of her bikini.

'Nico, no.'

This time she really did want him to stop. Was that a car engine she had just heard? If Chrissy caught them like this, she would put her on the next plane to Manchester.

'Nic.'

He stopped, laid down beside her, resting on his elbow and brushing a strand of hair out of her eyes. '*Sei bellissima*, Eloise.'

She looked away. They had gone too far, too fast.

He made a grab for her phone that was resting on top of her book.

'Hey, what are you doing?'

'We can make a photo together,' he said, moving in closer.

Eloise sat up, forgetting she was topless, and now it bothered her. 'Sorry,' she said, even though that was stupid. Covering herself with her T-shirt she took the phone and held it above their heads, trying to keep the T-shirt in place. 'You'll have to come a bit nearer,' she directed.

Nico moved down, placing his arm round her shoulders.

'Okay, now say Cheese Eloise.'

'What? What is this cheese?'

'It's what my dad used to say to make us smile. Ready?'

'Cheese Eloise!' they shouted together, laughing.

CLICK.

Nico stood up. 'See you tomorrow.'

'Oh. Well, don't you want to see the photo?'

'I know it will be beautiful. Tomorrow we will ride into the hills. Together. Far away. Never come back.'

'I'd like that.'

Definitely a car engine that time. Followed by the grinding of a handbrake.

'Nico, you have to go!'

She put her bikini top back on as quickly as she could, smoothed down her hair, put on her shades, and by the time she heard footsteps coming down the stairs she had her nose in her book.

'*Ciao, ciao,*' shouted Juliet.

'Gosh, you look like you've had a lot of sun, Eloise,' said Chrissy, dumping her things on the table. 'See how red your skin is. So how was it?'

Eloise felt a tiny bead of sweat trickle down her back. 'How was what?'

'Your day. Your ankle.'

'Oh. All good, thanks. How was yours?'

'*Have* to take you to Siena, Eloise,' said Juliet, slipping out of her shoes and dangling them off one finger. 'It's the most divine place.'

Chrissy nodded, letting Juliet carry on with the description. The Duomo, Palazzo, Piazza del Campo, the Torre del Mangia … the magic of those places, told in Juliet's seductive voice, allowed Eloise to slip into a fantasy all of her own. Going there with Nico on the back of his Vespa, wandering round the Piazza holding hands.

Lost in a daydream, Eloise missed what Chrissy and Juliet were saying, until her mother leaned in to kiss her cheek. Or, at least, she thought she was going to kiss her cheek. Instead she whispered: 'We need to talk, Eloise.'

***

Eloise was in bed, gazing at the image on her phone when she heard a light tapping on her door.

'Can I come in?'

'Yeah, 'course.' She fumbled with her phone, struggling to turn it off before her mother saw the photo of her and Nico by the pool.

'Anything interesting?' she asked, sitting beside her.

'Oh. No, just Anya.' Eloise slapped her phone face down on the bed. Chrissy didn't say anything, and it began to make her uncomfortable, unable to gauge her mother's mood. 'Sounds like you and Juliet had a good day, Mum.'

'Why didn't you tell me she'd put money into your account?'

The fierceness in her tone came as a shock.

'Erm. Well, because I knew you'd be cross? She said it was my uni fund and that she would be my sponsor. What could I say?'

'How much is it?'

'I – I don't know.'

'Yes, you do. How much?'

'Five thousand pounds. Please don't go mad with her, Mum. She just wants to help.'

Her eyes had turned a watery blue. Her voice softened. 'I don't want to lose you, Eloise.'

'Of course you won't lose me – that's the last thing I want. Look, I'll tell Juliet to take the money back again, if you like. Just don't make a deal of it. Please.'

'I'd give anything to turn the clock back,' she said, drifting.

'I know that, Mum.' Eloise gave her a moment. 'And I know you'd still be friends with Juliet, if it wasn't for France.'

It was her stare; one of those that just wouldn't let go. Eloise knew there was something else besides. And then she noticed her pulling something out of her back pocket, feeling sick when she saw what it was.

'You said this was lost.'

It was the yellow bear that Juliet had given to her dad all those years ago. Eloise's mind was like a jigsaw as she frantically tried to piece together how it had ended up in her mother's hands. Surely Juliet hadn't been stupid enough to tell her?

'I returned it to Juliet,' she began, praying this sounded plausible. 'When you told me the story of how she'd given it to my dad in Bristol, I just felt that it wasn't really mine. I knew how much my dad liked Juliet, what good mates they were, and I thought it was better to let her keep it from now on.'

She was struggling as she spoke to block out the memory of Anton breaking into their flat and taking it.

But that wasn't the issue.

'Why is it so bad that I gave it back to her?'

'Because your dad wouldn't want her to have it.'

'Why not?'

'Because he gave it to you.'

Her mother was holding it out to her.

'I don't even want that thing any more,' Eloise said, knocking it out of her hand. 'Is there something else you've not told me? There is, isn't there? What?'

Chrissy picked the yellow bear up off the floor, pulling its head so hard it became detached from the rest of the body, the stuffing hanging out of its neck.

CHAPTER 30

Bristol: 1989

The snow was only a light dusting, but lethal if it froze over. They lived on the steepest hill in Redland, and Dan was spotted doing wheel spins at the bottom of it. Everyone rushed out to push. Everyone except Chrissy. There was another person to think of now, besides herself, and she had to remember that.

As if she could forget.

It wasn't easy throwing up in the mornings so that no one else in the house would hear. Juliet had refused to leave her side these past few days, constantly begging her to stay. She had even wanted to sleep in her bed but Chrissy refused. For one thing, she didn't want Juliet knowing about her morning sickness. And for another, after today, they had to get used to being apart forever.

She threw herself into her arms, sobbing. 'I'm not sure I can survive without you, Chrissy. I just can't bear the thought.'

'Of course you will, Ju. You know I'll never forget you. And you'll always be my best friend.' She put her hand to her heart. 'In here.'

Dan was keen to get going as soon as the van was loaded. He

gave Juliet a brief hug goodbye. The snow was giving him a focus, which Chrissy was glad about because she knew how much Dan would miss Juliet, too. To think that Juliet would not be a part of their future, nor would they play any part in hers, was inconceivable right now. She didn't even have the faintest idea that Chrissy was pregnant. Her best friend; she couldn't even tell her that.

Dan started up the engine, and when Chrissy wound down the window Juliet stuck her hands through.

'Please, Chrissy. Can't we just stay in touch?'

'No. I told you, it's too dangerous.'

'But you're not leaving because of any other reason. Are you?

'Like what?'

Dan revved the engine. 'The snow's getting heavy,' he said.

Chrissy made sure her eyes were facing forwards and not on Juliet as they moved off slowly; Dan trying to get traction on the road. The yellow bear was on the dashboard. Chrissy picked it up and held it tightly to her chest. They were on their way.

'What do you think she meant? Have you any idea?' Chrissy asked, having reflected upon it a while. 'You don't think she suspects, do you?'

'No,' said Dan. Then: 'Yes.'

'Oh god, really?'

'No, not about the baby. But I know what she meant.'

'What?'

'She tried to kiss me. It was a moment, Chrissy. A stupid moment, and she apologized.'

'When?'

'The night of the party. She was drunk, worried about you, still traumatized about France. You know what a mess it all is. Everything's so screwed up.'

Chrissy let this filter through the chaos already tormenting her brain before she could respond.

'And, so, what if I asked Juliet? What would she say happened?'

'Look, I've told you, haven't I?' said Dan, hitting the steering wheel. 'Is that not good enough for you? If we can't trust one another, Chrissy, then we may as well quit now. The truth is there are bigger things to worry about than a kiss that never happened. We're going to be parents, fuck's sake. And we're never even going to see Juliet again.'

She tossed the bear into the back. She was sick of the truth.

Her tears were silent all the way back to Manchester, burning into her cheeks like acid.

CHAPTER 31

Tuscany: 2007

It was morning. It must be.

Eloise was aware of someone shouting, slowing pulling her back from sleep. '*Buongiorno*. Are you awake yet? Cuckoo.'

Chrissy was fast asleep next to her, fully clothed on top of the covers.

'Mum. Mum, wake up.'

'What?' she said, drowsily.

She felt her body go rigid as they heard voices in the next room. 'Who is it?' she asked.

'It's only Marianna. I think Juliet's with her.'

They could hear bits of their conversation drifting in, weather-related mostly. Marianna said something about the temperature set to rise above 40 degrees again, and then a joke about it being a very British talking point.

'I guess we ought to show our faces,' said Chrissy, getting up off the bed, rearranging her clothes.

Eloise noticed the yellow bear caught up in the sheet. Its head was hanging off. She kicked it onto the floor.

'Are you still angry with Juliet for trying to kiss my dad?'

Eloise wasn't sure how she felt about it herself. Of course, among her friends, snogging your mate's boyfriend was considered the ultimate betrayal. But, compared to everything else Juliet and Chrissy had been through, it didn't seem like such a big deal. Juliet had hinted at some mild flirtation when they were in Rome – that she had only wanted to test Dan's loyalty towards her mother.

Chrissy stood still for a moment, pensive.

'Oh, I suppose I was just angry with the world,' she said through a sigh. 'Your dad was right, I overreacted. And I'd no business to, not really. It's all in the past now anyway.'

She was making for the door.

'All Juliet wants to do now, though, Mum, is help us. Can't we just let her?'

'Come on, let's go.'

***

'Out!' said Chrissy.

They were attempting a game of tennis before the sun was fully ablaze. It was Eloise's idea, an attempt to lure Juliet away on her own, but Chrissy had installed herself at the side of the court in a chair that she found in the small hut nearby. Even though she was umpiring in Eloise's favour, Juliet was far too good and the heat was making Eloise lethargic. She used her ankle as an excuse and they abandoned the tennis for the pool, where Eloise hoped to get her moment with Juliet.

'Does anyone fancy pizza tonight?' Juliet asked after finishing her power lengths up and down. 'I quite fancy having a go with that oven.' It was a shrug from Chrissy and a nod from Eloise. 'I'll see about getting a scooter again then. Pop down into the village and get some provisions. Fancy joining me, Eloise?'

Then she felt torn. There were things she really wanted to clarify with Juliet, and Chrissy rarely gave them a moment, but Eloise had other plans for the rest of the day.

'I've arranged to go horse riding,' she replied, biting her lip. Nico might never ask her again.

'As you wish,' said Juliet.

'Wait,' shouted Eloise, chasing after her. 'I have a shopping list.'

She didn't. But when she reached Juliet she pretended to be writing things down, half-obscuring them both from Chrissy. 'I know you tried to kiss my dad, Juliet,' she whispered.

'She told you that?' Juliet considered it for a moment. 'Hey Chrissy,' she shouted.

'Juliet, what're you doing?' Eloise grabbed her arm, digging her nails in.

'Do you like anchovies on your pizza?'

'Don't mind,' Chrissy shouted back, peering over the top of her sunglasses.

Eloise let go of her arm with a huge sigh of relief. 'So why did you tell her about the money in my account? I thought we'd agreed not to say anything about that.'

'Your mother and I have always told each other everything, Eloise. And I thought she'd be pleased.'

'See if you can get some grenadine, Juliet,' Chrissy shouted over. 'For old times' sake.'

'What about the bear then?' Eloise asked, finding it harder to keep her voice down. 'Did you show her that, too?'

'Great idea, Chrissy,' Juliet shouted back. Then: 'No, 'course not. She just spotted it. I carry it around in my bag. I like to keep it close; it's a lovely reminder of those younger days. Look we're good, Eloise. You just have to trust me; it's all going to plan.'

'But what's the plan. Juliet?'

'These pizzas are going to be the best you've ever tasted,' she shouted, walking away.

Eloise returned to the pool, mulling things over.

'That must have been a long shopping list,' said her mother. 'You okay, Eloise?'

'Oh. Yeah, I realized I've run out of a few things. Trying to remember if I forgot anything.'

She did a couple more lengths of the pool. Chrissy was still lounging in the hammock with her book. Surprisingly, she seemed more relaxed today.

'Okay, well, I'm going to get ready,' Eloise announced, getting out of the pool and dripping over to her.

'Oh,' said Chrissy, peering over the rim of her sunglasses. 'That wasn't a joke then, about the horse riding?'

'Of course it wasn't a joke, Mum. It's good to try these things.'

'Who're you going with?'

'Marianna's sorting it for me.'

'Well, take some water from the fridge. And bring some down for me, would you?'

It was a relief to be back indoors where it was cool and peaceful. Having the place to herself gave her some time to shift her mind back into seeing Nico again.

After a cold shower she quickly got dressed. Pulling her ponytail through her Ricci baseball cap, checking her look in the mirror, she was ready to set off. As she passed Chrissy's room she was sure she heard a noise. 'Mum, is that you?' she said, edging towards the door, pushing it lightly with her finger.

'Juliet! I thought you'd gone. What are you doing in here?'

She was over by Chrissy's wardrobe. It looked like she was going through her clothes. She even had on one of her mother's old sweatshirts that she wore nearly all the time.

Juliet had been crying.

'I lost her,' she wailed. 'She saved me and then just … abandoned me.' She was clutching one of Chrissy's T-shirts, lifting it up to her face to breathe in her smell.

'She had to though,' said Eloise. Despite the bizarreness of the situation, she did understand her pain. 'It must have been awful for you, Juliet. I know if I lost my best friend I'd be devastated too. But you've found her again now.'

'The trouble is I don't know how to make her like me again.'

'Well, I guess things have to get worse before they can get better,' said Eloise, repeating Juliet's words back to her.

Juliet smiled. 'I'm sorry. I got overwhelmed all of a sudden. I was supposed to be going into town to get provisions, wasn't I? You won't say a word about this, will you?'

'Er, definitely not,' said Eloise. 'And you'd better take that off before she sees you in it, or she'll think you're taking the piss out of her clothes.'

**

'Here,' she said, slapping a cool bottle of water into her mother's hand. Eloise watched her glug it down. She kicked at the cracks in the sun-baked ground. 'You won't be mean to Juliet when I'm gone, will you?'

'It's too hot for that,' she replied. 'With any luck she'll set fire to herself with that pizza oven.'

Eloise took a moment to realize she was joking. She tutted and gave the hammock a shove.

'Just let me know when you're ready to go home, Eloise.'

'What? To Manchester?'

'Well, yes, that is where we live.'

'Already? Do you want to go home?'

'Are you going to be all right on horseback, do you think?'

'Come with me if you're so worried about me.' Eloise tried not sound too irritated. She knew full well that her mother wouldn't come, but the excuse she gave was a little unexpected.

'I'm allergic to horses,' she said.

'I never knew that.'

'You don't know everything, Eloise.'

'I thought I did now.'

Chrissy pushed her sunglasses back up her nose. 'Who're you going with again?'

'I told you, Marianna's sorting it for me.'

She returned to her book, cracking the spine.

Eloise gave the hammock a final shove and shouted: 'Enjoy!'

Chrissy reached over to hit her backside with the book but only succeeded in tipping herself out of the hammock.

'Fuck!' she heard her say.

'The word is *fluck*, Maman!'

***

Eloise ran towards the field where she could see Nico galloping about on a very impressive black beast. She hoped this was his horse and not the promised Cioccolato, especially when it suddenly flicked its back legs into the air jerking him forwards. Maybe she should have listened to her mother. She watched him take a series of jumps and he seemed at one with his horse. When she realized he was cantering towards her, she waved. 'Are we still going?' she shouted.

'I have prepared Cioccolato for you.'

Without warning, a hot flush consumed her entire body as she considered what they had been doing yesterday. She managed to recover as Nico began to explain the basics of how to hold onto the reins, how to start and stop, and how to turn. Then, with his help, she managed to get onto Cioccolato's back, alarmed at how high up she was.

'Okay, Eloise?'

'I – I think so.'

'So let's go.'

He swung himself up onto the black horse, steadying it with the reins. Cioccolato set off without any encouragement, which was just as well, as Eloise hadn't taken in a single instruction.

'Relax,' he shouted, waiting for them to catch up. 'Okay,' he continued. 'It's a little difficult to explain, but it's a feeling. You know?'

She didn't know what he was talking about and shook her head. 'Well, it's just you feel the movement of the horse but you don't think about it. It's like, you *just* feel.'

'I can feel something,' she said, her cheeks burning.

He spurred his horse on. She was relieved that he set a slow pace across the field, and they were soon out among vineyards and olive groves. Once she completely trusted that Cioccolato was perfectly capable of negotiating the narrow winding paths on his own, she actually began to enjoy it. They rode for about an hour, coming to a shallow stream with rocks clustered around its edges, an open view of the hillside tumbling all the way down to the valley. Nico dismounted, allowing his horse to dip its head in the stream before tossing the reins loosely over a jutting rock. He didn't come over to help and she struggled to get down.

They sat on a rock that had a flattish seat, and Eloise wondered who else had been here with him in this very spot. He offered her some water, but seemed abrupt with her now and she was confused.

Was it because she had refused to go any further yesterday?

They sat for a while, passing the bottle of water back and forth. She wanted to ask what was wrong, but ran the risk of upsetting him if she did. When the bottle was empty, he screwed the top on tightly and began tapping it against his knee. He looked at her, looked away again, tossing it to one side.

'When did your father die, Eloise?'

'What?'

'You told me he died, when we were at the lake.'

'Well, erm … I was eleven.' She was thrown by this sudden change in him. 'So – so nearly seven years ago.'

'What happened to him?'

She didn't like his tone. 'He got cancer. Testicular cancer. You know down—'

'Yes, yes I know where the testicles are.'

'Well, they said it was curable. Usually it is, but he had a rare form and it killed him. He was a musician. Dan, he was called Dan. I really miss him.'

As the tears welled up she became angry, feeling trampled. 'Why? What do you care anyway?'

He glanced at her. Then he dropped his head between his knees. 'Because mine is dead, too.'

It took her a moment to absorb what he had just said. 'Oh, Nico, I'm so sorry.' She put her hand on his shoulder. 'What happened to him? Do you want to talk about it?'

He picked up a stick, tracing it across the ground. 'No,' he said, throwing it away again. He got to his feet and went over to the horses. 'Time to go.'

After handing her the reins he gave her a sideways nod to get back on Cioccolato. Her foot found the stirrup easily and with a helpful push she was safely back in the saddle. They carried on in silence for another three quarters of an hour, but Eloise felt like her heart had been ripped out and rammed back in again. She wanted to head back now. They seemed to have covered some distance and she was annoyed with herself for not paying enough attention to the route. At the next opportunity she would tell him that she had had enough.

To her surprise, he suggested they make a stop at a viewing-point where she might want to take a photograph. She didn't protest when he helped her dismount but took a hasty picture on her phone so that they could start turning back. She was just about to say as much when Nico leant against the wooden barrier, and said: 'I was three years old.'

Eloise felt herself leaning into him. 'Really, Nico? God, that's so young. Do you remember him?'

'Sometimes. Maybe only through a picture.' He made as if he was holding up a camera. It reminded her of her own dad in the photos they had at home, frozen in time, always happy. Nico began to search for something in his pocket. 'I think I can remember him holding me,' he said. 'One second.' From the back of his shorts he pulled out his wallet, easing his fingers down into it. 'This is him …' He showed her a small, well-worn photograph, slightly creased in one corner. 'And me.'

His father had dark hair, a confident smile, and it was plain to see where Nico's good looks came from. He was cradling him to his chest, the white baby blanket falling over one arm. 'He looks like a lovely dad,' said Eloise. 'And you have his eyes. People say I have my dad's eyes, too, which I love. I suppose because he's not here any more.' She passed the photo back. 'I know how it feels, Nico.'

'Maybe.'

Everyone's pain was different, she knew that. She knew also that these moments could not be shared. Loss was a very lonely place. So it pleased her when he seemed to want to tell her more.

'He used to work away a lot. We lived in France then. His job was *sur la route*. You know, sales? Erm, driving.'

'A salesman.'

'*Si*. Exactly.'

'How did he die? Was he in an accident?'

He did that tutting noise again, followed by: 'No.'

'Was he ill?'

Again the tut. 'No.'

'Oh god, he didn't—?'

She hesitated.

'Kill himself? *Non*,' he replied.

The only other possibility she couldn't bring herself to say either. But she didn't need to.

'He was murdered.'

She had no words to offer him. How could she say that she understood this too? That her own mother had killed someone, and that she often thought of what that left in its wake.

He moved away, towards the horses.

279

'No, wait. Nico.'

'We should be heading back.'

'That must be so awful for you. And for Marianna, too. Do they know who did it? And why?'

She wasn't sure quite why she was asking, except that it seemed important if she was to understand him better.

He didn't answer.

They mounted their horses and headed back in silence. When they reached the field, Nico's horse broke into a gallop and she could feel Cioccolato pulling on the reins. She didn't know what to do. Tugging him back didn't seem to hold him. Nor did squeezing her legs into his sides, as Nico had showed her. In the end she had no alternative but to hang on as best she could to remain on his back.

Nico could see she was in difficulty, yet made no effort to stop. He may even have spurred his horse on faster, she wasn't sure. Each bounce jerked her more out of the saddle, and Cioccolato threw his head into the air as if deliberately trying to unseat her. Her right foot flew out of the stirrup. She tried to get it back in but failed. The muscles in her legs were screaming, and any moment now she would be thrown to the ground. 'Please Cioccolato. Stop!'

She was leaning too far over, and this time knew she couldn't pull herself back up. She would just have to let go. As she freed her hands from the reins she felt the horse slowing down.

Cioccolato shook his head, exhilarated, blowing air out of his huge nostrils. She saw that Nico had stopped too. His horse was panting heavily, steam coming off its body. As she tried to dismount, Cioccolato moved off again. Terrified of a repeat experience she clung on, trying to pull him back, relieved when he only wanted to be alongside the other horse.

'Fun, no?'

'You wanker!' she screamed, flinging herself down. 'You nearly fucking killed me.'

Nico was laughing. He was actually laughing. 'I don't know what that means but I can guess.' He got down from his horse.

'It means this,' she yelled, making the hand gesture right in his face.

He was still laughing. So she slapped him.

Hard.

He put his hand on his cheek, clicked his jaw side to side. 'I'm sorry,' he said. 'I'm very sorry. That was bad of me. A little cruel maybe.'

'A *little*?'

'I knew you wouldn't fall off, Eloise.'

'How could you possibly know that?'

'Because I can see that you are strong. When you have no father you have to be strong for your mother. Am I right? I am right, aren't I?'

He pulled her into him, gripping her firmly. It was rough the way he went about it, but she resisted only for a moment. When he pressed his mouth to hers she felt her anger subside. She was still confused by his awful cruelty one minute and such a raw tenderness the next.

'I wonder if your dead father is talking to my dead father?' he said, breaking the kiss and pointing towards the sky. 'What are they saying to each other, do you think?'

'My dad will be saying: *If your son does that to my daughter again I will kill you.*'

'Ah,' he replied. 'And then mine will say: *But I'm already dead.*'

She shook her head and smiled, pulling away to check the time on her phone. 'Oh my god, I have to go, Nico. I said I'd be back by five and it's already after six.' She helped him gather the horses, accompanying him to the stables but didn't go inside.

'What, you don't stay to help me?'

'I'm on holiday,' she replied.

He was already brushing down Cioccolato.

'What if I *had* fallen off?'

He didn't stop what he was doing. 'You were never going to. I already told you.'

'Wanker.'

'*Ah! Piacere di conoscerti*,' he said, bowing flamboyantly. 'Wanker at your service.'

She turned to go.

'You asked me who murdered him. My father.'

Eloise froze. 'Look, you don't have to tell me, Nico.'

'They think it was a prostitute.'

'Really?'

'They found him in a motel.'

'Oh.'

'He was *derubato*. How do you say that? *Volé*. Robbed. He was robbed.'

She felt the air being sucked out of her lungs.

'That's … awful. I'm so sorry. When did it happen?'

'It was 1989.'

'Here in Tuscany?'

Eloise couldn't imagine something so violent happening in such a beautiful, peaceful place. But as she well knew, people were capable of anything, anywhere.

'No, my dad was from France. We lived there for a while. He was murdered somewhere near Tours.' Nico's voice caught in his throat. 'It was my birthday.'

CHAPTER 32

Tuscany: 2007

Eloise stumbled her way home. The back of her throat was stinging with fear, and a searing pain shot up her leg each time her ankle gave way over loose stones. Her legs could not keep up with the rate her head wanted them to go. This was one hundred times worse than being on an out-of-control horse. Surely it was a coincidence. But she knew, deep down, that it wasn't. Then an even more awful thought struck her. Had Juliet known all along?

Chrissy was dozing in the hammock with her sunhat covering her face. Eloise wondered if she had actually moved in the four hours she had been gone, but she noticed a couple of empty beer bottles under the hammock and a succession of wet footprints leading back and forth to the pool. Her towel was drying on a branch in the early evening sun. The heat was just as intense.

She raced up the steps, hunting for Juliet. Carrier bags and brown paper bags were scattered about the place, some still unpacked, and Eloise noticed the wooden table in the kitchen was covered in flour. Juliet must have been making her pizza dough, as promised. Out on the terrace, a Vespa was resting on its kickstand, a red and blue helmet hooked over the handlebars. It must have escaped her notice when she had stormed inside. Eloise began to follow the floury trail snaking its way down the stone path to the bottom of their private garden. She might have found this amusing had she not been so furious with the person at the other end of it.

Juliet was bending over, peering into the pizza oven. As much as she adored her, at that moment in time she had only hatred for Juliet. She even hated the way she looked in her bikini, matching sarong and big curvy shades. Everything about her. Juliet was putting her mother's life at risk – was on the verge of ruining hers. Eloise managed to hold back her anger until she got close, checking behind for eavesdroppers. Anyone could be listening. And what if Chrissy had woken up and followed her?

'Eloise, *chérie*.' Juliet spotted her too soon. 'How was your horse ride? Were you with that gorgeous boy? What's his name again?'

'Did you know?'

Juliet raised her shades, casually securing them in her beehive. Eloise noticed that the trademark cat brooch was not in her hair today. Was that because she felt she was getting on better with Chrissy, and therefore no longer needed it? Or maybe the fact it was stolen had finally put her off?

Then she saw it pinned to her sarong.

It won't keep you safe now, Juliet.

'Did I know what exactly?'

'Did you know about Marianna's husband – Nico's father? Do you know what happened to him?

'Ah.'

Eloise felt her blood run cold. What was Juliet thinking? Was she insane?

'What the fuck are we doing here, Juliet?'

Juliet made Eloise sit down on the padded bench encircling the large marble table. A yellow parasol provided some much-needed shade above their heads. The pizza ingredients were set out ready to go, including three mounds of dough covered with tea cloths. Flies buzzed around them.

'We're on holiday, that's what we're doing here.'

Eloise began to shake. Juliet was out of her mind.

'This isn't a game, Juliet,' she said, her voice low. 'Nico told me his father was murdered by a prostitute in 1989 when he was three years old. In a motel. In France.' She banged her fist on the table to make each point. 'I'm not stupid, Juliet, and nor is my mum.'

Juliet was about to put her arm round her but Eloise was quick to edge away.

'Get the fuck off me. You're sick. You're twisted and sick. How could you do this to my mum – to me? I trusted you. I thought she was your friend. Your best friend.'

Juliet put some moments of silence between them, lighting up a cigarette. She let the smoke work its magic before forcing it out again in a long train. 'Okay, it's true. I knew,' she whispered, moving closer. Her tone was deeper, conspiratorial, and she dipped her head into Eloise's shoulder as she spoke. 'I admit it's a risk. But please, Eloise, hear me out.'

'A risk? It's downright mental, Juliet.'

Eloise stood up.

'We have to leave. If she finds out, she will totally freak and give herself away. We need to go now.'

'No. Wait, Eloise,' said Juliet, pulling her down. 'She won't find out until we want her to.'

'But what if she does? I did. It's too dangerous, Juliet. She could go to prison. I'll never see her again.'

Eloise was fighting her off.

'Hey, hey, hey. You really need to hear me out. Just hear me out, okay? And then we can decide what to do. Sit down. Eloise, please. Sit.'

Holding her stare, she did as she was told.

'Marianna and Nico aren't the only victims in all of this. Don't you see? We're *all* victims. You, me, Chrissy. All of us.'

Eloise had never considered Juliet a victim. She was right, of course she was a victim. She just didn't seem like one. Eloise guessed that was her point. But how could she possibly compare her suffering to Chrissy's?

'You've missed someone out,' she said sulkily.

Juliet had a look of panic, then she realized. 'Of course, your dad as well. Look, your poor mum has spent her whole life tormenting herself. That bastard deserved everything he got; we all know that. But Chrissy needs to see that his widow, of all people, has moved on. See it with her own eyes. And then maybe she can, too. Marianna has a great life here; she's made a great life for herself and for her son. I mean, she seems really happy, wouldn't you agree?'

Eloise kept quiet. And she wasn't sure about Nico. They hadn't been here long enough to know any of these things.

'Your mother deserves some happiness, that's all. She didn't do anything wrong.'

'She did kill someone, Juliet.'

'For me. She did it all for me. You must see that I have to at least try to set her free. Please let me try. The only person who hasn't moved on from any of this is Chrissy, because she hasn't allowed herself to.'

Eloise removed her baseball cap and placed it on the table. When she saw the Ricci logo she flicked it away.

'Listen, Eloise, your mum will continue to punish herself until the day she dies. You don't need me to tell you that. All I know is that it's not fair that the person who saved her best friend from getting raped should be the one to get the life sentence. She didn't mean to kill him; it was an accident. But you know as well as I do that she won't move on with her life unless she can see it's totally okay to do that. You don't deserve this either, Eloise. We have to fix her and set you free. You deserve so much more.'

Eloise poured herself some water from the jug on the table.

She drank some but it had got too warm in the sun. 'So when are you planning on telling my mum?'

'That, I don't know. Just when the time is right. Maybe only when we get home; I don't know. But trust me, I still think it's the right thing to do. Put it this way, Eloise, do you have a better suggestion?'

Of course she didn't.

'But what if Marianna finds out? It's just … unthinkable.'

'How can she? We're not likely to tell her, are we?'

'Tell me what?'

It was Chrissy. She was standing just behind them, holding a bottle of Pastis in one hand and a bottle of something very red in the other. 'I came to see if the chefs would like an aperitif.'

'Erm,' was all that Eloise could muster.

From the way she was behaving it seemed unlikely that Chrissy had heard any more of their conversation. She grinned, and like a magician produced a glass from each pocket of her shorts. A third one she plucked from her waistband. 'I see you bought grenadine, Ju. Shall I pour us *une tomate*?'

'*Bonne idée*,' said Juliet, bringing her hands together. She shot Eloise a glance. It said: *I think we got away with it*.

This was Eloise's moment to tell her mother everything, warn her of the betrayal by her best friend. 'What's a *tomate* when it's at home, Mum?'

'Pastis and grenadine,' replied Chrissy, pouring a little of each into the glasses. 'Not very Italian. But, for old times' sake.'

The grenadine was luminous red.

'Made from pomegranate,' said Juliet.

'*Comme ça*. Top it up with water … *et violà*.' Chrissy handed them both a glass and took one for herself. '*Santé*.'

Eloise watched the pair of them sipping the red liquid, but it reminded her of some creepy religious ritual. She tried it, nonetheless. First the hit of aniseed at the back of her throat, then the syrupy sweetness of the grenadine.

'Not bad, eh?' said Chrissy, smacking her lips. 'Okay. Now you can tell me.'

'Tell you what?' Eloise tried not to sound too panic-stricken.

'Whatever it was you said that you weren't likely to tell me.'

'Right.'

'It was a confession,' said Juliet.

Eloise almost passed out.

Chrissy put her hands on her hips, standing with her legs apart. 'Well, in that case, Juliet, I'm all ears.'

Eloise looked at Juliet in disbelief. What game were they playing now?

'I don't know how to light the pizza oven.'

Chrissy moved them both out of the way and peered inside the blackened dome of the oven which was slowly beginning to turn white, and there was a veil of smoke weaving out of the top of the chimney.

'It looks pretty lit to me. You're cleverer than you look, Juliet.' She went back up the path with her drink, shaking her head. 'Call me when it's ready,' she shouted.

Juliet sighed, one hand on her heart and the other fanning herself. Eloise was unsure if she had done a good thing or a terrible thing. She seriously did not know what was right or wrong any more.

'Will you give me a hand making the pizzas?' said Juliet. 'I've made the sauce – the tomatoes I bought at the market are absolutely divine. You won't believe how good this is going to taste. *Pizza à la Julietta*. Like you've never tasted in your life before. So,' she said, bringing her hands together with a puff of flour, 'it's just a case of slapping on the toppings. You up to that?'

Eloise glowered at Juliet.

'Eloise, I need you to be with me on this.' She lowered her voice again. 'I don't mean making pizza, I mean with your mum. We need to make this work. And *we* …' – she looked for somewhere to wipe her hands, deciding against her sarong – 'need to be a team.'

Juliet held out her hand. It felt like a handshake with the devil. Eloise's palm was hot and sticky; Juliet's, cool and floury.

'Should I prepare a salad?' said a voice.

They looked in horror at Chrissy heading towards them again.

'What're you two up to now?'

They snapped their hands free.

'We're just … we were just having a pizza stand-off,' said Eloise. 'Only, I think I might lose. You know how Dad used to be in the kitchen?' She pointed to Juliet. 'Well, she's the same.'

'Don't worry about it,' said Chrissy. 'You know I eat anything. Not sure why you're going to all this trouble in any case. Pizzas grow in cardboard boxes, don't they?'

***

They sat around the white marble table, the temperature more bearable in the retreating evening sun. In the end there was much to laugh about when Chrissy was assessing their pizzas. Rather predictably, she declared Eloise as the overall winner with her *Pizza Cheese Eloise*. Even if it had been burnt to a charred crisp she would still have awarded her the prize.

'Thanks, Mum,' she said, kissing her cheek. 'Good to know who your friends are round here.'

Juliet forced a smile.

They had drunk a whole bottle of wine, and before that several refills of aperitif. Now Chrissy was offering to go back up to the house to get more.

'That's a *bonne idée*,' said Juliet.

'I'm full of *bonnes idées*,' Chrissy replied, scraping her chair back. Eloise felt the noise claw through her insides.

'Bring an extra glass with you as well,' Juliet shouted.

'Why?' said Chrissy, looking puzzled. 'Do we have a mystery guest?'

Eloise was staring at Juliet, enough to bore a hole through her head. Only a couple of hours ago they had shaken on being a team. No more surprises.

'I've invited Marianna to come along and have a drink with us.'

'Marianna?' said Eloise, trying to compose herself. 'But she … I mean she wouldn't want to come and have a drink with us. *Surely*. Would she?'

'Well, why not?' said Chrissy. 'We don't bite.'

'Did she say she'd come?'

Juliet raised her eyebrows. Eloise could not bear to turn round.

'*Ah buonasera.* You are hiding down here.'

She had to warn her mother. Right now. But how could she? Juliet seemed intent on making them walk this tightrope and now there was no turning back.

'*Asseyez-vous*, Marianna,' said Chrissy, making a sweeping gesture with her arm. 'Oh god that's French, isn't it? I can't speak a word of Italian, I'm afraid.'

'Either is fine,' said Marianna.' Her loveliness was almost too cruel, and Eloise wanted to scream because of it. 'In this job we speak a little of everything.'

'*Moi, je vais chercher …*' said Chrissy. '*Je vais aller chercher … Merde.* Don't speak French when drunk! Forgive me, I'll just go and get that bottle of wine, shall I?'

'No need,' said Marianna, shaking the wine-carrier she was holding.

She sat down next to Eloise, taking out four bottles of Chianti and putting them on the table.

'We'll still need another glass,' said Chrissy. '*Une verre.* No! What am I talking about? I mean *un verre. Oh là là!*'

'Yes,' said Marianna. 'It's one to catch you out.'

Chrissy smiled, disappointed in herself. As she headed up the path Eloise ran after her.

She could have warned her then. She meant to.

But she didn't.

Instead, when they got to the kitchen she panicked, begging Chrissy to finish off her story in a play for more time.

'Not now, Eloise,' she said, opening the dishwasher.

'I need to know, Mum. I need to know the rest.'

'You know enough. There's no more I can tell you.'

She did know enough, but if she allowed her mother to go back out there and start drinking again it could be the end. And who could predict what sort of ending that might be? If she could keep Chrissy here a while longer, then Marianna would probably lose interest and go.

'They'll be fine those two,' she said. 'They'll be chatting. What about when I was born? Were you happy? Was Dad happy?'

Chrissy perched on a stool. 'Where do you want me to go from?'

'Sending Juliet that stupid brooch.'

CHAPTER 33

'That's a nice brooch. Who's it for?'

'Juliet. It's her birthday.'

Chrissy's mum inspected it more closely. 'Unusual,' she said. 'It's quite heavy. Looks expensive. Will you stay in touch, do you think, after the baby's born?'

'I doubt it. Our lives are too different now.'

Chrissy was not at all sure what to write on the card. There was so much to say and so much to ask Juliet. How was she? How was she coping? Did she suffer from panic attacks, night sweats and paranoia? Did she burst into tears for no reason, jump at the slightest thing, tear herself apart and lose her temper with those she loved? Or was she out partying every night, drinking and laughing, being the same old Juliet whom everyone adored and wanted to spend time with?

So much had changed for Chrissy. She had killed a man, dropped out of university and was going to have a baby. The world had gone mad in the space of only a few months.

She couldn't think straight. Her hand was trembling as she wrote:

'*HAPPY BIRTHDAY JULIET*
… one last time.
I'll never forget.
As long as we live,
Chrissy xxx'

***

On her way back from the post office she called by to see Dan. A small indie label had shown interest in signing his band and given them free rehearsal space in Hulme in a semi-derelict warehouse.

'Fag break soon, guys,' he announced when he saw her, mouthing the words *five minutes* whilst they finished off the song.

'We'll go outside,' he said as the others were lighting up. He had become very protective; it made her feel safe. 'So, how you feeling today?'

'Yeah, sick.'

Dan knew it was far more than just morning sickness, bad enough in itself, but the flashbacks were growing more and more graphic each day.

'I've decided to go and see that bloke this afternoon. You know, about doing some tutoring.'

'Really? Well, that's fantastic.' He kissed her forehead.

'Can't think straight, to be honest, but we need the money and it'll get me out of the house. Might stop me thinking too much.'

They were moving into Dan's grandmother's house just around the corner from the rehearsal studio. It was a temporary measure. His grandmother was going into a nursing home and her property would have to be sold. Their names were on a council house waiting list but they had been told it was clogged. Finding somewhere cheap to rent was probably their best option, but with Dan's band always on the verge of being signed, things were tight. Guitar and keyboard lessons brought in a bit of extra cash, and gigs too, although takings had to be shared between the five of them. The music store needed him only on a casual basis.

***

'It's for you, Chrissy,' her mother shouted.

They must not find her.

She would be thrown into jail, deported to France, the baby taken off her the moment it was born.

'Didn't you hear the phone ringing? It's for you.'

'Who is it?'

'Someone from the dole office. Are you all right, love?'

'Can you take a message?'

'Won't that seem a bit odd now? I've told her you're in.'

At least some of her behaviour could be explained through being pregnant, but it was only a matter of time before her mother would suspect there was something much deeper going on and begin to ask questions.

From the moment she discovered she was pregnant her feelings towards this baby had been erratic. It felt strange that something was growing inside her, feeding off her like some parasite. Each time she looked in the mirror her body had become more distorted, disfigured, stretched, swollen and sore, and she barely recognized herself. People assured her these feelings were normal. But her life was in such a mess after France, the last thing she wanted was to mess up someone else's as well.

When there was no sign of the baby a week and a half after the due date, a caesarean was threatened. She absolutely refused. The idea of being slashed open seemed the most violent way to bring her baby into the world.

***

'It's a girl!'

The nurse held up a peculiar-looking bundle streaked with blood and slime. It shocked Chrissy to see that it was still attached to her by some revolting slithery rope. Dan stroked her forehead, pushing away strands of sweat-soaked hair. 'Well done,' he kept saying, as if she had performed some miracle. She had, of course, but she had just wanted rid. Eighteen hours of sweating, pushing, swearing, screaming; an ordeal from start to finish.

The nurse, a smiling rosebud of a woman, placed the baby across her chest. Chrissy tensed against the pillow, turning her head away. If she had had one more scrap of energy left in her body she would have screamed. Dan leant over to give the baby's head a kiss, delicately, like he was afraid it might break; at the same time, stroking Chrissy's hair.

They were too young. Wouldn't it be better to give her away? Find parents who were better equipped to take care of her? Let her grow up with people who knew nothing of her mother's past and the terrible thing she had done.

Tell them that's what you want to happen. Tell them now. Then she will never have to know.

It was at that point the tiny creature screwed up its wrinkly, red face and let out a cry loud enough to wake the entire hospital: the sick, the dying and even its dead.

And Chrissy smiled.

Her reaction surprised her; she even heard herself saying 'Shush'. She closed her eyes and reached for Dan's hand across the bed as the baby nestled into her breast, vowing to protect her daughter from all of life's evils until her dying breath.

She was beautiful.

Eloise.

295

CHAPTER 34

Tuscany: 2007

'I love you more and more each day,' she said, coming over to give Eloise a kiss. 'We should go back. They'll be sending a search party out for us. We only came to get a glass.'

Her mother's arm slid around Eloise's waist; she was steering them straight into the ambush.

'We don't have to go!' said Eloise. 'Why don't we just stay here?' She even considered throwing herself onto the ground, pretending to be ill.

'Why would we want to stay here?' said Chrissy, laughing. She was drunk already, and there was something inevitable about all of this now. Juliet had pushed them to the edge of this precipice and there was no stepping back.

Marianna's voice could be heard quite clearly as they got closer.

'We can go for a walk, Mum. I can show you the lake.'

'Here they come. We thought you'd got lost,' said Juliet, putting a cigarette to her lips.

She gave Eloise a look of interrogation as they approached … *Had she said something to her mum? Did Chrissy know who*

Marianna was yet? Eloise responded with a discreet shake of her head and Juliet sat back looking pleased.

Where was this leading? Did Juliet even know?

She deeply regretted now not warning her mother. And why on earth had she trusted Juliet so implicitly? Eloise wiped the sweat off her face with her forearm, puffing up a breath of air to cool her forehead.

'It's still hot,' said Marianna. She didn't look hot, not to Eloise. The complete opposite, in fact – scarily cool. 'The storm is coming, you'll see,' she added, making it sound more like a threat. 'Then it will cool down.'

'When?' asked Eloise.

'I just hope it's not tomorrow night. We are having a party. Guests are very welcome. You must come along.' Marianna held her glass in the air. '*Santé*. Or should I say *salute*, as we are in Italy?'

'*Salute, santé*, cheers,' said Chrissy. 'Or should I say Cheese Eloise?'

Chrissy was the only one who laughed. As their glasses came together, Eloise prepared to hear them smash.

'So tell me,' said Marianna, addressing Chrissy, 'when were you last in France?'

Eloise watched any newfound confidence quickly seep out of her mother. The reminder of being in France was enough to traumatize.

'It was another lifetime ago,' she replied, kicking at a crack in the ground, probably wishing she could slither into it. Marianna was right, the rain was badly needed; there were cracks appearing everywhere and things hadn't even got started yet.

Eloise tried to distract. 'Do you miss France, Marianna?'

Marianna eyed her with suspicion.

'Oh. Er, Nico mentioned you used to live there,' she added nervously.

'Mm. Well, I needed a new start, so I came back to Italy. And it's very beautiful here.'

'Sure is,' said Chrissy, daydreaming.

297

To see her mother suddenly so relaxed again was worrying. She mustn't let her have any more wine. Nor have any more herself, for that matter. Eloise handed out the olives and nuts, going round the table three times.

Remember that Marianna doesn't know who we are.

Remember that.

Just like Mum doesn't have a clue who Marianna is.

'Sit still, Eloise,' said Chrissy. 'What's the matter with you? Do you have horseflies in your shorts or something?' She laughed, but no one else did.

'Nic said you'd been out today,' said Marianna. 'Did you enjoy it?'

'Yes,' she replied, blushing. Even now there was a confusing disconnect between the awful reality of Nico, who he really was, and the daydream of him. What if he were to find out who *they* were? She had seen what Nico was capable of, his wild streak, and it had scared her.

'It's just so peaceful, so perfect here,' said Chrissy, stretching out her arms. 'You're very lucky, Marianna.'

'That's what everyone says. Yes, it is, and I am very lucky. Some people come here to paint, some to write, some just to escape. I'm always curious what brings my guests here. So what brought you?'

'Definitely the last one,' said Chrissy. 'Escape.' She swished the wine around her glass. 'But actually, it was all her doing. My *best* friend over there.' She chinked her glass hard against Juliet's.

'What is it you want to escape from?' asked Marianna.

There was a silence that no one wanted to fill. Then Juliet came up with: 'Why don't we play the happiness game?'

'What the hell is that?' said Chrissy. 'Never heard of it.'

'My therapist taught me it.'

'Your therapist?' Chrissy guffawed. 'Bit late for that, isn't it?'

'You don't have to stay for this stupid game, Marianna,' said Eloise.

'Oh, I think I do. I am very intrigued.'

'Okay,' said Juliet, clapping her hands. 'Who shall we start with? You, Eloise.'

'Do we have to?' She glowered at Juliet. She could see where this was going. An image of Juliet was forming in her head. She pictured her chairing a meeting in one of her own designer suits, persuading people to do things they didn't want to do. This is what Juliet Ricci did all the time.

'So,' she said, 'on a scale of one to ten, how happy are you?'

'Is ten the best?' Eloise said, calmly. She was screaming inside.

'Ten is perfect, one is abysmal.'

'What if you're less than one?' asked Chrissy.

'Oh, don't be ridiculous,' Juliet snapped. 'You know you're not. Your fabulous daughter is here, next to you, for one thing. You're on holiday in a beautiful place …'

Chrissy put her hands up in submission. 'I was just querying.'

'Well, don't. You're not allowed to be minus. She's had some "stuff" going on.' Juliet drew quotation marks in the air. 'Lost her husband, gets a bit down. Just won't let things go.'

'Oh,' said Marianna. 'Well, I hope this holiday can go some way towards healing.'

Eloise held onto her breath, because Marianna seemed to have only paused, and Eloise was bracing herself for more words to come.

'I lost my husband too.'

'You did? Oh, I'm so sorry,' said Chrissy.

Actually, that was not such a bad thing for her mother to hear. Other people suffered as well. But the significance of it hit Eloise hard. Chrissy was the reason Marianna had lost her husband.

'Look, do we have to play this stupid game? I don't even know how happy I am. I just know that I am.'

'Sounds like an eight,' said Juliet.

'I guess,' said Eloise, reluctantly. 'I guess I'm an eight.' She should have left it there, diverted the conversation onto some completely new topic, but she wanted Juliet to know what it was like melting under the spotlight. 'So what about you, Juliet? You'll probably say you're a ten as you're such a positive person. But what are you really?'

Marianna topped up their glasses as they waited for her answer. Eloise took note that she would pour herself only a tiny amount, and none at all on this occasion. Perhaps she thought Eloise was older than seventeen. Did she have some agenda all of her own? But how could Marianna possibly know who they were?

'Go on then, what do you reckon I am?' Juliet challenged her. 'I'd be interested to know.'

'Ooh, well, let's see now.' Eloise swallowed a large mouthful of wine, forgetting that she was meant to be stopping. 'She's onto husband number four – I guess that tells us something. Rarely sees him though. He lives in Italy and she's in London, so hardly the perfect marriage.'

'Eloise!' said Chrissy, but she almost looked delighted.

'No, no. You carry on,' said Juliet, smiling at Marianna to indicate her willingness.

'Okay,' said Eloise. 'She doesn't have any kids. But, on the plus side, she's absolutely loaded and runs her own fashion company.'

'I adore your clothes, by the way,' said Marianna. 'They're a little expensive, but now and again I like to treat myself.'

'Well, who doesn't?' said Chrissy.

'Er, you, Mum!'

'Right,' said Juliet, raising her glass. 'Well thanks for the summary, Eloise. I love my life but I do spend too much time travelling. Always putting my career first has meant I've not had a conventional married life, and a family would have been nice, you're right. However, I'm never less than an eight.'

'It's not too late,' said Marianna. 'You're still young enough to have children.'

'It's not going to happen,' said Juliet. 'It can't.'

Even in her present mood, Eloise did not wish to delve into

that one. In fact, Juliet looked so upset she almost wanted to apologize for overstepping the mark. She watched her light up another cigarette as the cicadas did their usual clicking in the background, making a mockery of their silence. Marianna poured out more wine. Eloise managed to cover her glass just in time. She counted six bottles on the table: five empty, one half full. Was Marianna deliberately trying to loosen their tongues? Did she normally spend her evenings playing cruel party games with her guests? She was the only sober one among them and seemed to be playing some game all of her own.

But why?

'So what about you, Chrissy?' asked Marianna. 'How happy are you?'

Chrissy had drunk more than any of them. 'I'm nearer to one than ten, put it that way,' she said, slurring her words.

'And is that because of losing your husband, do you think?' Marianna's voice was gently soothing.

'He was a good man,' Chrissy replied.

'Oh, he was the best,' said Eloise, feeling the need to intervene. 'He was my dad.'

'I understand,' said Marianna. She stroked Eloise's hair in a genuinely kind way. 'But time heals.'

'It does if you let it,' said Juliet.

Chrissy ignored the dig. 'He was the love of my life,' she said, tapping the side of her glass with her chewed fingernails. 'But I lost the love *for* life when I was only a couple of years older than Eloise.'

'Oh. What happened?'

Marianna seemed to be weaving delicate threads around her.

'She gave birth to me I think!' said Eloise, gripping her mother's hands.

Juliet laughed, so too did Marianna. And Chrissy did seem grateful, although her lucky escape only made her drink more.

'That leaves you, Marianna,' said Juliet. 'How do you score on the happiness scale?'

Perhaps Juliet was more in control of this game after all. It was a masterstroke. If Marianna said the right things, it could be just what her mother needed to hear. Eloise crossed her fingers under the table until it actually hurt, crossing them even tighter.

'Life is never perfect, of course. But honestly, I think ten actually. Maybe nine on a not-so-good day.'

'Fantastic!' said Juliet, applauding. Eloise cringed at her over-the-top reaction, but she would have danced on the table herself if that had been any more appropriate.

Ten.

Maybe nine on a not-so-good day …

'Didn't you love your husband then?'

'Eloise!' said Chrissy, frowning at her. Even Juliet gave her a look to say: *Back off.*

'Oh, it's okay,' said Marianna. 'Yes. Yes, I did love him.'

Why couldn't she just admit that she hated his guts and wanted someone to bash his brains out?

Eloise knew Juliet was thinking that, too.

'How long ago did he die?' Chrissy asked.

'Oh, a long time ago now.'

'Time's obviously done its healing work,' said Juliet. 'I mean, for you to be a ten.'

'Well, yes, I suppose it has.' Marianna looked at them in turn, as if assessing whether to expand on that. 'I loved him but I didn't respect him.'

'Really? Why not?'

'Eloise, don't be so nosey. It's none of your business,' said Chrissy. 'I'm sorry. Maybe we should play charades instead. Do you know charades?'

'Because he didn't respect me,' said Marianna, trying to press one of the discarded corks into the table. She didn't make eye contact. This was the first time she had shown any signs of discomfort. The cicadas in the background seemed to get louder, a warning perhaps not to persist with this perverse game of

Juliet's. So now it was Marianna's turn to give away too much. As far as she was aware, they were merely holidaymakers staying in one of her properties, complete strangers. She also struck Eloise as someone who would normally maintain a professional distance.

It didn't make any sense.

'If he had still been alive I'd still be with him for sure, but I would have been crushed and humiliated. His death liberated me. To be perfectly honest, I don't regret that he died. He was a decent father but a terrible husband.'

Whatever her reasons, this was more like what they wanted to hear. Eloise beamed at Juliet. She was beginning to like this game after all.

'Why, what did he do?'

'Eloise! Really, just stop asking so many questions. You shouldn't have any more to drink.'

'I've already stopped, Mum.' She raised her eyebrows at Chrissy, hinting that she might wish to do the same.

'No, no, it's fine,' said Marianna. 'Really, it's okay. Sometimes it's good to share. Is it not? Share the pain, share the burden.'

How had Chrissy managed all these years to keep her guilt so tightly wrapped? And maybe Juliet was right. Maybe it did have to get much worse before it could get any better.

How would her mother take it, though, when she found out who Marianna really was? And when would that be? Eloise had already decided that she didn't want her to know until they were safely back in England. What would it matter to Juliet if her little scheme went up in smoke? It would change nothing for her. No matter what the outcome, Juliet would flit back to London, to Italy, carry on her glamorous lifestyle, perhaps feeling that bit better about herself because at least she had tried to repay her debt to Chrissy. Eloise was the one who had to be there for her mother long after this trip was over. And what if Chrissy went to prison?

She wanted to tell Juliet these things immediately, but their guest didn't seem to want to leave.

'My husband was very handsome,' she continued. 'Always flirting. He was not at all loyal. I don't think he was capable of it. I knew he had a mistress, at least one, but I chose to turn a blind eye, I suppose. I thought that was the best thing to do. We had a child and I didn't think I could cope alone.' Chrissy nodded. 'I had no family, what could I do? And as I said, I loved him.'

'What a complete and utter bastard,' said Juliet. 'He deserved all he got then.'

'Excuse me?' said Marianna.

'Er, you told us he died,' Eloise corrected. 'That's what she means.' She glared at Juliet.

Marianna ran her finger round the rim of her glass. 'Yes. We all have to die, don't we?'

Chrissy was crying. It was time to end this before it got out of control. Was she crying for Marianna's sake, or was it out of some form of release for herself? After all, if she ever did sit down opposite her victim's widow, however unlikely that was as far as Chrissy was concerned, these would be the exact words she would hope to hear.

Eloise stood up.

'Last one in the pool is a piece of *merde*!'

No one reacted. She sat back down, saying: 'It's just something we do, Marianna.'

In any case, Marianna was more interested in preparing Chrissy for the kill. She topped up her drink again. 'So, what is your story? Why isn't time healing you?'

'What is this, the Italian inquisition?' said Chrissy, finishing off her wine and slamming the glass on the table.

'Mum.'

Chrissy began rubbing her face until it turned red and angry. 'God, I'm so tired,' she said. 'Just so *fucking* tired.'

'Let's go to bed then, shall we?'

It was the best Eloise could do.

'What makes you so tired, Chrissy?' Marianna persisted.

'Look, she did it for me. It was an accident.'

'Juliet!' shouted Eloise. Any minute now the guillotine would come whistling down on the back of her mother's neck. And Juliet seemed to want to play the executioner.

Juliet was holding the cat brooch out for Chrissy. Chrissy closed her eyes when she saw it, and kept them closed even when she started speaking. 'You can still believe that's the reason if you want, Juliet. But that's not why I did it.'

'Mum, please.'

Chrissy had a chilling serenity about her now, and Eloise sensed this could not be stopped.

'I'm not a bad person. Not really,' she said. Her eyes were now locked onto Juliet's. 'I didn't do it for you.'

'You did it for both of us," Juliet replied. 'Anyway, you didn't mean to. She accidentally killed someone, Marianna.'

Eloise gasped. Right now she wanted to kill Juliet.

'It wasn't an accident!' Chrissy yelled, banging her fists on the table. The half-empty bottle spun round, spraying wine from its neck and spattering them in red spots. Marianna caught it and stood it upright again.

'Who did you kill?' she asked, coolly.

Chrissy shrugged. 'Doesn't matter. Just some worthless prick. We thought he was kind, offered us a lift to Paris. He saved us from another maniac too.'

'So you were hitch-hiking?'

'Yes,' Chrissy answered. 'Serves us right, eh?' She pointed at Juliet. 'Her idea.'

'He attacked me,' said Juliet. 'She did it to save her best friend.'

'No, Juliet. I did it for me.'

CHAPTER 35

France: summer 1989

She held her face up to the cool jet of water and closed her eyes. Tilting forwards, she could feel it running down the back of her neck and the rest of her tired, aching body. Her skin was glossy and tanned, the hairs on her arms bleached white from the sun. Dan was bound to say she was too skinny, but she quite liked her new shape. And Dan would love her whatever.

She hugged herself, imagining his arms around her.

Nudging the temperature up a notch, she began to wash away the sweat and grime of the day: standing by the side of the road trying to thumb a lift; the tension between her and Juliet; the sleazy pervert in his filthy truck; she watched all of that disappear down the plughole. Chrissy smiled to herself at the thought of home and of being in Dan's arms for real. There was her mother's home cooking to look forward to as well, and going down the pub with friends, not to mention starting her second year at Bristol.

The summer was almost at an end, and what a summer it had been, but she was more than ready now for the next chapter to begin.

Still luxuriating in the shower, she didn't hear him unlock the door. Or come into the room. And even when she saw a figure through the steam and condensation, she thought it must be Juliet. She banged on the cubicle door, shouting: 'Juliet! You frightened the life out of me,' rubbing away at a small area on the cracked plastic.

Only, it wasn't Juliet.

He was getting undressed, undoing his tie, unbuttoning his shirt. Removing his trousers. Couldn't he hear the shower still running? Maybe he thought it hadn't been turned off properly.

She banged on the door again. '*J'ai pas fini! J'ai pas fini!*'

He grinned at her.

Chrissy realized she was urinating, shocked to see the yellow liquid swirling around her toes. She covered herself with both hands. What else could she do?

She was trapped.

Juliet was probably asleep. And if she called out for help, they weren't meant to be here in the first place. Who would hear anyway from inside the shower cubicle?

Turn it off.

That seemed a logical thing to do. But before she could get her hand on the dial he was already in there with her. The door clunked shut behind him. He edged nearer.

Naked.

This big, powerful man. Married man. Father. Who, very proudly, had shown them a photo of his son. It was his birthday. Today, in fact. His son would be waiting for him to make it home. Tonight. To Paris. This man was their hero, too. Saved them from precisely this sort of danger. Now here he was, standing within a few inches of her, his athletic body, naked and solid, with a threatening-looking erection she felt sure he was going to use as a weapon against her.

'Please, Monsieur. Please don't do this. *S'il vous plaît. Monsieur.*'

She was trying to reach somewhere inside his heart not to hurt her. She also wanted to turn her back on him but felt that might be worse. Remaining face on, she pressed back against the tiles. The water gushed down between them. A barrier. But it was only water.

It was all starting to make sense now. He had put something in that wine. He must have.

He moved in closer. Closer still. The water was behind him, running down his back, his body firmly pressed against hers. He touched her. Breasts. Chin. Stomach. Face. Between her legs. He seemed to have more than one pair of hands. She tried to fend him off, cover herself, folding herself inwards, crossing her legs. She tried pushing him away time and again but, each time, he kept coming back.

'*N'aie pas peur*. Don't be afraid,' he whispered.

He tried to kiss her. She managed to cover her mouth and turn her face to the side. But he grabbed her chin, pulled it back and planted his mouth over hers. He needed a shave; his chin rubbed against hers like a scourer. She felt something inside her. It hurt, but not too much. It was only his finger. He was actually trying to turn her on, have sex with her.

Did he really think she would respond?

***

When it was over he released his grip that had been clamping her to the tiles, and took a step backwards. Gloating. She smacked him across the face, hard. He put his hand to his cheek, pushed his jaw side to side and then laughed as he pressed back against the cubicle door until it clicked open.

He stepped out.

The shower was still on, water coming down as if nothing had happened. Chrissy turned the temperature to max. Scalding. She wanted to wash away every last trace of him. There was blood running down between her legs. She was not a virgin; she had slept with Dan countless times. But Dan was the only guy she had ever slept with.

She watched the blood drain away.

Her insides were raw, like a knife had been thrust up inside her and twisted round, again and again.

Rubbing another tiny window in the condensation, she saw him wrap a towel around his waist. He was looking in the mirror to check his face where she had slapped him. Or perhaps to see if he needed a shave.

And then he went away.

Chrissy sank to the base of the shower cubicle, letting the water soothe and rinse. She wrapped her arms around her knees, allowing her head to slump, noticing that her fingers were shrivelled at the ends. Her toes, too. Funny, she thought, how she was focusing on those small details. Then she closed her eyes and drifted away, allowing the water to erase the nightmare, going somewhere else in her head. Back to Dan. She may even have fallen asleep.

And then, suddenly, she was jolted back to reality.

Juliet!

How long had she been in here like this? Ten minutes? Twenty? Maybe even half an hour. Too long. He must be in the bedroom. Where else could he have gone with only a towel round his waist? All she could think of was: *Oh god, please let Juliet be okay. Don't let him do to her what he's just done to me.*

She tugged the towel off the rail, securing it around herself as she hurried into the bedroom.

Juliet was lying on the bed. He was on top of her, tearing at her clothes. The TV was on.

'Stop!' she yelled, rushing towards him. 'Leave her alone.'

He turned, giving her that familiar look of contempt. What was she going to do exactly? Run out into Reception screaming – in a towel? It was only their word against his. They were nothing but a pair of cheap hookers.

He began to get rougher with Juliet.

Chrissy charged at him; he pushed her to the floor. Clawing

at the carpet for some inspiration, her eyes scanned the room, taking in the scene. The wine bottle was almost empty; she couldn't see any glasses. Juliet's flip-flops were over by the window where she had kicked them off. Her rucksack was on the bed, unopened. Chrissy's was on the floor, the top still undone from when she had extracted her washbag. Moving to the double bed, *his* bed, she saw his clothes neatly folded on the pillow. It incensed her that he had taken the time to do this.

She got up and tossed them to the floor, his belt coming loose in her hand.

Standing behind him, as close as she dared, she jerked the leather strap taut in her fingers.

Snap it round his neck and pull back hard.

She tried and tried. Each time, froze in the crucial moment.

Suddenly he turned and saw what she was up to. Moving quickly, he lunged at her. It came instinctively to use the belt as a whip and she lashed it against his face, catching his eye with the buckle. Blood spurted from behind his fingers, but he somehow managed to come at her again.

Chrissy took a step backwards to get away from him. She knew there was nowhere to go and felt her leg hit against the bed frame. It knocked her to the floor and she nearly gashed her arm on a piece of broken glass as she landed. This must have been from a previous struggle. Perhaps he had tried to force more wine down Juliet's throat.

She seized the jagged stem of the wineglass. She went for him, slashing his stomach. He tipped backwards towards the bed, splitting his head open on the chest of drawers as he went down.

Chrissy waited. Her breathing heavy from the exertion and the adrenalin coursing through her veins. She thought he might even be dead.

He wasn't. His pulse was still there. But he wasn't moving and it gave her time to concentrate on Juliet. When she roused her, she was bleary from the drug he had slipped into their drink and

310

wasn't making much sense. But enough to describe what had just happened to her.

He muttered something. It frightened Juliet, who wanted to know what he had said, but Chrissy sent her into the shower.

'Fuck you.'

He said it again and again. He seemed to be laughing at her.

The stem of the broken wineglass was on the floor where she had dropped it before. There was blood on its edges, and maybe a piece of flesh from his stomach. She picked it up and threw herself on top of him, pinning his arms to his sides with her knees, holding onto his nose. He began to struggle, refusing to open his mouth.

Sooner or later he had to take a breath.

'Little bit wider, *Monsieur*. Bit more ... Perfect.'

In it went.

There was a crunch when she snapped his jaws together. His body contorted; he tried to cough. Blood trickled down the sides of his mouth then appeared through his nostrils. It was hard to look at him, his looks completely destroyed; one eye bloody and swollen, and now this. When she finally released her hands he burbled like a baby. Gurgling and choking to death.

Removing her towel, she threw it over his face so she would never have to look at it again.

That face.

'No. Fuck you. Arsehole.'

CHAPTER 36

Tuscany: 2007

'Oh my god,' said Juliet, her fingers trembling across her mouth.

Eloise ran round the table and buried her head in her mother's shoulder.

'Why didn't you tell me?' said Juliet. 'Why?'

Only now did Marianna pour herself a glass of wine. She drank it in one go then poured herself another. Up until now, knowing what her mother had done, Eloise had felt nothing but sympathy for Marianna, but this new revelation turned her pity into something closer to hate. She knew it wasn't Marianna's fault, she wasn't responsible for what her husband did, but Marianna was the closest thing she had to blame.

So what happened now?

There was a coolness about her. She gave nothing away. Hearing the gruesome details of her husband's death, along with his alleged crimes, must have seemed like this was his murder trial. Would she even believe he was capable of rape?

If Nico had been present he would have worked it out by now; Eloise felt sure of that.

Juliet's head was bowed, her shoulders caved in. She seemed

to have aged in only quarter of an hour. What little use had she been to her best friend whilst all this was going on, lying on the bed with the TV on? She must finally recognize that Chrissy's torment, for all of these years, was not as simple as she thought.

As any of them thought.

Did Juliet regret bringing them to Tuscany now? If only she had stayed away from Chrissy in the first place, like she was meant to, she need never have discovered this terrible truth. By forcing Chrissy to relive her nightmare she had created one all of her own.

'Chrissy, I am so, so sorry.'

Juliet's words were faint, her voice broken.

'We both know he put something in the wine,' said Chrissy.

Juliet reached across the table and revealed the silver cat brooch in her palm. Chrissy stared at it. It was Marianna who took it. In that moment, Eloise saw how much older Chrissy looked compared to her best friend. Even now. What a difference a few minutes can make in a person's life.

Juliet left her hand on the table in the hope that Chrissy would take it.

She didn't.

'I couldn't move, Chrissy,' said Juliet. 'I heard nothing. That's why I did nothing.' With her other hand she wiped away the tears. 'I remember the smell of him. Garlic and wine on his breath. Expensive aftershave. He kept pushing his face into mine. I moved my head side to side, trying to avoid him. Everything was so slow and heavy, such an effort to do anything. I remember the room was pale lemon. Do you remember, Chrissy? Everything, pale lemon. Apart from the brown watermark on the ceiling. Even now I see that brown stain when I close my eyes. I have to fight to get rid of it. I remember staring at it the whole time it was going on.' She paused, shaking her head in tiny movements. '... And all the time, I kept thinking: *Where's Chrissy? Why isn't she coming to help me?*

Marianna put the brooch back on the table.

Eloise rubbed her mother's shoulders, wishing she could take away her pain. At least now she could truly understand it, now that she had *all* the truth. At long last.

'The word *rape* isn't enough to describe how it feels,' said Chrissy. The tears rolled down her cheeks but she barely noticed them. 'It's just not enough.'

'Did you respond in any way to his advances?'

They turned to Marianna.

Eloise wanted to yell at her: '*Don't you judge my mother. Don't you dare judge.*'

'Did you?' Marianna repeated.

'What?' said Chrissy. She started to tremble.

'I'm just asking.'

'No, I did not. Why? Have you ever been raped?'

They were back in the courtroom.

'It's a complicated word,' said Marianna.

'Believe me, if there had been any sort of implement in that fucking shower I would've given it to him then. Instead of having to wait until he raped me and started on my best friend.' Chrissy was too drunk and too angry to think why Marianna would be asking such a question, and carried on. 'If you'd seen how strong he was, how much bigger than me he was, you'd understand there's only so much fight you can give when you're trapped in a shower cubicle, naked, with someone overpowering you like that. I did think about kicking him in the balls but he was so firmly pressed against me I could barely breathe, let alone raise my knee. I bet the bastard had done it before.'

'How can you know that?' said Marianna.

'He seemed to know how to pin a woman down. Render her powerless.'

'To his advances or his strength?'

'What are you saying? That I didn't put up enough of a fight? That I wanted it really? Why are you drilling into me so much? The bastard raped me. He raped me. And then he started on

Juliet. Why do you care so fucking much anyway? Or not care, more like?'

She swiped at a bottle. It shattered a few feet away from them. No one got up to deal with the broken glass.

'I'm sorry,' said Marianna, quietly. 'It's difficult when there is no proof. And it's such a long time ago.'

'Proof.' Chrissy slapped the table and began to laugh crazily. 'You want proof. Well, that is a complicated word.' Her expression darkened. 'When he put himself inside me, the pain was worse than giving birth. You have a child; you know how much that hurts. Well, multiply that by a thousand, and then you'll know how it feels to be raped.'

Marianna nodded. She was only trying to defend her husband, or at least make sure that what Chrissy was telling her was the undisputed truth. 'I'm sorry,' she said, bowing her head.

Chrissy leant back against the chair. Her breathing was becoming erratic.

When Marianna realized she stood up. 'Are you okay? Should I call the doctor?'

'No, she'll be fine,' said Eloise. 'It happens sometimes.' She grabbed the chair by the pizza oven and made Chrissy straddle it.

'I can see it's very difficult for you,' said Marianna.

She could have said that over an hour ago. Then again, why should she let her husband's killer off so easily? This was her chance to find out what really happened, to see that justice would finally be done. Marianna knew exactly who they were now, Eloise felt sure of it. If she had only a very slight suspicion before, she could be in no doubt after what she had just heard.

She seemed in no hurry to call the police, however. Quite the opposite, in fact, appearing more concerned for Chrissy's welfare. She poured her a glass of water, even placed her hand on Chrissy's back in a comforting way. Eloise didn't trust her. She held onto her mother until her breathing began to return to normal.

315

'We were nineteen,' said Chrissy. 'Innocent, trusting and totally invincible.' She laughed at her foolish younger self. 'All I wanted was to get home. Back to Dan. To your dad.'

Eloise squeezed her hand. The night was starting to close in. A series of sunken lights dotted around the garden had come on automatically. Eloise had not even noticed until now. She stared at her mother, trying to make sense of it all. To think that she would be capable of such a violent, bloody act.

So Chrissy had killed a man and it *wasn't* an accident. But the man she had killed had raped her.

Silence fell over them, and it was Chrissy who was the first to break it. 'So now do you see why time isn't healing, Marianna?'

'What year was this?'

Eloise knew it was coming. Her toes curled, she screwed up her eyes, and didn't dare breathe.

'1989,' said Chrissy.

Of course, Marianna wanted to be sure. There could be no element of doubt that she had just extracted a confession from the woman who killed her husband all those years ago.

'You can call the police,' said Chrissy. 'I'm just so tired.'

'No, Mum! Marianna, please.'

'Maybe it's for the best. Maybe if I'd gone to prison I might not still feel this way.' She put her arm round Eloise, her eyes watery again. 'But I'm glad for your sake that I didn't.'

Eloise held onto her. Juliet came to join them and Chrissy didn't push her away.

When they eventually pulled apart, Marianna had gone.

***

Eloise ran up the path as fast as she could. The darkness seemed blacker than ever and she was without a torch. As her eyes grew accustomed, she could just pick out a figure moving in the distance. 'Marianna,' she called. But when she caught up, it wasn't

Marianna at all; it was one half of the fornicating couple from that first evening. The woman was startled by Eloise. '*Buonasera*,' she said as she shot past.

Eloise stumbled, picking herself up again, too frightened to stop even for a second. Marianna could be on the phone to the police right now. What if they were already on their way? In fact, what was she even doing going after her? They should be heading out of here immediately.

Her phone rang. It was Juliet.

'Eloise. Where are you? Are you okay?'

'I'm trying to find Marianna. How's Mum?'

'Calm. Remarkably so. Do you want me to come?'

'No, stay with my mum. I have to go.' She could see Marianna up ahead, almost at the stables. When Eloise called to her she turned round and waited.

'Please, Marianna,' she said, trying to catch her breath. 'Please don't call the police. My mum's serving her prison sentence. She lives it every day. Please.'

Marianna placed both hands on her shoulders. Her scent was orange blossom, so delicate it made her want to cry. 'I know,' said Marianna, almost in a whisper. 'I can see that she does.'

Her mind was in chaos. Eloise pushed her away again; she had to see her eyes. 'The thing is, Marianna, I know he was your husband.' She kept her voice low, as Marianna had, but the words spilled out regardless of who might be listening. 'And I know that you know who we are. I've no idea how. It was Juliet who found you on the internet. That's how she found my mum too. They haven't seen each other since it happened. Not until recently. You see, Mum dropped out of uni when they got back from France, never wanted anything more to do with Juliet because she was scared of being found out and because she was always a reminder of what she'd done. All this time Juliet never even knew that that bastard – I mean your husband – had raped my mum. Neither of us knew until tonight. We found out the same time as you did. Juliet thought that she'd killed him for her sake, to save her. Well she did. But I guess it was to punish him as well. Wasn't it?'

She had to stop, come up for air.

'It's okay, Eloise.'

'No, it's not. When Juliet got back in touch, she came to see us and saw what life is like for us, what it had done to my mum. So then she thought the only way to help her was to bring her here to see you, so Mum could see how you've managed to move on and get your life together again. See how happy you are. I don't think she properly thought it through.' Eloise shook her head. How could she have allowed Juliet to get them into this? Had she even considered that Chrissy might go to prison? 'I didn't know what was going on myself until I spoke to Nico earlier.'

'What? You told Nic about your mother?'

'No! I told him about my dad dying, and then it just came out about his. He said a few things; I asked more questions. It was so awful when I realized. I rushed back to Juliet. I couldn't believe that she'd done this. I told her she was crazy and that we had to leave straight away.'

'I'm glad you didn't,' said Marianna. 'You mustn't leave.'

Eloise nodded. She knew what was coming. She looked down at her trainers, scuffed from her horse-riding excursion with Nico only that afternoon. How things had moved on since then. She kicked at the ground.

'Look at me,' said Marianna.

Her face was so kind. Eloise knew it was about to betray them.

'I'm not going to call the police.'

'You're not? But … you're really not?'

'No.'

Eloise searched deeper into her eyes for the truth. What did she actually mean? The truth was never *that* simple. Could she trust her?

Blind trust. That was all she had to go on.

'Really? But what about Nico? Will you tell him?'

Marianna laughed, almost wildly.

'Never. It's the same as telling the police. Actually no, it's much worse. You see, he has an idealized version of his father that I can never alter. He'd never believe your mother's version of the truth.'

Eloise did not want to think about that right now. She had to keep Nico separate from any of this.

'But do *you* believe it, Marianna?'

Marianna's silence was unbearable and cruel. 'Believe,' she said with a long sigh. 'That's another complicated word.' She looked up at the dark universe, as if her answer was out there somewhere. 'Regrettably, yes. Yes, I do believe it.'

Eloise felt her lungs explode. She had to tell her mother immediately.

But tell her what exactly?

Chrissy still had no idea who Marianna was. She was oblivious to the fact that she had just confessed everything to her rapist's widow. If this came out at the wrong moment, then Chrissy would lose it altogether. They should still wait until they were safely back in England to tell her.

One thing still puzzled Eloise.

'Did you have any idea about us though, Marianna? I mean before tonight.'

Marianna gave her a half-smile. 'It was the brooch,' she said.

'What, that ugly thing Juliet always wears?'

Marianna laughed. 'Yes, that ugly cat thing.'

'But my mum said she stole it. I don't understand … Oh my god, is it yours? Did she steal it from—? No, she can't have.'

'I didn't much care for it either. He bought it for me from a little artisan in Paris. Each piece was very individual. He would stamp your initials on the back if you wanted. You will see the one your mother stole has 'ML' in tiny letters on it. I knew I'd lost it somewhere. I didn't know where. Earlier that day – the day he … the day he came upon your mother and her friend, he phoned me and said that he had found it in the car. She must have stolen it from him. I don't know when but she must have taken it.'

'Why would she do that?'

Eloise knew that was a foolish question. How would Marianna know the answer? Chrissy had stolen money from him so she must have taken the brooch too.

The roar of a motorbike engine shocked them into silence, the flood of its headlamp blinding them as it swerved around the corner. A tall, black leather-clad figure dismounted, pulled off his helmet, and said: '*Buonasera*.'

It was Nico.

'*Buona notte*,' said Marianna, giving Eloise a look of caution. And then to Nico: 'How is Sylvia?'

He laughed. 'She's fine.'

Marianna turned to go indoors, saying: 'Tell your mother I will call round as usual in the morning. I hope she feels better soon. We don't want it to spoil the rest of your holiday.'

'Thank you,' said Eloise. 'For everything.'

They watched Marianna go inside.

'Nothing serious I hope?' said Nico.

'Oh, erm. No, just … a headache. I've got to go.'

Eloise sped off. 'We go for another ride in the morning,' she heard him shout. 'With motorbike.' She carried on running, not even sure if they would still be here in the morning.

Their villa was in darkness. At first she thought they had done a flit, panicked and left without her. But she found them both in Chrissy's room, drinking strong black coffee.

'Thank goodness, Eloise,' said Chrissy. 'I've been calling you, left messages. I wanted to say goodbye before the police came.'

Eloise was so out of breath she could barely speak, but she was bursting to tell her the good news.

'Marianna isn't going to the police … She says she understands … what you've been through. And that she's coming round tomorrow as usual. And we all have to stay.'

Juliet got up. 'We can decide what to do in the morning,' she said. 'It's too late to do anything now.' She looked worn out. 'Goodnight.'

Eloise kicked off her trainers; one bounced off the wall. She was determined to remain positive. 'I'm staying here with you tonight, Mum' she said, climbing into her bed and pulling the sheet across herself. 'The police aren't coming, so you might as well get some sleep.'

Chrissy perched on the edge of the bed. 'I'm not going to run any more, Eloise. If that's what you think.' She began arranging Eloise's hair on the pillow. 'Whatever happens tomorrow, you know that I still love you, don't you?'

'You have to believe me, Marianna's on our side. And I love you too, Mum. Always.'

Chrissy finally got undressed and into bed. 'This could be our last night together,' she whispered.

Eloise knew that she would never convince her. Only Marianna could do that.

'Let me tell you about your first birthday, shall I?'

All Eloise wanted to do right now was sleep, but she had no choice. 'Okay,' she said, turning over to conceal her tears.

'The doorbell rang several times,' said Chrissy. 'I knew they'd come for me.'

CHAPTER 37

Manchester: 1991

'It'll be them,' said Dan. Chrissy held onto the kitchen unit. 'Hey, it's okay. We know who it is.' He was about to put his arms round her but the doorbell went again. 'I'd better get it before they break it down.'

'Happy birthday, Eloise!' She heard their cries in the hallway. 'Where is she? Where's the little lady?'

Chrissy hadn't wished to make a big fuss. She wanted it to be just the three of them. But both sets of parents had forced it and now it was a full-blown party with balloons and presents, and Dan had made a cake with a single candle stuck onto the nose of a big yellow smiley face. She could hear them in the lounge, cooing over Eloise. She would have to make the effort. They wouldn't just go away.

Glass of water. Straighten hair. Pinch some colour into the cheeks. Deep breaths.

'Chrissy, hello!' She got through all the kissing and hugging that had to be done. 'You all right? You look a bit peaky,' said her dad.

'Sleepless nights, you know how it is.'

'Oh, we remember that all right.'

Everyone laughed. It sparked a conversation about babies they had known – were they sleepers or shriekers, what techniques had they used to cope with the long nights – and Chrissy could edge away. Eloise was being passed around, gurgling and grinning, really quite the performer. She did seem a very happy child.

'We should eat,' Dan announced. 'Someone's got to shift all this grub!'

They milled around the table. Dan had done most of it, put the Paddington Bear tablecloth on, blown up the balloons, set out paper plates to save on the washing up, folded the green napkins into frogs. Chrissy had tipped crisps into bowls, her sole contribution.

'Smile!' someone shouted. 'Chrissy, come on. Stop hiding.'

'Oh. No, please.' She held her hands in front of her face as the camera flashed. 'I really don't – I'm sorry.'

'Eat. Come on, everyone,' Dan shouted.

Then, on top of all that fuss and commotion, the phone rang. And that was when it happened; always at the wrong time. Chrissy quickly sat down, hoping no one would see.

Dan did.

'Just get the phone,' she yelled at him when she saw him coming over, drawing attention to it even more.

It was no one important. Just someone from the band asking what time they could pop round. Dan came back, armed with kitchen roll and cloths. 'I knew you'd sit in it,' he said to Chrissy, but really it was for everyone else to hear. 'I knocked my beer over on that chair. Look at you, you're soaking.'

He made her stand up. She couldn't just sit there until everyone had gone home. There was a puddle on the carpet at her feet. 'I'll go change,' she said.

Chrissy dashed upstairs and threw herself onto the bed. When would this stop? She couldn't even cry. There were no more tears left inside her. She stood up, opened the wardrobe and shut herself inside. She had taken to doing this lately, burying her face in the purple raincoat that Juliet had given her in exchange for writing the essay that time. She could still smell her best friend. Juliet had not even known that she was pregnant when she left Bristol. She still wouldn't have any idea. Nor about their getting married. It was only a very small wedding but a best friend should have been there. Juliet should have been present when Eloise was born too. And today, on her first birthday, she really ought to be at this stupid party. If Juliet had been here it wouldn't have been a stupid party.

But it was all so screwed.

Whenever she drank a cup of coffee she would think of the two of them sitting in Gianni's; even smile at the thought of Juliet's lateness. Come the weekend, she would wonder whether Juliet was out partying, and who with. It was the little things, the unexpected triggers. A jar of Marmite on the supermarket shelf could send her to pieces. And she could never pass a second-hand shop without rummaging for a dress or a top that Juliet could turn into something really special.

That life was long gone. Even though Juliet was still living it.

Chrissy gathered up the purple raincoat, plus all the other clothes she had given her, and put them into a bin liner. Oxfam would be very grateful for them.

'What are you doing?' said Dan.

'This way we both forget her.'

***

'I want you to make an appointment to see the doctor,' said Dan, once their guests had all gone home.

They had discussed this before, but Chrissy was not in favour. 'You know I can't.'

'Well, I know you can't tell him what happened, but just say you're a bit down after having your first baby and he'll give you something. I'll come with you.'

'Unless he can remove my fucking conscience it's a waste of time,' she yelled, kicking the wardrobe door.

'Look at me,' Dan said. 'I said, *look at me*, Chrissy.' He sounded stern. Dan rarely sounded stern. Then he threw his arms in the air like he was giving up on her.

She buried her head in the pillow. 'I'm sorry. Forgive me. I'm just so fucking sorry.'

'You can't go on like this. We can't go on like this. Don't let him do this to you, Chrissy. Don't let him destroy you.' Dan's voice was shaky now. 'Because if you do …' – the pause frightened her – 'he will destroy me as well. And our daughter.'

Chrissy took deep breaths. It helped sometimes. 'Where is she?' she asked.

'I've put her down in her room.'

Dan followed her. Perhaps he was worried what she might do.

Chrissy reached into the cot and took Eloise in her arms. She looked down at her sleepy little face, oval-shaped like hers. She had the same nose too. Her mouth was thin, a different sort of a mouth. Brown eyes like Dan's. Everyone said she had Dan's eyes. And her cute, playful smile. She was always smiling. Just like Dan.

Dan was right. She would go and see the doctor and she would fight this. Eloise needed her. She needed to be a good mother to her daughter.

Kissing her delicate face, still fast asleep, Chrissy placed her back into the cot.

'Now what are you doing?' asked Dan. He had followed her back into their room.

'Looking for these,' she said, fishing out some old tracksuit bottoms and a pair of battered trainers. 'I'm going running.'

'Running?'

'It might just clear my head. And I'll make the doctor's appointment tomorrow first thing.'

CHAPTER 38

Tuscany: 2007

Eloise woke with a start. Her mother was throwing things into her suitcase.

'Mum? What're you doing?'

'We have to get out of here,' she said.

'But why? I told you last night that Marianna wants us to stay. Are you listening to me?'

'I don't know who that woman is but she was asking a lot of questions.'

'You said you wouldn't run away any more, Mum.'

'I need to go home.'

'Well, at least stay for the party.' Eloise knew how trivial that sounded after all that had gone on. Maybe she was being selfish, but then so was her mother. Last night was all in the past and they had to get on with the present. They had to trust Marianna. And no matter how warped it was, she wanted to see Nico again.

'What time is it?' she asked, searching for her phone. The last thing Eloise wanted was for Nico to show up here. He had said something about a motorbike ride. If she had been thinking straight last night she would have put him off that.

'Juliet's going to get Laura to sort our flights. We need to be ready by ten.'

She carried on stuffing things into the suitcase. Eloise got out of bed and kicked the lid down. 'I told you, it's fine,' she said.

'How can it be fine?' replied Chrissy. 'It's not fine. It'll never be fine.'

Eloise walked over to the window and pulled opened the blinds. The sunshine was burning through the mist. Tiny bundles of grapes, wet with morning dew, were hanging off the vines that twisted round the pergola. And red geraniums in wooden tubs waited patiently for their petals to dry out, their leaves threaded with shiny spiders' webs.

'What about Juliet? I bet she doesn't think we should go.'

'What's all this shouting?' Juliet peered round the door. 'Not doing my hangover any good, I can tell you.' Her hair was wild, still backcombed and pushed off her face with a black, glittery eye-mask. Clearly she had got her sparkle back, and even with a hangover she looked glamorous.

'Mum wants to go home.'

'Yes, I know. I've got Laura trying to sort something.'

'But Marianna says she's not going to do anything. Doesn't want us to leave.'

'It's not up to me,' said Juliet, stepping into the room. 'We'll go somewhere else, talk it all through. Somewhere more ...' She glanced at Eloise as she searched for the right word. '... more neutral.'

A loud knocking made all three of them freeze.

'*Buongiorno!*'

It was Marianna, bringing them their usual fresh *croissants* and bread.

True to her word.

She looked exactly the same as she had done the previous morning, smiling and radiant, and leaving a delicate trail of orange blossom wherever she went.

'So what have you got planned for today?' she asked, handing Juliet the *croissants* and bread.

'My mum wants to go home,' said Eloise, indicating to her that her mother was hiding in the bedroom.

'Already? What a pity.'

Juliet ushered them out onto the terrace and busied herself in the kitchen. The outside temperature was slowly creeping upwards, although for now it was tolerable. Soon the smell of coffee was released into the morning and Eloise gave Marianna a pleading smile. She seemed on the verge of saying something to Eloise when Chrissy suddenly appeared.

'So tell me,' said Chrissy, 'do all guests get a personal delivery service?'

She sat down next to Marianna, scraping her chair back on the tiles.

'Well, actually, I only do the ones I like or who have interesting stories to tell,' she replied.

'*Le petit déjeuner!*' Juliet announced. She had come out carrying a tray loaded with cups, plates, *croissants*, cutlery, butter, jam, bread and cheese. They helped her set it down and Eloise handed out plates.

Marianna held up her hand. '*Café*, only, for me. Really I came by to remind you about the party. I hope you're still going to come tonight. It's just a few people from the village, members of staff and some friends from Florence. There's food, and fireworks if it's not too wet, dancing too. It's just a thing we do every summer. I always invite my guests.' She turned to Chrissy, and added, 'I would like it very much if you would come.'

Juliet poured out the coffee. Marianna plopped in a sugar cube and began to stir. The sound of the spoon against the china cup became the only sound. She tapped the spoon a few times before putting it down on the saucer.

'How did you find me, Juliet?'

'What?'

'How did you know to come to Tuscany?'

Juliet wiped the sweat from her top lip.

'Well, I, erm … I was … Actually, I was trying to track down Chrissy and chanced upon an article that you were mentioned in …'

Chrissy was instantly on alert, and Juliet acting flustered was certainly not helping.

'And there you were. And … and here are we.' Juliet tried to give Chrissy a reassuring smile, taking a moment to think how to rescue the situation. 'At the end of the article it said how you now live in Italy and run a luxury holiday retreat. So I searched your name and 'Dream Tuscany' came up. I said to myself, *we simply have to come.*'

'I see.'

'You were much easier to find than my friend here.' Juliet laughed nervously.

'So where was the brooch when you stole it?'

Chrissy looked dazed. It took her a while to process the question, still trying to unravel the thread of what had already been said.

Eloise felt betrayed. Hadn't Marianna agreed last night that her mother had already suffered enough?

'What do you mean?' said Chrissy.

'Well, was it in the car? Or maybe in his wallet?'

'Erm. I don't—' There was panic in her eyes. 'It was in his jacket pocket. Which he'd put over the back of the chair. Why?'

'You stole the brooch from *him*?' said Juliet. 'Oh my god, so … So it's yours, Marianna? Those tiny letters on the back – "ML" – they're your initials.' Juliet gasped, covering her mouth with the back of her hand.

'Who *are* you?' said Chrissy, suddenly on her feet. Her hands felt for the wall behind her as she tried to keep Marianna in her sights. When her back thumped hard against it she realized she had nowhere to go and her breathing became frantic.

'As I told you last night, my life would have been very different if my husband were still alive. I cannot forgive *what* you did, but perhaps you should know that I forgive *you*.'

'But—,' said Chrissy, 'I don't—'

'Mum, come and sit down.'

Chrissy's eyes darted from Eloise to Juliet, and back to Eloise. It was already nearly forty degrees but Chrissy was shivering.

'Please don't waste any more of your life over this,' said Marianna. 'Your daughter needs you to be alive, not some shadow of yourself.'

Chrissy looked terrified as Marianna moved towards her.

'It's okay,' she said. 'You have my blessing to put this behind you now.' Then she placed her hand over Chrissy's. 'I forgive you,' she whispered.

Looking down at that hand, the hand of her rapist's widow, Chrissy allowed herself to be led over to a chair. Several minutes went by undisturbed as she sank deeper into her thoughts. When a lizard scampered across the terrace it seemed to bring her round slightly.

Chrissy turned to Marianna. She stared deep into her eyes. Finally, mouthing the words *thank you*. And then, more audibly, 'Thank you.'

'So … the party,' said Marianna, looking at her watch. 'You'll come? Of course, we hope the storm holds off or we won't be able to have any fireworks.'

She stood up. Holding her hand out to Chrissy in a business-like fashion.

Chrissy stared at it.

Her hand was trembling as it connected with Marianna's. They shook to seal up the past.

***

Marianna disappeared along the path. Watching her go it was as if in that moment time stood eerily still. The sky was dark and heavy over the hills. The *croissants* and coffee looked like they had been abandoned in a hurry, the occupants having fled in fear.

The same lizard scarpered out from under Chrissy's chair as she brought her legs into her chest, hugging her knees. Her forehead dropped down onto them.

'It's okay, Mum. Honestly.'

She had been waiting for one of them to speak so she could launch an attack. 'Was she talking about the same newspaper article that you saw, Juliet?'

'Well, erm, I suppose so,' said Juliet, cowering under Chrissy's furious stare. '"Victim's widow" it said. There was a photograph. It made me cry, made it seem real. She had a name and a face.'

'It was always real, Juliet.'

'Yes, I know but—'

'I killed her fucking husband.'

'Who was a fucking rapist. I still can't believe you never told me, Chrissy. All these years.'

'So then what did you do? After you saw her picture.'

'I did a search on her name.'

'As easy as that,' said Chrissy.

Juliet studied her. 'Why did you take it, Chrissy? The brooch. And then send it to *me*?'

'I didn't know you were going to wear it, day in, day out, did I? I had a lot on my mind too, you know,' she said, narrowing her eyes at her.

'Well, what did you expect me to do with it? It's all I had left of you.' Juliet's eyes filled with tears. 'Did you *want* me to get caught? Is that it?'

Chrissy stood up, and Eloise shuddered; the noise of the chair grating on her nerves.

'Let's face it, Juliet, you'd have told them it was me in any case.'

'You don't know that, Chrissy,' Juliet shouted after her. 'Chrissy.'

She was about to follow her but Eloise held her back.

***

The jet of water powered down over her body, suntanned and soft. Eloise had set the temperature to freezing but it still didn't feel cool enough. When the storm finally did come, it would certainly be a relief. For all of them. So they were staying here, at least for now. All her mother had wanted to do was just lie by the pool and think. She was still in a state of shock probably, but at least she seemed calm and more at peace with the world.

Eloise let her be. If Juliet wanted to seek her out, then it was up to her to take that risk. She couldn't intervene any more; she had played her part in bringing them together and now it was up to the two of them. If she had known, when Juliet first got in touch with that very first phone call, that it would be as painful a journey as this she might never have embarked upon it. But Eloise was glad that she had, because, at least now her mother had a chance to live her life properly again.

She allowed the drips to fall onto the white tiles, cool against her feet, intrigued by how quickly the drips became puddles. She wasn't sure what prompted it, perhaps the realization she was wandering about the place naked, but last night's conversation with Nico suddenly entered her mind. Quickly wrapping a towel around herself, she hurried to see what time it was.

Five past eleven.

'*Buongiorno*, Eloise.'

Nico had arrived carrying a spare helmet threaded through his arm.

CHAPTER 39

Tuscany: 2007

Eloise felt the towel slip. She caught it just in time and hitched it up, securing it under her arm. Running her fingers through her hair, teasing out the wet strands, it soon occurred to her that Nico had overstepped the privacy marker. No one had invited him in. She certainly hadn't.

'I didn't mean to intrude,' he said, sensing his mistake and stepping backwards. 'I did knock, but it was all open. So I just—'

'It's okay,' she said.

He put both helmets down carefully on the table and came towards her again. 'How is your mother?'

Eloise felt her legs weaken. 'Why?'

'The headache?'

'Oh. God, yeah, the headache. That's right. Well, she's okay now, thanks.'

Her mind was in a spin. What if her mother was to come back now?

'Okay,' he said, puffing out his cheeks. 'Well, maybe you have things to do today.' He picked up the helmets again, one on each arm.

'No! I can be ready in—'

'No, no, no. Today feels not good.'

She knew she had to let him go. Not just today, but forever. After all, he was the one person standing between her mother and a life sentence.

'*Domani*,' Eloise shouted. 'Perhaps we could go tomorrow?'

Nico spun round on his heel. 'But you're coming this evening, no?'

'Well, yes. I think so.'

He pulled something out of his pocket. 'This …' He held up another business card and placed it on the table, 'is my bar in Florence. If you want to go this afternoon you can go by Vespa. Or maybe—' He made a gesture as if thumbing a ride.

'Hitch-hiking! Oh god, no.'

'Or a cab maybe. Ask my mother for a telephone number.'

He was on his way out again.

'Nico. Nic!'

He turned round.

'Doesn't matter, it's nothing.'

'It's something,' he said, coming back towards her.

'No, I'll see you tonight at the party. That's if we don't make it to Florence.'

He stood with his arms across his chest, his hair falling messily over his face. She was wrestling with the truth of who he actually was. Again. *Remember, Eloise.*

'Is it Sylvia?' he asked. 'I told you, *come il vento*.' He made his hand soar like a bird. 'Or maybe I just don't meet the right girl yet. Without seeing inside someone's heart, you cannot really know. Don't you think?'

Suddenly she was gripped firmly in his arms. It happened so quickly, she wasn't really sure she wanted this, but as she tried to break free he pressed his mouth over hers. Then she found herself kissing him back.

She stopped, pulled away from him, holding onto the towel which had loosened slightly.

He gave her a moment, then said: 'I should go.'

'Yes. You should. You should go.'

Nico broke into a smile. 'Come like that to the party.'

'I don't think so!'

'It's up to you, Eloise. Of course.'

This time he did go. But immediately ran into Chrissy and Juliet.

Eloise hung back. She saw him wave, heard him say, '*Ciao*.' Juliet raised her sunglasses, checking him out. Her mother stormed inside.

'Is that who I think it is? Close the doors, Juliet.'

'Depends who you think it is,' said Eloise, retreating.

'Do not play games, Eloise. You know exactly what I'm asking. Is it?'

'If you're asking is he Marianna's son, then yes. That's Nic. Or Nico. He likes both,' she added, sarcastically.

Chrissy wanted to know what he was doing here, with Eloise in only a towel. Was she okay? She hated her mother for thinking along those lines. Did she think he would automatically be like his father? Juliet agreed she was being unfair.

'Well, just don't get any ideas about him, okay?' said Chrissy.

'Your mother's right,' Juliet pitched in. 'If you were to let anything slip—' She chewed one arm of her sunglasses. 'He's cute, though, I have to admit.'

'Juliet, for god's sake,' said Chrissy.

Eloise could see where her mother's fear was coming from, but she couldn't stop her hanging out with him. They would probably only stay one or two more days in Tuscany and then she would never see him again.

'Look, Mum, give me a break. He only came to drop off a card to invite us to his bar in Florence. If you don't believe me, it's on the table.' Eloise marched into her bedroom and shut the door harder than she intended. She opened it again. 'And he's got a girlfriend. Sylvia.'

She pulled on the cord above her bed, waiting for the ceiling fan to begin its whirring. The heat of this place. The storm could not come soon enough.

***

They had gone their separate ways again to cool off. Eloise was down at the pool, distracting herself by staring at the photo on her phone of her and Nico. She wished it was still only yesterday, when things were different. Before any of this happened. Then she sent a text to Anya to say that she had met someone. Sharing it with her best friend might just take away the awful reality of who Nico was. Almost immediately, a reply came back asking: '*who, what, where, when*' and '*Send me a pic.*'

Eloise put down her phone, shoving it away.

She would never be able to share any of this, not with anyone. Like her mother, she would spend the rest of her life with a secret locked up inside her. A secret which had to be buried right now, covered with earth and sealed up with concrete. Never dig it up.

Ever.

She texted Anya back to say she was joking and that she had gone off him already.

***

'Pack your bags, Eloise,' she heard her mother's voice over the loud banging on her door. Eloise had come inside for a siesta about an hour earlier to get some relief from the heat. Dazed, she got off the bed and stumbled to the door. Chrissy was standing there with her arms folded.

Eloise stepped into her face. 'If you leave now, Mum, you're on your own.'

She slammed the door and it went quiet for a while. Or at least, just muffled words from Chrissy and Juliet, which she couldn't even be bothered to decipher.

Not until their voices were raised. Then she couldn't fail to overhear.

'Don't blame me, Chrissy.'

'I don't. I blame myself for being swept along by you. And for what? A few good parties and a disastrous trip to France.'

Eloise shot out of her room. 'Mum. Please don't.'

'Get back in your *fucking* room, Eloise, and stay there.'

'Don't speak to her like that,' said Juliet.

'I'll speak to her how the hell I like, she's *my* daughter. Don't think I haven't seen what you've been up to either, manoeuvring your way in, trying to steal her away from me.'

'I only want to help, Chrissy. More than ever, now I know the truth of it.'

'You know fuck all, Juliet. And that's not what this is about, you know damn well it isn't. This is about *you*. It was always about you. And actually, I do blame you for what happened. I didn't, but I do now. You take and take and take and you ruined my sodding life.'

'I just want us to be friends again, Chrissy. Best friends – maybe, one day.'

Eloise could hear her mother's mocking laughter. 'Really? So why now? Tell me. The glitz and glamour wearing a bit thin, is it? Hm? Oh, and I know about Luca. I know he wants to abandon you as well. Divorce number four, is that? I've lost bloody count. Is that the reason? Poor Juliet feels lonely again. He told me about the divorce when we were in Rome so you needn't look so innocent.'

'I only want to help you, Chrissy.'

'By making me confess to the wife of the man I killed? You took a fucking risk there, even for you.'

Eloise was afraid of her mother's anger, where it might lead, but still didn't dare show her face.

'So I take risks,' said Juliet. 'That's who I am.'

'Or were you hoping to get me out of the way? Is that it? I confess to my crime and get carted off to prison.'

'No! I did it to save you, I swear.'

'But this is about saving you, Juliet. Not me. You're trying to fill a void in your life that's always been there. It always will be there.'

'No!'

'Well, let me make this clear; I am done saving you. Christ knows, I've done it enough times.'

There was a silence, and Eloise wondered whether to make an appearance but Juliet piped up again.

'I'd have done exactly the same for you in that motel room, Chrissy. If it had been the other way round. You know I would.'

'Now that is something I've wondered over the years,' said Chrissy.

'I'd do anything for you,' said Juliet. 'Anything. You should know that by now.'

'Well, let's see, shall we?'

Eloise didn't like her mother's tone. She was calmer but there was a menace to her voice.

'Right. I am going to call the police, and you, Juliet Ricci, are going to tell them that in 1989 you murdered Marianna's husband.'

'No, Mum! You can't do that.' Eloise rushed out. She had to intervene before it was too late.

Chrissy was holding Juliet's phone out to her. 'Do this for me, Juliet,' she said. 'Do it now.' But Juliet could only stare at it. 'No. I thought not.' Chrissy threw the phone against the glass doors. It bounced off, shattering into tiny pieces.

Juliet sank to her knees. 'I'd give my life for you, Chrissy,' she wailed.

'You're so full of shit, Juliet.'

Eloise wasn't sure which one to go to first. Loyalty prevailed, and she went to find her mother. Reluctantly, Eloise was beginning to see some of those things for herself about Juliet. Yet this was not the outcome she had hoped for.

'You know she doesn't really think things through properly, Mum.'

Chrissy was in her room, tossing more things into the suitcase. 'We're going home, Eloise, and that's that.'

Eloise swallowed. She didn't want to say it, and yet she had to. 'You can't make me.'

Chrissy stopped what she was doing and pushed her fingers deep into the grooves across her forehead. 'No. No, you're right, Eloise. I'm asking you to come with me.'

'I can't though, Mum. I just can't do this any more.' Eloise could hardly speak, choking on her sobs. 'I need you to be okay, to put all this behind you now.' She was coming towards her, but Eloise put her hand out to stop her. 'If Marianna can forgive you, I don't see why you can't forgive yourself. It's awful that you were raped, it makes me so angry and sad and I cannot even imagine what that must have been like for you. But for me that's even more reason to kill the person who did that to you.' She paused. Because this was the most important thing of all she had to say to her. 'Juliet is the only friend you have, Mum. You can carry on running if you like, but don't expect me to.'

Chrissy didn't respond. Her mother looked so wounded, and she hated having to heap even more onto her. But she had to, because this also needed to be said. 'In any case, you can't go.'

'Why can't I?'

'Because I promised Dad.'

'Promised Dad what?'

'He made me say that I'd always look after you, never leave you on your own. I was eleven years old and it wasn't fair.' Eloise broke down again. 'I just can't do it any more. I need you to be okay, Mum, otherwise what's the point of my life? You may as well never have had me.'

'I told you, don't ever say that. Don't you dare.'

'Well, it's true.'

'I've given up my whole life for you. I'd do anything for you.'

'Seriously, have you heard yourself? You sound just like Juliet. I am begging you, Mum. Just put on Juliet's dress, say you're sorry, and come to the party tonight. You have to draw a line under all of this now. Please, for my sake.'

***

The party was in a couple of hours. Eloise slid down the bathtub blowing clouds of white foam into the air with a sense of satisfaction. Clearly, they still had a long way to go – many hurtful things had been said which would not be forgotten in a hurry – but Eloise had managed to persuade Chrissy and Juliet to make a fresh start. She had even got them to shake on it.

With this all behind her now she could allow herself to daydream, just for a little while, about Nico. Distant rumblings of thunder brought her back to reality. Her head was telling her to steer clear of him. And what if her mother should catch them together this evening? But the rest of her body was screaming that it simply couldn't survive without him.

Then there was Sylvia. Who was Sylvia? Would she be at the party? What then?

As she stepped out of the bath she became aware of the darkening sky. It seemed to be getting lower, like a lid coming down on a box. The breeze had got up, too, and was mischievously trying to blow the window off its stay. Eloise went to close it, noticing the drop in temperature. Another roll of thunder clattered into the hills, lighting up the sky in the distance. She didn't mind the storm heading this way, just as long as they could get to the party without getting caught in it.

Chrissy avoided parties. She much preferred to lose herself in a crowd rather than engage with anyone in it. They had been waiting for her for over an hour. Juliet checked her watch again, looking anxiously at Eloise. She had chain-smoked at least four emergency cigarettes, and that was to Eloise's knowledge. Eloise noticed, too, that she had dispensed with the cat brooch and no longer wore it.

At last, Chrissy appeared.

'Mum, you look gorgeous!'

Juliet popped the champagne, rushing towards her with a glass. Then she stood back to admire, forcing Chrissy to unfold her arms. 'I hardly recognize you,' said Juliet, tearfully. This was the first time she had worn the Fifties-style black dress. It seemed so long ago now that Juliet had presented them with gifts on that first evening in Manchester. Everything about the dress was perfect. Chrissy's skin was tanned and toned, and it hugged her curves beautifully. A hint of cleavage was just visible through the V-shaped lace panel. The pinched in waist with full flowing skirt had a swirl of net underskirt beneath the hem, drawing the eye to her shapely, bronzed legs. Eloise recognized the familiar Ricci fragrance, too, which Chrissy had been refusing to wear until now.

Her mother was alive. She was finally being Chrissy.

'Both of you look stunning,' said Juliet, dabbing her eyes. With a sniff, she raised up her glass. 'To us. As long as we live.'

'As long as we live,' said Eloise, chinking glasses. She recognized those words from somewhere. Then she remembered. Her mother had written them in Juliet's twentieth birthday card.

'I'm not sure how long I'll stay tonight,' said Chrissy, fiddling with the dress.

CHAPTER 40

Tuscany: 2007

The storm held off until all the guests were safely under cover, as though politely waiting for everyone to arrive. Drinks in hand, they stood and watched a curtain of rain billowing across the hills. They could almost hear the trees and bushes sigh, holding out their leaves for their thirst to be quenched at long last.

A hundred or so people were milling about. The hippest crowd, from Florence presumably, were dressed in Ricci, according to Juliet. Others were distinctly rustic-looking from the neighbouring villages, but everyone seemed to mix and most people knew each other. There was a large screen set up at the far end showing a firework display to make up for the real thing being rained off.

Marianna came over to greet them. She made a point of holding onto Chrissy's arm. 'I'm so glad you've come,' she said, smiling at Chrissy as she spoke. 'You must *enjoy* yourself.' They were ushered to a long table where members of staff were serving drinks. 'Help yourselves to a glass of something.' Then she moved on to greet her other guests.

A man with a video camera was circulating through the crowd.

Eloise noticed that her mother didn't dodge out of his way. She also recognized the fornicating couple whose privacy she had trampled on that first evening. It seemed a long time ago now. The woman nodded, and Juliet struck up a conversation. Chrissy tapped the side of her glass, unable to join in as they were speaking German. Eloise searched for Nico among the crowd; she couldn't see him anywhere. When she turned back to her mother she was in conversation with a rather handsome Italian.

Eloise stepped away.

Chrissy seemed relaxed, smiling. Every now and then she would push her hair behind her ears, listening intently to what he was saying. She looked so lovely tonight and Eloise felt nothing but pride, especially when she considered how far her mother had come, after all she had been through. As she retreated further, confident she wasn't needed, she felt her arm suddenly forced up between her shoulder blades. She knew it was Nico even before he let go. He was so close she could feel his breath on her neck.

'Sorry,' she said, stepping backwards when he had released her. 'I just need to go and … I just need to go.'

Eloise spotted Juliet's beehive over the sea of heads. She made for that, weaving her way through the crowd. 'Talk to me, Juliet,' she said, reaching for her arm. 'And if Nico comes, just blank him.'

'Oh. You had a fall out?'

'She doesn't want me to go near him.'

'It's okay, he's talking to someone.' Juliet made the words come from the side of her mouth; another party game she had played before.

'What is she like?' asked Eloise. 'It doesn't matter. What do you think I should do, Juliet?'

She laughed. 'Don't ask me about men. I'm good at catching them, hopeless at keeping them.' But there was an underlying sadness to her words.

'I'm sorry about Luca,' said Eloise. She didn't know what else to say. The rain was still hammering down. She went to get herself another drink and then hid behind the Ricci lot from Florence to avoid the man with the camera. She just wanted to be alone and watch the storm. How different everything looked in the wet, like someone had turned the page to a totally new landscape.

Later in the evening people started dancing. It was Juliet who got things going, dragging Chrissy and Eloise with her. Once or twice, Eloise caught Nico staring at her. He had the video camera and was filming them at one point. She smiled briefly, trying not to look his way again. When her eyes wandered back to him he was kissing someone at the side of the bar. A pretty girl. Petite. Probably called Sylvia.

Eloise dropped out and went to sit by herself. Juliet and Chrissy were dancing to some Eighties' tunes. Her mother's Italian admirer seemed very keen. She was making out that she was more into the music but every now and then she would acknowledge him with a twist of her hips or a shake of her shoulders. Eloise smiled to herself. Seeing her mother happy was far more important. She had to forget Nico.

'Eloise, this is Sylvia. Sylvia, Eloise.'

'Oh.'

The pretty, petite girl was hanging onto his arm. '*Ciao*,' she said, coolly.

'Your mother seems to have made a good recovery,' said Nico.

'Yes. She's feeling much better now, thank you.'

Sylvia excused herself. Eloise stood up, about to say that she was going back to dance, when Nico grabbed her hand and kissed it. After a few seconds she pulled it away again. He was much quicker though. 'Got you,' he said, gripping her wrist. 'Now there is no escape.'

Whatever fantasies she may have in her head about him, she knew they could never be together. The terrible truth would never go away; she could never share any of it with him. Least of all with him. Eloise loved her mother too much to risk it; he loved his father too much to accept it.

'So what did I do?'

'What do you mean?'

'You didn't come to my bar in Florence. I call you many times.'

'My phone was on charge. Look, can we go somewhere less crowded?'

He didn't understand at first. The rain clattering down onto the roof and the rumble of thunder overhead made it difficult to hear. Every so often a flash of lightning would illuminate the sky. They needed to get out of sight. Eloise began to lead him in one direction but he somehow ended up guiding her to a secluded corner. He indicated to a low bench tucked away.

'So,' he said, stroking her arm. His whole body was pushing against hers. 'Something bothers you, no? Is it Sylvia?' It was simpler just to agree. 'I told you, I don't have girlfriends.'

'She seems to think so. I just saw you kissing her.'

He started laughing. 'Eloise. You and me, we—' He clicked his fists together to make them connect. 'No? You don't think so?' She shrugged. 'And you look so beautiful tonight.' She could feel herself turning towards him, at the very last second twisting away again. He pulled her chin back to him and pressed his mouth onto hers.

'What the hell do you think you are doing to my daughter?'

They sprung apart.

'Mum!'

Chrissy was standing over them. She sank her fingers painfully into the top of Eloise's arm, pulling her to her feet. As she was being dragged away she tried to get a last glimpse of Nico.

'Why did you do that, Mum? Get off me!'

'We need to talk.'

'What about? You only want to ruin it for me.'

Eloise shook her arm free. So she happened to like Nico. It was complicated, but was that such a crime?

345

Chrissy found them a spot well away from anyone. Her face was contorted, she looked in pain.

'Mum, are you all right?'

'I never wanted to have to say this, Eloise.'

Music from the party and bursts of laughter were carried to them in distorted bursts. The storm was slowly passing, although the rain still kept coming at short intervals. In between, they could hear the leaves dripping. Deep puddles were forming everywhere.

'Well, are you going to tell me, because if not—' Eloise was preparing herself for 'the lecture'.

'You cannot have anything to do with that boy. Do you understand me?'

'Mum, I'm not stupid. It's not as though I'm going to tell him anything.'

'That's not the issue.'

'Then what is?' Chrissy tried to hug her, but Eloise resisted. 'Please don't spoil it for me, okay?'

Her mother began squeezing the sides of her head as if it was about to erupt. Something was very wrong.

'I'm going to get Juliet.'

'No!' Chrissy lowered her voice to a whisper. 'No.'

This was more than just overprotective parenting. Eloise braced herself for yet another body blow.

'You cannot have anything to do with that boy because …' Chrissy faltered.

'Because what, Mum? For god's sake, please say whatever it is. This is killing me.'

'Because he's your brother.'

'What?'

'Ssh. You must stay calm.'

'*Calm*? But I don't understand what you're saying to me. You mean—?'

'His father raped me.'

Her words sounded blurred and far away, as if someone had pushed her head underwater.

'Oh my god, no. No, Mum. No!'

She ran off into the rain and into the darkness. Her mother shouted her name but didn't come after her. In any case, she was too quick. She cast off her shoes, tossing them into the air, wishing they would explode into little pieces. She wanted to break something. Hit something.

The water running down her face was a mixture of rainwater and tears. She wasn't cold but her dress was stuck to her skin, which was visible through the thin fabric. She didn't know where she was heading and somehow found herself by the side of the lake. How different it felt to the last time she was here.

She removed her clothes, all of them, ripping her dress in the process. What did it matter? What did any of this matter?

The rocks tore at her feet. But what couldn't be seen couldn't hurt you. She knew that now. It's what you *could* see. It's what you did know. That's what hurt the most.

The icy chill of the water seemed to take away some of her pain.

'*There is no better freedom,*' she wanted to say, but the words froze as soon as her lips tried to shape them. She swam to keep warm, soon becoming disorientated. Where was the shore and where was the middle of the lake? Impossible to tell with the darkness wrapped around her and the rain coming down again. The middle of the lake was too deep, she remembered. Soon she would be out of her depth and was already getting tired.

Did it matter? Did any of it matter?

Treading water she turned full circle on herself. The shadows and outlines all looked the same. Her knees scraped against rocks. Crawling over them she managed to stand up, the water to her waist, and she began to wade through it, pushing hard against the lake, feeling exhausted and numb with cold.

Gradually her steps became easier. Somehow she had reached

the lakeshore and looked around, hugging her shoulders, searching for her dress, swallowed up in the gloom. She ran. She must have, because suddenly she found herself at the tiny hut by the side of the tennis court where the racquets and balls were kept. The director's chair was in the doorway, wet beneath her skin when she sank into it. Pressing her hands hard against her ears she slumped over her knees. If only Chrissy's words would stop echoing inside her head.

She was shivering; naked, alone, and curled up like a foetus.

To think that only a few weeks ago she hadn't known any of this. Was it better now that she knew the truth? She had wanted it so desperately.

So she was the daughter of a rapist. Nico was her half-brother.

'I ruined my mother's life,' she said out loud. Every day Chrissy had to look at the consequence of being raped. Why hadn't she aborted her when she had the chance? How she must hate her, deep down.

Resent her.

Loathe her.

And Dan. Her darling dad, who was never her dad at all. Not her real one. She had saved his words to her heart:

'Take care of your mother, Eloise. See that she's never
alone. And no matter what you hear, always try
and forgive her. Don't be afraid to ask questions.
But remember, we both love you.
Always at your side,
Dad X'

The music from the party drifted over in waves. Then she heard a crack. Maybe a branch breaking as it was stepped on.

And another.

Someone was approaching. It didn't look like Chrissy or Juliet. Or Nico.

It was Marianna.

'Look at you. Where are your clothes, Eloise?'

Marianna unlocked a cupboard and pulled out a large blanket, which she wrapped around her. It smelt musty and was rough against her skin. Then Marianna perched on the arm of the chair.

'Did you know?' asked Eloise. Most likely Marianna would have no idea what she was talking about, but she wasn't thinking clearly enough to care. But to her surprise, Marianna shook her head slowly.

'No, but I wondered. You have the same eyes. You have his eyes.'

'A rapist's eyes,' Eloise whispered. She closed them, screwed them up so tight it hurt. She suddenly remembered something. 'Oh god, Marianna. I've seen those eyes. I've seen him, I've seen him.'

'How?'

'Nico showed me a photograph he has in his wallet. I feel sick.'

She retched, hunched over, but nothing came up. Then it came again. Nothing. He was in there, inside of her, like he had been inside her mother. Uninvited. Unwelcome.

Eloise knew now that he would be inside her forever.

She sat up, wiped her mouth. Marianna stroked her back. She was shivering again and pulled in the ends of the blanket under her chin. 'Everyone said I had my dad's eyes,' she said, rocking. 'My mum especially, she always said it. Even now. When, all the time she must have meant—'

'Your mother loves you. You shouldn't forget that.'

'She shouldn't have had me, Marianna.'

'But she wanted you. That's the whole point. You are the reason she carried on. I can see that she fought hard to keep you.'

It was a strange feeling, almost like *she* was the one violated.

'My husband did a terrible thing, but you are a beautiful young woman and you have your whole life in front of you. You have to live, Eloise. You have to laugh and cry and love and hope, and do all of those things you ever dream of doing. Grab it whilst you have it and don't waste a second. We all have something in our lives we'd like to change. You must never let it change you.'

Eloise looked out at the raindrops dripping down from the roof. The overspill from the storm, it had to go somewhere.

'What about Nico?'

Marianna was shaking her head emphatically. 'No. Never. He can never know. He will never forgive.'

'But he's my brother.'

'That would not matter. What matters to him is what your mother did.' She sighed. 'But at least I know now that his father chose to spend his son's third birthday with two English girls. We never came first.' She laughed to herself. 'He always did have a thing for English girls. But you mustn't get any ideas that we can all live happily ever after together, Eloise. It's not going to be like that. Nic is very bitter. If his father were still alive, he might have grown up hating him eventually. Instead, he's grown up hating you.'

'You mean my mother.'

'It's the same. If he ever finds out.'

She stood up, placed her hand on Eloise's shoulder. 'Are you okay?' When Marianna saw that she was still shivering, she said: 'There are more blankets in the cupboard. Shall I send for your mother?'

'Please don't do that.'

'Okay. I have to get back to the party.'

There was a crack, a branch snapping. They both heard it and froze. 'Who is it?' shouted Marianna. Then a rustling sound, as though someone was running away.

'Oh god, you don't think it was Nic, do you?' said Eloise.

'Probably wild boar. They like to sniff around in the woods just behind us.' Marianna rubbed Eloise's shoulder before departing, and said: 'Remember what I've told you, Eloise.'

The curtain of water still pouring off the roof seemed to warp Marianna as she walked away. Eloise ran after her. She went as far as the path then returned to the villa.

She didn't know quite what to do with herself when she got there. The emptiness of the place was unwelcoming. The silence that she had grown to love in those moments of peace and quiet when she had the place to herself was now unsettling.

She went into her room to find some warm clothes.

'Eloise.'

'Nico! What are you doing here? Get away from me.'

Not only had he let himself in again, he was standing in her bedroom. And he was the last person on earth she wanted to see right now.

'Where did you go, Eloise? Are you okay?'

She realized she had to calm down. 'I went to the lake. Please, Nico. Please go.'

'You went swimming without me?'

'I had a row with my mum.'

She wasn't sure if he had understood; rather than leave, he came towards her.

'Go away!'

'But I came to show you this,' he said, gesturing to his phone. 'It's something I think you should see.'

It was a video from the party, still in full swing, music playing in the background. People seemed to be gathering in one area.

'You're nothing but a sad, lonely cow,' Chrissy's voice could be heard saying angrily to someone. Then the camera caught up with the action and she was seen walking away from Juliet.

'Well, what about you?' Juliet shouted, pulling her back again. 'You've let your daughter down and you know it. She'd choose me over you any day. I can give Eloise the whole world. You've held her prisoner her whole life.'

351

Chrissy laughed mockingly. 'Why would she want your world? It's made of shit, Juliet.'

'Well, why don't we ask her? Let her decide whose world she wants to live in. I can guarantee it won't be yours.'

'Have you quite finished?'

'No. Actually. I was never going to tell you this, Chrissy, but fuck it. He did kiss me back that night. Your precious Dan. He didn't resist me at all. I could have taken him away from you any time I liked. And, believe me, there were lots of times. But I didn't. Because I wanted you to be happy. That's the sacrifice I made for you, Chrissy. She could so easily have been my daughter. Mine and Dan's.'

'What?' Chrissy glowered at her then slapped her hard across the face. 'You mad, selfish cow!'

Juliet clutched her cheek. She was stunned, tears weren't far off. 'But I meant what I said earlier. That I'd give my life for you, Chrissy. And if you want me to prove it, I will.'

'Big deal, Juliet. Big fucking deal.'

'Just try and stop me!' she yelled.

***

A commotion could be heard outside. When they went to investigate there were screams and voices being unleashed into the night, people seemed to be charging towards the lake. Nico grabbed her, but Eloise resisted because he was pulling her in the wrong direction. Then she saw his Vespa parked at the end of their path.

They followed the streaks of light made by torches and flares up ahead. The lake seemed much further than when they had made this journey together before. As they got nearer they could see the shape of someone standing by the water's edge and a crowd gathering around.

It already looked like it was too late.

'Mum!' Eloise cried out, jumping off the Vespa before it had even stopped. She stumbled and ran towards the crowd, praying that no harm had come to her mother. The terrible thing was, she already knew that it had.

'Mum! No.'

But it was Chrissy who was standing at the water's edge as people were making desperate attempts to resuscitate someone laid out on the ground.

Chrissy turned to her when she called.

Juliet was gone. Drowned.

'*Suicida*,' she heard someone say.

EPILOGUE

Manchester was enjoying a late September heatwave. Eloise had taken to sitting out on the walkway, imagining she was back in Rome, wondering if she would ever return there. If Chrissy felt inclined, she would come out to join her, as she was doing now. The neighbour's dog barked incessantly at being left on its own, the traffic thundered past on the Mancunian Way as it had always done, but there were so many other things to occupy their thoughts they barely noticed these more familiar ones.

Few words had been said, about anything, since their return. Yet Eloise wanted closure and two things still bothered her.

'Did Dad know, Mum? You know what I'm talking about and I don't want you to lie to me.'

Chrissy was used to being interrogated by now, and there was very little left that her daughter didn't know.

'Neither of us knew for sure,' she replied. 'It was only when you were growing up that we noticed you—'

Her head dropped. She didn't even have to say any more.

'I've seen his photo,' said Eloise, feeling that wave of nausea again. 'I know … I know that I look like him.'

'You were always Dan's daughter, Eloise. He was the one in a big hurry to get married.' She smiled at the memory. 'He loved you as much as I do.'

'How can you even bear to look at me though?'

'Oh, Eloise, I can't even remember now what that bastard looks like. When I look at you, I don't see him. I just see you.'

***

When she heard the rattle of the letterbox she rushed to see if there was anything from Bournemouth University about the open day.

'One for you,' she said, giving it to her mother. 'Hand delivered.'

Eloise darted out onto the walkway but there was no one there. Peering over the railings she saw Anton walking towards the car. She ought to have pulled back out of sight but couldn't move.

Anton looked up. She was determined to hold his stare. As long as it took.

Eloise watched him drive away then went back inside.

Chrissy's hands were shaking, opening the envelope. Eloise recognized the Ricci logo as her trembling fingers removed a small package wrapped in purple tissue.

'Is it from Luca?'

She didn't answer, taking her time to read the letter, and when she had finished she handed it to Eloise.

'I need some air,' said Chrissy, stepping outside.

My dear Chrissy

Despite all the years you were apart from Juliet, I know how much she meant to you and how deeply saddened you will be by her tragic death. She always regarded you as her closest friend and I never quite understood why it took her so long to track you down. It is a pity that, having only just found one another, you had to say goodbye so soon.

At least you got to spend these past couple of months with her, and it is of great comfort to me that you were with Juliet when she died. They told me you were unable to save her but I thank you with all my heart for trying.

It seems only right that I should return this brooch to you. Juliet would want you to have it. She wore it every day without fail. There is, however, one formal request she made in regard to her best friend. That, in the event of her death, I would do my utmost to find you, and ensure that you receive a sum of money from her estate along with any children you may have. Laura, who is helping me with this letter and with Juliet's affairs, will be in touch with you in due course.

As I told you in Rome, my lawyer had already served the divorce papers. Such a blessing Juliet will not have to go through this now. You know how much I still loved her, yet she was always looking for something I could not give her. She will no doubt have confided in her best friend about our marriage and perhaps you have a greater insight than I do.

My dear Chrissy, it was lovely to meet you finally. I enjoyed our morning runs together – even though you exhausted me! I know you will never forget Juliet and I am sure, like myself, that you will have many treasured memories which will keep her close to you forever more.

So all that remains for me is to wish you and Eloise many more years of happiness and success in your lives, and if there is ever anything I can assist you with, please do not hesitate to get in touch.

With much love to you both.
Your crazy Italian friend
Luca Ricci

PS I must also break the sad news to you that Chrissy the cat died a few days ago. She always did prefer Juliet to me.

Eloise stepped out onto the walkway and stood next to Chrissy.

'Did you try to save her, Mum? She was such a great swimmer; I just don't see how she could drown.'

Chrissy shook her head. 'She made no effort to swim. Carried rocks into the lake, like Virginia fucking Woolf.'

'But you tried to stop her though. You tried to reach her, tried to pull her out. Didn't you?'

Chrissy didn't answer. Eloise saw a strange look pass across her face. She shivered involuntarily then admonished herself for even asking that question. This was her mother she was talking about; she would never have let Juliet drown. Would she?

Her mother stared at the cat brooch, rubbing her thumb over the grooves, making it glint as it caught the morning sun. She tossed it over the walkway. 'Some things don't deserve to be saved,' she said, going back inside.

ACKNOWLEDGEMENTS

First of all, I'd like to thank Shelley Instone for being such a great supporter and believer in the early stages of this book. Your blood, sweat, toil and tears are very much within these pages. Such an amazing editor and motivator. I'd also like to thank Abi Fenton, who worked with Shelley in the days when she was a literary agent. The pair of you made it so much fun, but always professional. We were a good team, the Northern powerhouse in fact. And all the other readers Shelley got on board, your input really helped too.

I would have stopped writing years ago if it wasn't for Script Yorkshire. Yes, I got roped onto the Board and, several years on, still help run the Organisation, but it has enabled me to connect with other writers across the region and I've made some lovely friends along the way. I'd especially like to thank Sharon Oakes for your constant encouragement, Gary Brown for making that writing penny finally drop, plus the rest of he gang. You're the best. David Nobbs, former Patron, brilliant writer and all round lovely man, I miss you. I'll never forget your words when I asked if you had any tips: "Well, June. It never gets any easier!"

Also Fiona Gell of Leeds Big Bookend, whose enthusiasm for the local writing scene never seems to wane. I don't know where you get your energy from.

Lucy Dauman, you were the missing piece in my writing jigsaw for this book as Editor at HarperCollins. Special thanks to you, and for making the editing process so enjoyable. Thanks to the Killer Reads team in general.

To my family, thank you for never discouraging me and for putting up with me and my obsession. The ones who aren't around to see a book of mine actually get published, I'm sad about that, so this is for you. My dad would have been proud, I hope. My mum remains a constant pillar of strength in my life. You are truly amazing.

My friends, too many to name, but thanks for all your support over the years. With good people around you it's possible to get through the difficult things life throws at you. But a special thank you to fellow author Maria Malone who shares the writer's pain, and the two friends who have endured me the longest, Amanda and Al.

Finally, Tim, I cannot thank you enough. You sure as hell know why!

Printed by RR Donnelley at Glasgow, UK